The BARK CUTTERS

Also by Nicole Alexander

Divertissements: Love, War, Society – Selected Poems
A Changing Land

The BARK CUTTERS

NICOLE ALEXANDER

BANTAM

SYDNEY • AUCKLAND • TORONTO • NEW YORK • LONDON

A Bantam book
Published by Random House Australia Pty Ltd
Level 3, 100 Pacific Highway, North Sydney NSW 2060
www.randomhouse.com.au

First published by Bantam in 2010
This edition published by Bantam in 2011

Addresses for companies within the Random House Group can be found at
www.randomhouse.com.au/offices

National Library of Australia
Cataloguing-in-Publication Entry

Alexander, Nicole.
The bark cutters

ISBN 978 1 86471 162 2 (pbk).

A823.4

Cover images by Getty Images and Wildlight
Cover design by Blue Cork
Internal design and typesetting by Midland Typesetters, Australia
Printed in Australia by Griffin Press, an accredited ISO AS/NZS 14001:2004
Environmental Management System printer

10 9 8 7 6 5 4 3 2 1

The paper this book is printed on is certified against the
Forest Stewardship Council® Standards. Griffin Press holds
FSC chain of custody certification SGS-COC-005088. FSC
promotes environmentally responsible, socially beneficial
and economically viable management of the world's forests.

Part One

West Wangallon Homestead –
North-west New South Wales

Sarah stood quietly in the corner of the kitchen as her mother removed the piping hot scones from the oven and, wrapping a tea towel around them, rested them on the kitchen sink to cool.

'Jam.'

Obediently Sarah walked into the large pantry, reaching between packets of dried fruits and glacé cherries for the large tin of strawberry conserve. Her mother was particularly quiet this morning. She had barely complained about the colony of white cockatoos in the lemon-scented gum outside the kitchen window, even though they were intent on stripping the tree bare of its leaves. Already a layer of small branches littered the autumn paleness of the grass beneath. Sarah mentally reminded herself to tidy the mess up before dark, hopefully before her mother demanded to know why the chore had not already been done. Rummaging through the mess drawer, which held everything from egg flips to household screwdrivers, Sarah located the can-opener. Within a few seconds

1

the conserve was deposited into a small porcelain dish on the centre of the pale green linoleum-topped table.

'Cream.'

'Gee, Mum . . .'

'Yes?'

Sarah wanted to say that an occasional please would be nice but, at the sight of the deep frown lines between her mother's eyes, she reconsidered. 'The scones smell delicious,' Sarah finished as she fetched the freshly whipped cream from the fridge. At that moment the back gate swung shut with a loud clang. Sarah relaxed, listening as her father and brother's voices grew louder as they walked up the back path. Stopping to remove their riding-boots, they washed their hands before entering the kitchen. Sarah smelt the familiar tang of sheep manure and the slightly less invasive scent of lanolin-rich wool. They had been classing the rams since dawn; deciding which ones should be retained for breeding purposes based on Wangallon's strict wool characteristics and which would be considered culls to be sold.

'Just wait for the men first, Sarah.'

Sarah was adept at waiting. Waiting for cups, saucers and plates to be put out, waiting for the jug to boil, waiting for her father to remove his work boots, to wash his hands, waiting for him to start eating whatever was freshly baked. Even Cameron, though older by only a few years, ate before her. For as long as Sarah could remember her mother ensured she was always last to begin at every meal. Eventually, glancing remotely in her daughter's direction, she would give a sign and Sarah would take her seat at the table. Even now, at sixteen, she found it difficult to break the habit and ignore her mother.

'Scones, hey Mum, they're my favourite,' Cameron beamed as he dolloped a large spoonful of jam and cream onto the steaming dough and stuffed the entire scone into his mouth. Sue smiled, ruffling his hair before pouring tea for him. She sat the blue teapot directly in front of Ronald who, with a sigh, proceeded to pour his own.

'I know they are, darling.'

'You not having any, Sarah?'

'Of course I am, Dad.' Sarah answered with a covert smile, sitting quickly at the table and pouring tea from the pot. As soon as they were finished, she would be able to rejoin the men outside. It was not that she minded being indoors, it was just that cooking wasn't something she was really interested in. It was not a bad place to be when you were little, for biscuits, cakes and desserts were Sue's speciality. Main meals were a little less enticing and usually consisted of at least three stews a week. Unfortunately, if the recipe didn't call for dried fruit, chocolate, flour or glacé cherries, you could be sure you'd be gumming your food like a baby.

Sarah helped herself to another scone and waited for her mother's usual remark.

'Save them for the men, Sarah. They need them more than you.'

Right on cue she smiled to herself, meeting her brother's eyes as he crammed yet another scone into his mouth, winking at her.

'Would you like a doggy-bag, Cameron?'

'No.' He lent back comfortably in his chair and patted his stomach. 'I think I've had enough thanks, sis.'

'We'll move those sheep from the road paddock and walk them out to the big cultivation. Then you two can have the afternoon off,' Ronald said between slurps of black tea.

Sarah beamed. She couldn't wait to get out into the bush.

'I've got to see your grandfather this afternoon,' Ronald continued. 'He's just informed me that Wangallon is about to have a new jackaroo.'

'When?' Sarah and Cameron asked in unison, their slouching backs instantly stiff with interest.

'He's coming tomorrow. I'm to pick him up in Wangallon Town.'

'That was short notice,' Cameron replied. 'Where's he from?'

'What's he like?' Sarah added.

Ronald grinned, arching a bushy eyebrow. 'Well, I guess you two busybodies will know when I know.'

Sue coughed delicately into her hand. 'Well I hope the boy comes from a good family, I don't want any riffraff around my house.'

Bristling immediately, Ronald lifted his spade-like hand to scratch irritably at the thinning hair above his ear. 'I hardly think my father would employ riffraff, as you put it, Susan.' Demolishing another scone in one mouthful, he licked his fingers free of cream before pushing the wooden kitchen chair back from the table. 'And as you rarely deign to venture outside the back gate I hardly see how our staff choices are going to affect you.'

Grasping her teacup with both hands, Sue placed it firmly back on the pale pink saucer. 'Cameron, dear. Will you be a pet and give me a hand in the garden before lunch?'

'He can't, Sue, we're mustering sheep.'

'What about after lunch?'

'Well, I –' Cameron hesitated.

Sarah knew her brother longed for an afternoon off. One where he could sneak off to the creek, throw a line in and smoke one of the roll-your-owns he'd recently taken to.

'I said he could have the afternoon off. Come on, you two,' Ronald commanded flatly, getting to his feet so quickly that his chair squeaked across the surface of the worn vinyl tiles.

The jam and cream sitting in the pit of Sarah's stomach curdled. It was always the same. Her parents could argue over the smallest thing but mainly they fought over Cameron. Of course everyone held great hopes for him. As the eldest, his whole life was mapped out before him, and Sarah knew Cameron liked it that way.

'Are you coming?'

It was Cameron flipping her long pigtails and stirring her from her daydream. He gave her his distinctive *time to get out of here* look, as the back door slammed shut after their father and their mother splashed crockery in the sink.

'That's right. Go. Don't worry about helping with the tidying up,' their mother called after them. 'It's far more interesting outside than staying inside with your boring mother.'

Screwing up her nose and moving her lips in imitation, Sarah grabbed another scone, as her mother's rubber-gloved left hand reached for dirty crockery to plunge into the sink. A small tidal wave of bubbles and cream coloured dish water splashed over the edge to run forlornly down the door of the kitchen cupboard beneath.

For the briefest of moments, Sarah considered staying to help, but instead chose to follow her brother and father down to the stables, humming Michael Jackson's *Thriller*. 'What do you think he'll be like?' she asked when she finally caught up with their long strides.

'Who?' Cameron asked. 'And can you sing something else. You've been destroying that album ever since it came out.'

'The jackeroo, silly,' Sarah answered, her long legs matching her brother's fast walk. 'How about *Physical*?' She sang the first stanza. 'You know, Olivia Newton-John.'

Cameron shook his head in irritation. 'The usual: Two arms, legs. Dad, can you please tell her to stop?'

'Half a brain more likely,' their father called back to them as he entered the gloom of the stables to lead out their horses. A shaft of light filtered down from the roof through the open stable door where a piece of corrugated iron had recently lifted in the wind. Sarah found herself momentarily intrigued by the play of light on the hay-strewn floor, the delicate cross-hatch of a tiny spider web highlighted by the glow. If she owned a camera she would have taken a photo of it.

'I thought Grandfather said jackeroos were a waste of time,' Cameron queried as he took his horse's reins from his father.

'He does think that. We stopped getting jackeroos here about fifteen years ago, mainly because your grandfather got sick of having learners on the property. He reckoned that it was rare to find someone with ability and commonsense, who also fitted in with the family.'

Ronald led his and Sarah's mares from the stable, tethering both next to Cameron's mount on the old wooden hitching post that years ago carried ten horses with ease. 'And that's the calibre of men we've had in the past. Short of using the lad as a gardener . . .'

'Mum will be pleased,' Sarah interrupted, quickly noticing that her father's violet eyes weren't smiling.

'Or as an odd-jobber,' Ronald continued, 'unless he has a bit of go about him, I can't see him lasting.'

'Well maybe Grandfather thinks Wangallon needs a younger workforce,' Cameron added. He hoped he was a good bloke, this jackeroo, and wouldn't mind hanging out with Sarah. You couldn't hold his sixteen-year-old sister back with a stick if she wanted to do something.

Throwing the saddle blanket across the mare's back, Ronald pursed his lips thoughtfully. 'Whatever he's up to, son, we will know soon enough'. He picked up the saddle.

'Hey Dad, can I have a camera for my birthday?'

Ronald tightened the girth on the saddle and wondered what the girl was going to do with a camera. Although, as he'd dropped the last one in the cattle yards and broken it when he was taking shots of the bulls, a new one probably wouldn't go astray. 'If that's what you really want.'

Actually what she really wanted was a pair of wayfarer sunnies, purple stirrup pants and some ice-blue eye shadow. But a camera would be cool. 'Thanks, Dad.'

❈ *Autumn, 1854* ❈

The Scottish Highlands

*H*amish Gordon studied the prone figure lying on the thin pallet of grass. From the sweat-soaked bedding an acrid smell wafted about the small room. For days now his beloved Mary had lain motionless, appearing to study the lance of light rippling across the thatched roof of the small hut, eating nothing, unable to speak. He poured water from a leather pouch through her cracked lips and leaned back on his knees as the cool fluid trickled down her chin. The fever had finally broken – she would survive.

About him a brisk wind brought the smell of herbage, the lingering scent of the season's last before winter. In the past such smells delighted him. Now it only served to remind him of the bleak days ahead. With one last look at the young woman he once hoped would be his bride, Hamish left the hut. He walked down towards the loch, through rippling green and purple vegetation, his leather boots striking the soil that yielded so easily for his family. At the loch's edge he pulled off his shirt and kilt and walked waist high into the freezing water, splashing himself with the cold liquid, as if the action would cleanse him of Mary's betrayal. The coldness made his bladder empty itself immediately and as the warmth eddied about his thighs, he watched the clumps of purple on the land swell in the wind, the sprigs of violet seeming to dart towards him. Hamish knew he could no longer stay in this place, his home for the last seventeen years. Once he could have borne it. Even with the recent death of his mother. However, the dreadful pain of Mary's actions still burned in his chest and he knew it would never lessen if he remained.

Mary of Clanranald had appeared like a wisp of sunlight in the deepest fog only two months prior. Her voice reminded Hamish of the pure cadence of a flowing brook and she was the type of woman that others admired; pretty, strong and undemanding. She was the finest thing Hamish had ever seen. The fire-red lustre of her hair, the firm pink flesh of her parted lips, the strength of her fingers intertwined with his.

Hamish wiped at the tears welling in his eyes. He would have died for her. Returning to the hut, he slung a water pouch and his rolled bedding over the shoulder of his thick woollen tunic, before tucking his knife securely in his kilt, along with a small portion of dry oatmeal from their precious stores. A dense fog was rolling in across the loch this morning and he intended to be across the trickling burn and traversing the hill before it arrived to engulf their thatched hut. Outside, his father barred his path.

'You'll be lost to me then, lad.'

Adjusting the leather straps across the broad wedge of his chest, Hamish considered the violet-eyed man whose resemblance to the father of his boyhood now lay depleted by injustice.

'Aren't you forgetting the dead? What of your wee sisters?' his father persevered.

'They're gone, Father, and not to be coming back,' Hamish answered curtly, brushing past him to leave the hut of his birth for the last time.

'And what would you be expecting? That your ma and wee sisters will not know you've left them? They'll know, lad.'

Hamish listened to the puff of his father's breath as he laboured up the hill behind him. 'Aye, and they know what type of father you've been also.'

Silence answered him.

Hamish thought of the brief respite summer brought before winter descended upon them. Soon enough the remaining inhabitants of the hut would be bringing the cow in for the winter. Sharing their meagre dwelling with their prized possession, they would spend freezing days with pitchfork in hand, scooping the animal's shit off the dirt floor and out onto the heather.

'Many of our neighbours have managed to stay on.'

Hamish stopped abruptly and turned. His father's eyes remained steely, unrepentant. He recalled the great bear hugs of his youth. The harsh red-gold of his father's beard on his cheek stinging like a burst of sharp sleet-peppered rain. It was all too late. The chilling water of the loch seemed to have lodged itself in his gut. 'Aye, and many have been forced to settle on the coast as crofters. I have heard the stories, Father, eking out a subsistence living from fish and farming, a small holding with high rents and starvation for company. I have no taste for such things.'

'You imagine to be a drover then?' His father's voice grew tight with sarcasm. 'Have you listened to nothing I've said?'

He wondered if his father honestly believed he was only leaving home to find a different type of work. 'What, and receive the generous sum of one shilling a day, driving cattle purchased by the English at Falkirk to England?' Hamish had scoffed.

'Aye, and they would not trust you, lad. You are a Highlander. They would clap irons on you for theft whether you were responsible or not.' His father's chaffed and cracked hands took him by the shoulders. 'I know you grieve, lad, but give it time.'

Hamish shrugged him off. 'I can't forgive you,' he said roughly.

The anger surging through his body begged for revenge. He must leave before his fury caused actions he would ultimately regret. He turned his back on his father. One goodbye remained. Regardless of what he thought of his younger brother's role in his betrayal, he did need to see the lad. Hamish thought of their short years together. To the illness that young Charlie suffered every winter. To his tendency to get lost, not listen nor follow advice. It was best to leave the boy behind, besides Hamish was past caring for anyone anymore. With a swipe at the tears gathering in his eyes he turned in the opposite direction to his father.

The springy turf of autumn already grown sparse with the season crackled beneath Hamish's feet. The top of their hill was only a few strides away when Charlie's tear-bloated face appeared before him, his young lips trembling.

'I'll come too.' Charlie's eyes trailed their father's progress downhill to their hut.

'No, lad.' Hamish tried to curb the anger of the past few weeks.

'Yes.' Charlie swiped at the moisture tumbling freely down his cheeks. 'Please.'

'It will not be an easy journey. I've no idea where I'm going. I may leave this country altogether. Goodbye lad and take care.' Hamish shifted his belongings into a more comfortable position and trudged on upwards into the gathering fog, his feet following the path worn bare by their traffic. He looked behind only once. The figure of his father disappeared as a sheet of whiteness descended into the valley below, obliterating the hut from view. Closer, he could see Charlie following at a cautious pace.

'Leave me, Charlie,' his voice echoed in the whiteness. Surely the lad would become disorientated and be forced to return to their valley. The persistent *shush shush* of stamped vegetation answered him. Hamish grunted and increased his pace.

❈ Spring, 1982 ❈

Wangallon Station –
North-west New South Wales

'These two are my children, Sarah and Cameron.'

They had been out riding early, aware that their father would soon be turning up the back road with the new jackeroo. Taking a short cut across the corner paddock through a clump of black wattle, they had arrived at the boundary gate just in time to find the Toyota pulling up and a tall guy opening the gate. They urged their horses forward a little further until they were just a few feet away and Sarah caught the deep brown of the jackeroo's eyes. She found herself thinking of rich chocolate icing and she pulled her Akubra further down on her head, suddenly self-conscious.

Cameron pulled his left leg across his horse and casually rested it on the pummel of the saddle before sliding off, his jeans brushing his mount fleetingly. 'Hi there.'

'You must be Cameron, I'm Anthony.' They shook hands warmly.

Sliding her foot out of the stirrup to dismount, Sarah stopped herself quickly. Sometimes Oscar didn't go much on being remounted, invariably the old bugger would wait until she had one boot in the stirrup and then trot away, leaving her hopping stupidly until she could either jump up on him, untangle her boot or he decided to stop. Deciding not to let fate cheat her of her dignity, Sarah satisfied herself with a perfect view of Wangallon's new recruit. Anthony and her brother were the same height, tall and lanky, with the same laconic grins and expressions of mischief on their tanned faces. Yet where Cameron's light brown hair was sun-streaked, Anthony's was glossy and verging on the rusty brown sheen of a bronze-wing pigeon.

'And this is my sister, Sarah.' Cameron clapped Anthony hard on the back. 'She's looking for a husband. You know, nice family, bush heritage, a bit of ability.'

'Cameron!' Yelling in embarrassment Sarah quickly removed her hat, walking Oscar over to where her brother stood to belt him over the head with it. At that moment, a pair of kookaburras burst into laughter. *Bugger*, she thought with discomfit, maybe she would have been better off to let old Oscar drag her into the sunset. At the thought the kookaburras' noise increased, echoing through the morning air.

'She's already got a good temper,' Cameron chuckled as he swung neatly onto his horse, his pale eyes lighting up. 'Oh, and she likes singing, although I can't seem to wean her off Michael Jackson.' With a casual tug on the reins he trotted off into the scrub in the direction of the homestead.

'Nice to meet you,' Sarah said, replacing her hat firmly on her head. When she got home she was going to hide Cameron's Springsteen cassette.

'Likewise.' Anthony touched the brim of his hat. When his fingers left the felt Sarah noticed that a slight dip remained. Perhaps it was a remnant of the red-tinged months of summer when his hat rested on the edge of a table or maybe it was a lasting impression of continued politeness. For a moment she hesitated, twisting her fingers through the knotty chestnut mane of her horse, wishing she had put a comb through it. As if sensing her indecision the kookaburras stopped their laughter. Sarah listened as the crackling of dry undergrowth signalled the growing distance of her brother. 'So, is your family from the bush?' she blurted out, as she took in the length of his legs and the faded blue of his shirt.

'The Monaro. Down South,' he smiled. 'I'm suffering from the younger brother syndrome. The place isn't big enough for both of us.'

'How long are you working for us?' There was just the slightest tinge of blue beneath his eyes.

'Why? You're not trying to get rid of me already? I kinda like this climate; nice and green, regular rainfall and all that.'

His eyes were so dark, almost decadent in their depth. He had taken a step closer. Close enough for the slight etching of a scar to be revealed. It highlighted the arc of his cheekbone, the inverted crescent shape ending with the tail of a question mark. Even as she stared Sarah could imagine her forefinger deftly examining the slight indentation, caressing the pale thin line surrounded as it was by the darker hue marking a life lived outdoors. His face, strong and composed, fell to a sculptor's vision of a jawline before his body disappeared into the duck-egg blue of his shirt.

'Come on, you two, that's enough fraternising between camps for one day.'

It was her father calling out, revving the engine and winding up his window.

'Better go,' Anthony said, not moving. She was a cute-looking kid.

'Yep, hope you like it here, Anthony.' Sarah turned her horse. She flicked the rump of the gelding, riding faster than usual, wondering if he was watching, but not daring to look back.

'Well, is anyone going to enlighten me as to our new employee?' Sue enquired across the kitchen table at dinner.

Sarah and her brother continued to chew steadily on their steak and salad. Having already both been reprimanded for speaking with their mouths full they were loath to answer. Instead, they concentrated on hiding their respective grimaces from their mother as they bit into uncooked flowerets of broccoli mixed in with iceberg lettuce, home-grown vine tomatoes and thick rings of red salad onion.

'He's from the Monaro. Good family. Has ability. Nice kid,' Ronald concluded. Having finished his dinner he poured himself another glass of wine. 'Actually I think Anthony will fit in quite well here although it's early days yet. He's quite mature for his age and he gets on very well with my father.'

Sue folded her napkin into its customary elongated triangle. 'Well God forbid if he didn't prostrate himself in front of the mighty Angus Gordon.' Tilting her head, she gave a tight smile that encompassed her children's partially eaten meals. Her hand surfaced from her lap to rest on the table and the slow, expectant tapping of her fingers indicated she was ready for an argument.

Taking two large mouthfuls in quick succession, Sarah looked across the table to where, sure enough, her brother's stealthy *let's get out of here look* waited.

'Sarah, tomorrow I expect you to read up on your correspondence lessons for Monday. The booklet came in the mail yesterday.'

'Okay,' Sarah glumly agreed. Her brother, having finished his schooling nearly two years ago, was free to work alongside their father and spend his spare time as he wished; which usually involved being as far away from the house as possible.

'Someone's gotta do it, Sarah,' Cameron remarked happily, pointedly folding and re-folding his napkin in a poor attempt at an origami swan. While he'd only just managed to pass his Higher School Certificate, Sarah didn't seem to have any problems with her studies. 'By the way, have you seen my Bruce Springsteen tape?'

'Hmm.' Sarah took another mouthful of food and chewed thoughtfully. 'Why? You're not missing it, are you?'

Cameron screwed up his eyes as if he could mentally extract an answer. 'Sarah?'

'Anyway,' Ronald interrupted, 'Anthony's a good bloke, Sue. You'll like him.'

'Maybe. In the meantime your father is coming to dinner tomorrow night.'

'What, here?' Sarah asked. She couldn't recall the last time their grandfather had visited them midyear. She had not seen him for a month. In fact even before Granny Angie died of asthma he was a rare sighting at their home. Their grandfather, when not out on the property, tended to hunker down at the main homestead, Wangallon. Sarah couldn't blame him. It was a sprawling homestead filled with the Gordon heirlooms and apart from relatively new paint and wallpaper, remarkably intact; which apparently was just how the National Trust liked their heritage-listed buildings. Cameron believed their grandfather's scarcity was a good thing, for it meant their father was able to manage his own block of land, West Wangallon, without interference. Yet Sarah knew better. Angus Gordon was forever roaming the property, checking on staff, stock, equipment and the condition of boundary fences.

'Yes. Something important. Well important enough to have him leave the big house and venture down here to our humble abode.'

'Geez,' Cameron exclaimed. 'The old fella coming here for dinner. We'll have to kill the fatted calf.'

'Don't be cheeky,' Ronald chastised.

'No need for that,' Sue answered quite seriously, 'we're having mutton stew.'

'Great,' Sarah and her brother chimed in unison.

After dinner Sarah and Cameron raced to the television set. A *Country Practice* was about to start and Sarah loved the programme.

'*The Leyland Brothers* are on tonight,' Cameron reminded her.

'Good luck. *Dallas* is on too.'

'No way.' He liked *The Leyland Brothers*. They invariably got stuck somewhere out in the middle of nowhere.

Sarah squirreled down further into the lime green beanbag. 'Maybe Mum will forget. She doesn't always remember things these days.'

Cameron looked at her and rolled his eyes. 'Big hair, big shoulders and plastered-on makeup? She'll remember.' Cameron leaned back in his own beanbag and, reaching for a cushion decorating one of the chairs behind him, threw it at his sister. His aim was perfect, hitting her fair in the head.

'Hey!' She lifted the cushion and pelted it back at him.

Cameron caught it. 'If you give me back my cassette, you can have a cigarette.'

'True?'

'True.'

Sarah considered the trade. 'It's worth two.'

'Okay.' Cameron laughed. 'Geez you're a hard bargainer.'

Sarah smiled sweetly. She had a nice little stack of cigarettes under her bed, which was a handy stockpile to have on the occasions when her brother's supply ran out and she needed a favour.

◆

Angus Gordon strode up the back path of West Wangallon at 6.30 p.m. sharp. He noted the freshly mown lawn and just-watered geranium-filled terracotta pots before a whiff of jasmine circulating in the soft breeze caught him off guard. The scent drew memories of freshly cut flowers, the soft tinkle of piano music and the lavender water that once wafted in a trail behind his beloved wife. He knew it was time to let her go, to restart his life even if he was pushing eighty, yet somehow her image was stronger than ever, his memories alive and vital. At any time of the day she could appear miraculously, catching him unawares in a haze of heat, reflected in a window or in the birdsong of the tiny darting jenny wrens she loved so much. At such moments it was easy to imagine her in her garden, chasing the work dogs with a stiff straw broom when they invaded her domain, her wispy white halo of hair coming askew from beneath her wide-brimmed straw hat.

Perhaps it was just as well that she shadowed him, for it was not his intention to remarry. He had no time for such luxuries anymore and even less for the blossoming and nurturing of a new love incapable of equalling his first. It had taken three long years to let her go and now, having finally accepted that he would be alone for the rest of his life, it was time to move on. There were other far weightier matters to oversee, highlighted by the uncertainty of his life span. In truth he guessed he was lucky to be here. He was the only surviving son from his father's second wife, a late addition after a couple of stillbirths; although his solitary presence ensured Wangallon's continuation. There had been no splitting of land required for recalcitrant siblings.

Tonight he intended to pass the baton to the next custodian of Wangallon. The challenges facing the heir apparent lay shrouded in the future and would only be realised with his own personal demise, yet his choice required advance notice, both for the longevity of the property and for his own satisfaction. After all, he *was* Wangallon and like his father before him, this decision was his alone. He just wished that things could have been different. But the past could not be revisited. He had to make do with the here and now. So he chose to feign ignorance and do what both the family and the outside world expected. It was the only way to protect the Gordon name and reputation.

At the three cement steps leading to the back door of the house Angus paused for his dog, Shrapnel. The part kelpie, part blue cattle dog was a sappy young pup with more bounce than a kangaroo in him and the type of surly loyalty that Angus appreciated.

'Sit.'

The dog, wagging its tail, took up position on the top step and gave a low growl. Angus cocked his left eyebrow. 'Got a bit of attitude, have we?' Patting the pup roughly on the head, he grinned, showing irregular shaped teeth tinged yellow by time. 'Good.'

'Evening all.' Angus greeted his family in the kitchen where they were assembled like a flock of sulphur-crested cockatoos suddenly gone quiet. The table was set for dinner and a passable bottle of merlot lay open and waiting. 'If we could all sit,' he suggested. He sniffed the air, taking in the large pot on the stove and the saucepan of peas next to it. His preferred meal of steak, fried eggs and coleslaw was looking mighty appealing. Accepting a glass of wine from his son, Angus waited for his two grandchildren to stop fidgeting. It had been some time since his last visit to West Wangallon, firstly because this was another man's castle and secondly because of his absolute inability to suffer stupidity.

'Angus, I thought perhaps we could have dinner first.'

The wine wasn't half bad, so Angus helped himself to a top-up. 'Thank you, Sue, however I've never been a great fan of stew –' he paused, the momentary silence emphasising his disdain – 'as you well know.' He watched as his daughter-in-law's features tightened on her face until she was all parallel lines, with a smear of red lipstick. 'This won't take long. I don't want to deprive the rest of you from your evening meal.' Winking at Sarah he leant forward in his chair. 'First, I would like Sarah to have these.' From his pocket he withdrew a long strand of opera-length pearls. Placing them firmly in his granddaughter's palm, he cupped a sun-mottled hand over hers and looked deep into the violet eyes that were the one sure indication of the girl's Scottish lineage. 'She wanted you to have them, dear girl. They were her favourites.'

'Thank you, Grandfather,' Sarah beamed, her fingers brushing the luminous nacre of each pearl.

'She's a little young, Angus, for such gifts,' Sue interrupted.

Angus countered the woman's tone with a deep scowl, his eyes remaining fixed on her until she turned towards the stove and the bubbling mutton.

'Second, her apartment in Centennial Park in Sydney is also yours, Sarah.'

'Well, I never,' Sue mumbled.

Sarah felt her breath catch in her throat. 'But Grandfather . . .'

'It's currently being rented. After body corporate fees and agency charges etcetera have been deducted, the rental income is being deposited into an account in your name. You can't touch it until you're twenty, however. Agreed?'

Sarah nodded her head vigorously. Fabulous jewels and now an apartment of her very own. Heavens, she really couldn't believe it.

'That's very generous, Dad,' Ronald said slowly.

Angus stifled a cough. 'Yes, well, been meaning to do it. I've a mind to keep hold of the rest of Angie's trinkets for a bit longer. A man can't let go of too much too soon.'

'It's been three years,' Sue reminded him.

Angus stared in reply until Sue's plump middle-aged arse turned quickly from the table back to the stove.

'We understand, Dad,' Ronald said softly.

'Yes, well.' Angus cleared his throat and took another sip of wine. 'Now, Cameron my boy, what are your plans?'

'My plans? Well, um . . .'

'Everyone has plans, lad,' he interrupted impatiently. 'You've finished your schooling. So what do you want to do? Agricultural college, business administration in the city for twelve months, two years on a big holding in the territory?'

'Actually I'd rather stay here,' Cameron said quickly. Only last week he had overheard his father on the telephone discussing the merits of various agricultural colleges and he could not think of anything worse. None of those places could teach him anything that he couldn't learn on Wangallon.

'Of course you would, darling,' Sue smiled, coming to rest her hand on her son's shoulder.

'A bit of experience probably wouldn't hurt,' Ronald suggested.

'I totally disagree,' Sue pounced. 'There's absolutely no need for that, Ronald.'

'Save the bickering for when I'm out of earshot, will you, Sue,' Angus stood abruptly facing his grandson, who was equal in height if, he decided, not quite in intelligence. 'Wangallon and West Wangallon will be yours one day, lad. It's taken our family a mighty effort to be able to pass it on to a fourth generation, so –' he paused for emphasis, waiting until the only noise audible in the kitchen was the sizzling of simmering packet peas – 'don't piss it up against a wall.'

Cameron squared his shoulders and looked his grandfather directly in the eye. 'I won't, Grandfather.' The weight of responsibility crossed the few feet between them. Cameron felt it hover undecided before him, before reversing in direction. It was easy to say yes when he was third in line, for if anything happened to his grandfather, Cameron figured his father would swoop on the opportunity to manage the sprawling property.

'It's a mighty responsibility. My father, Hamish, did it hard, really hard, don't you forget it. And I have to make sure that you're equal to the task, so if you want extra experience you let me know.'

'I'll do that. Thank you.' They shook on it.

Angus placed his hand on the boy's shoulder; pale blue pupils blinked back at him. 'I suggest you do a correspondence book-keeping course. Next year I'll send you down to Sydney for six weeks to a friend of mine who runs an accountancy firm.'

'Okay,' Cameron answered a little less enthusiastically. He knew Sarah should be the one doing all the technical stuff. Bench-marking, new innovations and financial things were subjects he'd never been good at, besides, it made sense, Sarah wanted to stay at Wangallon as well. 'What about –'

'You might know a bit about stock, lad,' Angus continued, 'but you need to know a fair bit more about budgets, projected cash flows and general bookkeeping procedures. As of next week I expect you to spend the last Friday of each month in the station office with my bookkeeper. She'll familiarise you with our general office procedures.' With his business completed, Angus recovered his wine glass, swirling the contents contemplatively. 'Good, that's settled.' A dry aftertaste sat unquenched in his throat, he decided against another top-up, a very fine Grange awaited him at his home. 'Well, Anthony seems to be handling himself.'

'Yes,' Ronald agreed. 'The lad's quite capable.'

'The boy has ability and brains. I thought you two could use someone your own age around here for a change,' he concluded, directing this last comment towards his two grandchildren. 'I expect him to be treated like a member of the family, with respect and courtesy. I have a few things in mind for young Anthony. Well, I'll be leaving you to it then. Goodnight.'

Sarah walked her grandfather to the back door. 'Thank you,' she whispered, standing on her toes to kiss his sun-baked cheek.

'Consider it a bit of extra security, girl.'

'I will.'

'Good. Well then you better go and have some of your mother's infamous stew.'

Sarah turned her nose up as he winked, opening the back door.

'Wait,' Angus fumbled in his pocket, holding out a beaten gold bracelet. 'Just a trinket. It belonged to your great-grandfather's first wife I think. Anyway, thought you should have it,' he finished gruffly.

Sarah closed the door, watching his figure merge into the darkness of the night, his voice low and melodic as he spoke quietly to his new pup. At the kitchen doorway, she watched as Cameron quickly shovelled stew and peas into his mouth, their parents already arguing. He looked up once, rolled his eyes at her and then resumed eating, using his fork and index finger to scoop up bits of onion and carrot. Walking slowly back to her own seat, Sarah poked disinterestedly at her meal. A momentous event still hung in the Gravox-infused air of the kitchen, yet nothing was altered. Her parents were still arguing and her brother, having scoffed down his dinner, would soon disappear for a secret roll-your-own ciggie behind the old iron rainwater tank at the rear of the garden. She felt his elbow in her ribs and knew he would be giving her the two finger lazy victory sign for a quiet smoke. Shaking her head, Sarah reached across to take her mother's untouched glass of wine. Throwing the contents back she swallowed a mouthful of the dark red liquid in a peppery gulp, ignoring the urgent swivelling action of her brother's head. In front of her lay the pearls that had belonged to her grandmother and a rather beaten-up gold bangle. Before her brother lay Wangallon. The wine left a slight burning sensation in her throat.

Ronald sat quietly in his office, sipping freshly brewed coffee, as a light breeze stirred the papers on his desk. Through the venetian blinds wild budgerigars were busy fluffing their feathers in a tall stringy bark, as willy-wagtails dive bombed the sprinkler on the lawn. The seasons were kind to the inhabitants of the north-west at the moment. Over the past year, above-average rainfall had increased the natural feed in the paddocks, ensuring well fed cattle and sheep, optimising the growth of grain. The ledger said it all: a year of sweet green grass and excellent clover cover, of wheat and barley crops exceeding normal expectations at harvest, of sheep nearing a record lambing, of cattle not far behind. Even the prices were positive at the moment, which meant Sue could travel to Sydney for ten days and give everyone a break.

God it was peaceful this morning, Ronald mused, as he finished paying the monthly fuel account. He had given himself a timeline of about ten years; he then intended to retire to the coast. He figured by that stage Cameron would be running the property, Sarah would probably be married and he could escape the land he'd been tied to all his life. Sometimes his situation reminded him of the British monarchy. He had waited half a lifetime to inherit, only to realise that his own father was never going to abdicate. Some years ago he would have been jealous of Cameron, but not now.

Years ago he believed that his father knew of the error of judgement that had been made within the walls of his marriage. There appeared to be no other possible explanation for his refusal to allow him more freedom to manage the property. And it would be characteristic of Angus to exact some type of payback for the detriment past actions could cause to the family name. Yet over time Ronald could not be sure, for Angus never broached the subject. Eventually Ronald simply assumed that his father was more interested in a lump of dirt than his own family. Angus gifted him the 5,000 acres dubbed West Wangallon on which to build his marital home, however, the 120,000 odd acres that comprised Wangallon remained tightly within his control.

Yet Ronald still loved Wangallon, especially now when her fertile earth swelled with life and he could actually plan and see a positive result from his labours. At night he dreamed of fields of golden wheat, awakening to find himself lying on his side with his hand outstretched, his fingers brushing the heads of imaginary grain laden with the prime hard wheat so loved by the flour mills. At other times sheep leaped into his subconscious to munch on spring herbage as he sat beneath the protective arms of an old coolibah in a rattan chair. Such dreams, such moments, were made more beautiful when contrasted with the endless hot, drought ridden months experienced intermittently over the last forty years. The memory of riding his horse back through a biting westerly wind, his face and eyes stinging from sunburn and flying grit after arduous hours of checking bore drains and dams for bogged stock – this was reality on Wangallon. Yes, Ronald mused, if he had his life over, Wangallon's enticements would fail to entrap him a second time. She was a hard mistress, and unlike Sue, could not be calmed with valium and an extra shot of whiskey in the evening.

A zephyr of air flowed through the gauze window to gently vibrate the blinds. Putting the station cheque book to one side, he breathed in the morning stillness and rummaged in the desk drawer to retrieve a selection of black and white photographs secreted beneath a wad of yellowing bank statements. There were pictures of small crofters' cottages, shots of the Scottish

Highlands and one of a young woman smiling brightly into the camera. He thumbed through the ageing photographs, pausing at last at the neat cottage and the slim beauty standing outside the front door. Turning the picture over, a burly thumb traced the ink writing: *Outskirts of the village of Tongue, Scotland 1961.*

With a shake of his head, Ronald drained his now cold mug of coffee. Beneath the photos lay the leather folio gifted to him by his father on his twenty-first birthday. Resting proudly between protective folds of cream tissue paper lay a black and white photograph of Hamish Gordon, his grandfather. The white-bearded, wedge-chested giant was pictured sitting on the verandah at Wangallon homestead, a dog by his feet, a pipe in his hand and a scowl on his face. Perhaps, Ronald mused, Angus believed the essence of the man within would, via some mysterious form of osmosis, permeate the soft skin of his only child. Ronald closed the folio and buried it deep beneath his treasured photographs. Some genetics were best not passed on.

❈ Summer, 1983 ❈

West Wangallon Homestead

Sarah didn't hear the knock on the back door. Busy unpacking groceries in the walk-in pantry, she was intent on finishing the job before her mother reappeared. The trip to town had lasted a good part of the day and her mum, having complained for almost the entire 150 km return journey, was medicating herself with paracetamol and Staminade.

'Hello, anyone there?'

Sarah started at the voice coming from outside the screen door.

'Sorry, didn't mean to scare you.' Anthony gave a lopsided grin and took a step back as she opened the door. 'You look nice.'

'Thanks.' Sarah fidgeted with the empty plastic shopping bag in her hand.

'Shopping day?' Anthony asked.

She felt his eyes skim over her pale jeans and bright pink, oversized sweatshirt. She finally had her ice-blue eye shadow and a new bright pink lipstick and she'd actually felt pretty trendy in town today. His hat was tilted towards the back of his head revealing a sweep of sun-burnished hair. She held the door open. 'Machinery parts day,' Sarah replied. 'Hydraulic hose, o-rings . . .'

Anthony nodded. 'For the tractor.'

'Engine oil, grease gun cartridges, 12-volt car battery,' Sarah elaborated, finishing with a roll of her eyes.

Anthony shook his head. 'What, no good stuff?'

'Nothing. Oh except for mum. She got herself a few things and a potplant. Oh, I got more film for my camera.'

'You'll be broke getting all those photos you take, developed.'

He was right. Since the gift of the camera for her birthday last year, she had taken heaps of shots, most of which had ended up in the bin.

'You not into the post-Christmas sales?'

'Not really.' Her mouth was beginning to feel a little dry.

Anthony cocked his head to one side. 'There should be more women like you, Sarah.'

Sarah felt her cheeks warm, 'Yeah, right.' The awkward silence that followed was broken by her mother's voice demanding to know where the dried peas were.

'Dinner speciality?' Anthony queried.

Sarah nodded. 'In the pantry, Mum,' she called out over her shoulder.

'Anyway, I just wanted to give you this. Merry Christmas.'

Sarah accepted the small red tissue-paper-wrapped gift. 'Anthony, you didn't have to get me something.' She'd not bought him anything for Christmas. He had spent two weeks with his own family down south over the holiday period and although she had thought about getting him something on more than one occasion, finally she'd decided that by the time he returned to Wangallon it would be too late.

'I wanted to give you something. It's just a bit late.'

Sarah squashed the small, soft parcel between her fingers. 'No, it's not.'

Anthony raised an eyebrow, the action sending the crescent-shaped scar on his cheek into a squirrelly line. 'It *is* the third week of January. Well? Open it.'

'Sarah, are you going to finish unpacking these groceries?'

'Yes, Mum,' she answered loudly, her fingers quickly tearing at the tissue paper to reveal a bright blue silk neck scarf. 'It's beautiful.'

He shoved his hands into the pockets of his blue jeans. 'Anyway, I hope you like it.'

'I love it.'

'Good.'

'Thank you.'

Anthony smiled. Pulling his akubra down a little on his forehead, he walked down the back path. Sarah watched him leave, the scarf clutched tightly in her hand.

'I'll be seeing you, then,' he called out mid-stride.

'Okay.' Sarah ran the material through her fingers, her stomach warm with delight.

⪻ *Spring, 1857* ⪼

The Victorian Goldfields

Having taken to sleeping outside with the onset of warmer weather, Hamish struggled down into the soft sandy hollow. A few feet away the remains of the camp fire flickered restlessly; further on the soft glow from a tent dimmed to darkness. Pulling coarse blankets about his stubbly chin, he rocked slowly in the depression, the warmth of the dirt massaging the continual ache of his back. Gradually his spine eased into the earth and he sensed his body succumbing to the day's exertions. Only his hand betrayed his tiredness, the muscles trembling spasmodically from overuse. He yawned loudly, the noise as familiar to him as the jerking movements of his body as his muscles eased from their daily state of tension. The release of sleep was only temporary. It did, however, herald a ritualistic moment of reflection.

The creek was proving useless. For the last ten days their panning had yielded only the barest traces of gold dust. It was enough to keep him and Charlie fed but not enough to keep Hamish satisfied. One didn't travel to the other side of the world for scraps and that is exactly what the goldfields were yielding. Hamish grunted as he turned on his side, wedging his hip into the dirt he once believed would make his fortune. He would give the place one more try, he decided, one more attempt before moving on. He had to explore every option if he was to make a life for himself in this new country.

His fingers clawed at the cool dirt beneath his touch and instantly he was back by Mary's side. Turning towards him, her smile bright and brimming with happiness, he kissed her, the unruly strands of her red hair whipping his face in the morning wind. That first sweet taste of her had blinded him to everything except her happiness and irretrievably changed his life. From the depths of bush outside the shadow of the fire's embers, a small creature scuttled in dry foliage. Hamish stirred in his bedroll, rolling onto his back. If his time could be had again he would not have nursed Mary through the fever. Yet he believed her to be dying, like his wee sisters and mother. With the prospect of her passing, his love for her kept him by her side when he should have left. In death there may have been forgiveness. In life there could be none.

Hamish sensed the void about him. Thousands were gathered together, yet still Hamish knew each and every man felt lonely, for he sensed their desolation in the tight blanket of the air. This was a place to swallow your soul. A night owl swooped low, a mouse squealed and then the whoosh of wings was replaced by silence. Yes, it was time to leave, Hamish concluded, as he stared upwards into a maze of brightly burning specks of light. Soon they would head north. He recalled the drover's stories of travelling by the stars; of the *Elfgin's* crew navigating by the constellations. The bible told of a star leading the three wise men to Jesus. Hamish drifted. He too would follow the stars, even if he had to drag his young brother behind him. Sleep wafted over him. Only a gentle sway was required and it would be as if he were still aboard the

Elfgin, soothed by the lap of water on her hull, buoyed by each passing day as he worked for his passage to the new country.

A little before dawn, Hamish rubbed crusted sleep from his eyes and stoked up the fire as a streak of muted pink smudged the horizon. From a hessian bag he pulled free a lump of meat and, with a curved blade, cut it into two large pieces. The billy can, already wedged above the fire, sizzled steadily, small bubbles forming and reforming on the surface of the water. He threw together flour and water and knocked it into a rough loaf, which he then sat in the coals.

Six months they had been on the fields. The winter, a harsh one even by Scottish standards, took many lives. Sickness came as fast and unbidden as a rich deposit and disappeared just as unexpectedly. Charlie remained touched by one such malady. Trust the lad, Hamish thought gloomily, to have the sickly disposition of a girl. As if aware of his thoughts, his younger brother struggled through the flap of the tent. Gaunt and yellow-eyed, he stooped to splash dawn-chilled water on his face from a cast-iron bucket.

'I've been thinking, lad, we'll leave in two months.' Hamish passed his brother a mug of tea, before tossing a lump of lard into a cast-iron fry pan on the fire and then the two pieces of meat. He prodded fiercely at the lumps of sizzling, salted mutton. Meat for breakfast was an indulgence. This lot, brokered from a new arrival in exchange for a small pick, was the last of it and was near past eating.

Burning his tongue on the boiling liquid, Charlie squatted heavily on an upturned cooking pot. 'And why are ye up and changing our plans? Always it's been a year.'

Hamish hunched his shoulders, turning the coal-covered bread with his knife. He was damn hungry this morning, his ribs were sticking to his noisy gut and convoluted talk was not something he needed.

Charlie let out a cough, a long, racking procedure that shook the length of his sinewy body. When the convulsion relented he sent a green globule of spittle into the dirt behind him. 'It's me? But winter's near over, and Lee will be back today with more herbs.'

'Aye, he will be,' Hamish agreed. If one person could be relied upon it was Lee. Having finally relented to the Chinaman's endless pestering to help the two brothers with their washing, cooking and other chores, Hamish now gave Lee his protection. In return he cared and cooked for them, while the herbs he boiled made a bitter drink that eased the lad's cough. Lee was bound to a headman in Southern China and had travelled from some obscure village in a cargo hold along with seven hundred countrymen, to work on the fields to repay debts in his homeland. Perhaps that was the reason Hamish felt so protective of the Chinaman. He had made that journey alone.

Spring was with them now, yet Hamish doubted the warming of the land would ease his brother's ailments or cure him of his whining. It was definitely near their time to be bidding the gold-fields goodbye. Besides, the thought of panning and digging and fighting and near starving had lost its appeal to him.

'So we'll stay?'

'You've been bickering since the first month, Charlie. First it was the seasickness, then Melbourne you didn't take to. You pushed hard to get here and then complain is all you've done. Now I say we are to leave and you disagree. You should not have come.'

'You should not have left, for what was I to do?' He screwed his face tightly.

Always their arguments returned in a circle to the beginning of their adventure. 'Made your own life,' Hamish said tightly as fat spurted out from the pan to burn the back of his hand.

'Who with? They were all dead, Hamish,' Charlie stated sadly. 'Five piles of stone on the edge of the loch.'

'You could have stayed with your father.'

'He's your father too,' Charlie replied softly.

'He's no kin to me. Decisions made, lad,' he growled. 'We'll be leaving when I give the word.' How he longed to remind his brother that he'd not invited him on this journey.

'You should not have put Mary before your own family, nor forced me to take sides.'

Selecting a chunk of sizzling meat, Hamish skewered it with a knife. 'Firstly, no-one asked you to take sides and secondly, never mention her name again.'

Charlie looked about the waking goldfields and winced at the thought of another day. He should have stayed in Melbourne. There was good work to be had there and loading supplies and chopping wood were chores he could manage. 'I should have told you,' he said simply, 'about what I saw that afternoon.'

Hamish glared at him, his lips greasy from the meat. 'Yes. You should have.'

❈ *Autumn, 1983* ❧

West Wangallon Homestead

Sarah flung the louvered doors open onto the verandah and walked out of her bedroom. The morning sun was just beginning to skirt the trees on the horizon. As she waited patiently for the first rays to flicker across the countryside, a flock of lorikeets flew overhead. She followed the formation of brilliant colour until they landed with a chorus of squeaks in a gum tree at the end of the garden. She didn't expect her mother to be very impressed with their return. Twelve months ago they had managed to decimate one of Sue's favourite trees directly outside the kitchen window, condemning them immediately to abuse should they ever return. Sarah lifted a finger to her lips, willing them to quietness. The birds would forever remind her of the day she learned that Wangallon was to have a new jackeroo.

With a smile she breathed in the dawn moist air, her eyes surveying the distant paddocks dotted with merino sheep. Their bodies moved effortlessly through the swaying grasses, their heads obscured as they munched with military precision.

The sun was climbing faster now, turning the distant skyline from a smudge of rose pink to a widening streak of red and blue. With its ascent came the almost imperceptible change in smell that Sarah knew so well. It reminded her of a basket of flowers, herbs and grasses. A tangy potpourri of scents growing in intensity as the slumbering countryside woke to a new day. It was this moment she loved best, even more than sunset when the animals quieted for the night and the shadows lengthened into the memory of the day. The constant majesty of the bush would always delight her.

Constancy within her family, however, was a totally different matter. Returning to her bedroom, Sarah tucked her pale yellow shirt into blue jeans and, not bothering to look in the mirror, gathered her hair back into a loose ponytail. After her grandfather's visit to their kitchen the previous year, Sarah had expected a shift in attitude amongst the inhabitants of the property, yet nothing altered. Indeed, her grandfather's presence only grew stronger. In some ways it was a relief. Cameron was still the same brother, dependable and fun. But it bothered Sarah that Cameron didn't change one bit with the formal notification of his eventual succession. In fact she had begun to worry whether he took the responsibility seriously, for if it had been her she doubted she would ever have felt the same again. Of course Cameron spoke often enough of sharing the running of Wangallon with her. He even went so far as to cheekily suggest that Anthony would be an excellent permanent addition. However, the fact remained that the property belonged to him.

As her thoughts threatened to ruin a perfect morning, Cameron's voice echoed loudly through the three-bedroom house. Sarah glanced at the small metal alarm clock on her dressing table. He too was an early riser, content to hunker down with a coffee in the kitchen with his cassette deck blaring out Bowie or Men At Work. That was until their parents appeared for breakfast. West Wangallon was much smaller than the main Wangallon homestead where her grandfather lived, which meant privacy was restricted to either the bedrooms or outdoors. Sarah grinned. She'd choose outdoors every time. Cameron yelled again. At this rate, Sarah thought, their mother would wake any minute. Today she was going riding with her brother and Anthony, but if Cameron succeeded in waking their parents they would certainly be delayed. She opened her bedroom door leading out into the hallway, surprised by the sound of her parents' voices. They were standing together at the end of the hallway where a closed door led to the living areas and kitchen.

'I don't care what you think, Ronald. The fact is that Cameron is the eldest. If it's good enough for your own father . . .'

Her parents' voices carried clearly down the hallway.

'If he knew the truth . . .' Ronald replied with a definite edge to his voice.

'Well he doesn't and we both know you're not going to tell him. The time for that is long past and the consequences for Cameron are too risky.'

'What about –'

'You forget,' Sue said silkily. 'None of this is Cameron's fault. Why should he suffer because you've suddenly developed a sense of honesty?'

Sarah shut the door slowly, trying to understand what she had just overheard. None of it made any sense. It sounded as if her parents had kept a secret from either her grandfather or Cameron. She searched her mind for any snippet of information she may have heard in the past. There was nothing, only the certain knowledge that Cameron was the only son recently crowned heir to Wangallon.

Glancing quickly in her bedroom mirror, she smoothed her hair with her hand before turning the collar up slightly on her cotton shirt. She studied herself again, freed her thick red-gold hair, flipped her head over and fluffed it with her fingers. Retying it she pulled a few wisps of hair free so that they hung delicately around her face. 'Better,' she decided. With only a slight pause she rifled through the top drawer of her hardwood dresser and retrieved a small pine box. Inside lay her grandmother's pearls, the beaten gold bangle and the bright blue scarf Anthony had given her in January. The silk was cool to the touch as she tied it carefully around her neck. She listened at her door and, although hearing nothing, decided not to risk a confrontation with her mother. Grabbing her camera, Sarah slipped through the louvered doors onto the verandah and walked quietly across the floor boards, out the gauze door, and ran around the side of the house.

Touching the flanks of her horse with the heels of her riding boots, Sarah trotted behind her brother and Anthony, finally catching up to the boys as they walked their horses through the thick lignum. The lignum grew like a hedge on the creek's edge, extending through the shallow water and out onto the opposite bank, reminding Sarah of a giant woody animal that had sprawled itself across the waterway. Their horses' hooves sunk into the soft sand of the creek bed as they began to cross it, water swirling only a couple of feet below their feet in the stirrups. Small water birds scuttled away as they reached the opposite bank, a pair of black swans lifting into the air before dropping again to the water's surface a few metres on.

'What kept you?'

'Nothing,' Sarah answered Cameron, adjusting the camera strap on her shoulder. She longed to blurt out what she had overheard her parents arguing about, however, with Cameron at the very centre of their discussion, it seemed wrong to mention it to him.

Dismounting, they tethered their horses to a tall gum and walked to the edge of the lignum. The myriad branches of each plant rose from ground level to weave thickly with its neighbour forming a dense barrier between the creek and the paddock. Cameron squatted, sniffing the dirt at the edge of the scrub. The lignum in this particular area had been knocked aside so that it resembled a cave opening.

'See where it's bashed down,' Cameron said, pointing to the obvious tunnel that led into the depths of the lignum.

'Feral pig,' Anthony said, squatting down beside him. 'They sure like their holes. At this time of the day I reckon there will be at least one of them camped in there in the shade.'

'Do you think it's the one Dad was after?' Sarah asked, resting her hands on both their shoulders, as they peered into the pig tunnel.

'Probably,' the boys answered in unison.

'Big one.' Cameron pointed at the thickness of the lignum. The woody plant had been broken off in a number of places. 'Good track.' The expectation in their voices matched their expressions as the boys looked at each other simultaneously and grinned.

'What?' Sarah queried. She could smell trouble, like the tang of burning twigs and brittle leaves.

'Be a good show,' Anthony announced, walking towards the nearest tree. 'We'll throw to decide who gets to crawl in after the pig.'

Cameron tilted his head to one side, a lock of hair catching in the thick length of his lashes. 'Fair enough.'

Both boys drew their pocket knives from the leather sheaths attached to their belts. They paced out four feet and then speared the small knives into the tree trunk. The blades held fast, quivering slightly, then Anthony's face fell as his blade dropped to the ground. Cameron cried out delightedly, springing to the tree to retrieve both blades. He passed over Anthony's knife, his face glowing.

'Be careful, Cameron,' Sarah called, as he made his way to the lignum. Gripping the knife between his teeth, he winked once at her before crawling into the scrub tunnel.

Wordlessly Sarah remounted her mare and, gathering the other horses' reins, waited. Cattle called loudly along the creek, a bull bellowing fanatically to his wandering harem. Anthony crouched to one side of the tunnel entrance, knife ready, just in case he ended up being charged by the wild pig. On the far creek bank, a four-foot goanna ambled slowly up a tree trunk. Sarah shifted in the well-oiled saddle; the horses, sensing her growing anxiety, stirred uneasily.

From the direction of the dense lignum, Sarah heard a soft thrashing sound. The noise grew louder, quickly becoming a crashing noise that vibrated out from the lignum tunnel and through the air. She lifted her camera and started taking shots; the surface of the lignum swayed thickly, gathering momentum as whatever moved through it increased its speed and headed for daylight.

'Holy shit!' It was Cameron's voice, loud and excited.

Holding tightly to the reins as the horses snorted and pawed the dirt, Sarah hoped it was only a little pig, not the one with the two-inch tusks her grandfather had confronted, which had ripped Shrapnel, her grandfather's young pup. Shrapnel had needed twenty stitches. She rubbed her hand against Oscar's flank to steady him.

Anthony yelled into the tunnel, 'Hey, what's happening?' Suddenly, the guttural sound of pigs squealing and her brother yelling abuse were terribly loud.

Anthony was smiling broadly. 'By the sounds of that, Cameron must have got him.'

'Great, great,' Sarah murmured her heart pounding in

anticipation. She pointed the camera towards the mouth of the lignum.

The crashing grew louder and louder, then Cameron re-appeared in a flash of pale blue shirt and dark denim. 'Run!' he yelled, his eyes wide. 'They're coming straight for us.' He bolted from the mouth of the lignum, Anthony matching his long strides.

The horses reared instinctively as Sarah finished taking a couple of shots and pulled hard on their reins, but the horses galloped across the creek, water splashing high in a great arch, soaking her jeans and shirt. To the right, a hundred metres or so, seven squat dark bodies hurtled out of the lignum tunnel and along the creek bank before disappearing from sight. Sarah burst out laughing before recrossing the creek as Cameron and Anthony climbed down from their respective trees. Only when she drew level with them did she see the bright smears of blood across her brother's face and shirt.

'Almost got the smaller one in the leg,' he grinned.

'I think I got some really cool photos,' Sarah replied.

'Same thing happened last time.' Cameron swiped at the perspiration running down his face. 'They're heading straight for you, then, just at the last moment, the sow turns, angles off to one side and tries to sideswipe your ribs or arms. Damn hard to get a kill.'

Anthony added, 'Same thing happened to me down by the river, remember?'

'What if you ended up with a broken leg or something, Cameron? What would happen to the property then?'

'Well that's bloody lovely,' Cameron grinned. 'She's more worried about the dirt than me.'

'Oh, you know what I mean,' Sarah answered, checking her camera. She had taken fifteen photos.

'I'll look after it,' Anthony said quickly, referring to Wangallon.

Cameron frowned briefly in Anthony's direction before raising his eyebrows. 'Nice scarf.'

Sarah felt her cheeks warm and immediately fussed with her hat. 'I didn't want my neck to get burnt.'

As Cameron trotted off ahead on his horse, Sarah held her breath as Anthony moved his own mount close enough so that their legs touched. 'It suits you,' he said slowly.

'Thanks.' His leg was warm against hers.

'You're welcome.' He leant forward in his saddle, his hand stretching across the short space between them to touch the silken material. Sarah felt his finger tips brush the warm softness of her neck.

Anthony finally spoke. 'I owe your brother a race.' He smiled at her, a soft smile that crinkled the corners of his eyes. 'And I want copies of those photos, particularly if they show Cameron being chased by that pig.' Any other girl would have taken off at the first sight of those pigs, he thought as he trotted after Cameron. At the very least she would have fallen off when the horses reared up; but not Sarah. There she was, cool as anything, taking photos as the pigs charged out, just as excited as they were. Anthony flicked his mount with his spurs, breaking into a canter.

As she watched him go Sarah let her breath out very slowly.

≪ *Summer, 1857* ≫

The Victorian Goldfields

S ix days a week they toiled; digging, panning, shifting dirt. On the Sabbath they bathed and read the bible, and then Hamish, practising his reading, would study any material he could obtain as Charlie slept the day away, exhausted. They found no rich deposits, yet what they did mine was enough for food and they managed to save a little. Hamish kept the small wad of notes in his boots. As Hamish suspected, Charlie's health was not improving. However, having decided on a departure date, he ensured the few remaining weeks spent at the fields did not go to waste. He perfected his habit of eavesdropping on conversations, becoming so observant that his nickname, 'silent one', became commonplace. He watched other teams bickering and learnt to soothe things in his own. Before punishment was meted out to thieves, he asked what drove them to commit such acts, and all the while he watched the Chinese labouring with diligence, wincing at the savage treatment they received.

It was at night though, with the stars illuminating his imagination, that Hamish sought the answers to an unknown land and marvelled that he lay cocooned in such vastness. For settled on the outer limits of a stranger's campfire, in a landscape peppered by the bodies and small lives of the desperate and the adventurous, he discovered the magnificent tracts of land waiting unclaimed beyond the hills of the known. These wild, unimaginable spaces were stalked upon by the dark peoples who roamed the bush. There were renegades, the old-timers told him; starving renegades, anxious to protect their land from settlers, wary of the whites. He learned of the mass killings of the blacks in the early days of settlement, of white settlers murdered in revenge, and of the convicts: those who continued to steal, those who had been freed, those who were forced to cut a swathe in the bush and those, woman and man alike, who rotted in chains.

This then was his new country and Hamish embraced it like a father to a first born, for within its sour interior lay the sweetest of fruit – livestock. Only cattle and sheep enchanted Hamish. Everything else, imperative to learn though it was, merely served his survival in this wild place he had chosen to ride. He clung to the stories surrounding the great mobs of stock traversing the inland. The ex-drovers reeled him in like a slumbering yellow belly and through them he learned of the huge numbers of cattle traversing the country to saleyards, and of the sheep, the Merino. This creamy gold, buried beneath the daggy exterior of dirt and mud and urine and burr, would be his salvation.

❖

It was an old shaft, left in disgust some six months back, yet Hamish had a feeling about it: a deep feeling in his gut that it would change his life. He began repairing it as best as possible. The timber supports took time, but they now lined twenty-five feet of the old mine. Lamps placed every six feet illuminated the dank tunnel. At the end of it lay a further five feet of dirt, then rock. This was the culmination of a week's work.

'Let us go back to the creek, Hamish,' Charlie pleaded. He was not yet sixteen years, yet his brother's daily battle for gold was now beyond his endurance. In truth the illness crept upon him so slowly that he had not realised the extent of the sickness until it was too late. Now his nights were sweat-inducing nightmares, his days, ribbons of pain that struck at his joints. At least panning in the creek gave him sun and fresh air. 'There was dust enough there to keep us fed.'

Lifting his pick, Hamish struck the surface in swift movements. One day he hoped for bigger concerns than the neverending quest to keep bellies full and his young brother quiet. To his left, a further five feet on, the sounds of Charlie shovelling carried eerily in the gloom.

'Are you trying to kill us both then?' Charlie called out into the darkness.

'I'm trying to make money, lad.' Hitching slipping braces over his calico shirt, Hamish brought his lamp closer to the rock. The seam once dreamt about did not appear beneath the flickering light. 'Damn it!' In response the dank cavern rumbled.

'Did you want me to admit then that I was wrong? Is that what you've been waiting to hear these past three years?' Charlie continued.

Scrunching his head down deep into his shoulder blades, Hamish considered what it would mean to go back to panning in the cold water to the jeers and scornful asides of those older hands who advised to leave the useless mine alone. Dirt trickled from the roof, gathering beneath his shirt collar, crusting the sweat in the hollow of his back before landing in the waistband of his trousers. The lamp flickered, threatened to go out, then it regained its former brightness.

'Tell me then, brother,' Charlie persevered, 'what would you have done?'

Hamish sighed and lifted the wooden handles of his barrow. He'd managed to avoid this conversation for months and he intended to keep doing so. To reopen the wound would surely damage his relationship with his brother.

The rush of clean air and unrestricted light struck Hamish as he strode from the opening of the mine with a barrow of dirt, his chest easing as the constriction of the tunnel released its grasp. Dumping the earthy contents in a nearby pile, he sat heavily on downtrodden vegetation only twenty feet from the reinforced entrance. The time drew close for their departure, and it was none too soon for Hamish. It wasn't just the rough winter and the unceasing digging for little reward; his brother's health demanded it. Already 1857 was near halfway through, as good a time as any to move on. Loath to admit it, the thought of leaving Charlie safe in a small town appealed to him, not just for the boy's own health, either. How much faster the trip north would be, how unencumbered.

The sound, loud as the crashing of waves, rolled towards him where he lay sprawled in crushed spinifex grass, an index finger searching out wax from his ear.

'Charlie!' he roared, scrambling to his feet. Dirt and dust billowed out as if from a dropped bag of flour, engulfing his body, nose, eyes and throat; as if the ground swayed beneath his very feet.

Charlie lay flat on his back in a low-slung camp bed, the flicker of an oil lamp forming intricate patterns of light and shade on his pained face. Outside, a shadow rippled past the canvas wall and Lee entered the tent with broth. He removed Hamish's untouched plate of dripping and bread as Hamish poured the green trickle of the broth into his brother's mouth, rubbing his throat to make him swallow.

'I didn't know what to do,' Charlie whispered. 'I felt I had to follow ye, Hamish. I would have stayed in Scotland if not for ye.'

Hamish leaned over his brother, ready to pour more broth, 'It'll help your pain, Charlie. Lee said it would.' The liquid bubbled and spluttered across the boy's face. 'Damn.' Placing the small wooden bowl on the dirt floor, he wiped the boy's face roughly.

Charlie's eyes darted about the room. 'And having stayed I'd have seen nothing of this life. I'm sorry not to see your sheep, Hamish.' The creases around his eyes smoothed.

Hamish wiped a damp cloth across an almost unrecognisable forehead, recalling each long mile travelled.

'I remember sitting at Mother's feet . . .'

'Save your breath, lad.' He did not want the boy's last thoughts to be that of their miserable life in the Highlands. Yet, he thought sadly, he had not been able to replace that life with something better, at least not in Charlie's eyes.

'Father knew he'd not be seeing us again,' Charlie whispered. 'The day we left, the way he looked at us, he was still watching when we crossed the second burn.' His voice wavered. 'Do ye think Ma and the wee ones were watching? Sometimes I thought Ma was here with us.'

Hamish nodded. There was no minister, Presbyterian, Catholic, nothing. The priest had died two months earlier of the sickness, and the other had vanished some weeks back, some say killed by blacks. Hamish searched frantically for a word of comfort. 'God bless.'

Charlie's eyes crinkled in a half-smile of sympathy and regret. 'It was not just Mary's fault you know.'

'Quiet, lad.'

'Father kissed her back.'

47

So then, that was the truth of it.

'You loved her so. I wanted your image of her to remain untainted, but I was wrong to do so. Forgive them, Hamish.'

They had both betrayed him.

'I wish I were going with you.' Charlie's voice dropped away like a coin down a well.

Hamish pulled his little brother roughly to his chest, the movement sending the lad unconscious. Frantically he tried to force more of Lee's drug down the boy's throat, until the insistent pressure of the Chinaman's grip on his shoulder caused him to stop. Gradually the lad's eyes flickered and reopened. His clammy skin, yellow in the light, appeared to cool ever so gently as Hamish held him close.

'I'll be watching, Hamish. I've walked through your dream, tasted it. You have to live your life for the two of us.'

When the night was at its blackest, Charlie drew his last breath. Behind him Hamish heard the barely audible sigh of Lee. Carefully he laid his brother down on the camp bed. With a nod he left the body in the care of the Chinaman.

The grave was deep. Much deeper than the usual plots scattered on the far northern boundary of the goldfields. Hamish, Lee and Dave, a loner who had elected to join them, lifted Charlie's body above the pit. It was not yet dawn.

'Are ye ready then?' Dave asked. His impatience, evident since birth some twenty-five years prior, currently lay curled in his throat, along with the aching beat of his one-inch-shorter left leg. Had humour ever rested within his small frame, the hanging of his father for theft and the death of his mother in some tavern further south had surely drowned all hope of character reformation. He cleared his throat, once, twice. The dawn mist lifted steadily, removing its wet cloak from their faces and clothes. Dave dared not move, yet the lad grew heavy between them, heavier and stiffer.

A few feet away wallabies hopped shyly from sleep into the new day and stopped to nibble tentatively at the green butts of grass. Dave watched the small animals hungrily, his nostrils flaring at the thought of the young flesh roasting succulently. A small pan to catch the juices, a chunk of doughy bread, he could feel the fat glazing his lips and whiskers. His stomach rumbled noisily. 'An unnatural time for a burial,' he grunted as they finally lowered the hessian-swaddled body into the damp soil. Disturbed, the wallabies crept quickly into the ridge of trees behind them.

Hamish concentrated on shovelling the clods of dirt over his brother until the earth was mounded above him and the stirrings of the cramped quarters of the fields could be heard below.

'A far distance we travelled and this . . .' Hamish gestured towards the glowing dawn sun. 'Anyway,' he turned towards Dave, 'now he has seen the start of a new day.'

Lee touched his arm. 'He good man.'

'Yes,' Hamish agreed. Charlie had followed him to the other side of the world out of a sense of loyalty. And out of love he had kept his own council regarding Mary's betrayal.

Dave backed away silently to join Lee who, having finished burning a fragrant offering in the cold air, stamped it out with his sandalled foot before walking to the dray. Scooping up a fistful of dirt from the burial mound, Hamish placed it in his pocket and turned his back on the fields below.

❧ *Winter, 1983* ❧

West Wangallon

*A*nthony walked towards the stables, aware Sarah would be feeding the mare. Charlotte was due to foal within the next few months and looked forward to her nightly stabling and bucket of oats. At least once a fortnight Anthony found an excuse to be nearby, even though he lived in the jackeroo's quarters on Wangallon, a good few miles from Sarah's home. He approached quietly, watching as Sarah pulled her pocket knife from the soft pouch at her waist to cut open the feed bag. Her hands worked quickly, fingers nimbly pulling the hessian apart as Charlotte nudged both Sarah and the bag as the bucket was filled.

'Steady, girl, let me get it in the bucket first.' Sarah carried the bucket into the stables, Charlotte following closely, her muzzle resting on Sarah's shoulder.

Anthony could hear the horses munching, interspersed with Sarah's reassuring voice. It was nearing dusk, the day's sounds dwindling as small creatures readied themselves for night. Crickets chirped noisily while the rising hum of cicadas could be heard from the pine ridge beyond.

Only three years separated them, Anthony thought. Not a lot really. He and Cameron were nearing twenty-one, while Sarah was soon to turn eighteen. He stuffed his hands in his pockets; a year he'd been at Wangallon, the best year of his life. The responsibility old Angus gave him was enormous and he considered Cameron a close mate. The fact Sarah Gordon completed his small circle of station friends only added to his everyday enjoyment. Sure he'd been sad on accepting the position at Wangallon, for only a chance of birth meant that it was he who left his home and not his older brother, yet now he couldn't imagine living anywhere else. Being employed by Angus Gordon still caused a lump of pride to rise in his throat and he admitted finding it difficult not to appear arrogant when discussing his job with the few other jackeroos about the district. Even his own father had congratulated him on being 'chosen' by the Wangallon Gordons. Friends questioned him on whether the old squatter really was a mean-hearted old bastard with a mind as sharp as a tack, while the mail lady – as she was known – took great joy in relating a story to Anthony that she said was common knowledge in the district. 'Got a match?' a passerby requesting a light had asked Angus, 'Yeah, your face and my arse,' had come the unwavering reply.

Anthony prised as much as he could out of Cameron, but it was impossible to decipher the legend from the reality. There were the stories, the rumours, connecting Angus's father, Hamish, with stock theft and illegal dealings, with deaths of family members and Aborigines alike, yet even Cameron admitted that some things were best left in the past. So Anthony had to satisfy himself with the basics. Angus was the product of a second marriage, born when his father was in his early sixties, and the locals reckoned he was as wealthy and as scheming as his father had been.

❖

'Hi.' Sarah appeared from the stable, bucket in hand, her pale blue jersey filthy, her eyes bright. 'What are you up to?'

'Returning these.' He held out a white and yellow envelope.

Tossing the bucket into the shed with the feed bag, Sarah grasped the worn door knob, nervousness attacking her stomach as she slammed the door shut, bolting it against roaming animals. Since Cameron's mad dash through the lignum a few months earlier, her school work had increased dramatically. She was to sit the Higher School Certificate later in the year, which effectively meant free time was almost non-existent. Yet somehow she still managed to see Anthony every week and usually it was here at the stables. She wiped her hands on her jeans and took the envelope from him. They were the photos she'd taken during their morning at the lignum. 'Thanks.'

'I got some copies made. You know they're really excellent shots. Especially the one showing Cameron after he stopped running.'

That was Sarah's favourite as well. 'He sure looked scared.'

'You should enter a photographic competition, you know.'

'Well, I'm really only mucking about.'

It didn't look like it to Anthony. He'd shown the photos to a photographer in town and he reckoned Sarah had a real eye for composition. 'How's the study going?'

'I had English and maths, missed the muster in the stud paddock, but you know what Mum's like.' Sarah folded her arms across her chest, and then let them fall to her side before finally jamming them deep into the pockets of her jeans. It gave her a bit of a thrill to see Anthony alone like this.

'Yep,' Anthony agreed. Sarah's mother was definitely a bit loopy, and he instinctively knew that she didn't like her kids fraternising with the hired help, even if he too was from a respected grazing family.

Sarah knew he liked her. Well, at least a bit, otherwise they wouldn't keep bumping into each other at the stables. He was hardly detouring all the way from the jackeroo's quarters to talk to the horses. Surely he would ask her out. Heavens she wished they lived closer to a bigger town. She'd had her eye on a purple dress with ruching down the front and a sort of tulip style skirt and she figured it would suit her. She pulled the elastic from her hair, shaking it loose about her shoulders before gathering it up again into a rough ponytail.

Anthony moved to sit on the old cement block that served as a step into the feed shed. Already the sky had darkened, leaving only a thin pale streak beyond the distant trees to show the sun's path. He beckoned Sarah to his side. She wavered momentarily as she wet her lips, before walking over and sitting down beside him. They sat silently, Sarah drawing her knees closer to ward off the chill of the night air, terribly aware of their arms touching.

So when had he lost his heart to the girl beside him? Anthony wondered. No longer did he see the tomboy, the girl in patched jeans, a sheathed pocket knife hanging from her plaited leather belt. He could mesmerise himself by examining the pale pink ovals of her nails, dream of his hands resting on her hips and imagine the rich scent of her hair as it cascaded through his fingers. His hand brushed an imaginary streak of grime from his jeans, a half-smile sneaking across his lips as he acknowledged how wimpy he sounded.

'Only a few months back and we were down by the river,' Sarah said, tucking her hands under her jumper. It was going to be a cold night.

Anthony recalled the afternoon, the last before the cool of autumn struck; the three of them splashing about in the brown water of the creek, their toes being sucked down into sludgy mud as they cooled off. Later, half asleep, he'd turned on his towel and caught the last of the sun's rays reflecting off Sarah's body. Her lean form, tanned and wet, had become a recurring image in his mind. Sure he'd experienced something of women but things were a little different at Wangallon, for she was the grand-daughter of his boss.

'Did you hear about old Ronnie Reagan? Apparently he's going to launch all these satellites that will be able to shoot down incoming nuclear missiles.'

Sarah looked skywards. 'You're not serious.' Above where they sat, the stars appeared gradually, drawn out one by one until they sprinkled the dark space above them like pearls. 'Is he that worried about the Russians?'

'Seems like it.'

'Hey, it would sort of be like *Star Wars*.'

'Actually that's exactly what some people are calling it.'

Sarah shook her head. 'Amazing. Here we are watching this stuff at the drive-in and it could be happening in real life. Thank heavens we're here.'

'You'll never leave here, will you, Sarah?'

'No, never. Like Grandfather says, once you have this place in your blood, neither will work without the other. That's why the family has been here for so long. To leave is to leave yourself.' She wanted to tell him that she liked him, although maybe he thought her too young. Perhaps that was the reason he had not asked her out? After all, she was still at school.

'I'd better go, it's late.' Sarah stood reluctantly. Through the line of trees bordering the rear of West Wangallon homestead, lights beckoned. Soon it would be dinner.

'Sarah.' Anthony moved to stand beside her. He wanted to kiss her, to hold her slight body against his. To smell the scent of sandalwood and saddle grease. He doubted if she had ever been kissed and certainly not by someone with a bit of experience. While he imagined his hands and arms encircling her, he touched her shoulder lightly. If his advances were not accepted by either Sarah or the family, he would be out of a job in a heartbeat and he did love it here. Being a part of Wangallon was very important to him. 'Better let you get home. We start shearing in a couple of days, so I probably won't see much of you once it starts.'

'Probably not.' Something made her turn to face him. His hair ruffled by the wind, the nonchalant lean of his body, the pull of his jumper across his shoulders, a queer sensation filled her.

'No, probably not,' Anthony repeated, taking a step towards her. His heart pounding, he lifted his hand and let his fingers gently run down her face, following the curve of her cheekbone to the soft hollow at the base of her throat. Reluctantly, he stepped back. He needed time to consolidate his position on the property, time to see if their feelings were mutual, to discover if Sarah wanted him as much as he yearned for her.

Her body mechanically turned towards the lights of her home, while her mind focused on the nearness of him, on the look in his eyes, on the thought of him kissing her. Her feet led her away. However, at the line of trees bordering the rear of the homestead, Sarah dawdled beneath the softly rustling foliage. Darkness had descended and with it would come her mother's taunts of lateness. She briefly rested her palm against the rough bark of an athel tree, the knobbly surface calming the emotions inside her as Anthony's utility roared to life. She recalled Cameron's light-hearted teasing about whether she had given Anthony a Christmas present and his remark about Anthony becoming a permanent addition at Wangallon.

At the timber gate to her home she lifted the latch, remembering the brief lecture on risk she and her brother had been subjected to only yesterday by their grandfather.

'Yer not going anywhere, lass, if you don't have a debt on the place. No point living comfortable and paying cash, for that means yer not a risk taker. The bush isn't the place for people who don't like risk.'

'Risk,' Sarah repeated softly, walking the few steps up the cracked cement path. There were different types of risk. One of which was being keen on the jackaroo. At the back door, she scraped the heel of her work boots against the step.

'Would you mind hurrying it up a little, Sarah? Your father and brother would like to eat before midnight.'

Taking a deep breath, Sarah walked into the kitchen.

Birds and lizards scattered as the chainsaw ripped noisily through the box tree. Anthony pushed the chainsaw harder against the trunk, the blade finally meeting with the cut Cameron had made on the opposite side. A loud crackle sounded as the tree swayed, the rustle of leaves and the accompanying whoosh of wind ending with a resounding crash as twenty feet of timber fell heavily into dense scrub.

Deftly, Cameron cut the top of the tree free of all branches, leaving a good twelve feet of perfectly straight trunk. Wiping the sweat from his brow, his hat tipping back off his forehead with the movement, he caught the water bottle Anthony threw and took a long swig. He remained sitting on the decapitated crown of the tree as Anthony, with chainsaw in hand, strad-dled the trunk and began to cut a straight line through the bark lengthwise. Eyes focused, woodchips flying, Anthony's hands were steady as the saw ran precisely down the length of the trunk. With the first cut completed, he rolled the trunk over with Cameron's help and proceeded to cut the other side. Later, when they were back at the yards, they would remove the bark. Leaving it on made the tree easier to carry and transport without the slippery under-skin of the woody plant impeding their progress.

'That's six. Should do it, don't you think?' Anthony asked

Cameron as they heaved under the strain of the tree, pushing it onto the back of the Land Cruiser.

'Yep.'

Anthony drove carefully through the scrub, avoiding the fallen timber that could stake an unsuspecting tyre, the vehicle bumping roughly over undulating ground. Locating the barely visible track serving as the main road for this part of the property, they settled back for the thirty-minute drive to the sheep yards.

'So, what's the story?' Cameron enquired nonchalantly, turning up the radio and changing the station.

'About what?'

'You know. That lame excuse about Sarah not needing to come with us this morning. She'll be pissed when we get back.'

'Probably,' Anthony agreed, his hand moving to adjust the volume.

'So, you gonna share?' Cameron continued, his fingers drumming with anticipation on the dash. 'I heard your ute last night. Sarah was late for dinner.'

'Share what?' Anthony attempted to answer with disinterest as three kangaroos bounded across their path. Sure, he and Cameron had spoken occasionally about Sarah, but it was usually his mate giving him a hard time. Surely Sarah hadn't told him about last night. Not that there was anything to tell. Anthony peered intently at the dirt track ahead wondering how he could worm his way out of his mate's fact-finding mission.

'How long have you been here for?'

'Okay, okay I give up.' Anthony tapped the radio on/off switch with his forefinger. Suddenly it was deathly quiet. He glanced at Cameron, whose eyes were crinkling in amusement. 'If you've got something to say, I'd prefer it if you just came straight out with it.'

'What do you mean?'

'If you want to ask me something, ask me.' Anthony gritted his teeth. It was possible Cameron didn't like the idea of him being keen on his sister. If so maybe it was better if Cameron told him how he felt, for Anthony had no intention of jeopardising his position at Wangallon.

'Okay then, I will. No need to get all feminine on me. I was just wondering how long you've been here at Wangallon?'

'Over a year, you know that.'

Cameron bolted upright in his seat. 'A whole year. It took a year for you to make a pass at my sister!'

Anthony gripped the steering wheel, hastily accelerating with a quick gear change. 'She tell you that?'

'What? That it took you a whole year or that you actually did make a pass at her?'

About to answer, Anthony looked across to find his friend's face red with suppressed laughter.

'Well, you are enjoying yourself, aren't you?'

Cameron's chuckling continued until they reached the sheep yards. His face, usually so tanned beneath his blonde hair, remained red for a good minute before gradually resuming its normal colouring.

'It wasn't actually a pass,' Anthony answered quickly, as they pulled a trunk from the rear of the vehicle and carried it, one on either end, into the yards.

Cameron nodded over his shoulder to where Sarah was pulling up on a quad-runner on the other side of the yards. 'What was it then?'

'Well, you two took long enough. Thanks for leaving me behind.' Sarah walked briskly towards them.

'Told you she would be pissed off,' Cameron stated knowingly, as he watched his sister swing her long legs over each railing. 'Well, if it was a pass, it wasn't a very good one by the looks of her mood. Need some pointers?'

'Maybe,' Anthony agreed with a shrug and a grin. They dropped the trunk near the broken railing.

Cameron clapped his mate on the back. 'Anthony was just telling me that, well, it was nothing really,' he finished lamely at the hostile look in Anthony's eyes. 'Let's get going.'

Axe in hand, Cameron began to prise the bark away from the trunk. With short taps and a twist of the axe-head, the blade slipped neatly into the incision down the length of the trunk, pulling the bark neatly away. When one side was completed, Anthony and Cameron rolled the tree over to reveal the other incision. Within moments the bark had separated neatly from the trunk and lay in two curled pieces.

'You would think someone would invent a quicker method,' Sarah exclaimed, when the last trunk had been de-barked and the boys set about positioning the new upright post.

'Imagine building a house using this method, like the old-timers did,' Anthony commented.

'Yeah, well, Wangallon homestead is still standing. It may have taken them a bloody long time, but what they built sure lasted.' Cameron continued to shovel dirt into the four-foot-deep hole in which the new post sat.

Confident it was sturdy enough, Anthony measured the replacement railing and, with a smaller chainsaw, cut a ten-inch wedge into the face of the new upright. Another length of wood fitted neatly into the wedge and was secured at either end with a double twist of wire.

Sarah patted the new rail. 'Makes a difference with the chainsaw. I don't think building a house with a couple of axes would have been easy.'

Cameron stood back to admire the new rail and upright post. It was a beaut day, bright and clear. He watched Anthony measuring up another length of timber, his sister watching him carefully from under the brim of her hat. They would be great together. He certainly agreed with his grandfather on that score.

'Hey, Cameron, you gonna pass me the pliers or what?'

'Sure, sure.' He threw them across to where Anthony was uncoiling a length of wire. 'So, Anthony, you gonna ask Sarah out?'

The tinny snap of wire being cut answered Cameron. For a moment he thought Anthony was going to throw the pliers at him, instead he concentrated on twisting a double length of wire securely around a loose railing and another upright post.

'Well, what do you think?' Anthony finally blurted out. When his question continued to hang in the air unanswered, he took a deep breath, turning towards Sarah.

'Too slow,' Cameron stated laconically as the quad-runner started up in the distance and disappeared around the corner of the shed.

'How did you know?' Anthony watched her go, his clenched knuckles the only sign of misgiving.

Cameron thought about the question for a moment. 'The way you look at each other. Like there could be a party going on but you two might as well be in the bloody desert. Besides, you gave her a pretty nice scarf and she wears it.'

'Let's finish the yards.'

'Sure, just remember one thing.' Cameron grasped his friend's shoulder firmly. 'Don't let the grass grow under your feet, Anthony.'

'Cam, old mate, I appreciate your interest but have you thought this out. Your mother would chuck a spastic if she thought anything was going on between Sarah and me.' Anthony scratched his temple, the action tilting his hat slightly to one side. 'Besides, there's my job.' Slipping off the railing, Anthony began to work on the next upright post. Twisting the wire firmly across the timber, he began talking of the next day's mustering job. It was far easier to discuss the trek from the southern boundary than to continue a topic he had not quite got his head around.

⪻ *Summer, 1857* ⪼

Central Western New South Wales

*T*he scent of stagnant water assaulted Hamish's nostrils two miles before his sullen party were in sight of the river. Ducking his head to bypass a low hanging limb, he looked ahead to where Dave trotted at the lead, his stocky body weaving in and out of barrel-sized tree trunks, the occasional screech of a bird registering their imminent intrusion as they completed their descent down the slight hill. Their mounts, slow and deliberate in gait, increased their pace a little as the ground evened and, with the thinning out of trees, they struck the softer soil indicative of a waterway. Pulling up a short distance from the river, Hamish indicated with a nod to Lee that this would be their campsite. Daylight was receding and this narrow trickle of mud that was to have provided water for all would be their sleeping companion, at least for this night. It had been a rough trip. The dray had been lost crossing the Broken River. Hamish had watched as his only spare shirt, his small collection of books and his tent and tools had either sunk to the bottom of the river or been swept away in

the fast flowing water. Ahead he watched the Chinaman mutter-
ing under his breath as he rubbed his arse, inspected the creek
and rubbed his arse again. It had taken some cajoling to get him
aboard the old mare he'd bartered half a pound of rendered sheep
fat for. Still, with the loss of the dray, the man surely couldn't
walk around this great land.

Dave dismounted, leading his horse to the drying creek before
stretching out his stiff leg. The horse snuffled miserably at the
stagnant pool as Dave removed both saddle and saddlecloth and
placed them beneath the sprawling branches of an ancient gum
tree. Dropping his swag to the ground, he poured water from
a leather-bound bottle into his hat, his mount drinking thirstily as he took a swig himself. Close by, Hamish and Jasperson
were doing the same, the muffled snorting of the horses as they
snuffled up their paltry share echoing along the river bank. With
a deep sigh, Dave patted his horse's muzzle, then removed the
bridle before gathering his swag and limping to the base of the
gum. A few feet away Hamish and Jasperson settled on respective trees, one swishing at the flies and poking a pointy stick in
the dirt, the other thumbing through a well-worn book that Dave
suspected Hamish had read near one hundred times.

'Mister Hamish, we have little water.'

The complaining Chinese for once was right, Dave decided
as he stretched out in silence. Lee set about gathering small
twigs and dried leaves to start a fire. They had bashed across the
swollen Broken River, losing their dray and most of their supplies
in the process, picked up another mouth to feed in the likes of
Jasperson and then four days after finally crossing the Broken,
they had reached heaven. Groves of ancient eucalypts concealed
kangaroos, pigs, emus and foxes. Fish and mussels appeared
fresh and sparkling from rivers and streams and they breathed
crisp fresh air with no bleak outcrops of weathered rock to hinder
their line of sight. And the sheep; for the sheep alone Dave was

certain Hamish would pull up. They dusted the soft undulating country like wisps of cloud dotting the expanse of sky. 'Not here,' had been Hamish's only remark, as if there were better things in store for them. Two weeks was all that lay between the flooded Broken River and this excuse for a river, two weeks of fine grassed country. Country glistening as morning dew draped its arms about it and embraced it as a lover and Hamish had deserted it.

'Better things indeed,' Dave mumbled, squirming his arse in the dirt in an effort to find a modicum of relief. He was keen to stop moving. He was sure he'd be nearing thirty soon and after all his years of wandering, he was partial to the idea of return-ing to the land to work for one of the squatters on a big sheep spread. A boundary rider, yes, that would suit him fine. He had mentioned it to Jasperson, but that one was a strange char-acter. Lost his party, he'd said; all drowned, he'd said, crossing the Broken; seeking his fortune, he'd said, or seeking it back, for he claimed he and his family were free passengers out from England.

Lee deftly stoked the fire's coals before wedging in a rounded shape of dough and a billycan of precious water for tea. Then he sat cross-legged with his saddle bag beside him and, from a tanned piece of kangaroo hide, unwrapped a collection of dried meats. In fact all their bags held the remains of smoked emu, roo, fish and lamb meat. Begrudgingly, Dave admitted that Lee took his self-imposed position of cook seriously, which was damn lucky, for Hamish never thought of food until mealtime and then he expected Lee to provide it.

'Well, Dave, I can hear your brain ticking over, and I'm sure if I can, Jasperson can too,' Hamish said suddenly, breaking the silence.

Lee, who was carefully pouring tea into four tin mugs, waited expectantly. Dave poked the dirt between his legs with his fore-finger as Hamish closed his book.

'Dave, it's not like you to not speak your mind.' He had chosen Dave particularly at the camp and Jasperson's presence was decided upon for the same reason – they were men without ambition or direction. Accepting the tea Lee offered, Hamish slurped at the scalding contents before wedging it securely in the dirt by his side. They were the type of men he needed, men scared of decision-making, men who wouldn't go back or forwards without a leader.

'A boundary rider, Hamish. I'd been thinking of it, not to leave you, Hamish, no, but to settle down for a while. Maybe go back a week or so, to that Englishman's station, the squatter.' Dave wet his lips, glancing quickly at Jasperson in the hope of support.

Walking across to the fire, Hamish picked up a sharpened stick and hunkered down in a squatting position to spear a sliver of smoked roo meat from the leather hide on which it rested. He held the meat over the fire for a minute or so before chewing it thoughtfully.

Dave gulped his watery tea, scalding his throat. Damn Jasperson, he was sure the man would agree, for who wanted to put up with this ceaseless roaming? He could see no point in it. He was tired, of his leg, of the travel, of the riding, and he was lonely. He had need of a woman, someone to cook, something soft to paw at night. Damn long it was since he had been with a woman.

'Two days' travel to the next mail run. There'll be water there if we've enough to last,' Hamish replied, spitting gristle from his mouth.

'Lee?' Hamish asked.

'There will be enough.'

'Enough for the horses too, Lee?'

Lee nodded as Dave and Jasperson came forward to pick at the thin strips of meat by the camp fire. Lee took a selection of emu flesh for himself and lay down in the soft hollow he had carved out under a bulbous tree trunk.

Hamish continued squatting by the campfire, poking disinterestedly at the lumpy dough, thinking of the rendered fat swapped to keep Lee's arse off the ground. The thought of the dripping lying warm and tasty on a chunk of bread caused his stomach to growl nastily. 'The best of the land we've travelled through has been taken.' A lone star flickered through the thick leaves overhead as the sky settled into a smudge of pink and blue. 'I have a mind to own my own piece of dirt. Somewhere we can all call home.' He glanced around at the stunned faces. Hamish figured as much. These were the type of men who needed to belong, but more importantly they needed a goal. 'Two days then, Dave?'

'Aye,' Dave agreed. 'Two days.'

The Hill was little less than a mail point. A small building served as Post Office and General Store, a hotel provided alcohol, meals and beds, while three small humpies housed an old man, a tracker and two prostitutes. In all, this monument to isolation and ruination was a poor reward for the men he had sent on ahead to the hotel. Scratching his head thoughtfully, Hamish spun around in the middle of the track that separated bunks and whiskey from boiled lollies and soiled women, and then looked further afield to the trees and swaying grasses at the very edges of the settlement. This was a place where few would notice a man's comings and goings.

A few feet away, the store's flaking red and white signboard announced the proprietor, Todd Reynolds. It rattled with the arrival of a dirty southerly wind. Carried along with it in a flurry of grit, came the cackle of a well used woman and the hoarse cry of a familiar voice: Jasperson's needs were clearly far greater than Dave's. Hamish clucked his tongue, the action dislodging a piece of emu gristle from a back molar. One day he would have to acquire some ability in that department as well although, at the moment, a book, a feed and some information were his ultimate priorities.

Hamish entered the store, noting the whistling of the wind as it speared through gaping holes in the wooden walls. Within the dim interior he could see rough shelving and cupboards – most were partially empty except for great dust-covered cobwebs. The storekeeper looked up once before returning to his polishing cloth, which he rubbed in a circular motion across the long wooden counter, empty except for two large jars of boiled sweets and a ledger.

'What do you sell here, then?' Hamish enquired of the stocky man.

'M-m-many things, b-bolts of cloth, l-lamps, l-lard.'

Hamish glanced around the gloomy interior, 'Aye, I see.'

'Tea, flour, tobacco. W-we don't get much p-passing trade. There's a town, you see, and an agency, Stock and Station, a-a day's ride s-south.'

'An agency. So they buy and sell sheep, do they?' Hamish asked.

'Aye, m-my brother owns it and the s-s-store and the-the hotel.'

'Owns it all?'

'Yes.'

The shopkeeper's hand stilled. His lips twitched as if he had more to say. Hamish got the impression the man had not had a conversation with another person for some time.

'What do they call this town?'

The shopkeeper spoke slowly, as if the giving of so much information at once demanded every ounce of his concentration. 'Ridge Gully. T-they're building a lumberyard, there are many houses. M-my brother Matthew lives in a mud-brick house. M-money there, there is.'

Indeed there would be, Hamish decided as he ambled up the dirt track, a wedge of boiled sweet glued to the side of his mouth and the same apiece for his team seconded in his pocket. Todd Reynolds, or Tootles as he apparently preferred to be called, was certainly full of information, yet there was the question of how Hamish could best make use of it. He could be like the others, he scratched his whiskers thoughtfully, use his savings to buy a few head, but how would he get land? And if he did, well, what use would a small plot be? The wind continued to blow up, heaving gritty dirt into his eyes and ears. To his left, the older of the two prostitutes, dressed only in a filthy chemise, waved disinterestedly at him, while the younger allowed Jasperson to lead her away, again. Hamish stuffed his hand inside his shirt to touch the pouch of money secreted there; his boots were no longer solid enough to carry it safely.

On the rickety steps of the Hill Hotel and Board, Hamish paused to brush the dust from his clothes. His left boot, the sole half torn off, was held in place by a piece of twine. His trousers were near threadbare, and his shirt, dirty and badly patched, stunk like the rest of him. His eyes stung, a filmy sheen blurring his vision. Diagonally opposite him, the remaining prostitute whistled shrilly, clutching herself between her legs. The task ahead of him suddenly seemed insurmountable. He'd left his home country because of a woman. He'd spent three months on board a ship crowded together like rats, lost his brother . . . Sitting heavily on the steps, Hamish lifted his head to stare directly across at the whore. The woman sat in the dirt outside her bark lean-to, mouth open, rum dribbling down her chin.

The step creaked beside him. Hamish opened his hands and looked carefully at the dirt-scoured lines crisscrossing his palms, at the torn fingernails embedded with the dirt of his journey. This then was the essence of being alone and it was of his doing. The smell of herbage washed about him, filling his eyes, nose and mouth with the thick scents and images of his home country; lochs and burns, the thick smell of burning peat, of the mounds of rock shielding the dead, of Mary's willowy form walking away from him. Then there was Charlie, as clear in his mind as if he sat next to him still; laughing on the fields one day, complaining the next. The step creaked.

'Are you coming in then?'

Hamish ignored Dave, concentrating instead on a formless shape only feet from where he sat. The shadow swirled away from him, merging with the dust of The Hill's main street. Charlie was with him still, as he'd promised. And it was a promise undeserved.

'Dave, first we'll get cleaned up. Then it's Tootles from the store we'll be needing with cloth for shirts and such. And tell Lee to mix a brew for that old moll across the street. I'm hoping she can hold a needle and thread.'

Hamish could do nothing about the past, but he could do as Charlie asked. He would live his life for the two of them and be successful no matter what. He would create a legacy in memory of his brother and no-one would stop him.

Ridge Gully bustled with wagons and drays. The main street, wide and hot, held one tall coolibah tree, beneath which children loitered to play knuckles and argue over precious boiled lollies. Hamish rode sedately down the main street, freshly attired in waistcoat, suit and repaired, polished boots. The clothing, fashioned after an ageing catalogue sketch, required some making, delaying their arrival substantially, yet it ensured his arrival would not go unnoticed, a fact confirmed by the stares of the townsfolk intrigued by his appearance and that of the Chinaman walking two paces behind. Hamish quickly noted that Tootles' information was not a recent report. A second general store stood next to a bank, and further on was a new building that was soon to be the District Lands Department. Dave and Jasperson tied their horses opposite Matthew Reynolds' hotel and set about locating the whereabouts of a certain English squatter, a Sir Malcolm Wiley, to whom they were to present themselves as reliable boundary riders from Victoria. Their letter of introduction, penned with great deliberation by Hamish, was constructed with the assistance of a year-old newspaper from Tootles' store.

Hamish found lodgings in a small guesthouse owned by one Lorna Sutton, and secured a laundry room out the back for Lee.

'She is bringing daughter home.'

'Eavesdropping are we, Lee?'

'You,' Lee chuckled, 'very wealthy. Buy up all the land. You are a very good catch.'

Hamish inspected the mouldy dampness of Lee's one room located at the far end of the small house block and the outside copper for the boiling of clothes. He decided being wealthy would be a very good thing.

'You be all right here, Lee?'

'Landlady busy.' Lee thrust his hips backwards and forwards, his pigtails flapping over his shoulders in tandem with his stilted movements. 'Missus very busy.'

Hamish couldn't help but chuckle at Lee's animated actions. 'I don't think so, Lee. Mrs Sutton seems like a respectable gentlewoman to me.'

'Ah, Mister Hamish,' Lee shook his head, 'are you an expert now?'

'Expert enough to know that Lorna Sutton makes her money from taking in borders.'

❖

Hamish grasped the brass knocker outside Matthew Reynolds' residence and knocked twice. A surly pimple-faced girl greeted him in starched apron and cap and led him into the parlour in which a small fire barely fought the chill. The wood-panelled room, with heavy burgundy velvet curtains and matching covered armchairs, carried the stale odour of food, and Hamish scrunched his nose at the ancient aromas stalking the room. Apart from the dining table, chairs and a number of portraits, the subjects of which were definitely not relatives given Tootles' account of the family history, the room was remarkably bare.

'Ah, Mr Gordon, welcome to Ridge Gully. A toast to your arrival.'

Hamish accepted the small dram of rum and sat down, realising instantly that he was indeed in the company of a thief. Tootles, only too eager to help dislodge his bloated half-brother, had happily revealed over a meal at the Hill Hotel and Board the source of Matthew's wealth: stock theft – although such an accusation remained relegated to whispered asides, for the man was yet to be caught. Matthew Reynolds was dressed in a stylish dark suit with scarlet waistcoat. A thick watch-chain hung from his pocket and on more than one occasion, he removed the watch from his pocket and polished it absently on his sleeve. For all the spotlessness of the man's attire, his nails were filthy and he lounged sideways in his chair as if lying in his swag.

Hamish sipped at his glass of rum. Not used to the power of such liquor, he was cautious of losing his faculties although he found himself enjoying the drink all the same. His host carried Tootles' anxious air about him, but his was the demeanour of a bully built more for a street fight than for storekeeping and, unlike Tootles he couldn't hold Hamish's gaze, continually shifting his eyes about the room.

'The old days have gone, Mr Gordon. The common people aren't prepared to take the slops anymore. Tis hard enough to get decent staff these days and if you do, sooner or later you find them rooting about. Then they're with child. Well, I hear you have a loyal man. Hang on to him's my advice, indeed, hang on.'

'Indeed.' Hamish lifted his glass and instantly it was refilled. It appeared he was to be the recipient of a lesson in servitude.

'Thing is, it's hard for the likes of us, Mr Gordon. My ancestors,' Matthew gestured towards the portraits and then genuflected, 'may they rest in peace, never haggled with the common people. Now it's daily.'

'And land?' Hamish queried, eager to divert the subject to an area he understood.

'Yes, well, that's just the thing. The squatters have it all and you being a buying man, like myself, will know the difficulties acquiring it.'

Hamish leaned forward in the well padded chair. 'So what do you suggest?'

Carefully spitting into his palm, Matthew patted his thinning hair flat. Rarely did the opportunity present itself to entertain the likes of polite society. 'There is talk, they tell me, of the Government freeing up the land. It can't last, they say. Every year more arrive in our ports, and you cannot have the squatters owning all of it.' Matthew gulped at his rum, his Adam's apple bobbing impressively.

'No, it can't last.'

'So I agree with the agitators; unlock the land, I say. Damn the squatters and their arguments over the destruction of the country. Bugger them all, I say. Give everybody some dirt.'

'Aye, but with land you need stock,' Hamish countered cautiously.

'Exactly, Mr Gordon.' Matthew jumped up from his seat, his jowls quivering with both the movement and anticipation. 'Food!' he bellowed through the dining room door, before removing a yellow-stained handkerchief to mop his brow and slumping back in his chair. 'And if, for example you were looking for some, I, myself, could be of assistance there.'

'Good stock.' Hamish set his glass down on the small leather topped table. 'I know the price of stock, Mr Reynolds, but as a successful man, perhaps you could provide me with cheap, good stock, if you get my meaning.'

'Absolutely, Mr Gordon, absolutely,' Matthew beamed. 'Now please, do me the honour of taking a little dinner with me.'

The meal consisted of boiled mutton and potatoes, a delight in itself though there were oranges for dessert, the likes of which Hamish had never tasted. He found himself eating heartily and in spite of himself returned his host's fat-glazed smile as their meal came to an end. The visit alone was worth it for the food, Hamish decided as the hours stretched and his host regaled him with stories and snippets worth storing. It seemed Matthew Reynolds heard a great deal of news from his whore, who worked at Sir Malcolm Wiley's and waited on him at bed and table alike. The squatters spent their days arguing with the politicians over the proposed changes to land ownership, and there was no doubt in Sir Malcolm's mind that a war would ensue. Only last week, 'Unlock the land' flyers had been nailed up outside the soon-to-be-opened Lands Department.

'Buying and selling is the future,' Matthew emphasised, his podgy hands battling with the rubbery skin of his third orange. 'Here, you're probably a little better in the wrist department than me.' Reynolds' handed Hamish one of the small silver knives resting with the platter of oranges.

Hamish ran his finger along the small blade, admiring the smooth white stone of the handle.

'Mother of pearl they call it. Anyway, buy land now, sell later. A man's future can be made on that. And stock?' Leaning heavily on his fine oak table, Matthew banged his fist hard on the surface. 'Borrow it, carefully, is my advice.'

Hamish choked on the citrus flesh mangled decisively in the back of his throat. Surely Reynolds' had not just admitted to theft.

Reynolds' nodded knowingly. 'I know, I myself never had similar inclinations, being a gentleman and all, but mark this well, Mr Gordon, this is a new country with new rules. How do you, Mr Gordon, society man that you are, reckon the squatters obtained these vast landholdings in the first place? It was a matter of timing. They arrived first and, with their airs and graces, ingratiated themselves, and now they have it all – land and stock.'

Hamish swallowed the last of his orange and pocketed the fruit knife.

A few weeks later Dave and Jasperson used the light of the full moon to travel from Sir Malcolm Wiley's holding back to Ridge Gully. It was a clear night, one ripe with anticipation for Hamish. His need for further information was vital if his plan had any chance of coming to fruition. The three men stood out the back of Lorna's guesthouse, near the beginnings of Lee's vegetable garden, their faces illuminated by the moon.

'Well?' Hamish asked, barely giving the two men time to acknowledge him.

'Well, we're boundary riders now at the Englishman's run,' Jasperson began. 'It's a poor excuse for a property although only Sir Malcolm Wiley himself can be blamed, for he is rarely home.'

'He'd be bleeding money,' Dave revealed, pleased at last to be spending each night under a roof, even if it was a bark humpy with five other men snoring and farting beside him. 'It did not take long to learn the scheme of things.' Dave leant closer, dropped his voice lower. 'Stock theft, all the boundary riders are in it. Each receives a cut and they keep quiet about it.'

'All of them?' Hamish asked somewhat amazed at the extent of such unlawful activities.

Jasperson scowled at Dave. 'The northern and western boundaries only, Hamish. There are ten men involved; twice a year, after lambing.'

'Reynolds?'

'Aye, I'd reckon he'd be the mastermind,' Dave confirmed. 'No-one much else is mentioned.'

'And Sir Malcolm knows nothing?' Hamish asked.

Jasperson sneered. 'Bloody toff's too busy in Sydney. Reckon he's going to lose his place to the shit of the world, so Reynolds' whore says.'

'Reynolds' whore is also Sir Malcolm's whore. If she be yours, too, Jasperson, you'd do well to find another at the end of this business,' Hamish advised. 'Whoring women who play for both sides are likely to be thinking of an advantage to be had.'

Jasperson grunted, scratching his crotch irritably. 'He's repairing all the old log fences. I heard he's even gonna divide the place up into smaller paddocks.'

Hamish nodded, 'Less men needed that way. The stock are more secure and it's only the outside boundaries that need watching.'

'So, Reynolds is gonna do one more lift in two months' time. Five thousand head to be driven up north to Queensland.' Jasperson snorted down the mucus stuck in his throat. 'Reckon he'll clear out then. The troopers have had their eye on 'im.'

'Aye, I reckon he will,' Hamish agreed. 'Jasperson, ride to The Hill and tell Tootles I have a business proposition.'

Dave grimaced, the corners of his mouth drooping. 'Why would the likes of him come here for us?'

Hamish's eyebrows lifted in amusement. 'Money.'

❈ *Winter, 1983* ❈

Wangallon Woolshed

'If you would stop procrastinating over the cost of the upgrade, you wouldn't be in this predicament.' With a deep sigh Angus looked from Ronald and beckoned to Anthony, who appeared around the side of the woolshed in the Toyota, towing a trailer with a generator on board. It was the last day of shearing and the main electrical board had blown, cutting the power to Wangallon homestead, the shearer's quarters, three station-hand residences, the cook house, cottage and the shearing shed itself. Angus scratched his head irritably, aware of the smirks and just audible comments coming from where twenty-six shearers and assorted rouseabouts, board boys and shed hands waited inside the shed. The men were beginning to grumble about the possibility of having to work late on a Friday to get the job finished.

'What happened?' Sarah asked her brother when he appeared from the far side of the sheep yards on his motorbike.

'There's no power at the cook house to boil water for the men's tea. Clayton really has the shits about it because he had a cake in the oven as well.' Cameron got off his bike, put the stand down, and continued. 'The board blew. Grandfather told Dad to upgrade the board last year. Dad ignored the suggestion, reckoning on another twelve months out of the old girl. The ten grand allocated for the upgrade went toward purchasing panels so we could enlarge the cattle yards. Other than that, well, they're arguing about it. Nothing new there.'

They watched as Anthony reversed the trailer to the door of the shed, both their father and grandfather standing angrily to one side as a shed hand unrolled a power cord and tried to plug it into the generator; the lead was a good foot too short.

'Better give Ant a hand,' Cameron said aloud, walking over to where Anthony was reversing the trailer again in order to get closer to the shed. At the angle Anthony was forced to reverse, the trailer was partially jack-knifed.

'Dad, Clayton's mad about the power,' Sarah said meekly as she approached her grandfather and father. Both men were frowning, the deep furrows between their eyes reminiscent of angry twins.

'I'll go see him once we're up and running. Unhook her when you're set up, Anthony.' Ronald walked towards the Toyota. 'I'll have to go and calm Clayton.'

'Righto.'

'Watch out that doesn't spring back on you, mate,' Cameron yelled out as Anthony undid the tow-hitch. A second later Anthony was lying flat on his back, the trailer having sprung to one side once it had been disconnected from the Toyota.

'Shit.' Cameron was by Anthony's side in a second. 'Anything busted?'

'No, nothing.' Anthony rubbed his shin roughly as he squinted through the pain of the impact.

'Anthony, are you all right? Are you hurt? We better get him to the house, Dad.' Sarah dropped to her knees, touching Anthony's face in concern.

'I haven't got a temperature, you know,' he complained, pushing her arm away. 'I'm not an invalid.' Some of the shearers were sniggering in the background. 'I'm all right, Sarah.' He rubbed his hand down the side of his calf muscle to gingerly check the surrounding area.

'Fine.' Sarah took a step back, watching as her father and brother pulled Anthony up off the ground. Anthony's eyes found hers. For just a moment Sarah thought she saw something fleeting cross his face, then just as quickly his expression changed again and he threw her a cocky smile. Frowning, Sarah turned from him and began walking away from the woolshed.

'Well, Cameron,' Angus called out gruffly, 'you're not part of the local rescue team. Hook that generator up and get the shed going.'

'You were bloody lucky that didn't break your leg in two,' Ronald said. 'Jump in the Toyota with me, Anthony, and we'll go put some ice on that,' he suggested as the generator kicked over and the comforting whirr of the shears echoed from deep inside the woolshed.

Ronald watched his father in the driver's side mirror, the image of him decreasing in size, his bulky form leaning nonchalantly on the side of his Land Cruiser, the muzzle of his dog, Shrapnel, resting in the crook of his arm. 'Fucking old master and bloody commander,' Ronald muttered. A simple nod of approval was beyond the old bastard. How hard would it have been? No-one was badly injured, the shearers were going again and by nightfall the ewes would be back in their paddock.

'Right then, we'll get you that ice and then all that is left to do is calm the cook, call the electrician and hope to hell he makes it out here in the next hour or so, otherwise Clayton will probably bugger off.'

'Pretty much a normal day then, Ronald,' Anthony grinned.

'Pretty much. Sarah, do you want a lift?' he called out to his daughter as he slowed his vehicle on the road leading from the woolshed.

'Hop in,' Anthony agreed.

'I'd rather walk, thanks.'

'Suit yourself.' Ronald wasn't much in the mood for surly women.

Sarah trudged on up the road, shutting her eyes against the flying grit. She was hardly going to sit in the same vehicle with Anthony after the way he had just spoken to her.

'You'll have to go back you know, girl.'

It was her grandfather, driving at a snail's pace beside her.

'Men, particularly young men, don't take too kindly to being fussed over.'

'I didn't fuss over him.'

Angus lifted his forefinger for silence. The only Gordon that ever interrupted him was young Sarah and he admired her for that. 'They don't take kindly to being fussed over in front of anyone who could give them a hard time about it later. And those shearers will give Anthony a hard time about it. He works for me, remember, and you're my granddaughter.'

'But . . .'

'Don't argue. Secretly we like the fussing. Just make sure you go back to the shed this afternoon.'

'Why?'

Angus lifted his eyes skyward. 'Because otherwise you'll be surly with Anthony for the next week. Then you'll get surly with your mother. Then Sue will complain more than usual, your father and I will argue . . .'

'Again.' Sarah smiled.

Angus stopped his vehicle. 'Yes, again, and Anthony will ask your brother what's going on and he'll come to me. And we are running a business here, not an agony aunt column.'

'Grandfather,' Sarah hesitated, resting her arms on the open window of the passenger door, 'I wanted to ask you . . .'

'Yes?'

'Well, I heard something the other morning. Mum and Dad were arguing. It was something about Cameron. It sounded strange, like they had this secret they were keeping from everybody.' She hesitated. 'Even you.'

'Ridiculous. Your mother has a fixation regarding Cameron. Everyone knows that.'

'But –'

'You don't want to pay attention to her.'

'But –'

'I have to attend to a few things.'

Sarah was left standing in a cloud of dust.

Shearing was finished. The team had already packed up and were enjoying a well-earned beer. Some of the men, lining up empty tins at the end of the lanolin-smoothed board, were playing bowls; others were cleaning and packing away the metal combs they used for shearing. Cameron was urging the men to join him at the closest village, Wangallon Town. Few needed convincing. Sarah sat quietly on a large wool bale, enjoying the smell of wool, manure and powdery soil trampled ceaselessly by yarded sheep. The men talked and laughed, spun stories and mostly ignored her, not quite sure how to include the boss's granddaughter. Sarah observed their easy banter for a few more minutes before leaving the shed to cross the wooden fences of the sheep yards. Scuffing the dirt with her boots, she muttered angrily under her breath. She had gone back as her grandfather had ordered and Anthony was nowhere to be seen.

'Where you off to?' Cameron grinned, his battered army green jeep shuddering as it idled to a stop next to her.

'Jump in,' Anthony called, opening the door for her. Sarah smiled – maybe her grandfather was right.

◈

Back at the house, Cameron coerced their parents into agreement. Tonight they were off to the pub.

Sarah spent the night in the ladies bar, drinking lemonade. Cameron sat cross-legged on the corner counter that separated the bar itself from the public drinking area and the ladies lounge. He occasionally slipped her a rum and coke, watching over her, entertaining everyone with his stories and jokes. Between Sarah and the shearers in the public bar, Cameron held court while Anthony jumped the bar, deciding he would help pull beers during the evening.

'Tell us another one, Cameron,' one of the shearers enthused, a schooner of beer in hand.

'Well . . .' Cameron scratched his head, his face widening into a mischievous grin. He skolled his rum and coke and, within minutes, the young barmaid, all heaving bosom and bottle-blonde hair, was holding another one towards him.

'There you go, Cameron,' she sighed, her free hand coming to rest on his thigh. 'I never charge my special customers.'

Cameron pinched her cheek playfully, the soft skin yielding easily under his touch as it had only last weekend.

'That's enough, Lottie,' the publican bellowed, as he tucked a pristine white shirt into skinny-legged cowboy jeans. 'There are a few other blokes here that need some attention.'

With a quick smile at Cameron, Lottie moved to collect empty glasses from along the bar.

'You're not wrong there,' one of the patrons yelled from the opposite end of the bar, holding up his empty schooner glass. 'A little service wouldn't go astray.'

'No soliciting allowed at this pub,' another boomed. 'Now what about that joke?'

'What do blondes and cow shit have in common?' Cameron called loudly across the crowded bar.

The barmaid narrowed her eyes.

'The older they get, the easier they are to pick up.'

The bar erupted into bellows of laughter. Lottie stared hard at Cameron and poked her tongue out at Sarah, who was doubled up in mirth. Instantly Cameron slipped off the bar to give the girl a quick hug. She grudgingly responded, eventually pushing at him a little with her well padded hips.

'Oh, Lottie, I wasn't referring to you, my bonnie lass,' he said softly, putting on a very poor Scottish accent. Then, more loudly, 'I was talking about real blondes.'

'Oh, get away. I would rather spend my time with Anthony.'

'Sorry.' Anthony gave an apologetic grin and took his elbows off the bar as she approached him. 'I'm too busy working for the Gordons to have any spare time for romancing.' Plus, he was hardly going to cut Cameron's lunch.

'Really?' Lottie responded, her grey eyes crinkling up under a thoughtful frown as she threw Sarah another kiss-of-death stare. 'Suppose that depends on your definition of working.'

The bar erupted again into bellows of laughter.

'She's got you there, Anthony,' Cameron nodded towards his sister.

Sarah took a gulp of her drink. She could feel her face heating up under the room's scrutiny.

'Less travel involved,' one of the shearers commented. 'And you know what they say about the end of the rainbow.' He sniggered into his schooner glass.

'All right, all right, enough speculation on my sister's list of suitors. We should be discussing mine.' Cameron quickly diverted the conversation to himself and away from Sarah, whose face was now the colour of a tomato.

❧ *Summer, 1857* ❧

Ridge Gully – Central Western New South Wales

Lorna Sutton, forty years of age with the fatty folds of an overfed pig, knew breeding. The Scot, well, he was breeding. They said he came from just over the border from England, had been raised near Sir Malcolm himself in a fine manor house and, upon the loss of his family in a terrible fire, come to start anew in Australia. Wasn't it just God himself bringing the man to her door and she with a learned daughter? Lorna crossed herself in thanks, her pudgy fingers patting dry her sweating chest with the bed linen.

'Well?'

The man's voice startled her from her daydreams.

Lorna rolled off the bed. Kneeling on the floor she positioned herself between his thighs. What about his money? She'd not been able to find out where he kept it. Not that she felt the temptation to steal it, mind. She was not a thief. It was just that she believed she would feel so much better if it was safe. A hand pulled her head harder towards him, twisting his fingers through her hair.

Grimacing, Lorna did as she was bidden, sucking harder until he gripped her head tightly between his palms, before pushing her sprawling to the floor.

Wiping her lips and chin, Lorna scurried into a shift, before pouring water into the porcelain basin on the washstand.

'Nothing else has come to hand?' Matthew Reynolds asked as he wrung out the wash cloth in the cool water and swiped roughly at his body.

Lorna shook her head, no.

He splashed water beneath each hairy armpit and then rubbed his member vigorously.

'Well, stupid or not, the man's got money. You keep him here, Lorna. Make sure he takes up with that lass of yours. If he's gonna be a-spending his money, in Ridge Gully it will be.' Matthew Reynolds pulled his clothes on, placed some coins on the bed in his spare room and walked out.

Closing the door quietly, Lorna began to wash carefully, lifting the folds of her skin to remove all traces of his scent. So, she had lain with him for that. He knew as much about the Scot as she did, and he too wanted his money. Well, her intent remained firm. Mr Gordon would take up with her Rose; the girl had the looks and was untouched, unlike her mother, Lorna giggled to herself. But that was all she could be expected to do. After all, she had a daughter to marry off and her own comforts to be thinking of. Stepping into her dress, Lorna smiled demurely at her surroundings. The nice wooden bedhead with the carved ball posts, the matching washstand, even a marginally fine wardrobe and the bedspread. She ran pudgy fingers over the patchwork of green, blues and reds. Oh, she so liked fine things. Lorna snatched up the coins and counted them twice. She'd be needing to purchase a few items if she were to pass as somewhat gentrified.

❖

'Nice,' Lorna commented as her daughter descended from the two-horse dray like a lady. The girl's brown wool dress, relieved with tuffs of white at collar and wrist, displayed a rather large gold brooch with intricate filigree work, a green stone flashing at its centre.

Rose immediately noticed her mother's pointed interest in the jewel. 'A birthday gift from Sir Malcolm, Mama. He says I may stay until his return from the Parliament; six weeks, Mama, although I may return sooner.'

'Hmm, and what of your resigning and returning here to me?' Lorna queried, her arms bulging at the seams of her tightly fitted bodice. 'You read my letter?' She surveyed the slim-waisted, ample-chested fifteen-year-old she had created.

'I shall marry for both position and love, Mama, and my best chances for both remain with Sir Malcolm.' Rose observed with some distaste the deepening stains around the arm holes of her mother's dress.

'What's this? You think I'd be happy with a jumped-up gardener or overseer? Your best chance is currently holed up here, a Scottish gentleman if you don't mind, with his man-servant. So leave your airs and graces in that cart and come inside and ready yourself to make his acquaintance. This is our chance, for both of us and I'm not having your *if you please* airs ruining my plans.'

Rose gave her mother her best look of disdain and addressed the red-faced driver of the cart, one of the many staff employed by Sir Malcolm Wiley. 'Would you kindly carry my baggage inside the house, please?'

The man reached around from where he had been adjusting one of the horse's harnesses and with a bemused expression, lifted the two leather and fabric bags, dumping them unceremoniously in the dirt. 'This ain't the estate now, Miss.'

Rose looked dismally at her mother as the dray rolled away.

'Now if you've spare coin, I'll be needing that,' Lorna puffed as she helped her daughter drag her belongings into the two-bedroom timber cottage. 'I've been a bit poorly myself and unable to take in the laundry as usual.'

'I had planned . . .' Rose began.

'Leave the planning to me. I've purchased a few essentials, but we will be needing brandy. Every person knows these gentlemen prefer it to the rough rum the common folk drink. And you and I will be sharing my room.'

'Actually,' Rose begged to differ, dusting one of the kitchen chairs with a tea-towel before sitting, 'Sir Malcolm drinks . . .'

Lorna plopped down on Rose's trunk, mopping her brow with a handkerchief retrieved from the folds of her ample bosom. 'Brandy, Rose. This is a house of gentrified females. Now, the money, if you please.'

Rose handed over a drawstring bag with a sigh. 'What if I don't like him?'

Lorna pursed her lips together until her face was drawn into a series of small circles. 'You'll like him, Rose.'

Hamish, discovering himself dumbstruck in the company of womenfolk, immersed himself in dinner. Their rather plain meal of mutton, damper and glasses of sherry was enlivened with a highly seasoned parrot pie. Lee's contribution certainly appeared to intrigue his dining companions, for a good part of their meal was taken up with exclamations of delight. Hamish found Rose's intricate rendering of her daily routine charming, and the minute details of the running of Sir Malcolm's household allowed him the luxury of listening rather than having to add to the conversation. By the end of dinner he envied the lifestyle Rose's employer enjoyed.

'With such knowledge, Mr Gordon, you can appreciate my Rose would have the capabilities to manage any sized household and, of course, she is used to staff; a most important qualification these days.'

'Indeed,' Hamish agreed amiably, patting his moustache with a linen napkin. It appeared one's staff were a major consideration in any household.

'And you, Mr Gordon. Was your estate very large?'

'Large enough to demand staff, Mrs Sutton,' Hamish answered smoothly.

'Why, of course,' his hostess smiled coyly, her head tilting coquettishly to one side. 'More tea?'

'Thank you, no.'

'Perhaps then a stroll would be in order. Certainly it is a usual occurrence in this household.' Lorna fetched her daughter's shawl. The evening had gone remarkably well. Having purchased three stemmed glasses and some new linen, her small dining table now emanated a more gentrified air. A little light fingering led to three sets of cutlery and a rather nice sterling silver bowl care of Mr Reynolds' fine house. It was surprising the type of impression one could conjure with a little enterprise.

Rose found herself being pulled bodily from her chair; the best of her two shawls thrust around her shoulders. 'Mr Gordon may not care for an evening stroll, Mama,' she answered, not quite able to keep the twitch of annoyance from her voice. One did not entrance a man by being so terribly forward. Besides, she barely knew him and as yet was unable to form an opinion as to his character. He was undoubtedly ambitious and clever, two characteristics one must admire. And he commanded respect. It was not one single aspect of his person but rather a combination. He was tall and broad-shouldered, well dressed and pleasing to look at. As for his education, Rose could only assume it would have been substantial, although his conversation revealed little of his former life. Understandable considering the personal losses he had suffered in the great fire on his own Scottish estate. It was this aura of sadness she believed she found most attractive.

'Nonsense, it is a fine, clear evening. Is that not so, Mr Gordon?'

'And you, Mrs Sutton, will you not be joining us?' Hamish enquired.

'No. Evening walks are for young people, not respectable matrons, Mr Gordon.'

Lorna shuffled her charges out quickly, peering through the faded floral curtain in the cramped dining room to check their progress. At the front gate, her house guest awkwardly offered his arm and Rose, with little enthusiasm, linked her thin arm through his. 'Smile, girl, smile,' Lorna encouraged quietly as she slipped back into the kitchen to pour herself a small brandy. Her evening was to be spent in the company of Matthew Reynolds. A somewhat disenchanting prospect made palatable by being finally able to pay for the new dress recently ordered. And, Lorna thought, pouring herself another drink, providing her future son-in-law with a tasty cut of meat for tomorrow's dinner.

'As a governess, most of your time is spent with children?' Hamish finally said as he rather roughly took Rose's elbow to cross the street, doffing his hat to another couple as they passed. His schooling with women remained limited, but surely a girl of this character with a mother running a respectable boarding house was a rare find. He studied her profile as she smiled prettily at a passer-by. Rose was finely featured and well proportioned. Indeed she was the very opposite of his beguiling Mary; slim, educated and pretty. Fair-haired and oval-faced, she moved gracefully, clearly thought before she spoke and, he believed, knew right from wrong. But she was also a soft, frail thing: an unwanted quality in Highland women.

'Not at all, Mr Gordon. In fact, I have only one charge now and spend equal time with Sir Malcolm. His wife is dead, you see, and his remaining three children, of the nine she bore him, have all returned to the family estate in England.'

'I see.' Hamish studied the girl's chest, paying particular attention to the large gold and green jewelled brooch pinned near her breast.

'I fear I shall lose my position within the year. A most unhappy occurrence.'

'Most.' Deftly changing direction, Hamish steered his young companion back towards her home.

'And your plans, Mr Gordon, if I may. There is talk of you buying property, sir. May I ask if that will be here in Ridge Gully?'

'Aye, or perhaps further north.'

'So you too wait for the great land rush, for the squatters to be divided and their land redistributed. It may happen sooner than you think, though Sir Malcolm feels it will be war.'

Hamish opened the door to the guesthouse, stopping to stare at the moist young lips, momentarily regretting the lateness of the hour and the mother inside, waiting.

'I see by your silence you find me too forthright, sir. Perhaps Sir Malcolm's allowances are not so easily accepted outside his home.'

'You must forgive me. It is the company of women I am not used to.' Hamish stepped aside for Rose to enter. 'There are many who will fight.' He bowed his head briefly, referring quickly back to their conversation.

Rose inclined her head. 'Many will lose, although I don't expect you to be one of them. Goodnight, Mr Gordon.'

Hamish nodded, latching the front door as the sound of the girl's footsteps echoed down the narrow wooden hallway.

Removing his jacket and waistcoat in the solitude of his bedroom, Hamish stripped off the rest of his clothes, pulled back pale pink curtains and lifted the sash to the window near his narrow bed. Lying down, he struggled to find comfort on the thin mattress sagging beneath his weight, as a freshening breeze skimmed the hairs on his chest. The last woman Hamish walked with had been his beloved Mary. Running alongside a small brook, he had caught her hand as she tried to overtake him and they'd fallen into the springy heather. Pushing the picture of his lost love aside, he reminded himself of Charlie's words. His Mary was not blameless. It was time to let go of her. If they were still alive and were yet to succumb to the harshness of life in the Highlands, his father and Mary would be married by now and there would be children. Was it not time to forget Mary and move on? Especially now, when having not expected to appreciate a woman's company again, he'd met young Rose Sutton.

Tootles Reynolds arrived quietly at Ridge Gully one dusty afternoon, his well worn coat pockets stuffed with boiled sweets and his head swimming with anticipation. In truth, the thought of bolting the door of his little shop and following the man Jasperson into the expanse of the bush was tantamount to madness, yet within the curl of fear shivering in his gut also lay a feeling of excitement. A man rarely found himself called upon, especially at The Hill, to perform an urgent service for which money would be provided. Nor could one expect a guarantee of safe passage and accommodation at the final destination. Yet the Scot, Hamish Gordon, promised all this and by the time Tootles' inner thighs escaped his horse's flanks and found themselves in a warm bathtub with a tray of supper waiting on the high table next to his bed, he had become a firm believer in Jasperson's original entreaty. Hamish Gordon had provided Tootles Reynolds his word as a gentleman if he would only come. And indeed he had not been left wanting.

❖

'Your brother is a thief, Tootles. He intends to sell his agency after stealing stock from further south. At such a time I intend to purchase the agency and I require you to run it for me.' Hamish poured a neat shot of brandy into a cracked glass and swallowed the liquid amber in one bitter gulp. One day, fine crystal and even finer brandy, such as that slurped by Matthew Reynolds, would be his.

Carefully removing his glasses, Tootles cleaned them and then wiped his brow with the same filthy handkerchief. Ordered to stay inside his hotel room lest his brother see him, Tootles had enjoyed eggs for breakfast, a visit from a tailor with the promise of a new suit by morning, a passable stew for lunch and even managed to rut with a whore delivered to his door by the Chinaman. Simple he might be, but he knew enough to consider his own well-being. He could gain much from this adventure.

'How will you p-pay for i-it?' Tootles asked cautiously, admiring the new suit his benefactor wore, the freshly laundered white shirt and the waxed tips of a meticulously clipped moustache. Could he dare to believe that this fine gentleman was the same filthy, battered man who had chanced upon his small store not two months earlier?

Hamish recognised the flame of interest in the brown eyes opposite as that very ambition he himself harboured in his gut. This man, slighted by his own brother, would do very well indeed. He would covet his brother's life to the advantage of all. Hamish nodded briefly to Lee, and the Chinaman stepped forward to place a large gold brooch with a green stone on the table between them. Surrounded as it was by the virgin timber lining the room and mismatched furniture of bed, dresser and washstand, the stone shone like a beacon.

'Tomorrow morning I want you to present yourself to the manager at The First Gully Bank. That brooch is to be exchanged for a quantity of pound notes, say, forty pounds, with the money delivered to Lee, the remainder for a note of credit, which you can call upon when you inform the manager of what type of business you are interested in acquiring.'

Tootles reached out a pale hand and stroked the fine green centre. 'He's my half-brother, he is. Threatened me with death just this year past when I came to town. Threatened all and sundry not to frequent The Hill store.'

Hamish nodded. No answer was expected of him, only a kindly ear as the man justified his actions.

'Done.' Slowly Tootles' mouth broadened into a gappy grin. 'We'll spit on it.' Loosening a sloppy globule from his mouth, he held his hand out firmly to shake Hamish's.

'Anything else you need?' Hamish asked when he had succeeded in freeing his hand from Tootles' slimy grip.

'A barber and I've a hankering for some chicken.' Tootles drooled in anticipation.

Hamish wiped his palm on the food-streaked remains of Tootles' luncheon napkin, which rested next to his licked-clean plate on the end of the table. 'Well, Lee, you heard the man.'

'Yes, Mister Gordon, one hair chop and chicken.'

'Good. Well I'll let you know when the transaction is to go through.'

'I'll be fine.' Tootles crossed his fingers across his stomach and gave a satisfied belch. 'A home away from h-home it is here, Mr Gordon, a h-home away from h-home.' He glanced appreciatively around the sparsely furnished but spotless room.

Placing his palms flat on the table between them, Hamish

spread his fingers as he stood, his tall frame shadowing the newest addition to his growing staff. 'Good, I look after those that look after me. You do get my meaning, Tootles?'

Tootles sank bodily back into his chair. 'Yes, of c-course. I mean, I'm h-here aren't I?'

Hamish walked to the door. 'Excellent. Lee, keep an eye on our friend here.'

'Yes, Mister Hamish,' Lee answered, following his boss to close the door after him.

Opening his mouth in a gappy, half-hearted grin, Tootles nervously tapped his fingers on the table.

'Hair chop?' Lee walked towards him grinning, his bony right hand landing in the middle of his left in a firm chopping movement.

Hamish received word that Matthew Reynolds needed to see him as he was walking through the front gate of Lorna Sutton's guest house the next morning. The message was delivered by a scraggly youth lolling on the picket fence in anticipation of his return. Immediately Hamish began the half-mile walk to the other side of Ridge Gully.

'Thank you for coming on such short notice,' Matthew Reynolds announced as Hamish settled again in an oversized leather chair in the drawing room. A dram of rum already resting in his stomach, Hamish waited for his host to reveal what he already knew – that there were five thousand head of sheep for sale. Reynolds smiled, the effort revealing a blackened mass at the back of his mouth where teeth should have been.

'Seven thousand sheep ready for delivery in three weeks, one hundred miles north of Ridge Gully. If you would be so kind to deposit the monies in full by week's end.'

'Of course.' Hamish shook Reynolds' sweaty hand. Tootles had already introduced himself to the bank manager and deposited the magnificent brooch Lorna had so thoroughly chastised her daughter for losing the night before. He allowed himself a slight smile. Hamish presented his glass for a refill. So Reynolds would steal from Sir Malcolm, trust Hamish to pay for seven thousand head, when in truth there were but five thousand, and then no doubt escape Ridge Gully with Hamish's money and the sheep as well. Fine crooks they were, all.

'Friday it will be then, Mr Reynolds.' They shook hands, Reynolds spitting on his palm first to seal the bargain. 'I like the style of your house, Reynolds,' Hamish said admiringly as they farewelled in the entrance hallway.

'A gentleman's compliment is made more worthy by its sincerity, Mr Gordon. Good day.'

Hamish walked down the swept dirt path of Reynolds' residence and out onto the rutted street of Ridge Gully. The only thing he did like about Reynolds was his house. He had a mind to own it. In fact he would, he determined, as he walked towards the newly opened Lands Department, his hand patting the bulge of pound notes in his pocket.

The gaunt youth creeping behind the desk approached, round-shouldered and coughing.

'I wish to purchase some land,' Hamish began, placing the stack of pound notes on the counter. The youth eyed the money, his crooked top teeth biting down on his lower lip. 'There are three small parcels on the southern end of town,' Hamish said, his hand resting securely on the cash.

The youth pulled a brown ledger and three title deeds from beneath the counter.

'It's not usual practice I'm sure, sir.'

Hamish pulled some coins from his pocket and pushed the money in the youth's direction. 'Spare your poor mother more grief and buy her some tasty morsel for her supper.'

The youth coughed tenderly into a soiled handkerchief.

'A little mutton perhaps, or some eggs for her breakfast.' Hamish added to the pile of coins. 'I would be concealing that if I were you, lad. I can't be helping every waif I come across.'

A bony hand scraped the coinage off the counter top and deposited it into a grimy pocket.

'Good. Now if we could –' Hamish gestured at the paperwork.

'Three small parcels you say, sir. Well, if you look here . . .'

Hamish followed the ragged ink-stained thumbnail to where the three lots were allocated and due to go up for sale after lunch, along with a number of other small buildings.

'The southern end of the town, sir. There's been quite some interest what with the growth we're experiencing.'

Hamish studied the pile of pound notes on the counter and began to count out his preferred buying price. 'Obviously as I'm buying all three blocks simultaneously there would be a discount for that. Plus I'm paying cash.'

'It's not enough, sir,' the youth said as he counted the money.

'Then note me down as owing the Department.'

'But, sir . . .'

'And of course then there's the matter of the bribe you took.'

'The bribe?' The youth stuttered.

'Come, now. I knew you were a man of intelligence when I first walked in. No-one does business without benefit, but of course you know this, so . . .' Hamish held out his hand and found it gripped rather nervously. 'And the deeds?'

'The deeds? Yes, of course the deeds.' The youth noted Hamish as the new owner for all three blocks for the price of two and scrawled his own signature in scratchy copperplate beneath.

'And a receipt.'

'A receipt,' the youth repeated, automatically filling in the required paperwork.

'Very good, boy,' Hamish muttered as he strode from the building, adjusting his hat against the angle of the noon sun. If he walked quickly he would have his business done before the heat of the day arrived, leaving him the afternoon at his leisure. He fingered the coin in his pocket and thought of Rose.

'Flowers last Friday, and now this.' Rose smiled demurely, opening the small box that held a thick length of fine green velvet ribbon. 'I accept this gift as part of your courtship, sir.' Rose smiled beatifically.

Hamish was not sure when he'd decided to take Rose Sutton as his wife. He certainly did not love her. At least not in the way he knew from the past. But her youth and innocence were attractive and he cared for her. Besides, first-hand experience had taught him that love was an overrated commodity. There were other reasons to form unions; respectability, for one. The Suttons were by no means impoverished. Lorna's table was dressed with care and they lived and dressed well, although conservatively. There being no Mr Sutton also gave Hamish a modicum of power for there was no-one to question his past or make demands on his future. As gentlewomen Rose and her mother were content to accept the rumours circulating about him and to this end Hamish found himself pictured in a most positive light.

'I am away on business this evening and shall return tomorrow,' Hamish offered. He had sold the three small blocks within the hour to speculators, doubling his money, and went on to purchase a fine watch and chain for himself. The ribbon was something he believed his Mary would have liked. 'So you will excuse me?'

'Of course.' Rose smiled, a rather becoming blush spreading across her fair skin.

He watched the slight figure as it retreated back to the sanctity of her mother's house, momentarily intrigued by the perfect sway of her gown.

'Very much you want a wife, Mister Hamish?' Lee grinned cheekily, appearing from the street, a pouch of tobacco in his hand.

'In truth, I had not been seeking one,' Hamish admitted as he strolled from the front of the house around to the side to where Lorna's small but sufficient vegetable garden had recently been introduced to some of Lee's more exotic herbs. 'But it appears Miss Rose Sutton is prepared to accept the task.'

'You get in trouble quick,' Lee grinned again, patting his stomach with enthusiasm before removing a chunk of tobacco from the pouch he carried and stuffing it into his mouth.

'Perhaps,' said Hamish as he clapped his friend on the shoulder. 'We shall see.' With a wife, perhaps a child eventually and Lorna to mind both, he planned to continue the establishment of his business, whilst presenting himself to society in a favourable light. Unplanned though the union was, respectability was fast becoming a commodity Hamish knew he needed in the rough days ahead.

❧ *Autumn, 1857* ☙

200 *Miles West of Ridge Gully*

*D*ave watched Hamish as he skinned the two hind legs of the kangaroo, using his knife to run around each knee-joint before twisting and snapping the bone. Deftly he skewered the meaty thighs with a long stick and rested them above the flame of the fire. Within seconds Lee bustled him aside to sit the billycan next to the meat. Dave slurped his tea loudly. He rather liked the old Chinaman. He had a knack of keeping things steady. Hell, even Tootles liked him. He was their good luck charm, he reckoned. No wonder everything was going to plan. They had walked the merino sheep some twenty miles west of Sir Malcolm's property before driving them in a northerly direction and seen not a soul in the last week. A few more days and they would be forty miles north of The Hill and into relative safety.

Dave rubbed his back roughly against the tree trunk behind him, aware his movements were being followed. Opposite him, hunched low on the edge of the light from Lee's fire, the two weedy recruits collected some days prior, sons of convicts both, stared at him. Dave lifted his nose in imitation of a pig's snout and proceeded to stare them both down.

The tall boy, the talker, drooled at the mention of food and the other had to piss every five minutes. Jasperson didn't want to know about it. Said it didn't matter. Dave guessed he was right. They could ride and control a wing apiece of the sheep and mostly were too scared to speak, instead taking to picking their noses and farting the rest of the time. Dave reckoned Jasperson used the boys like the whores in Ridge Gully, except the kids didn't cost him a cent. Disgusting was what Dave thought of it. Still, if it kept Jasperson happy and off his back, he could live with it. Besides, the boys could work and he reckoned that was all that mattered.

With the meat finally cooked, Lee divided the food up equally, dumping a wedge of warm damper on each man's plate. The Chinaman had arrived only that morning, having ensured Tootles Reynolds had played his part to completion. The men pulled apart the juicy flesh with their teeth, using the doughy bread to slop up any juices. They ate ravenously, each keeping an eye on Lee, who safeguarded the remains until all were finished, before offering scant seconds. There would only be bones tonight, Dave concluded, rubbing his filled stomach. Lee tossed a bone apiece to the two lads, who fell upon them like starving dogs.

In the quiet of early evening, as Lee made more tea and filled their leather water pouches from the small creek only a few feet from their camp, Hamish studied his resting team. Dave, already lying flat on his back, snored quietly, while Jasperson threw a small log onto the fire and began whittling a stick with a knife he kept hidden in his boot. The blade winked in the firelight, the sharp pointy end making quick work of the wood. When he had finished, he picked a few strings of meat from his teeth. The two lads, having withdrawn slightly further away from the ring of light, slept close together, as if needing protection. Hamish knew that once all were asleep Jasperson would take one of the boys off into the scrub. He leant forward to warm his palms against the remaining heat of the dying coals. It was a mild evening and Jasperson's appetites were none of his concern. The man was loyal and, like Dave, had ability – that was all that mattered. His plan had been accomplished and very soon he would return to Ridge Gully, a wealthy man with a wife to warm his bed.

Hamish knew he had timed everything perfectly. Tootles Reynolds would now be the owner of Ridge Gully Stock and Station. The bank manager, having approached Matthew Reynolds with a buyer, would have been surprised to find Reynolds not only interested, but agreeable to the first offer. For some hours earlier Reynolds would have discovered his sheep stolen and his own plan gone awry. This mishap would have then been complicated by Reynolds learning that Sir Malcolm Wiley had been sent word that his trusted agent was indeed his robber. Hamish decided Reynolds would have wasted no time in packing his belongings and disappearing under cover of night. Happily, Tootles would now find himself a well respected business man.

The Ridge Gully Commerce Society would welcome Tootles with open arms and the bank manager would place the gold and jade brooch back in the safe at Ridge Gully Bank. Good for another major transaction at some point in the future. Perhaps the General Store, Hamish considered, with Lorna Sutton at its helm. Yes, the woman would be astute enough for that.

Hamish stretched out flat on his blanket. The last of the business, Sir Malcolm's sheep, were on their way back to Sir Malcolm, at least five thousand of them. The remaining two thousand, their current charges, had already been sold to an agent from Queensland. And by the week's end, having fulfilled the contract, Hamish expected to be ensconced in Reynolds' brick residence. Lee was to return to Ridge Gully tomorrow to ensure Tootles carried out this next transaction. Hamish closed his eyes.

Respectability was his, although he would decline the personal invitation expected from Sir Malcolm on his return. Being feted by an Englishman would only sour his achievements and reveal that he was not the wealthy Scottish neighbour the inhabitants of Ridge Gully had so helpfully announced. He yawned. Tomorrow he would give the order for Jasperson to cut the throats of the two lads they had hired not two weeks back. It couldn't be helped. They were uneducated youths, the sons of convicts and not to be trusted.

❖

'She Reynolds' whore,' Lee uttered quietly, a bulbous mass of chewing tobacco lodged firmly in his left cheek.

Hamish sat upright. 'Whore? What are you talking about, Lee?' He'd been dozing by the remains of the fire, awaking periodically to the rustling sounds of creatures beyond the rim of their camp site.

'Lorna is a whore,' Lee repeated, dragging a night log onto the glowing embers.

'How do you know this?' Hamish asked, glancing around at the sleeping bodies. Dave was asleep while Jasperson and one of the youths were missing.

'I followed her.'

Distracted, Hamish waved his friend away. Lorna, short, pudgy, unattractive, and a whore. He scanned the evenings spent in her company, sifting through their conversations with minute precision, but there was nothing there; nothing that would be useful to Reynolds anyway. 'Damn her,' Hamish said aloud. Somehow the woman had managed to breed a fine daughter and play him the fool. 'Damn!' He swept his fingers through his hair with irritation, and then just as quickly relaxed. The daughter was an innocent and once Ridge Gully lay like an empty well behind

101

him, not one person would know what stock his wife had come from. Lorna would do his bidding and she would ensure Rose stayed in line as well. Hamish lay back down, cocooning himself between soil and blanket. There was time enough to contemplate that every negative could indeed prove useful when it came to creating an empire.

Summer, 1858

Ridge Gully

Rose Gordon sponged her body carefully, the warm water soothing the swell of her stomach. In the lamplight the drops of water joined at her breasts and, gathering momentum, ran down in rivulets to the cotton of her petticoat. The moisture accumulated, a large dampness forming. Irritably wiping her body dry, she got into bed, pulling the coverlets up high to her chin. Nine months of marriage, most of which she had been with child. Were it not for some pressing business on the day of their wedding that kept him away for nearly two weeks, the weight of his child would already have left her.

Oh God, how had she, schooled as she was, managed to deceive herself into believing marriage to this invisible Scot was what she wanted? There had been hopes, nothing grand, no, a modest wedding, with perhaps a carriage, a white dress, with just a little lace. Perhaps Sir Malcolm would pay for it, or send a gift, for it had often been said at the big house that she had been his favourite. However, nothing came. Much later her new husband's ignorant refusal of an invitation to the estate was finally revealed to her. It would appear that he had been of some assistance to Sir Malcolm in a matter of stock theft, yet Hamish had refused a titled man, someone their better.

So there was no gift. And the brooch from which she could gain a loan for the wedding she wanted had never reappeared after it went missing from her small box of keepsakes. Inside the box there only remained a scrap of copied poetry, a dried flower and length of green velvet ribbon. But there was no brooch. She and Hamish married in a quiet ceremony in their street clothes. And now all these months later, growing heavier with child, with no-one but her mother and a serving girl for company, she wandered the badly furnished brick residence of Matthew Reynolds. Four times Hamish came back to her bearing gifts. First a slim gold finger ring inlaid with turquoise, then a pair of gold earrings, a length of silk and a striking ivory-handled fan. Each gift was repaid by her in their bedroom. Within days he was gone, his presence only noticeable by the smell of cigar smoke and the return to the dull food the serving girl prepared without the watchful eye of Lee. And, of course, there was the emptiness. For people only visited when Hamish was about, and then they were all male.

The brick residence was her domain, the two houses either side hers also, a belated wedding gift. Immediately she had rented them both, depositing the returns into the bank for her child's schooling. The Stock and Station Agency, now owned by Reynolds' brother, appeared also to be owned by her husband, as did the General Store and the lumberyard. In the street there was talk of stock theft, of Sir Malcolm retiring to Sydney, of the land her husband accumulated, of his entry into a war zone with squatter and selector fighting for land.

Rose rolled onto her side. NSW parliament had passed two acts that had changed her life in Ridge Gully forever. A selector was now able to purchase 40 to 320 acres of crown land at twenty shillings per acre. All that was required was a deposit of twenty-five per cent of the purchase price, the balance to be paid to the Colonial Treasurer over three years. So while the squatters argued over the destruction of their fledging colony and the 'Unlock the land' cries continued, Todd Reynolds charged interest rates of eighty per cent to selectors, who accepted the terms when the banks turned them down. When the selectors could not meet their commitments, Ridge Gully Stock and Station foreclosed and Hamish Gordon became wealthier as his land holdings increased.

'Rose?'

Hamish's voice startled her. She hunkered down further beneath the bedclothes.

'Rose, are you awake?'

A streak of light shone through the open door. 'Your mother says you've not left your room all day.'

Rose felt the weight of his body as he sat on the bed next to her.

'Are you ill?' Hamish rested his hand on her brow. He turned up the oil lamp on the pine bedside table until a weak light spluttered across the white linen and the huddle beneath.

'I am heavy with child.'

'A ready excuse you have availed yourself of these past months.' Hamish's fingers retreated to his pocket, curling around the gold brooch. Having decided to return her possession now it was no longer required, his mind flicked over the story he'd concocted. Stumbling upon it at a money lender's establishment seemed the best of limited alternatives. 'I hope after the birth you will be more rested.'

'Surely you have more important things to attend to.'

Hamish frowned at her harsh tone. 'I thought you would be happy here. I know the wedding was not as you'd hoped for. Your mother told me as much. However you have to understand, Rose, that I'm building a future not only for us but for our children as well.'

Rose sat upright in her bed. 'You lied to me. You were never any Scottish gentleman. Gentlemen with honour don't behave the way you have. Why, I can't hold my head up in the street anymore.'

Hamish thought of mentioning Lorna's prostitution. It seemed her mother was equally adept at obscuring reality. However, he doubted Rose was even aware of Lorna's extra-curricular activities. 'You took me on face value, as you took Sir Malcolm Wiley.'

'What's that meant to mean?'

'That you believed him to be a decent, honest man.' Hamish couldn't help but chuckle. This new country was full of illegal dealings and hypocrisy at all levels of society.

'He is,' Rose replied with an adamant nod of her head.

'I had no idea you were so naive.'

'I don't love you.' There, she had said it. The relief was palpable.

'We married because we cared for each other.'

'I was wrong.'

'People marry for different reasons, Rose,' Hamish said as tenderly as he could. 'You married me because you cared for me and knew I could care for you. You married me with the firm assumption that I would be able to provide you with the type of material possessions that you grew to enjoy under the employ of Sir Malcolm. Well, am I wrong?'

'I thought you were different,' Rose said sullenly.

'You have money and position. Wealth is position. And now you complain about how your comforts were acquired?'

'You don't love me.'

Hamish touched her cheek. The pregnancy had rounded her

face and lent some maturity to the previously delicate bone structure. 'I do care.' He had grown fond of her over the preceding months and was sorry for his continued absences. 'You will feel better once the child is born.' Yet he couldn't say the word love. He'd only used it once before, a long time ago in another country. 'Won't you come downstairs for a little while, Rose? I must leave in the morning.' He wanted to share his news with her. Finally a magnificent property some five hundred miles to the north of Ridge Gully was his. The original homestead had been destroyed in a fire and Hamish thought Rose would take great delight in discussing his plans for their new home. Women had a talent for decorating and Hamish hoped Rose would be enthralled for months choosing furnishings and wallpaper. 'Please come downstairs. I have news.'

Her eyes, wide and accusing, stared back into his. 'Go away.'

Hamish thought of the brooch in his pocket and quietly left the room.

❖

Downstairs in the dining room he removed the decanter and glasses holding down the drawing of Wangallon homestead and rolled the paper up. His mind knew every detail – the thick mud brick walls white plastered, the large dining room and drawing room, the bedrooms, a place for Lee at the rear of the house near a vegetable garden and, of course, a separate kitchen with a covered walkway to the main house. His home would not be burning down due to an untended cooking fire. His hands twisted the paper tightly before throwing the sketches on the fire. It seemed Rose wouldn't need a copy.

❖

Rose listened to the footsteps downstairs. She supposed she would just have to get used to being a Gordon. At least she would have a child to care for and love and she did have money, so she would not be wanting in that department but, as for her husband, well, he was that in name only. 'Looks like it will just be you and me, little one.' As if in agreement, the child kicked fiercely. It was a kick that lasted into the late afternoon the following day, when not one, but two Gordon children cried for attention at the top of their lungs.

❧ *Spring, 1983* ❧

West Wangallon

'Cameron, let's go for a ride.'

'Go by yourself, Sarah. You are, after all, old enough not to need an escort.' Sue's mouth flickered in a tight smile.

Cameron took a bite of his vegemite toast. 'Do you need me, Dad?'

Sarah turned to her father, imploring him with an earnest gaze. On the opposite side of the kitchen, Sue folded her arms in annoyance. Her once smooth hands squeezed her forearms, rough and sun-spotted from years in the garden. Her parents had been arguing again. This time it had something to do with Bob Hawke beating Malcolm Fraser's Liberal Party. Her mother liked Bob, while her father was adamant that Labor wasn't interested in the bush. Across the grey and white splotches of the plastic tablecloth Cameron slurped his coffee. Sarah concentrated on her milky tea. She wanted to try to get some shots of the creek in the morning light. Maybe she should go alone.

'You can both go,' Ronald said quietly, before turning the morning news up on the radio and pouring more tea.

'Ronald?' Sue's voice rose in pitch. She placed a protective hand on her son's shoulder. Her look, sharp and aggressive, turned her pinched face red. Small veins flickered on her neck, her mouth opened slightly, beads of perspiration breaking out on her forehead. 'It is quite obvious he's overtired.'

Cameron rolled his eyes and Sarah tried not to giggle. It was the only defence they had against their mother's increasingly weird behaviour.

'I don't want my son out.' Sue picked up a cup and, with a look of superiority, let it drop from her hands. It shattered as it hit the floor. Cameron and Sarah looked from the white shards on the black and white vinyl back to their mother, their mouths agape.

'Sue, please. As much as you would like to think he is still a boy, he's a grown lad. If he has time to take Sarah for a ride, well, that's up to him.' Ronald spoke evenly. 'Maybe Anthony would like to go along,' he added to his two stunned children.

Sarah nodded in his direction, admiring the control in her father's voice.

'There's no need for the jackeroo to be included in everything. In fact I've been thinking Sarah should spend the remainder of her school year in Sydney. The HSC is less than two months away. We could both go. I'll speak to Angus about moving into the apartment down there.'

'But there are tenants living there, Mum,' Sarah quickly objected.

'Sarah has a point, Sue. You can't exactly evict them,' Ronald added with a hint of weary impatience.

'Can't I?' Sue challenged everyone at the table with raised eyebrows and a mouth that looked like a heart monitor gone flat. 'You've had enough correspondence lessons, my girl. Time to learn some discipline.'

'Forget it, Mother, I'm not going.' Sarah pushed her chair back abruptly, sending it crashing to the kitchen floor.

'You come back here, young lady.'

Pulling on her riding-boots Sarah rushed out the back door. Behind her she could hear Cameron calling out, telling her to wait, but she kept on walking towards the stables. She couldn't do it. She wouldn't leave Wangallon, especially if her mother was going with her.

Anthony watched Sarah and Cameron as they trotted off in the direction of the creek. Once they reached the tree line they would disappear from sight as they wound their way through the sand ridge. He wished he was with them. Instead he was on his way into town to collect some parts for the John Deere tractor. Unfortunately his knuckles were about to knock at the back door when the argument started and by the time Mrs Gordon had finished relegating him to working-class status, he had retreated to his vehicle. Sue Gordon was a moody woman all right; one day all smiles and compliments, the next going off at the slightest thing.

He had heard the rumours, of course. Sue had been a real sort when she and Ronald first married; all legs and teeth, with a fondness for Vodka martinis and red lipstick. It did not seem to be the type of description you would expect of a woman who lived out in the North West, but she was still here. The publican talked of a bout of severe depression, followed by hospitalisation, followed by Sarah's birth. Yet the real eye-opener was the quietly held belief that Sue had an affair with a wool-buyer, which Anthony thought pretty much accounted for Ronald and Sue's prickly relationship.

Anthony looked out the window of the utility at the countryside spinning past him. His family owned a pretty nice property, but as the youngest brother he knew his inheritance would come in the form of a small amount of money, not land and it was unlikely he would ever have enough to buy his own property. His best option was to ensure he became indispensable at Wangallon, for he doubted if he would ever get a better job. If he hung on long enough, said yes to everything, he had a good chance of becoming a long-term employee. The problem was Sarah. He liked her, a lot, but he hadn't been on the place long enough to risk everything he was working towards by asking her out on a date. 'Idiot,' he said aloud. He was getting a bit ahead of himself. Still, sometimes he just couldn't help himself. Sarah was like a roast dinner, a cold beer and the sound of rain on a corrugated iron roof all at once. Would it really hurt if he asked her out? He thought of the jump she'd taken on Oscar only yesterday; a five-foot hurdle she'd rigged with a fallen tree branch and two forty-four gallon drums. She had cleared it effortlessly.

The air was cold, Cameron's horse flighty. As they wound their way through the sand ridge, disturbing rabbits, lizards and the odd fox, the large gelding snorted and started to pig-root in a half-hearted manner. Cameron laughed at the animal's attempts to dislodge him. Gathering his reins, he forced his mount into a gallop, swishing his battered hat behind him as he went.

Sarah followed at a fast trot. She glanced ahead to where her brother galloped and increased her own pace. Finally the dust settled as her brother slowed his mount, patting his horse's neck. They rode side by side, moving easily through the long grass, Cameron whistling.

'They can't make you go, Sarah.'

'Geez! Can you imagine me living with Mum in a small apartment?'

Cameron grinned. 'I've got to admit it could be messy.'

'Messy? She doesn't really like me, you know,' Sarah admitted.

'She does care. Mum is just one of those people who woke up one morning, decided they didn't like their life, and concentrated on being in a bad mood for the rest of it.'

Sure, Sarah thought. It was the day I was born. She flicked at a passing blowfly.

'I'll make sure they don't send you away, sis. Things just wouldn't be the same without you.' The last thing Cameron wanted was to be left holding the reins of the property. Being wholly responsible for the machine that was Wangallon scared the crap out of him. 'Besides, you've got too many reasons to stay, and Anthony is one of them.'

Sarah sighed. She had put up with her brother's good-natured taunts regarding Anthony for over a year now.

'It would just be beaut if you two got together. Imagine the three of us working together.'

It was one of Cameron's many plans for the future, Sarah knew that, but Anthony hadn't even asked her out on a date yet. In fact, since the night at the stables and the innuendo at the sheep yards, he had barely been around.

'I saw Blaze today. He's looking good.'

'Yeah, I gave Charlotte some extra oats last night,' Sarah added, grateful for the distraction.

Charlotte had given birth to a fine colt. Upon sight of the small foal balancing precariously on wobbly legs, Cameron had named him Blaze. Not very original, he had admitted to Anthony's jibes, but appropriate, considering the large white patch on the small muzzle.

'I'm looking forward to the day when I can ride him. You know, teach him to be easy with a rifle fired from the saddle when I chase pigs, get him used to roping, hell, maybe he'll even be a fine camp drafter.'

They broke their horses into a trot. They were out in the start of the swamp country, where a large paddock held a twisting river in one corner.

'Time to turn back, sis. Gotta be back to move the stud rams before lunch.'

'We can keep heading this way and take the short cut through the scrubby paddock,' Sarah insisted, trying to delay the inevitable return home. The sooner they got home the sooner Sarah would have to face her mother. She dreaded the thought of another argument.

'Okay. No harm in giving the folks a bit of extra time to cool down.'

'Thanks.' She smiled at Cameron. He was a pretty good brother when he wanted to be.

Sarah trailed behind Cameron as he turned towards home. She watched his lean form in front of her, the way he swayed ever so slightly with the gait of his mount, her mind formulating a plan. Hopefully Cameron would be able to change their mother's mind. A little of the fear gripping her heart loosened and a sigh escaped from her lips.

Kangaroos bounced off into the scrub and foxes sniffed the wind on the rough track ahead, before catching their scent and racing away. They moved carefully, peering at the clumps of grass concealing rugged holes that could be traps for hooves. Rising quickly, the sun flashed off tall blades of grass. Sarah squinted against the glare, sweat gathering in the creases of her soft skin. It was going to be a hot one today. Easing back into the saddle, she concentrated on eradicating the tension from her neck and back. Maybe it was time to confront her mother. Maybe she could move in with her grandfather. She and Cameron had to assert themselves a bit. They were old enough not to be bossed around. 'I'm going to go overseas when I finish school. Want to come?'

Cameron dismounted, checking the girth on his saddle before springing lightly onto his horse's back. 'Absolutely.'

'Excellent,' Sarah called out, drawing level with him and taking some close-up photos of him and his horse.

'A couple of months would do me fine. Let's go to the Highlands, see where the Gordons came from.' He held his hat to his chest. 'Oh, fanciful Scotland, land of burns, rivers and lochs! Mist-shrouded stones of hill and moorland.'

'When we come back everyone will have missed us,' Sarah enthused.

'I reckon we'll miss Wangallon more.' Turning his horse, he trotted ahead of Sarah through a clump of young belah trees, the denseness of the woody plants scrapping at his arms and legs.

Sarah screamed. Cameron's horse, having shied at something in the long grass, took off at a gallop; suddenly the animal stumbled, and Cameron flew out of the saddle. Sarah watched in horror as his right foot caught in the stirrup and he hit the ground hard, his body bouncing fiercely. Burying the heels of her boots into the flanks of her horse, she raced after him. She followed the runaway horse through the dense belah, losing sight of Cameron's trailing body as she passed through the thickest point, then she was out the other side, her own horse stumbling in the rough terrain.

Ahead she could see Cameron trying to turn, trying to keep his face free of the rushing, tearing ground. His hands were scrambling uselessly at the thick grass covering the hard cushion of earth. As she gained on the fleeing animal, she hoped she would be strong enough to grab the reins. She concentrated on willing her horse to go faster. She needed to overtake Cameron's horse. There was nothing else she could do, short of waiting for

Cameron's mount to slow down, but Cameron continued to be dragged over the ground at a horrifying speed.

'Come on,' she cried. Her horse was nearly level with Cameron's horse. With an almighty stretch her fingers reached for the loose reins just as a large log came into view. She watched uselessly as the horse cleared the fallen timber. Cameron rose slightly into the air before hitting the log with a sickening crunch. The force of the impact tore the stirrup trapping Cameron's foot from the saddle. As Cameron's horse cantered off, Sarah turned back towards where her brother lay. She jumped from her horse. Gingerly, wordlessly, she pushed him onto his back. His face was pale, scratched and bloody, his long-sleeved blue shirt in threads, moleskin trousers ripped. Blood oozed from deep wounds in both legs.

'Shit,' Cameron mumbled amid wheezing gasps of air.

Sarah held his hand, gently touching his cheek. From the wound near his temple, blood and white muscle meshed together to run freely into his eye and hair, and began to pool in the grass. Removing her camera hanging from her shoulder and light sweater, Sarah tore strips of material from her shirt-tail, ripping madly at the cotton with her teeth. Cameron's head, angled slightly to one side, revealed the lump of a broken collarbone; a leg and arm were angled awkwardly away from his body. Sarah looked down at the scrap of material and pulled her shirt off.

'Cam, everything will be fine. Really,' she swallowed as she wadded her shirt on the head wound and lay her sweater across his chest. The injuries were bad. She would have to leave him to get help. It was then that she noticed the sharp end of a small sandalwood stump protruding from his stomach. About her, the paddock was quiet, the birds still. They were a good few miles from the house, from the two-way radio, from help.

'I'm cold, Sarah.'

'I know, I know.' She squeezed his hand. His eyes were filling with tears. Sarah wiped blood from his face. 'I love you.' The words seemed too little. She leaned close to his face, his hand tight in hers. This wasn't happening. How could this be possible? They had just been talking. How could her brother possibly be hurt? 'Cameron, can you hear me? How bad is the pain?' Should she leave him and ride for help? Her horse was grazing only a few metres away. Unsheathing her pocket knife, she cut the arm off her sweater and gently mounded the material around the stomach wound.

'Anthony,' he whispered, 'loves you. He'll watch out for you, always.'

As a rush of blood trickled from his mouth, Sarah bent low, closer to his face, her long hair resting on his shoulder. His breath sounded like a rush of wind hurrying to pass through the drying stems of grass.

'Cameron?'

Lying in the grass in the mid-morning sun, Cameron looked beyond her towards some distant object. Then his breathing stilled.

Sarah followed her father and Anthony as they carried him through her grandfather's house. At each step they staggered, their boots dragging, their faces pale and sweaty with shock. Her mother was screaming, screaming and bashing the walls. Sarah wanted to hit her, to stuff her mouth with a towel to stop her from crying out as her own body swayed from side to side, like a ride at an amusement park. She felt the adrenalin surge, but there was nowhere for it to escape. Palpitations rose in her chest.

Her grandfather cleared his oak dining room table of its solid silver candelabra with one almighty swipe. It was there they laid Cameron, his spurs, a tenth-birthday present, striking deep into the same wood that had embraced previous generations. His hands quivering like bowls of Anzac Day jelly, her father kept patting him, as if making sure he was comfortable. Ronald's face was red and bloated, oozing tears of disbelief.

'Christ Almighty!' he cried. 'Christ Almighty!'

Angus studied the distorted angle of his grandson's beautiful head. With a devastated look at Ronald, his face creased in distress, from incomprehension to profound sadness. The old man removed the bloody shirt and, with a damp washer, gently wiped blood and dirt from Cameron's mouth, eyes and cheeks. Finally he placed a clean folded tea towel across the stomach wound.

'My boy, my dear boy.' Sue began repeating the words like a mantra, as if only just realising that her son was dead. 'I told you, Sarah, I told you I didn't want him to go.'

Sarah watched as her mother repeatedly touched Cameron's cold face. If anyone could will her brother back to life it would be their mother, and for a brief fantastical moment, Sarah believed it possible. Sarah let her eyes roam over the length of the body before her. She studied the moleskin legs and riding boots, stared at the tanned skin turned pale, at the blue-grey fingernails. She reached out to hold fast to his left leg, dimly aware of Anthony's grip on her shoulder as he placed a blanket across her shoulders and bloody white singlet.

'Oh God, Cameron.' She couldn't look at his face or into his eyes, those same eyes that had begun to fade as he lay in the spinafex under a hot mid-morning sun. They were the eyes of the person who loved her most in the world, whom she adored in return. She was afraid of what she wouldn't see.

'You stupid girl.'

Sarah looked blankly at her mother.

Sue pulled herself up from where she had crumpled onto the floor. 'You've done this.'

'For heaven's sake, Ronald,' Angus shouted, 'get Sue out of here.'

'Let go of me.' Sue tried to extricate herself from Ronald's restraining arms. 'You don't care about him,' she spat at her husband. 'How could you? You're not his father!'

'My God, Sue. Think about what you're saying,' Ronald exclaimed sadly.

'It doesn't matter anymore. Nothing matters.' Pulling herself free of her husband Sue straightened her back and, with a last desolate look at her son, walked from the room.

Sarah looked from her father to her grandfather. 'What?' Instantly her grandfather took her in his arms, her body engulfed by his strong, burly frame.

'Cameron was your half-brother, girl,' Angus said gruffly. 'Sue had an affair.'

Sarah's brain was filled with moving pictures. Her head began to pound; a baby screaming, a man, a stranger, the brother who was not her brother.

'Sarah? Sarah, are you all right?'

Her chest felt tight, her lungs constricted.

'Anthony, look after her, will you,' Angus passed Sarah into his arms. 'We have to . . .' he hesitated. 'Ronald, you better get a sheet, lad.'

Ronald, his whole body shaking, could only nod.

'It's okay, son,' Angus took his own son into his arms. 'It's okay.'

'But you knew he wasn't mine.'

Angus patted his son's back roughly. 'It's okay. It's okay.'

❖

Sarah let Anthony wash the blood from her hands. She put on the shirt he offered, drank water from the glass he brought. Later, after the ambulance took Cameron away, Anthony stayed with her. They held each other long into the night, leaning against the wall of the dining room, the room to which her brother would never return.

❖

Sue Gordon dressed carefully. From her wardrobe she selected a navy skirt and matching jacket – the shoulder padding adding form to her plump figure. A white shirt, gold earrings and a gold ring completed her outfit. Without bothering to check her appearance in the full-length mirror, she walked sedately to Cameron's bedroom, closed the door and sat quietly on his bed. His dirty clothes still sat in a heap in the corner of his room, his bed remained unmade and the dressing table with its cut-off cotton reels, a remnant of his great-grandfather's , lay strewn with cassettes. Her fingers clutched at the bedclothes, the material scrunching between the tightness of her grasp. Only last night her boy had come to her in her dreams. They both had.

Sue first looked into the unfathomable blue of Tom Conroy's eyes at her wedding. Later she would recall the exact moment as a small gift from the angels, if there were such things. Walking down the aisle arm in arm with her new husband, Tom, a stranger to her then, had smiled and winked at her. It was as if they shared a secret, some tremendous thing known only to them. Later, at the reception, they had danced. Not once out of politeness, but twice. Even now it seemed such an innocent thing to do. After all he was Wangallon's wool buyer, a position that held much credence in bush society circles. On honeymoon in Fiji, Ronald later complimented her on the courtesy she extended to their business associates and clients. In the months ahead he would come to understand the extent of her largesse.

Sue never intended to betray her husband. Ronald was a good, honest man, simple in his desires and pleasantly outgoing in character. A chance meeting at the now defunct Australia Hotel graduated swiftly to dinners in Sydney, trips to the theatre and nights of dancing. It was the type of lifestyle Sue was not only used to, being the daughter of a barrister, but one she attended to with delight. Of course her parents' aspirations were limited by their desire to see her well matched, and Ronald Gordon, as heir to Wangallon Station, was certainly one of the catches of the sixties.

Two visits later it was the Wangallon homestead that won her over. It was a gorgeous symphony of faded elegance. Solid silver items were strewn deliciously through a series of inter-connected entertaining rooms that fanned out from the original dining room like an enticing jigsaw. Ancient oil paintings of family members, objets d'art in the form of porcelain figurines and art deco pieces, complete sets of French crystal stemware and English crockery all competed for her attention. And the furnishings – two-seater couches, armchairs, settees and daybeds – the majority covered in rich brocades. Of course there was also a cook and a gardener as her mother-in-law, Angie, was involved in any number of causes.

Only after their engagement did Sue discover that a simple three-bedroom house, unimaginatively dubbed West Wangallon, was to be her home. Ronald's answer to her arch complaint consisted of an incredulous: 'What did you expect?' Indeed, for some weeks Sue repeatedly asked herself the very same question. Her assumptions included regular trips to Sydney, which, she was advised, were only once a year at Easter for two weeks. And there were no staff. Sue was young, after all. Her home and garden were less than a third of the size of Wangallon homestead. Ronald asked her why would they need staff? Sue had no answer.

When Tom visited six months later during shearing, Sue's initial disappointment had grown to frustration. What on earth was she really expected to do out here in the middle of nowhere? The men worked from dawn to dusk. There was no corner store, no theatre and certainly no fashionable shops. She was bored and disinterested. She had taken to sleeping in the spare room, for she realised her imagined fairytale was non-existent.

Her beautiful Cameron was the result of her and Tom's consuming passion. Her pregnancy took Ronald by surprise; they both knew the child wasn't his and his hastily planned trip to Scotland amid unspoken accusations gave Sue the space and clarity she needed. Not once did she consider the ramifications of her affair. Indeed Sue's only thought was for Tom. However, she waited for her husband's return, knowing she owed Ronald an explanation. Yet by the time Ronald returned Tom was already gone. His life had been destroyed by a low-life thief, just when Sue decided to flee Wangallon and run to him. She learnt of Tom's death nearly a week after he had been found in some alley in Sydney. Ronald's brief explanation started with: 'Oh, I forgot to tell you, remember Tom Conroy . . .' *Her* Tom killed in a robbery. His money and watch stolen, his head bashed in. 'Found in Kings Cross. Can you believe it?' Ronald elaborated a day or so later, remarking on why a man like that would be visiting such a place. Yet he had spoken of Tom kindly and Sue recalled, waited on her with the doting expectation of a father-to-be.

That was the beginning of the end for her. She knew then she would have to live out her days on Wangallon, her body growing parched and wrinkly as the harsh sun dried up the land around her. She stayed for Cameron, for her love of him, to ensure his rightful place in the family remained secure. Now Sue's beloved boy was gone.

With great effort, Sue collected herself and looked once more around her dead son's room. It was time to say goodbye to him, to both the past and the future. She was too old to begin her life anew. Even if she wished it, her mind felt, on occasion, as if it were being carefully torn into tiny shreds of paper. Sue knew she was being skilfully invaded. It was as if another person, having taken up residence in the smallest recess of her brain, remained intent on methodically ravaging the remainder of her thoughts. It was just as well, she decided, closing the bedroom door behind her. Some things were too painful to remember.

❖

Half-hidden behind a large gum, Sarah watched as Anthony dismounted, picked up a stick and threw it into the muddy water. Her mind was a blur. She still found it incomprehensible that her brother had been buried nearly a week ago. She felt weak and cheated, yet her thoughts kept returning to Cameron's wild pranks, silly jokes and endless horseback rides into the blue haze of the bush. Resting her cheek against the cool bark of the gum, Sarah gazed beyond horse and rider. Her life was now engulfed by her parents' devastation, Sue's downward spiral from reality and the knowledge that the truth had been kept hidden from her. Cameron had been her half-brother.

Sarah followed Anthony's movements to the very tree the two friends had thrown their knives into before Cameron's mad chase into the lignum. Anthony walked slowly around the gnarled trunk, but she knew he would not find the blade marks, her own hands had already examined every inch. She watched him running his hands over the bark for fruitless minutes before kneeling to pick up a stone, weighing it carefully in both hands, then throwing it deep into the lignum beyond.

When he doubled over, his face in his hands, birds escaped hurriedly from their trees, squawking loudly. Sarah had never heard such a cry, nor did she ever expect to hear such a piercing death wail again. It was then she knew how much Anthony had loved her brother.

He was gone, Cameron was truly gone. From a web of pain the memory of his funeral came to her: Sue, prostrate on his coffin; Ronald, crumpled, supported by unknown relatives. There had been many words, although none had touched her. When the cars drove off in procession, Sarah knelt at the foot of his grave. She could recall the damp earthiness of the freshly turned soil and the melancholy birdsong of a lone Bower bird as she imagined the heart of Wangallon wrapping her arms about her brother. And she also remembered a coldness; the chill of being alone.

Yet Anthony had remained to watch over her. A broad hand resting on her shoulder, fingers supporting her elbow as she rose, the caress of his face as his hand brushed dirt from her stockinged legs. Only when he rose, straightening his broad back, did Sarah recognise his anguish, the wretchedness. Even beyond her own pain she could sense his. He was there that day when all the others disappeared. He was there for *her*, Sarah reminded herself. Did he know then? Was he conscious of a recess deep within her heart, narrowing silently, sealing itself forever? By Cameron's grave, in the midday sun, Sarah had taken Anthony's hand. Why could she not do it again?

'You all right?' she asked, finally summoning the courage to speak with him.

'No. Your grandfather says you're leaving. You told me you would never leave Wangallon, Sarah.' He looked straight ahead, his gaze somewhere between the far bank and a black wattle tree. 'I know how hard it has been on you, but surely if we try . . .'

'Try what? Things will never be the same here for me, Anthony.' She moved to the water's edge, the toes of her riding boots sinking into the sandy mud of the creek's edge. The water rushed past her. A brolga stalked the opposite bank, his mate appearing from behind fallen timber in a flurry of blue grey. The pair were joined by another six birds, their graceful landings soon forming an elegant grouping. The flock began dancing, long legs sinking into soft mud, fluttering wings and arching necks moving in a form of corroboree.

They had laid here, Sarah recalled, the three of them. Only yesterday, it seemed. While they rested after cooling down in the river, Cameron had stripped naked, covered himself with mud, and jumped out in front of them like some deranged native. He had succeeded in scaring both her and Anthony so completely that they eventually slapped him hard on the back several times to stop him choking on his own laughter. In spite of herself, Sarah smiled.

'Everywhere I turn he's around me – his laugh, his voice, in the trees, on the wind. It hurts too much to stay.'

'I'm staying. I love this place like my own home. It's your home too, Sarah.'

'Before you came, Anthony, it was just my brother and me. Our parents, well . . . Grandfather agrees I should leave for a while, get some perspective.'

Anthony was now behind her. Sarah smelt the closeness of him. She could turn and hug him as she had so desperately wanted to the day of the funeral, yet somehow hugging him would not make things better. Whatever they had once shared now lay stagnant, buried in the past with her beloved Cameron.

'I don't want you to leave, Sarah, I'm asking you not to leave.'

His fingers were insistent on her shoulder, the tips plying the fine bone beneath. 'Don't ask me that, Anthony,' she turned to him, brushing aside his touch. 'I have to leave. I can't stay here with grieving parents.'

'You are not alone.' Anthony raised a finger to trace the path of a tear falling down her cheek.

Sarah moved back quickly. Dreaming of Anthony all those months ago, wanting him, she had waited for some definite sign from him and it had never come. Damn it all, now he wanted her to stay, and she couldn't. She felt at odds with herself, adrift.

Remaining on Wangallon at this time in her life was the last thing she needed. She couldn't spend each waking moment dreaming of the old days. She couldn't spend each evening with her mother's unceasing hostility or her father's blank stare.

'Bloody hell, Cameron was everything to me. He taught me what love and loyalty mean. He looked after me. He was my friend. Nothing can replace him. No-one can make things better for me at the moment, Anthony.' She looked beyond the water to the distant memory of her childhood.

The once welcoming warmth of those extraordinary violet eyes stared back with a determination unknown to him and, Anthony now knew he was too late. So he left her standing by the creek, her face pale, her eyes rimmed by dark circles. He left her knowing that with Sarah's departure and Cameron's death, the future of Wangallon was unknown.

≪ *Summer, 1859* ≫

Wangallon Station

*T*he horsemen stopped in the shade of a large Wilga tree and dismounted in a haze of flying grit and biting black flies. Hamish sprang lightly down from the saddle and turned to face his assortment of men. The sun's apex ate their shadows as smoke rose thinly in the distance.

'This is it.' He spat the stub of his cigarette from his mouth and raised an arm, gesturing in a wide arc. 'The boundaries are fenced. We'll drive the sheep straight up, then . . .'

'Boss?' Jasperson queried, his hand straying to scratch at the perpetual itch in his crotch. 'Why did you choose this piece? There's nothing here. It is so bloody flat.' He gazed disinterestedly at the land about him. Certainly with the number of sheep thefts neatly accomplished over the last year, distance provided security, yet here in this place Jasperson felt removed from humanity. 'No hills. Nothing.'

Hamish only smiled. 'We will ride towards that smoke.' Remounting his horse, Hamish led Jasperson, Dave and two other ringers slowly across crackling grasses as a biting westerly blistered their faces. The property comprised a large tract of land reclaimed from a previous pastoralist gone bust. Crows cried out above them. The land was heavily timbered in spots, the tall trees blocking the horizon. Hamish cursed under his breath at this wild, lonely country now belonging to him alone. It was not unlike the land of his forefathers in its harsh beauty. He liked a battle and by God this wily piece of fertile dirt would give him one. It was a long hard ride from his exploits at Ridge Gully and even further from the goldfields of Victoria, the place where his brother rested. New South Wales was his country now and it had been dearly paid for.

Hamish directed his men towards the smoke. A huddle of figures came slowly into view.

'Aborigines,' Jasperson whispered.

Hamish nodded as the group stood on their approach. 'Be on your guard, men.' There had been many incidents of altercations between the blacks and the whites and death had been the result on both sides. He was the owner of this land, but these people had been here first and he reckoned their knowledge of the bush would be invaluable. He was not prepared to risk his new life through arrogance. On reaching the group of Aborigines camped under a box tree Hamish spoke slowly, aware of his heavy accent, wary of their guarded eyes as he dismounted and removed a quantity of tobacco from his saddlebag. There were six of them, tall, lean, dark. Two of the men wore white man's clothes and had thick leather belts and wide-brimmed hats. They nodded, accepting the dark moist shreds before their teeth began chewing at the wads growing sodden with spittle in their bulging cheeks. Flies settled over the group, crawling over backs, hands and faces. The horses shuffled in the heat. Using a filthy forefinger, Hamish drew a map in the dirt, roughly drawing the borders of his land. Instinctively, one of the blacks leaned over and added extra bends to the river and a number of creeks. Extending his hand outwards, he then pressed his thumb into the dirt; their exact position.

'You boss of Wangallon now?' White teeth smeared brown with tobacco juice winked from a midnight skin. 'You need men, boss?' he enquired shrewdly, not waiting for an answer, 'you come to me. Plenty of help and no problems if you look after tribe.' He pushed his wide-brimmed hat so that it perched rakishly on the back of his head.

'Jesus, Mary and Joseph,' Dave exclaimed, spitting his own chewing tobacco into the dirt at his feet. Black ants immediately began crawling towards his offering. 'He's asking for terms.'

Hamish chuckled. 'What do they call you?'

'Boxer.'

'And you worked for McInnes?' Hamish asked, calling the previous owner by name.

Boxer gave a single nod. 'Good man, but weak here.' He thumped his chest.

'How many of you are there?' Hamish figured that he would need as many men as he could get.

Boxer squinted his eyes as a willy-willy of dust lifted upwards not three feet away from them and blew through the group. 'Enough.'

Later that night, camped in the open, Hamish watched the mesmerising stars for long hours, the strange southern stars of a foreign land. There was no breeze, only the faint rustling of creatures in the drying grasses, the call of an owl claiming his domain. He turned on his side, still half-expecting Charlie to be lying beside him, talking of the old country and of their place in the new. It was no small thing for a brother to have loved him so that he would forsake the only life he wanted, to follow him to the edge of the world.

Hamish sat up silently, careful not to disturb his sleeping men as the moon's shadow crept in and out of the rim bordering their campfire. The night air, having cooled a little, wiped a layer of exhaustion from his body as he suddenly envisaged the large homestead. A copy of the house plans were in his saddle-bag. Tomorrow they would begin pegging out the foundations.

There was a ridge of cypress pine not a half day's ride from the homestead site. It was from here Hamish would start cutting timber for the frame, the pines used ensuring his home would not be destroyed by the interminable white ants of this country. He would fell trees from two other ridges so that no one area was denuded of trees, using a pitsaw to cut lengths; each man taking turns to stand in the hole beneath, calloused hands grasping one end of the two-handled saw, wood chips, saw dust and dirt crusting eyes and caking faces. The felled logs would then be loaded onto a dray and carted back to the site to be barked. The barking of the timber to reveal the creamy wood was a tedious job but the reward lay in the virgin timber beneath. The bark itself, once dried and flattened, made an excellent waterproof roof, although Hamish considered such a measure temporary. He had a mind to transport shingles from Sydney when funds would allow it, beneath which he would eventually have cedar ceilings, cut by his own hands.

Hamish figured he and his men would have the frame up within a week, and by then the extra labourers from Ridge Gully would have arrived. They had been hired to help with the barking of the timber and the sawing of lengths for the ceilings and floors. The walls were to be constructed of pisé, a concoction of mud and grass bricks that once dried, a process of some months, would be indented all over with a hammer before being painted with a couple of layers of mortar and lime. By month's end the cedar doors would be built, with the main structure close to completion. It would be a proud building, one to last over one hundred years. Yet in the meantime he needed a simple bark hut for himself and his men, and there were outbuildings, men's quarters, a shearing shed, horse yards and drafting yards that either needed to be repaired or built.

'Wangallon is your memorial, Charlie lad,' Hamish mumbled softly. 'No matter what happens I swear Wangallon will be held by a Gordon for all eternity.' Removing his pocket knife from the worn leather pouch at his waist, Hamish flicked open the blade, spitting on it he rubbed the metal firmly against his trouser leg. Cutting a deep gash in the palm of his left hand, he then clenched his fist tightly. Hamish watched as blood ran freely from his flesh to stain the soil of Wangallon.

Winter, 1862

Ridge Gully

Rose lifted Elizabeth into her arms and held the sleeping child close. Her daughter snuggled tightly against her and Rose smelt the fresh scent of bath water and the milky remnants of her dinner. On the other side of the nursery, two-year-old William slept soundly beside Elizabeth's twin brother, Howard. The boys were easily disturbed and on more than one occasion the nanny had chastised Rose for waking them. For now they were quiet, lulled by food and a late afternoon playtime.

Rose settled her cheek gently against Elizabeth's smooth forehead and swayed softly to an unspoken lullaby. The children's nanny was eating dinner in the kitchen with the rest of the staff and would not return to her domain for at least an hour. This was the most wondrous part of Rose's day, when the three miracles she had created were hers alone to enjoy. Their births, particularly Elizabeth's, helped to calm Rose's unhappiness and her devotion to her children eased the pain of a marriage she wished she could escape from. No matter what Hamish did or said to try to ease the discontent between them, Rose was unable to forgive him. She considered her husband a formidable businessman, but the fact remained that Hamish was a most unscrupulous individual.

Only his continued absences made her daily life enjoyable, for Rose had settled into a happy existence revolving around her children, the smooth running of her household and the twice-weekly morning teas she held, to which she invited only the most prominent matrons of the district. After all, the Gordon money might well be tainted but Rose considered it a duty to uphold the good name of Sutton. Combined with her weekly piano lessons, Rose felt herself content and at long last, thanks to her darling children, both loved and needed. With the cessation of her physical relationship with Hamish, accomplished by letting out such a scream of abhorrence one night that he moved into another bedroom, life had finally became quite agreeable. Until last night.

Hamish returned unannounced after an eight-month absence. In the four years of their marriage she had grown accustomed to his irregular visits, however this last absence had been one of the longest. The hour was late when he demanded entry to her bedroom, stripped her of her fine lace nightgown and proceeded to ravish her. The whole event completed wordlessly and with little fanfare had taken Rose so by surprise that she never uttered a word, even when Hamish kissed her gently on the cheek, turned on his side and slept soundly until dawn.

Elizabeth now squirmed in her arms.

'Shh, baby. Mama's here.' Placing a soft kiss on the pale crown of hair, Rose placed her daughter back in her crib. She was due downstairs in the drawing room at Hamish's behest and while promptness was important to her, she refused to give Hamish what he apparently felt his due – obedience. The household was under her control, not his and just because the two of them managed a passable night together did not mean for one instant that she would relinquish control of her domain.

◆

Hamish paced the panelled lounge room, noticing the concessions to femininity. Reynolds family portraits, long disposed of, had been replaced by large oil paintings depicting idyllic rural scenes, crystal vases held fresh flowers and the very leather chairs he so admired now graced with embroidered cushions. Already his mother-in-law sat happily in one of the armchairs, dozing under the combined influence of weight and the heat of the fire. Her hair was carefully arranged into a fashionable style that quite flattered the otherwise plump face. Hamish considered the cut-glass decanter with its enviable contents, simultaneously deciding against another dram. He expected a scene, for there was always some type of one, in one form or another.

At least the children were asleep, saving him the effort of inspection. With the twins nearing four years of age and young William, two, the thought of subjecting himself to the noise and general havoc of their company elicited an ill-tempered scowl borne of previous encounters. He hoped for better things from them soon, of which only age would determine. Now that he had a family and the respectability he believed an influential man required, he did not know what to do with them. Clearly they were happiest here and Rose still knew nothing of Wangallon Station. Her lack of interest had so deflated his pride in the purchase that he'd not bothered to raise the subject again, yet now his home was built. He wanted his family about him and still hoped for some form of reconciliation with his wife. Hamish scratched the thickness of hair at the nape of his neck.

Rose shut the panelled door quietly and, smoothing the heavy material of her skirt, sat in the leather chair next to her mother.

134

No doubt he would reveal that the rumours circulating in the kitchen were true, that his business up north had outgrown Ridge Gully. Rose hoped that her life would go on unchanged. She dearly wished to be left here with her mother and her children and truly believed that considering her husband's infrequent visits home, that their lives would go on unaltered. Why was there a need to change a domestic situation that was almost agreeable? She could do little about how her wealth had been accumulated, so instead she had determined to create a genteel world redolent of the peaceful restfulness of Sir Malcolm's home. Gradually she hoped the shadow of her husband's dealings would fade as her children grew. She was in discussion already with the housekeeper with regard to furnishings and had ordered some fine curtain material for her bedroom, which she determined to redecorate in a pink and white brocade.

Hamish observed his young wife carefully. The business of mothering agreed with her and he experienced a renewed interest in a face grown more attractive and a fuller figure. Unfortunately she had lost none of her attitude, despite her reluctant acceptance of his advances the previous evening. If they were to be reconciled, changes would have to be made, regardless of Rose's inclinations. The woman agreed to be his wife. One could not change one's mind on a whim.

Moving to the fireplace, he poked a stray log into the embers, turning as the flames lit both the room and the face of his wife seen only briefly in daylight since their marriage.

'There have been significant changes in my business over the last months.'

At his voice, Lorna woke immediately, struggling to attention. Rose glanced at her mother, at the pale pink of her gown and the matching shade that now graced her lips and cheeks daily. 'Indeed, sir, and whose stock have you stolen today?'

'Rose, mind your tongue! You are speaking to the father of your children, your husband and provider.'

Removing a pouch of tobacco, Hamish began to carefully pack the pipe he had taken to smoking only recently. 'No, Lorna, the lass is angry and well she should be, for I have not been the husband I promised.' He stated this purely for the girl's benefit.

'You promised nothing and it is less than that I have received these last months. It is only through the gossip of the townsfolk, of the servants who come to this house, that I have become aware that you, Mr Gordon, are a thief of stock, property and land.'

Puffing at his pipe, Hamish concentrated on the curl of smoke rising towards the ceiling. Rose's petulant outbursts were unchanged since their first bitter argument prior to the twins' births. He ran his eyes over the heavy leaf green silk of her gown.

'I find your comments amusing, my dear, considering how easily you spend my money.' For the first time, Hamish saw his wife for what she really was: the daughter of a prostitute, well skilled as a tutor in polite society, yet now too high principled to value her husband's increasing wealth, nor for that matter, her own and her mother's good fortune.

'Good gracious, forgive my daughter, sir,' Lorna exclaimed as she stood. 'We are most grateful . . .'

'Enough! I will not endure this conversation any longer, my decision is made.' Tapping out the remains of his pipe into the hearth, Hamish rested a long muscular arm along the mantelpiece, his fingers brushing the base of a fine porcelain urn acquired on one of his many trips. Regardless of Rose's feelings towards him, he could not bring himself to desert her. He had spent too many months regretting his relationship with his dead brother. Rose was his family now. He owed it to his brother's memory to try to remedy this failing marriage and ensure his future relationship with his children was not tainted by his past mistakes. More importantly, it was imperative the Gordon blood-line continued. It would be a new start in a new country far removed from the father he'd left behind.

'This should be fascinating,' Rose answered with feigned politeness.

'I have sold the agency and the general store to Todd Reynolds and the houses either side of the main residence.'

'But they were your wedding gift to me,' Rose uttered as she grasped the arms of her chair.

'Aye, and the money will be invested elsewhere, along with the income received from them these past months.'

Moving swiftly to her feet, Rose's hands formed small, tight fists. 'That money was for Elizabeth, Howard and William, for their learning. I will not let you . . .'

The darkness crossed his face suddenly. Lorna, having risen in excitement, pulled lightly at her daughter's sleeve, entreating her to sit.

'When Howard and William require schooling they will receive the best. Young Elizabeth will receive instruction in those areas deemed appropriate for a gentlewoman; enough to find a suitable husband. I have purchased land, a large portion five hundred miles northwest of Ridge Gully, and tomorrow we leave for it. My daughter will stay here with you, Lorna, in this house. I have hired an extra servant and, of course, a monthly allowance will be yours in repayment.'

Rose felt as if someone had placed a stake in her chest. 'My Elizabeth?' She looked helplessly at her mother but there was no mistaking Lorna's relief. The woman glowed happily as she lifted a lace-edged handkerchief to her eyes.

'Of course the sale of the General Store means you will be relieved of the more mundane day-to-day duties associated with it, Lorna, however I have informed Tootles that you will remain the overall manager. He's purchased only half of the business. I gift the other half to you.'

Lorna, turning puce with the news, rose instantly to kiss her beloved son-in-law, only regaining her senses at the last second as Hamish drew away from the advancing figure.

'Rose will join me and my sons, of course.' It was done, the boys would be safe. There would be a second generation of Gordons in this country.

Lorna Sutton knew fortune when it came to her. Rose would be better under the guidance of her husband and, if that meant separation from her child, although she wondered at the reasoning of it, well so be it. Inclining her head as sweetly as possible, Lorna excused herself from the room. 'I'll see to the packing for the child then. Please excuse me.' At week's end she would have a dinner, perhaps invite Mr Todd Reynolds. Then there were new gowns to decide upon, the menu for the following week . . . Oh, she would so enjoy being mistress of this grand house for a change.

Hamish waited for the door to click shut. 'A drink?' His question ignored, he poured a small whisky and passed the fine-cut glass to his wife. She accepted it with shaking hands. 'This is for the best, you know, for our family, for our future.'

Rose stood unsteadily. Composing herself she joined her husband before the fireplace on the handsome red, blue and gold rug retrieved from Matthew Reynolds' former bedroom. She studied the tall man beside her. Flecks of grey speckled his whiskers and hair, fine creases hung about his eyes. 'I don't know you,' she found herself saying.

'You knew enough to marry me.' Hamish took her hand. It was cold to the touch. 'I did try to tell you about Wangallon, but you weren't interested.'

'I can't leave Elizabeth.' She felt unsteady, her hand reached for the mantelpiece.

'Your daughter will be safe here,' Hamish said quietly. His wife looked very pale. 'And Ridge Gully is the best place for her to receive the proper education.'

'Don't take her from me. Please.'

'Are you unwell? Perhaps you should sit, Rose.'

'She's all I have.'

Hamish took his wife's hand. 'I'm not trying to punish you, Rose. You and I have to make a life for ourselves, together, and the bush is no place for a baby girl. Not for little Elizabeth. In the future, should her husband's business lead her to a life on a property then so be it. In the meantime I wish her to stay here and enjoy the advantages of a feminine education.'

'And me?' Rose pulled her hand free of his grasp.

'Rose, you are being melodramatic. You're my wife.' Hamish drained his glass. 'I would hardly leave you here or my sons. Besides, there will be more children.'

'I hate you!'

'No, you don't,' Hamish said patiently. 'Don't you want Elizabeth to play the pianoforte and have singing lessons? Those options will not be available to her where we are going.'

'I do, I tell you. I hate you and I won't let you take Elizabeth from me.'

Hamish threw his glass into the hearth, the pieces smashing violently. 'You, Howard and William will be coming with me and that's an end to it, Rose.'

Rose's slight hand slapped hard against her husband's face.

Immediately Hamish experienced that same feeling of smothering sadness that seeped into him prior to the birth of the twins. 'Why did you ever agree to marry me?' His wife shook her head as if unable to formulate an answer. 'Have I not cared for you? Have you not been provided for in the best possible way in comparison to your former life?' Rose merely stared at him. She was like a porcelain doll. Golden hair and light-coloured eyes and the flush of youth highlighting her fair skin. Whatever Hamish expected from a companion in life, this cold young woman would never give it to him. There was a cost to respectability, one that would shadow him for the rest of his days. 'I have something of yours.' He had not intended to return it this way, but he was angry at his petulant wife and his own misjudgement of her. As she opened the small box, her eyes falling on the gold and jade brooch, her initial expression of surprise quickly changed to suspicion.

'You see, you do know me.'

The pale eyes narrowed, an angry redness crawling childishly from the high collar of her dress.

'You stole this?'

'Perhaps you will feel more comfortable knowing your dear Sir Malcolm assisted in creating the wealth you and yours now enjoy.'

Rose snatched at the piece, cradling the brooch in her hands. 'It was a gift, a gift from a kind, honest gentleman.'

Hamish could not live with such naivety anymore. 'Indeed, the same kind, honest gentleman who bribed members of Parliament and the Lands Department to secure one of the largest tracts of land in New South Wales. The same man who forced two daughters to return from England, to marry one to the son of the Manager of the Bank of New South Wales, and the other to the owner of his wool-broking house. How convenient to have one's fortunes intermarried with the two major institutions in this country.'

Rose glared at him, her fine nostrils flaring with each breath.

'Instantly the continued success of three major businesses is dependent upon each other.' Hamish pulled at the servants' bell. The swag of stiffened material hung from the ceiling and wound its way via an intricate pulley system to the kitchen. Walking through to the adjoining dining room, he had barely seated himself when a red-haired youngster appeared with a curtsy.

'Cured ham, some edam and bread, fresh baked now. Don't bring any of yesterday's. Oh, and tell Lee I want him to join me in around –' he looked contemplatively at his wife – 'say ten minutes, and that's supper for one.' Pouring a glass of brandy from his favourite decanter, cut crystal etched with a fine engraving from which the wine came forth from its sterling silver rim, Hamish waited for Rose to retaliate. Having followed him she stood at the far end of the dining table like a condemning judge. Far better the lass understood the way business was done these days, Hamish decided, than to continue her sentimental attachment to a man who, but for a chance of birth, could have been born poor like the rest of them.

He tapped his fingers impatiently on the fine grain of the burr-walnut table. This interview was beginning to tire him. 'And this same kind, honest man sent his wife back to England so he could indulge himself in the flesh of his housemaids while he treated his convict labour like animals.'

The brooch burnt her hand, burnt her deeply. Was everyone in her small circle unscrupulous? Her mind returned to Sir Malcolm's estate, recalling every detail as if she still resided there. Her gowns laundered, the tinkle of piano music after dinner, the time spent reading to Sir Malcolm in the library, the quiet elegance of the frequent daily visitors when Sir Malcolm was in residence, the fresh flowers.

'Incidentally your dear, honest Sir Malcolm died of the pox in Sydney last month. Ridge Gully Stock and Station is handling the sale of his estate, sixty thousand head of sheep, of which we now own half, and the land is to be broken up into parcels, subdivided into thirty lots for sale.'

Rose found herself mesmerised by a streak of dirt on the collar of her husband's shirt. 'Is there anything else?' she enquired in a small voice.

'Yes, my dear. Spare me the virgin innocence and the complaints. You may consider me unworthy compared to your own high morals but I notice that that same morality does not extend to the spending of my money.'

'You are a –'

'A bastard? If I am you have made me so. I have only ever shown you kindness.'

'I detest you.'

Hamish slammed his fist on the table top, the action rattling crockery and cutlery alike. 'And you are the daughter of a whore or did you conveniently decide to forget that fact?'

Two weeks later Rose stood in the middle of the nursery. In the small box, the box her mother told Rose many years ago belonged to her unknown father, she placed the gold and jade brooch. Beside it lay a dried flower, a length of green velvet ribbon and a love poem copied in her youth. It was a plain wooden box with neat brass hinges and a worn piece of red cloth to hide the scratched bottom. It was an old box, a relic from a childhood she could barely recall. With shaking hands Rose closed the lid and threw it in the small fire in the nursery.

Checking her reflection in the heavy gilt mirror above the nursery mantlepiece, Rose tied a firm bow beneath her chin. The loop of ribbon held her brown travelling bonnet tightly in place. Tucking a stray wisp of hair back into place, with shaking hands she took a sip of brandy from the sterling silver flask before replacing it on the mantlepiece. She had considered secreting the flask in the folds of her brown wool dress but the thought of Howard and William stopped her. Rose dabbed at her lips with a lace handkerchief, her pale hands fluttering in the reflection of the mirror. Coal-smudged eyes stared back at her with a vacancy that scared her. Even her weight, in the past so constant, was dropping. By the time they travelled the five hundred miles northwest, Rose wondered if there would be anything left of her at all. Certainly part of her heart would remain in Ridge Gully.

She gently lifted the sleeping Elizabeth into her arms and with a sigh, sat down in the rocking chair with her daughter. 'I will always love you,' Rose said softly as her daughter's almond-shaped eyes fluttered to wakefulness. Elizabeth's pudgy finger traced the path of a tear as it rolled down Rose's cheek. Rose grasped the finger before hugging her daughter fiercely. 'Be good for Nanny and remember I love you.' Rose dearly wished to tell her young daughter that they would be together again soon. Her intuition told her otherwise.

❧ PART TWO ❧

≪ Summer, 1985/86 ≫

Wangallon Station

*A*ngus looked past the brittle garden through the house
paddock, across to the line of trees spanning the horizon.
The floodwater was moving fast. It glistened in the distance, the
shimmering blanket mesmerising in its beauty. Trees appeared
to bathe delightedly, long, thirsty branches leaning deep towards
the earth intent on scooping armfuls of blessed water into their
ancient hearts. Angus shook his head slowly, this entrancing
mirage hid a swirl of mud and debris, beneath which the scales
of this water-creature grew, sucking at the soft earth, waiting
to consume. No inhabitant of the bush ever said no to a fall of
rain, for you could do more with moisture than crumbling dirt.
However, floods, like fire, were ruinous. The season had started
perfectly, Angus recalled. A good fall of rain in the spring, some
welcome storm showers in November to freshen the countryside
as summer's heat increased and then another good downfall mid-
December. Invariably it was only when the dams and low-lying
areas were filled and the rivers and creeks brimming that there

was heavy rain upstream that had the potential to swell the waterways downstream.

He rubbed his knuckles together, the bones scraping noisily. Twenty years since a flood of this magnitude, twenty years! The family would have to move in with him at Wangallon homestead to escape the rising waters. 'God forbid,' he voiced softly, wincing at the assortment of fractured human beings soon to descend upon him. He glanced across to the creeping liquid, clicking his tongue. Why he had tried to convince his son not to build here, he didn't know. Had Ronald listened? It didn't matter what age your kids were, they never listened.

Returning inside, Angus strode through the house, passing the greying Christmas tree in the lounge room where Sarah and her excuse for a boyfriend, Jeremy, stared dismally at the brittle branches sagging under the weight of decoration. Once it had been white; the kids used to play at its base with a small Frosty the Snowman, laughing at the concocted stories their mother would devise with the help of tinsel and a few of the less precious baubles. He caught Sarah's attention as he passed her and gave a brief, curt nod. She knew he was not impressed with Jeremy's presence and he'd told her as much. Bloody ridiculous dragging the boy all the way up here to the bush, even if Angus did suspect Sarah cajoled him into coming so that she would not be subjected to a week's holiday alone with her parents. Christmas had become his granddaughter's yearly penance. And unfortunately it was the one time of year when Anthony took his holidays as well.

The breaking of crockery echoed from the kitchen. Angus waited a few seconds before entering, willing himself not to compound the calamity of the coming flood by allowing his irritation to get the better of him. Sue's mouth twitched nervously; the bobbed brown hair, dyed weekly to hide minute strands of grey, tucked continuously behind her ears. The woman rambled incoherently although Sarah, following him into the kitchen with an attached-at-the-hip Jeremy, appeared to understand what her mother said. With Ronald still on the telephone, Angus returned to his partially eaten Christmas lunch to munch loudly on a leg of roast turkey pulled directly from the bird still sitting on the table. The grease settled into a thick smear on his lips and fingers as the meat slid down his throat. He could give orders, or he could wait to see if sanity prevailed. He sucked his fingers appreciatively.

'What about the scraps, Ronald?' Sue asked, her voice high-pitched. 'Where will we put the scraps?'

Ronald finished his telephone call and rested a consoling hand on his wife's shoulder, as the agitated woman scraped barely touched turkey and salads into a large red plastic scrap bucket on the sink. 'The water is being directed by the cotton levee banks,' Ronald said.

'Really,' Angus encouraged, stunned by such useless information extracted after a twenty-minute conversation.

'Yeah, all those bastards and their irrigation developments have altered the entire flood plain in this part of the country.'

'Well, you're not telling me anything I didn't already know,' Angus countered, letting out a turkey-enriched belch.

'Usually they go into the compost bin, but . . . but will it be washed away?' Sue continued.

'I'll just be in the lounge room, reading,' Jeremy announced quickly, 'if anyone needs me.'

Angus huffed noisily. 'We'll be sure to holler if we need your services, lad,' Angus called out to the man-about-town lawyer, solicitor or whatever the boy was or did. Yes he was polite, well-mannered and all that crap, but was he any use to Wangallon? Or, for that matter, his granddaughter? Across the room, Sarah smiled at him as if in apology. Angus nodded, they both knew that this life was disintegrating. Like rats, they sensed the impending doom.

◈

The next day Sarah and her father travelled by flood boat straight up the centre of the twenty-kilometre dirt road from Wangallon homestead to West Wangallon, the home deserted on Christmas Day. Along the way the stench of death washed over them. At the boundary gate, drowned sheep hung, caught on the barbed wire. Their sodden, twisted bodies, eye sockets bloodied by feeding crows, clung to the barrier that marked the end of their Styx crossing. The majority of sheep were theirs, but some belonged to neighbours many kilometres away.

The tall belah trees lining the road served as watery guideposts. Though the water level was now stationary, their bark showed the flood's peak and Sarah marvelled at this new unknown seascape where familiar features, such as anthills, scrubby bushes and tree stumps, were obliterated as if they'd never been there. They covered the distance between the houses in silence as the outboard rippled the water in the eerie landscape, small creatures wiggling at the waterline of trees. Above, shuddering branches held a menagerie; cockatoos, jenny wrens and hawks competed with goannas and lizards for space on sagging branches. Snakes wove in and out. Bottles, tins, paper, branches, even children's toys, floated on the muddy water, along with the decaying carcasses of sheep, birds and stray dogs.

The bloated animals floated past like lifebuoys. Two sheep, weighed down by the weight of their wool, covered in a myriad of spiders, centipedes and other insects, stood hopelessly in their path. Their gait was laboured, their nostrils and mouths bleeding. Ronald lifted his rifle, and within seconds blood trickled from their matted foreheads. As if in relief, the animals slumped, passengers searching for dryness, the weakest to drown or be eaten.

West Wangallon, the eerie monolith built thirty years prior, rose dismally from the floodwater. Father and daughter stared. If a man's home truly was his castle, theirs lay under siege, the outcome already rising, phantom-like, before them. For whether or not the house before them lay wasted by the force of the flood, the true victim was Sarah's mother. Sarah understood how her mother felt. Sue still grieved for Cameron as she did and their home held every single item of his clothing, his books, his cassette collection. If you opened his bedroom door and walked into his room you could almost breathe in the scent of him. No-one wanted that last remnant of his short life to be washed away.

Sarah tied the boat to the gatepost, four thick knots holding the rope. Turning, she lifted her face into the lifeless ears of a joey just visible from its mother's submerged pouch. She slapped at the sandflies and mosquitoes, felt the stinking water seep upwards towards her thighs and wished she had not come. Only ten days ago she had been in her darkroom developing a photograph of a young family. The shoot, held in Centennial Park among picnicking families, cyclists, walkers and young lovers, had been a dream of a job. It had served as a gentle reminder that her bread-and-butter jobs weren't that bad, particularly as the money earnt from them allowed her to pursue her real passion, landscape photography.

'You lead the way, Dad,' Sarah found herself saying as the image of a sunny day in Centennial Park was replaced by reality.

'Don't touch anything, and look out for snakes and spiders.'

Sarah shivered as she waded up the back path and thought of the one person who would have been able to lighten the situation – Anthony. They still sent each other Christmas cards, but she had not laid eyes on him for nearly three years. Her Christmas holidays were his also and when she came north he went south. They were living different lives now. Time changed everything and everyone.

The interior was gloomy, as if a sunken wreck. Even the air smelt stagnant, with undercurrents of rotten egg stench. The kitchen and dining room still held the remains of Christmas lunch. Chairs and other furnishings rested on top of platters and cutlery. Blowflies buzzed overhead. Sarah waded after her father through a swirl of wrapping paper, tinsel and the smashed remains of precious baubles, the beam of her torch catching small gift cards, their depictions of Santa blurred and grey.

Not one room had been left undamaged and most of the furniture that could not be stacked up on something else had been toppled by the force of the flood and ruined. Water ran freely through the house, and the stench of decaying small animals and furnishings brought bile to her throat. In the hallway Sarah halted outside Cameron's room. The door was closed. Gritting her teeth, she moved onwards. In her old bedroom she checked her chest of drawers now resting lengthways on her bed. She didn't think she'd forgotten anything important, but there was something rattling around in the top drawer: the gold bangle. She pulled it out, shoved it in her jeans pocket and left her bedroom.

'There's a snake!'

'Shit! Where?' Sarah's kneecaps marked the water level.

'It's gone towards the spare room.'

The gauze on the front verandah heaved under a mound of lizards, spiders, ants and centipedes crawling over each other in a seething mass. Beyond was the space where the garden used to be. The only things visible were trees.

'It'll be too much for your mother.'

Through the blur of water, Sarah imagined her mother's lone silhouette at the end of her garden. A garden created from the dirt of the outback, created from buckets of water carried in the early days before the garden pipes were laid. How many trees and shrubs had died over the years and been replanted? In her memory, gums, box, sandalwood, poplar, bougainvillea, pansies and geranium merged in shape and colour. Only one stood out in Sarah's memory, one that kept dying, one Sue continued to buy for years: *cestrum nocturnum*. Even now she could taste the night scent of the dollopy thick fragrance, imagine it lingering out there somewhere with the coastal childhood of her mother.

'There's not much to save, Dad.'

'No.' Leaving the verandah they carefully waded down the hallway, over rotting floorboards, tracing the increasing line of wetness sucking up papered walls. 'Still it's mainly just clothes and the few bits of furniture that we couldn't move in time. The carpets are ruined, the wallpaper and I'd say the foundations and the floorboards will need major work but other than that there are only memories.'

Sarah caught the sadness in the lowering of her father's voice. For once they understood each other, memories cemented their existence.

'I'll just check the office.'

'I'm sure I got everything, Dad.'

'Not quite.'

Ronald waded into his office and from his jacket pulled a waterproof envelope. Into it he placed the entire contents of a drawer. Sarah saw a conglomeration of old letters and photographs all tied neatly together in separate bundles with twine.

'They're of Scotland,' he offered, aware of his daughter's interest. 'I went there once.'

'I know, you told me.'

Ronald sealed the envelope. 'Our forefathers came from there.'

'I might go there one day. You liked it.'

Ronald shook his head. 'There are better places to visit, Sarah.'

'But you kept the photos.'

'Yes,' he agreed, 'I kept the photos.'

'There are a lot of memories in this house, Dad.'

Ronald's heavy hand rested briefly on her shoulder. Sarah thought of her beloved brother and smiled sadly.

'Let's get you back to that boyfriend of yours.'

On the return journey Sarah sat quietly, lulled into contemplation by the whirr of the outboard. It was difficult coming home at the best of times, but this Christmas was proving especially hard. Since Cameron's death her yearly visit at Christmas was all she could endure, and returning was like revisiting the scene of a crime. She would spend her days roaming the countryside, revisiting the creek, the lignum, the woolshed; all the places that held memories of her brother, documenting their lives with her new Pentax camera. Then she would relive that last fatal day and the words of accusation shouted at her by her mother. Initially Sarah believed her departure from Wangallon would only be temporary but nearly three years on she still felt estranged from the land she had once cherished.

Her relationship with her mother now verged on non-existent, and her father had taken to long drives across Wangallon, often not returning until dusk. Not once in all the months that stretched between Cameron's death and now had the subject of his true parentage been discussed. She tried once, twice, with her father yet a glazed look frosted his eyes and silence greeted her frustrated attempts for knowledge.

'Drop it,' he commanded one late afternoon. 'He's dead. It doesn't matter anymore.'

But it mattered to Sarah. She wanted to know why it had happened. Why she had been deceived since birth.

'Bad?' Jeremy knew he had to ask, but by the expressions on their faces as father and daughter walked through the back door, he rather hoped they wouldn't be forthcoming with detail. Sarah slapped sandflies from her neck before sitting heavily at the kitchen table. Of course he had been warned what to expect; that was one thing he could count on with Sarah, she was always big on detail, but in truth he hadn't really listened or, more correctly, had been unable to understand the true definition of a flood. Jeremy gave Ronald a sympathetic glance and then concentrated on the desolate looking creature that seemed to carry the rotten stench of filthy water on her clothing.

'You should change, you know,' he suggested, coming to sit by her side.

'Have a shower,' Ronald agreed. 'Use that disinfectant in case you've got any small cuts. Make her a coffee will you, Jeremy, while I shower.'

'Of course.' Glad to be useful, Jeremy topped up the stainless steel kettle and plugged it in.

Sarah swiped at a mosquito. 'Sorry, had I known this was going to happen I never would have dragged you up here for Christmas.'

They had been introduced at an art gallery opening. Sarah hedged around Jeremy's frequent telephone calls, citing work-loads and out-of-town shoots, joking for some time that his photo should be in the dictionary under 'p' for persistence.

Most of the time she was holed up in her grandmother's apartment trying to make sense of the world. Eventually Sarah relented and agreed to one date. Two months later she agreed to another.

'Well, I have to admit I didn't expect this,' Jeremy agreed. He brushed his white T-shirt, his acid wash jeans spotless compared to Sarah's flood-filthy clothes. 'It's staggering how quickly things change. One minute everything is green and lush, the next a flood is on its way.'

'Well I should have listened to Grandfather. He did warn me that heavy rain was falling up in the catchment area two days before we left Sydney.'

He brushed a bloodthirsty mosquito from her cheek. 'I won't stay, Sarah. There is nothing I can do to help. Besides, I think both your father and grandfather consider me a bit of a liability.' And wasn't that the understatement of the year. Angus Gordon had the uncanny ability of making him feel like a leper just by looking at him.

Sarah frowned.

'Hang on, before you speak, please let me say that if I thought that there was anything remotely constructive I could do to help, I would, but I really don't want to add to the angst in this household.'

Sarah reached out and touched his hand. 'I'd rather you stayed, but I understand. I can't say I'd want to spend my holiday surrounded by stinking sludge when I could be back in Sydney partying and going to the beach.'

'That's unfair.'

'Sorry,' Sarah answered.

'You asked me to come here. It took me a while, I know, but I figured as you only venture up here at Christmas I could at least support you. I don't understand why you keep coming though, Sarah. Even if there wasn't a flood, everyone just seems to be very distant and disinterested. I'm not from the bush so maybe I'm missing something but has anyone asked how you are? How your work is going? It's like we live in another world.'

'Well, as you can see, we do.' Sarah gestured to the massed insects crawling on the gauze kitchen windows.

'Yeah, well. I suppose you're just a better person than me. I wouldn't put up with any of this crap from my parents. It was tragic what happened to your brother, but life goes on and if you're only coming up here once a year out of some sense of family duty . . . well, why bother?'

Jeremy warmed the cups with hot water before adding coffee and then milk.

'I'm sorry,' Sarah answered again.

'Hey kiddo,' he ruffled her hair. 'You don't have to say sorry to me. It's just that I don't understand the family dynamics and with the flood and all I do think it's better if I leave. You can stay and support your family without worrying about me. It makes sense, doesn't it?' Jeremy knew she was torn. He'd rather she return to Sydney with him, but her allegiance this time was to her family. A skewed sense of family loyalty shadowed her trips north, but he'd also seen the look in her eyes when their car drove through Wangallon's boundary gate. It was pure love.

'One hundred and twenty-five years this house of Grand-father's has been here,' Sarah said thoughtfully.

'What about your old home? It is salvageable, isn't it?' Jeremy licked his teaspoon, absently sticking it back in the sugar pot.

Sarah traced the length of his forefinger as it rested on the tabletop. 'No, yes . . . well, not for me.' In each room they had lifted chairs onto tables, gathering clothes and shoes from the bottom of wardrobes, pulling the culmination of thirty years from beneath beds and within linen closets. 'Even the Christmas tree, all ruined. Nothing was left untouched.'

'And your brother's room?'

'I didn't go in,' Sarah took a sip of her coffee. 'It's her mausoleum, you know, Sue's shrine. She made it off limits years ago.'

'But you've been inside?'

'Sure,' Sarah smiled softly, 'I've been in there.' From it she had salvaged the old packing-case desk once used by her great-grandfather Hamish, her brother's favourite Bruce Springsteen and The E Street Band cassette collection and a clean blue work shirt he once wore. This last item was stored in a plastic bag with the silk scarf Anthony had given her years before.

Five days into the flood, having organised a lift in a State Emergency Services helicopter, Anthony arrived. He jumped from the machine as it touched down briefly onto the only patch of dry ground, the uneven bank of Wangallon's large house dam. Sarah, sent by her grandfather to check which supplies were arriving, watched as the familiar figure appeared on the dam bank. At first she thought she was hallucinating.

'Anthony?' she half-whispered, his name catching in her throat. He was wading towards the small tinnie where she sat, a large wooden crate in his hands, his akubra cocked back on his head, his lopsided grin oozing goodwill.

'Well, Sarah Gordon, came back for the show, did we?'

Sarah found herself suddenly speechless. She watched his capable hands grasp the boat as the helicopter dipped, lifting into the air, the wind whipping the water.

'Anthony,' she said slowly. She brushed at the moisture rising in her eyes. He grinned as he sat gingerly in the boat, dumping the crate between them.

'Hey, it's okay.' He leaned forward, kissing her on the cheek. 'Everything will be fine.'

Sarah experienced a welling of emotion in her stomach. His hands reached for hers.

'Is everyone okay?'

Sarah scanned his face, soaking up the tan of his skin, her eyes flickering to the small scar on his cheek. 'Everyone is fine,' she said softly. 'It's really good to see you.'

'It's been a long time, Sarah Gordon.' He gave the old outboard motor two quick pulls.

'Too long,' she replied, the words blown away by the engine noise.

With the flood water swirling about them as they moved off, Sarah focused her eyes on the rushing liquid, her heart quickening its beat, her hands subconsciously grasping the sides of the old boat. Eventually she found herself looking directly into his eyes again. Anthony was smiling, an expression of contentment resting in the soft creases about his dark blue eyes and around his full lips. She smiled automatically in return. The dogs barked loudly at their approach, the noise waking Sarah from a memory of that last day by the creek. With a rush of nervousness, her thoughts turned to Jeremy, reading quietly on the main verandah.

'Well,' Anthony stretched out a little, his leather work boots resting on the wooden crate separating him from Sarah, 'when your grandfather called me, I figured things up here must be pretty bad.'

'He called you? He never said you were coming.'

'Well, maybe he wanted to surprise you.'

He sure managed to do that, Sarah thought, aware that there was a broad smile plastered over her face like a kid just given a bag of fairy floss. 'Thanks for coming.'

'No problem. Things look a bit ordinary.'

'It's not good, Anthony. Not good at all.' Confusion was seeping into her body. She was so pleased and happy to see

Anthony after so many years, but Jeremy waited for her inside the homestead.

Anthony nodded, acknowledging the calamity as he took in the wreckage of the soil, the lapping of the water against outbuildings and trees, the destruction of the main homestead's beautiful garden, the terrible stench of decay. The stock losses would be atrocious. Jumping from the tinnie, he tied the boat to the back gate and extended his hand to Sarah. He felt the sweet pleasure of her soft skin against his and then she was gone.

'This is Jeremy. Jeremy, this is Anthony.'

Sarah waited awkwardly as her grandfather did the introductions. He was smiling, telling everyone to sit. For a moment Sarah wondered if her grandfather had intentionally arranged Anthony's visit just to make Jeremy feel uncomfortable and for that matter, her as well. Certainly the atmosphere in the kitchen was one of unease. Sarah busied herself prising the lid off the crate with a flathead screwdriver.

'Well, about time you arrived,' Angus said to Anthony. 'Maybe we can get a bit of order going again on Wangallon.' He looked squarely at Jeremy as if suggesting he was adding to the current disorder. 'I'll let you young people get acquainted,' Angus grinned, 'then I want Anthony and Ronald to meet me in my office in ten minutes.' He tapped Anthony briefly on the shoulder as he left the kitchen.

'Be right with you, Angus,' Anthony answered.

'By helicopter?' Jeremy repeated, upon learning of Anthony's mode of transport. He couldn't help expressing the surprise he felt. Angus had promised he would get Jeremy back to Sydney as soon as possible and considering how ill at ease he felt in the presence of the old patriarch, he half-expected to be rowed out by the old bugger himself. Instead he was politely watching his girlfriend unwrap chunks of cheddar, long-life milk and tinned goods in an environment as about as welcoming as a Doberman convention. 'I'm trying to get back to Sydney.'

'Well, Jeremy,' Anthony began, 'the telephone line dropped out before I could let Angus know an arrival time and secondly, I had no idea that you were even here. Quite frankly, it was a fluke I caught those blokes heading in this direction.'

'I'm prepared to pay if they'll take me.' Jeremy leaned across the table, his arms spread, palms down.

Sarah looked through the long window above the sink outside to where dirty water glistened in the noon sun. 'Lunch anyone?' she asked lamely.

'I'm sure you are but, at the moment, emergencies come first. That helicopter, along with every other available aircraft, is busy rescuing people who have lost their businesses.'

Anthony sounded very sure of himself, Sarah decided, as she placed insect repellent, water purification tablets and generic antibiotics on the kitchen sink. He was right – emergencies came first.

'Anyway,' Ronald interrupted, 'the helicopter will return in a couple of days, that's standard procedure, so we can contact the SES beforehand and let them know we want to do a lift.'

'Right, thanks for that, Ronald,' Jeremy answered.

'No problem. Sarah, why don't you go check on your mother, see if she wants some lunch?'

'Okay, Dad.' Sarah didn't particularly want to leave Jeremy and Anthony alone together but on the other hand she didn't want her mother coming into the kitchen and giving Anthony the third degree either. She had calmed down since their evacuation from

West Wangallon, but her mind seemed a little more confused than usual. 'Right then, I'll just go check on Mum.' Her father followed her out of the kitchen. Anthony smiled in her direction. Jeremy's glance was far more subdued.

◆

Sue was in one of the spare bedrooms knitting a jumper. Sarah was pretty sure she'd been working on the same piece last Christmas. 'How you doing, Mum? Do you need anything?'

Sue stopped the click clack of the knitting needles and looked over her shoulder through the window. 'Angie was just telling me that we should plant some pansies after the water recedes. It's a good idea, don't you think?'

Sarah followed her mother's gaze out the window. 'Angie? Do you mean Granny Angie?'

'Well, of course, Sarah. Who else would I be talking about?'

Sarah pulled the thick yellow curtains wider. Outside the water was brown in colour. 'Mum, Granny Angie died, remember? She had asthma. The doctor said it was environmental, from the dust and everything.'

Sue resumed knitting. 'Well, she never left and we are going to plant pansies.'

To some extent her mother was right. Granny Angie suffered from asthma all her life yet she flatly refused to leave Wangallon. She died one afternoon when Angus was out mustering. Her puffer had run out. They found her lying in her beloved garden among the geraniums, a basket of cuttings by her side. 'Pansies are a very good idea,' Sarah said as she patted her mother's shoulder. 'Granny Angie would like that.'

◆

Left alone in the kitchen, Jeremy and Anthony looked at each other for a minute or two before Jeremy decided to break the silence. 'So, I was wondering when we'd eventually meet. You seem to figure fairly prominently in the goings-on up here. Sarah's told me a lot about Wangallon and you.'

Anthony poured himself a glass of water from the plastic jug on the table. 'Well, I've been here for a while.' So, Sarah's current flame was a yuppie. He had that man-about-town, no-dirt-under-my-nails look about him.

'And you knew Cameron?' Jeremy persisted. Chatting with Anthony wasn't exactly on his list of top ten hits. Sarah talked of the old days and Anthony like they were joined at the hip and Jeremy knew how much she loved getting his yearly Christmas card. He wondered if their relationship had ever gone beyond friendship.

'Yeah. He was a good mate of mine.'

'Sarah talks about him all the time. I worry she can't let go. It doesn't seem healthy to me.'

'Well, they were really close. It's not like living in the city, you don't mix with a lot of people on a regular basis, so you tend to make your own fun and have very close relationships with family members. And those two were close. Cameron looked after her like a true big brother but they were best friends as well.'

'What was he like?'

'Cameron? Probably about the best person you could meet. Funny, considerate, reliable and a damn good stockman. Even old Angus respected him for that.'

'He must have been good.'

Anthony laughed. 'Angus is tough, it's true, but his life is about survival. About keeping Wangallon alive and breathing. He wants to hand it on to the next generation, as his father, Hamish, handed it to him.'

'That's going to be pretty difficult with Sarah in Sydney.'

Anthony began transferring the remainder of the contents of the crate from the table to the sink. 'That depends on Sarah. Standard issue baked beans.' Anthony rolled his eyes as he held the cans aloft before setting them alongside the other foodstuffs on the sink.

'You think she should be back here, don't you?'

'Sarah knows it as well. She's tied to Wangallon by blood. It's her birthright. You must be able to see that.'

'Actually I only see a young woman tied to a piece of dirt that's holding her back from her life.'

Anthony gave a sour laugh. The bloke had some audacity, waltzing in here and imagining he knew what was best for Sarah. Or maybe he was more worried about what was best for himself. 'Well some of us are blind to reality.'

Jeremy stood up. 'And some are blinded by what they can't have.'

Anthony figured one quick jab to the nose would do it, but while the thought of walloping Jeremy one really appealed to him, he didn't take the baited line. This was Angus's house and there was no damn way he would disrespect him or Sarah by arguing with this upstart. Besides, he reckoned that this round was already won. Gathering up the opened crate under one arm, he left the kitchen grinning. 'See you later, Jeremy.' He wasn't the one catching the next flight out.

Sarah waved goodbye to Jeremy from the dam bank. The bubble dome of the SES helicopter glinted brightly in the sun and then gradually disappeared from sight. Shoving her hands deep into the pockets of her jeans, she listened to the dogs howling. God, she couldn't stand the noise they made anymore. Having sprayed their bodies and makeshift kennels on the back of the cattle truck with insect repellent, hoping it would ease their faces swollen by insect bites, she hoped for some quiet but the plaintive yelps continued. Maybe she should have returned to Sydney with Jeremy. She felt strung out, exhausted and everywhere she went she was encircled by bloody, stinking water.

'Watch you don't end up with a crate on your head.'

Sarah started at Anthony's voice.

'Sorry.' He squatted beside her on the bank, slapping at the mosquitoes feasting on his neck and face. Anthony pointed skyward. 'They radioed in to say they were coming and they've done their circle, Sarah.'

The RAAF *Hercules* flew low, its noise deafening as it made its approach towards them. The dogs recommenced their howling and as if in sympathy, birds screeched from nearby trees. Sarah watched in anticipation as two crew members, secured by lines, pushed a small crate from the plane. It landed with a thud, the heavy wood splintering, leaving deep cracks in the timber. Sarah set off to retrieve the damaged crate, praying that the medications ordered for her mother arrived safely.

'Good one, fellas,' Anthony called after the plane, over-taking Sarah as he waved a salute. 'These crates are meant to be unbreakable.' Hoisting the crate onto his shoulder, he ignored Sarah's outstretched hands – the girl still felt she had to do every-thing. 'It's a bit heavy.' He stumbled down the bank and then, wrestling with his small boat, he deposited the crate within. 'Hope old Angus wasn't expecting a ten-year-old whiskey with this lot.' Tying his boat to Sarah's, he became aware of her eyes on him. 'Thought we better be a bit cautious with the fuel situation.'

Sarah opened her mouth to speak.

'I know, you're gonna say there's heaps, but we just don't know how long the water will stay here. Angus said during the last flood the water lapped the floorboards for nearly six weeks.' He patted the aluminium seat opposite him.

Sarah remained standing on the dam bank. Why couldn't people just give her a bit of space? That was all she wanted, room to breathe. Instead she felt surrounded. The house was claustrophobic, her father and grandfather argued, her mother was starting to get under her skin and to compound everything she felt guilty about staying on at Wangallon now Jeremy was en route to Sydney.

'You coming?'

And now here was Anthony, grinning like some schoolkid with an icy-pole to lick. 'I can manage this, Anthony,' she answered brusquely. 'Why don't you have the day off? I'm sure Grandfather won't be needing you.' She didn't mean to sound dismissive however she just couldn't handle Anthony today. She'd been so happy to see him, but then guilt speared through her when she thought of Jeremy. It was stupid, she knew that. Jeremy was the one she loved and he understood why she needed to stay on.

The contours of Anthony's face, partially shaded by day-old growth, tightened as he clambered awkwardly out of Sarah's boat. 'Nice tone of voice. What am I? The hired help to you now?' Grabbing the crate Anthony dropped it into Sarah's tinnie, the small vessel dropping half a foot into the murky water with the weight. As he swiftly untied the rope that bound the two boats together, Sarah rushed to jump into her tinnie as it began to drift away from the bank.

'I'm sorry, I didn't mean to –'

'I'm a little surprised you didn't go as well,' Anthony talked over the top of her. 'Not much you can do here and I'd imagine you're a little out of practice.' Anthony climbed into his own boat and, tipping the brim of his hat down further over his face, started the outboard. 'Don't think you have to stay.'

'What do you mean, "Don't think I have to stay"? Of course I want to stay.' Sarah yanked miserably on the starter cord of the outboard motor. 'Just because you're back doesn't mean I'm defunct.' Did he hear her? Shit. How could anyone hear a bloody thing over the twin engines.

'Anyhow, no doubt old fig jam will be pleased to be outta here,' Anthony yelled.

Sarah stared after Anthony as he directed his boat in the opposite direction. He had just called Jeremy fig jam. Everyone knows what that means, she thought to herself: Fuck I'm Good, Just Ask Me.

Cocking his akubra back on his head Anthony swatted at a mosquito. 'This place is more than just a breeding ground for you, mate.' He sniffed at the festering river of moulding vegetation.

A few days later they stopped listening to the radio. One lunch hour, halfway through the rural news report, Angus switched off the station.

'I think we have all had quite enough of the daily horror stories floating over the air like spectres. We know how bad it is and we certainly don't need to be constantly reminded of the losses.'

Sarah looked across the kitchen table at her mother. She rarely involved herself in any of their conversations. She was adrift in her own thoughts. She meandered through the house, spending her days knitting and watching the soapies on TV. She cooked meals when no-one was present to stop her, baked beans, runny fried eggs dripping in fat and lettuce and made polite conversation when required, but that was the extent of her life. Sarah found herself questioning her father's patience daily. The close proximity of the flood meant there was no escaping her mother's changed personality, but even making allowances for that it was difficult to reconcile her mother's deterioration. Her father asked for her understanding, especially when Sarah told him how Sue had taken to having gardening conversations with Granny Angie;

yet understanding was the one thing Sarah was unable to give her mother. This was the same woman who had had an affair. She'd not been a true mother, obsessed as she was with Cameron then, lastly and most cruelly, Sue blamed her for Cameron's death.

'How will she survive this tragedy, the loss of her home,' Ronald tried to explain to Sarah one day, 'when she has never recovered from the last?'

Sarah recalled biting her tongue. She was at a loss to understand her father's continued loyalty to a woman who had betrayed both him and his daughter.

Climbing into the helicopter hired to check stock, Sarah squeezed in next to her father. From above, the expanse of territory covered by the flat muddy water was daunting. Trees guarded the clogged land like sentinels in a surreal world. As the helicopter dropped closer, hundreds of sulphur-crested cockatoos and wild budgies flashed through leaves heavy with insects. Last night three generations of Gordons had pored over bank statements, discussed expected losses and the insurmountable debt required to restock with cattle and sheep. Their most immediate concern, however, was where they could purchase fodder. The SES was assisting with initial stock feed requirements, with more Hercules dropping bales of feed to stranded animals, but once the waters receded Sarah knew they would be on their own unless the government offered some form of assistance. It all depended on how widespread the damage was.

They ventured further into the more distant parts of Wangallon, observing what they could not alter, haunted by helplessness. Dam banks and small rises provided the only refuge for the starving, waterlogged animals. Herds of cattle stood quietly, heads down. Mobs of sheep clung tenaciously to the few dry ridges available. There were very few lambs to be seen. In one large paddock, more than two hundred cattle were moving steadily through the water. Their backs formed an arrowhead formation, rippling the otherwise still surface. The helicopter hovered above the pitiful sight.

'They're canny old girls,' her father said into his headset. 'They'll be heading for Boxer's Ridge.'

The pilot answered and in seconds they were above a dry area, empty except for half a dozen kangaroos and a fox.

'That'll make for interesting dinner conversation when they get there.'

'Well, at least we know there's still stock out there to be fed, Dad.'

'That's right, Sarah. That is exactly bloody right.'

That night the sky was luminous with stars. Brushing her shirt-sleeves free of sandflies, Sarah resumed her stance, gumboots swallowed in mud, arms resting on the back gate. It was strange how many times the image of dead sheep came to her. In her dreams their backs disappeared, their once soft white faces crying out as they sank slowly out of sight. Reminding herself that they still had stock that were alive and well helped her sadness. Still, their losses remained as unsalvageable and as irreplaceable as West Wangallon.

Sarah needed to apologise to Anthony for the way she had spoken to him earlier in the week. The last thing she wanted was to hurt him. There had been far too much of it in her life. She needed to be honest with herself and admit that she missed Anthony, but since her brother's death she had been unable to make sense of her feelings. Her desire for Anthony seemed to be irrevocably caught up with the past and it was a past too painful to revisit. No-one knew what a basket case she'd been on first arriving in Sydney, how many listless, friendless days she'd spent judging herself for her brother's death and the mess both her life and her family's had become. She had closed the door on her beloved Wangallon to survive and that same door had also closed on Anthony. At least in Sydney with Jeremy, stability, fun and security were hers. She knew where she stood with Jeremy. She was finally experiencing some control and direction in her life.

The night air, heavy with heat and moisture, draped her body. The earth was close tonight, its hot, moist breath bringing a sheen to her skin. A trickle of sweat escaped from her matted hair to run down her neck, gathering between her breasts.

'If you gaze up long enough, especially in the quiet, all the things you don't want to remember come back,' Anthony said quietly. ·

With the swish of water he was beside her. He smelt clean like mown lawn, his hands gripping the fence, the iron straining under the lean of his body. If she turned ever so slightly, she knew he would turn to look at her, soaking up her face with the dark blue of his eyes as he had in the past.

'In the bush there is always too much time to remember,' Sarah answered. In Sydney, she was too busy to dwell on the past, too preoccupied with her life. Here, with Anthony beside her, she almost expected her brother to appear with a couple of beers and a ready joke.

It was hot and uncomfortable, Anthony decided, slapping at mosquitoes as he wondered what had possessed him to follow Sarah outside. Now leaning next to her he allowed himself the luxury of studying her profile in the dark, the smooth curved bones and long swan's neck. Perspiration, staining the pale cream of her shirt so tantalisingly sheer on her skin, highlighted the strap of her bra beneath.

Anthony still marvelled at how easily Sarah left Wangallon. He'd heard snippets of her life through Angus. The months she'd spent unemployed, her growing skill as a landscape photographer and her increasing demand at the small photographic studio in

Surry Hills where she worked. It amazed Anthony how quickly she'd adjusted to city life. But then it struck him that she hadn't adjusted, Sarah had simply run away. And he was not surprised that someone had taken a fancy to her and she to him. Sarah was trying to create an entirely new life for herself.

If he only knew what to say to her, but they had both changed. He had cared for her once, but it was so long ago and so much had happened in their lives since Cameron's death that there was a gulf between them now. It would have been better if she had stayed in Sydney, Anthony decided, walking away.

❧ Summer, 1866 ❧

George Street – Sydney

Hamish stepped out of the Bank of New South Wales building in George Street, into the grey morning where covered wagons stocked with produce unloaded across the busy street, a shop owner checking the delivery of cases of flour and sugar. A highly polished black carriage pulled by matching bays headed down the slope towards Circular Quay, scattering three open drays hauling timber for the many buildings going up. Careful not to slip on the dirty cobblestones, Hamish skirted through the busy traffic, avoided a group of ragged children rushing past him with a trooper in pursuit, and sidestepped the tattered workers off-loading coal and firewood for heating. Gingerly stepping over puddles of water, horse shit and other refuse, he crossed safely to the other side of the street. It was mid-morning. He'd time enough to walk to the auction house, purchase the fine oak dining table he wanted and still be back at the club for lunch.

Hamish was inordinately pleased with his business meetings to date. Especially rewarding was the time spent with his old acquaintance, Tootles Reynolds, from Ridge Gully Stock and Station, whose surprisingly fertile business mind had allowed him to prosper and acquire two further agencies: one in Sydney, the other in Bathurst. Tootles, whose business network naturally included colonial merchants and import houses – the main buyers of wool – was the obvious man for the task of organising the consignment of Wangallon's wool-clip, which this very year could possibly exceed the largest ever in New South Wales. Consigning his clip with Sydney's leading wool store, Hamish obtained excellent foreign exchange rates and promptly received substantial monetary backing from another agent in London, immediately gaining purchasing power overseas by selling his wool in London.

With his main business completed, he had banked his sizeable advance and enjoyed a lengthy stay at a gentleman's club in Sydney, purchased some pieces of furniture and other household items, subscribed to a selection of local and European magazines and purchased a trunk of books from an estate sale. The trip also afforded him the chance to meet the Abishara brothers, owners of the Bourke Carrying Company, to whom he had consigned his wool clip for the arduous trip south to Sydney. All that remained was to obtain a nanny for his children. Once organised, all his new belongings were to be packed up to begin the arduous wagon journey north.

The young girl walked briskly out of the butcher's shop and stepped up into an open dray. Hamish noted the grey-haired man, his sickly pallor and the look of concern on the girl's face as she turned, touching his arm lightly. Her eyes caught Hamish's and she smiled brightly.

'Good morning, sir.'

'Good morning to you, Miss,' Hamish responded, surprised by her confidence.

'If you are visiting Mr Harrow, the butcher, do ask for his freshest cuts. He has a fondness for saving the best for the

Governor's kitchen, regardless of whether he is called upon to provide for his Excellency or not.' Ensuring her companion was settled, she placed a paper parcel between them on the seat. Then lifting her small hand, the lass tenderly caressed his cheek and rested her fingers momentarily on his shoulder. Taking the reins confidently from the man beside her, she twitched the horse's flank lightly with a short-plaited crop.

A strong sense of familiarity came over Hamish, a feeling of continuity, as if whatever he had sought or expected upon arriving in this distant country had at last presented itself. The journey was complete. Yet the girl he stared at so frankly could not have been more than fifteen. Even more astonishing was that she not only met his gaze but continued to stare back at him with a mixture of admiration and curiosity. Hamish found his arm lifting briefly in a wave; the girl's eyes flickered with delight. Her wide unblemished face, graced by large eyes and a generous mouth, promised in a single glance both strength of heart and honesty. Hamish wished he knew the lovely creature. Tendrils of dark hair shone black against the whiteness of her neck. It was not the fire red of Mary's or the light blonde of Rose's, but a luscious deep black blue. The girl smiled delightedly, as if pleased with her older admirer, before concentrating on manoeuvring the dray into the traffic.

Hamish stepped back under the awning of the butcher shop as rain began to fall, the street clearing quickly of pedestrians. The splash of rain hit the canvas awning above his head, falling in a veil when it reached the edge. He watched the dray until it disappeared from sight. This is ridiculous, he thought to himself. Nonetheless he found himself walking into the butcher shop and enquiring after the young woman.

The butcher answered Hamish's questions with little reluctance. The girl in question was Claire Whittaker. Following the outbreak of fever, she and her father were the only ones left of a family of eight. They owned land at Parramatta and were of respectable stock, though the butcher doubted an abundance of money for, although the slender frame of the young girl was always neatly dressed, she never carried the style of a moneyed lady. Hamish left the shop clutching the girl's address on a square of paper.

The girl was probably half his age, Hamish thought as he walked back up George Street. His fingers curled around the slip of paper in his pocket. That night he dreamt of a young girl full grown into a woman, wearing a crinoline not quite two yards in diameter. The skirt, dark blue, was complemented with a paler blue blouse, and around her neck was a blue velvet neck ribbon. In his last sight of her, the dream presented her in a brown pork-pie hat, with several coloured streamers falling from it at the back.

❦ *Autumn, 1866* ❧

Wangallon Station

*H*amish sniffed the wind carefully, his nostrils flaring. The dry scent of dirt caked each breath he took and he longed to wash himself clean of his long journey. The inside of his thighs ached and his lower back harboured a constant pain, which heralded a previously unknown stiffness sure to invade his body tomorrow. With a groan he stretched out his shoulder blades and arched his neck. He would be pleased to be home.

Boxer, the head stockman, waited with an assortment of Aboriginal ringers, as Hamish approached the entrance to Wangallon Station homestead after an absence of four months.

'Boss.' Boxer tipped his wide-brimmed hat; the others, numbering ten, stared in return.

'No problems, then, Boxer?' Hamish inquired, knowing if there had been, he would not be told.

Boxer grinned cheekily, displaying a marvellous set of teeth faintly stained by the tobacco he chewed religiously. They rode side by side along the track that forked half a mile from the main house.

A well worn track veering to the left led to the twenty-six-stand shearing shed, its encompassing sheep yards only a short distance from the rough bark humpies that served as accommodation for the shearers and rouseabouts. Boxer pulled himself upright in his saddle as he left the other members of his tribe behind. The late morning wind rustled the grass, green clumps visible at the base of the plants where the recent rain had refreshed them.

Spitting a gob of tobacco clear of his horse, Boxer wiped spittle from his chin with a grubby shirtsleeve. 'More tribe coming, boss. Wanna be with mine.'

'Camp with yours, Boxer?'

'Yeah, boss. More family.'

'How many?' Hamish asked, removing his riding glove to smooth his immaculate moustache.

'Ten, maybe less.'

Or maybe more, Hamish thought. Boxer's tribe, the Kamilaroi, were a close-knit community and not adverse to work. Their numbers had swollen since Hamish's arrival, due in part to his fair treatment and the safety they felt, for skirmishes between blacks and whites continued unabated. Replacing the glove, he loosened his grip on the reins, the ache across his shoulder blades dulling instantly. Hamish considered the Crawfords over the Wangallon River. This great sweep of water ran the length of Wangallon's western boundary. An English family of some standing, the Crawfords were their closest neighbours, however the property was often left in the hands of their stockmen and an apparently untested manager. Another three boundary riders would tighten things up considerably.

'Work?'

'Yes, boss, three. First wife's boys and one girl to help the missus with new youngin.'

Hamish looked at his head stockman briefly – a child. So it seemed Rose had already given birth. 'Train them to shoot.'

'Yes, boss.'

'To wound only.' He hoped it was another boy, one could never have too many out here. Their last child, Luke, a brother for Howard, William and his daughter Elizabeth, was now four.

Boxer grinned, the deep lines around his eyes bunching thickly. 'Wound only, boss? Not very good shots sometimes, boss.'

'Don't tell me what I don't need to know, Boxer.'

'Yes, boss.'

Holding the reins tightly, Boxer ensured his old mare did not edge in front of his master. It was time the Boss returned. Boxer knew a place was no good without a leader. No problems while he was away, Boxer made sure of that, still it was better for him, for the camp and for the Missus. Boxer worried about that pale lady. From the beginning the Missus was sad most days, sad, even though the white spirits gave boys. Patting his old horse roughly on the neck, his knobbly dark fingers picked at the mud matted in the thick mane. He remembered in the beginning his women went to her, to bring gifts and to see the children, but they saw the look in her eyes. The look of a rabbit when the women, waiting patiently at one end of the burrow on the sandy ridges near the river, catch the animal as it is driven out. Nearing the large gum tree that marked the half mile to the homestead, Boxer tipped his hat to Hamish, riding off in the direction of his camp.

Although tired from his travels, Hamish scanned the countryside like a mother inspecting a wayward child. It felt good to be back, to breathe the clean air and taste the dry dust slightly moistened by recent rain. About him his land stretched to the horizon, a large expanse of open plains to the east and north and more heavily timbered areas in the west and south. Prickly briar bush, wattle, belah and box trees, the thrashing of grass in the wind – this had been the ache in his heart since leaving Sydney. Stretching his shoulders, Hamish eased back in the saddle. Every reason he ever needed to leave Scotland surrounded him and it was his.

Ahead, the homestead glistened in the midday heat. How long ago his leaving seemed. Now it was near lunch hour at Wangallon, and the heat seared through his suit, one of three made for him by his new tailor in George Street. With his purchases boxed securely, a velvet smoking jacket, a number of crisp white linen shirts and a large quantity of fine cigars, the addition of his portrait finally completed three days in advance was welcome indeed. He would have to ensure Lee trained the maids appropriately in the care of his wardrobe. And of course the painting would hang in the dining room.

A slight curve of the left corner of his mouth betrayed the satisfaction he felt as he entered Wangallon's picket fence house yard. Immediately he felt the relief of a clump of gum trees that sheltered the final few steps. This was his house. Not the dirt floor of a crofter's house in Scotland, nor the canvas sides of the camp on the outskirts of Melbourne, nor the later one of the goldfields. No, this was his house, not another man's home, like Matthew Reynolds' mud-brick residence, a building he had barely slept in for more than two days straight, with months between visits.

The house, low and white-washed, consisted of six bedrooms and dining, sitting, library and office. A sewing room, large pantry, the nanny's room and station storeroom completed the current structure, although Hamish intended adding a music room and a school room in the new year. A wide, open verandah ringed it. The kitchen joined the main building through a narrow walkway, which also housed the adjoining sleep-out for the four scullery maids. Dave and Jasperson, who shared the responsibilities of joint overseers on Wangallon, had separate accommodation a mile or so away.

Dismounting, Hamish tied his horse to a long low railing. He turned to survey the flat, featureless country surrounding him. Yes, it was good to be back.

A succession of quick steps broke Hamish's concentration. A young boy dressed in a pale blue sailor's pinafore ran strongly towards him. Startled by the sudden appearance of his eldest, Howard, Hamish laughed with amusement as the child stopped a few feet away from where he stood. Hamish held out his hand, smiling warmly as his son shook his hand in greeting. 'Hello, Howard.'

'Hello, Father.'

A series of loud squeals broke their brief meeting. The square-sided matron, Mrs Cudlow, appeared with one child, William, by her side and another boy covered in dirt clasped firmly by the elbow.

'Oh, Mr Gordon, sir. I swear young Luke was bathed and dressed for your arrival, sir, but the lad's nothing but trouble.' The nanny moaned as Luke kicked and struggled before aiming a mighty kick at his captor's shin. With a quick grin to his father, Luke tore off around the side of the house.

'I am sorry, Mr Gordon.'

Hamish shrugged his shoulders. Luke showed promise for a four-year-old.

A figure in a long cream over-shirt covering dark trousers raced out of the house. 'Boss, it's very good you are home,' Lee stated, a huge grin spreading from ear to ear. The Chinaman stood with his hands clasped together, while behind him two young Aboriginal girls giggled and fidgeted with the white aprons that covered their long grey dresses.

'Yes, Lee, and how are you?'

'Good, good.' He glanced towards the women. 'Can chop but not cook,' he said sadly.

'Aye, well, Lee, that is why you are in charge. Everything

else running smoothly?' Hamish noticed that one of the girls was new.

'Missus,' Lee nodded with dissatisfaction, his arms folding abruptly across his chest, 'she cook.'

Hamish thought for a moment that he might have been referring to his wife, however Mrs Cudlow thrust out her formidable chest.

'She wants to cook, cook, cook . . .'

'Well, Lee, you will have to sort that out with Mrs Cudlow.' Hamish nodded towards Mrs Cudlow before sitting down on one of the three chairs Dave had constructed over four years ago. The seat and back were sides from packing cases and the stout legs and spindly arms had been cut from the remaining pieces. Lee quickly knelt and began expertly removing Hamish's knee-high black patent leather riding boots.

Hamish would be pleased to be rid of this second-hand furniture. Another dray-load of fine timber chairs and occasional tables had been ordered on his trip and he hoped for their arrival within the next few months.

'If you'll excuse me, then?' Mrs Cudlow hoisted her charge high on her hip and, with a sigh, left the verandah with a vertical line of disapproval marking the place where her mouth should have been.

Lee grinned. Over his shoulder he gestured to one of the young black girls. The youngest, petite and ebony in colour, took the boots carefully and, following a flurry of Chinese gestures and words, fled the verandah with the other girl.

Hamish followed the slight figure with his eyes as she disappeared inside the house and stretched his legs. 'Any problems with the maids?'

Lee sat cross-legged on the verandah. 'No, boss. Milly is new, boss.' He grinned.

Hamish removed a pouch of tobacco from his inside coat pocket. 'You like?'

Lee jumped to his feet, grasped the pouch, inhaled the contents heavily and had the gift hidden before anyone chanced to see the exchange. 'Thank you, boss.'

Hamish grinned at his old friend. They were a long way from the goldfields and the headman to whom Lee had been bound in China. Grinning and bowing, Lee disappeared around the corner of the verandah. Hamish knew he would be running to his bark humpy behind the vegetable garden to savour the tobacco.

'If only everyone were that easy,' Hamish mumbled as he rose from his seat to stretch his lower back. In repaying Lee's debts and freeing his family from servitude, Hamish was now rewarded with a loyal cook, companion and manservant. Lee was the closest thing Hamish had to a true friend. The man had known his brother and watched him die. He knew what it was like to be displaced in the world, and most importantly, he knew what loyalty was.

'And now for the welcome home,' Hamish announced flatly as he pulled his aching body from the comforts of his chair and strode indoors.

The windows were drawn with thick cream lace, yellow cotton tie-backs hanging from a nail secreted somewhere near the window frame, adding colour to the pale timber walls. Next time, Hamish thought to himself, he would purchase wallpaper for this room as well. Something patterned, maybe like the rows of red roses on a cream background that covered the walls of his room at the gentle-man's club. The fine porcelain washbowl, jug and soap stand, white with a surround of pale pink and yellow roses, rested atop the large oak dresser purchased in Sydney. A soft-coloured quilt rested on his wife's legs, and a small cross-stitch of a house lay beside her on the bed. The face, partially covered by long fine hair, sunk deep into the pillow, as if a small animal had burrowed in for warmth.

Removing his jacket, fob watch and waistcoat, Hamish turned up his shirtsleeves and, pouring water into the basin, washed the morning's grime from his hands, arms and neck. Only when he had finished redressing did he turn to the corner where the wooden crib sat. The child, only days old, was small and bald, with a screwed-up face. Ugly kid, Hamish thought to himself, having produced better. Roughly he pulled down the tight swaddling and touched the small penis with a large forefinger.

'Yes, another boy,' Rose spoke wearily, the disinterest clear in her voice.

'So it seems. He looks strong and healthy, my dear.'

Leaving the child, Hamish stood awkwardly by his wife's bed. Glazed eyes peered from sallow skin. 'The furniture arrived in good condition?' A whiff of sour breath carried across to him.

'Yes.'

'The books and magazines?' The barest scent of lavender water wafted in the cloying air.

'Yes.'

'And you are feeling –' He searched for the right word – 'more rested?'

'A little.'

'Good, good.' Hamish glanced about the room uneasily. Striding across to the window, he drew the curtains and lifted the sash. Immediately the harsh midday sun entered the room, accompanied by a blast of hot air. 'That's better.' Ignoring the frown on his wife's face he leaned down carefully to give her a kiss on the forehead. 'An Afghan merchant will be arriving here in two months. I expect you up and about to entertain him. You will be ready?' He added a little more gently, 'And Luke, he appears a bit unruly.'

'He is four, Hamish,' Rose pointed out, struggling to sit up in the bed. 'Who is this merchant? We've not had a visitor recently.'

'Well, no doubt Mrs Cudlow will cure him.' A thought occurred to him. 'You received the material?'

Rose smoothed the bedcover about her waist. 'The children needed clothes. There was not enough to go around.'

'I'm sorry. Sailor suits?' Hamish queried, his full lips turning upwards briefly at the sight of her firm breasts straining against the material of her nightgown.

'Yes.' Rose pulled herself up further in bed. 'You mentioned we were to have visitors?'

Hamish noticed a hint of colour in her cheeks, she appeared almost interested. 'Yes. We will talk of that tomorrow. When you are rested.'

Rose sighed. 'Of course.'

The minutes stretched. Hamish listened to the soft pat of bare feet in the hallway. The servants were bringing in his luggage.

'Hamish, I was hoping that perhaps you would take me on your next trip to Ridge Gully to see my Elizabeth. I miss my darling daughter so much.' Her voice grew softer, almost pleading in tone.

Hamish watched as beads of sweat formed on her brow. The baby began to mew softly. 'I have seen both your mother and our daughter. They are in good health. Surprisingly, our daughter is well mannered.' Indeed his daughter was almost entertaining in her coy questioning about his travels.

'Oh.'

He lifted the child from the crib, the slight body enveloped by Hamish's large forearm. 'Good lad,' he said with a proud smile when the baby ceased crying and returned his father's stare. 'This lad will be both confident and obedient, I can sense these things.' He passed his new son to his wife.

'Has she grown much? Is she tall like Howard?'

Hamish frowned at talk more suited to women. His gaze

followed Rose's movements as she pulled at the ribbon at her neck and, with her gown loosening, lifted a breast, heavy with milk, towards her child.

'I would like so much to see her.'

'My dear, we have already lost one child through too much exertion on your behalf. You must learn to rest. It is a long tiring journey to Ridge Gully. Do you not remember how you complained when we left?'

Rose settled back in the pillows, the baby gazing at her quietly. 'Yes.'

'You complained of the ceaseless swaying of the carriage, then the dray. You complained of the food served at the coach stops and of the beds we slept in. And what of your own children here? Three fine boys and now this one, a fourth.'

Hamish thought of Lorna, resplendent in her silks and with a reputation for outrageous dinner parties. The General Store was now a thriving Emporium, owned entirely by Lorna, whose staff of five appeared loyal, knowledgeable and discreet. Hamish, suitably impressed, found his visit refreshingly pleasant. Lorna only requested an interview once to briefly send her regards to her only daughter and to commiserate over the death of his son Matthew at birth, some two years prior.

The boy mouthed disinterestedly at Rose's nipple. 'You should have a wet nurse. This mothering seems to keep you confined to your bed when you should be up and about.' The pale eyes studying him were disbelieving.

Rose settled herself into the pillows supporting her back and waited patiently. Gradually the child began sucking smoothly. The children at least filled in the endless hours for her. 'I don't think I could bear being bandaged in this heat, Hamish.'

'Bandaged?' Hamish coughed. 'Yes, well that's something best discussed with Mrs Cudlow.'

Rose closed her eyes. 'Of course.'

'As for a trip, Rose, the children are far too young to be left alone without one of us, and I certainly couldn't risk taking them on a journey. I don't think you realise, my dear, the dangers nor . . .'

'Perhaps you are right,' Rose answered wearily, 'after all I am busy also. Seven children later, I have one stillborn, one dead and my beautiful Elizabeth, not seen for near four years, the same length of time since my arrival in this godforsaken place. But you, Hamish, you have your business and four healthy boys, the beginning of your little dynasty.'

Hamish backed away from the sarcasm in his wife's voice. What was he meant to do, he wondered? Risk the lives of his children and send them all south so Rose could visit her daughter? Apart from the tiring journey, what if his wife and young sons encountered bushrangers or worse, some of the renegade Aborigines that had attacked a settlement only 200 miles north of Ridge Gully last spring? The only other possibility was to let Rose travel south by herself and leave his boys in the hands of Aborigines and a nanny. That was not an option. The children needed their mother, besides which he could not risk his wife's safety. They were married and regardless of Rose's clear disdain towards him, he was duty bound to protect her. Elizabeth was safe and well used to her grandmother. Quite frankly, Elizabeth was the most secure of all his family, but Rose only saw what she wanted to see.

'I'll let you rest,' Hamish said quietly, closing the door. Marriage was not as he had expected it to be, for no matter what he did it was never enough.

'There is little else to do,' Rose replied to his retreating figure.

Hamish's fingers tightened on the doorknob. Surely there was to be more to his personal life than this detached relationship.

≪ Winter, 1986 ≫

Sydney

Sarah walked out of the cinema with her two girlfriends, Shelley and Kate.

'Loved it,' Shelley exclaimed, huddling into her white jacket as they hit the bracing wind funnelling up George Street. 'Tom Cruise was just so cool and that Val Kilmer . . .'

'Now, *there* is a body,' Kate agreed, managing to light her cigarette as they walked. 'Still my favourite movie remains *Ferris Bueller's Day Off.*'

'You *are* joking? You would choose that over *Top Gun?*' Sarah linked arms with both of them and they crossed at the lights. 'Bueller, Bueller, Bueller,' she joked, steering them into their monthly haunt, a small Italian restaurant chosen more for convenience than the food. They were ushered to a corner table and before the girls could decide what they were having, Sarah ordered three West Coast Coolers.

'I'm so parched.' Shelley drank hers almost immediately and ordered another round. 'So, have you photographed any delicious male models recently?'

'I wish. But I have helped on two model portfolios. They were female,' she revealed to the expectant look on Kate's face. 'It's good money.' She stood to briefly show off her new Guess jeans and purple Swatch watch.

'Gorgeous,' Shelley held out her own wrist. 'Me too.' Her Swatch was fire engine red. 'Don't you just love this brand? Tomorrow we just have to go shopping. I saw this unbelievable acqua suit – it would be just perfect for the office.'

'Done,' Kate clinked her glass against Shelley's. 'I'm booked for a manicure at nine though. Sometimes I wish I'd never done that damn typing course.'

'Oh,' Shelley pouted, 'then you never would have met us.'

'I could meet you both in the city at 10.30?' Sarah suggested. 'I want to go to Centennial Park first thing in the morning and try out the new lens on my camera.'

'Well, remember us when you're rich and famous.' Shelly raised her glass to Sarah.

'So are we on for The Aussie Rules Club at the Cross?' Shelley was picking at a piece of complimentary garlic bread. 'It's a verit-able smorgasbord there, girls,' she giggled.

'Nothing like a bit of eye candy,' Sarah agreed.

Kate pointed a finger at her. 'You just behave yourself. You already have a man. I love that whole preppy college thing Jeremy has going with the blazer and open-neck shirts.'

'I can look, can't I?'

'I thought you got enough eye relief, Sarah, when you were home last.' Shelley teased her. 'You said Anthony came back while the flood was on.'

'Is he still just as good looking now he's older?' Kate asked. 'It must be a few years since you last saw him?'

Shelley leaned forward. 'You never did get around to telling us.'

Sarah smiled blandly and took another sip of her drink, aware that the girls were waiting for a response.

'Well?' Shelley persisted.

'Are you ready to order?'

Their regular waiter, a man in his sixties with the annoying habit of soundlessly appearing at the table, poised a pen over his order pad. Sarah turned her attention to the menu, grateful for the distraction. When she next looked up, three pairs of eyes were staring at her expectantly. 'Sorry, I wasn't listening.'

Shelley looked at her with a knowing gaze.

'Well, as my friends can't decide and I'm starving we will have –' Kate skimmed the menu – 'spaghetti marinara, and some red wine. You know the Italian stuff; the green bottle in the little wicker thingy.'

'Of course.'

When the waiter left, Sarah lifted her glass. 'A toast to us.'

'To us.' Kate and Shelley lifted their glasses.

'And to the men in our lives,' Shelley continued. 'We may not be able to live with them –' she looked pointedly at Sarah – 'but we can't always live without them either.'

Spring, 1986

Wangallon Station

*A*ngus knew his granddaughter had not been consulted about her parents' decision to leave West Wangallon. Sure he could have telephoned her, advised her of Ronald's decision, but in truth he had never thought today would become a reality. He had been reared on the epic stories of his own father's arrival in Australia, of his uncle's death on the goldfields, of a man who created a huge empire, losing much of his family along the way. Angus knew too well what the Gordons had gone through to survive on Wangallon. No, with a history the likes of the Gordons', one simply didn't leave. A mad daughter-in-law and a dead grandson notwithstanding, one simply did not.

Angus stood next to his granddaughter outside West Wangallon homestead. They were waiting for Ronald to appear from the house one final time before saying goodbye to him. He was moving north to the coast to join Sue, who had left some weeks earlier.

'It's done now. It's beaten them, well probably more your mother than Ronald. Still, the end result is the same.' There was only the barest trembling of Angus' hands as he lit a cigarette, his fourth in as many minutes. He drew back heavily, the action causing the constant phlegm his nightly cigar seemed to have created, catching in his throat.

'Grandfather, when did you start smoking?' Sarah's question went unanswered. While resentment ebbed in her chest, she knew her grandfather was disappointed and hurting in his own way as well.

From where they stood, West Wangallon appeared to glare defiantly at them both. Light traced the gutters overflowing with twigs and leaves and a disused air seeped outwards, a mouldering scent of dampness and neglect. Most of the furniture had been transported up north a few weeks ago. Industrial cleaners had returned again, their second visit since the flood, and now there was only an empty shell. Her father had made some bad choices in his life, but this was a selfish, bloody-minded choice, Sarah decided. At least she knew the regard in which she was held, the place on the food chain she occupied. Fine, she thought angrily, she'd done her duty and was here to wave her father goodbye.

Angus lit another cigarette, dragging heavily until his lungs filled with smoke. Sarah had moved to lean on the back gate. He watched her slim figure, her boots shuffling nervously in the dirt, the way her right hand fiddled with the latch, opening and closing the squeaky mechanism with monotonous repetition. The girl was damaged. They had been close, his grandchildren, no one doubted that and he had expected the lass to suffer as they all had, but he had never reckoned on her leaving. Sarah was strong, capable, with a sense of humour and loyalty not found in the young today, but she carried an over-sensitive streak and the damn Gordon pride. In truth he'd figured on Sarah helping to run the place in the years to come with her brother as right hand. She was the one with the brains, Cameron the brawn, plus the boy knew stock. With Sarah married and living on Wangallon with Cameron and his eventual wife, they would have worked the land together, ensuring another generation would keep the property going, instead of one of them buggering off to the city and then putting their hand up for cash when things didn't work out the way they'd planned. What was not so obvious, what God himself could not have foretold, was that the boy's death had buggered her.

God, every day he wondered how things could have gone so pear-shaped. Of course he couldn't blame his grandson for his stupid death. Storm clouds were brewing as soon as Sue appeared on the property and Ronald didn't have the balls to handle things in the proper manner. Angus took a last drag of his cigarette before crushing the stub out with the heel of his boot. His eyes met Shrapnel's and the dog whimpered in shared annoyance. Short of getting rid of that Jeremy cove and forcing Sarah to return to Wangallon, things were now out of his hands. It wasn't like the old days when all it took was money to get things done. Still, he wasn't dead yet. Sarah was back home again and this time so was Anthony.

Surely something could be done, Angus thought. He didn't for a second believe that it was the photography thing she called employment keeping her away and nor, he hoped, was it Jeremy. It was about time he learnt a little about his granddaughter's life away from Wangallon and, he decided, a lot about her relationship with the anaemic accountant. Angus prised free a sliver of dried snot from his nostril, rubbing the small ball between thumb and forefinger. It was time to call in a favour. He silently ran through a list of names and settled on Matt Leach. He needed to know if there was anything he could do to entice his granddaughter back to Wangallon. He needed to secure the future of the property. But just in case his own family couldn't see the damn forest for the trees, Angus figured that there was no harm in a bit of healthy competition. Yesterday he had made Anthony manager of the entire property.

Ronald, a cardboard box in hand, appeared from the house and walked silently down the back path, past his daughter to where his station wagon was parked. *A happy lot*, Angus mumbled, rubbing his hands brusquely. The air carried an unseasonal chill for late spring but by noon the day's heat would be upon them. He needed a drink, a good whiskey, no ice and no water, then something to fill his gut. Out of the corner of his eye, he noticed Anthony standing off to one side, half hidden among trees. In spite of himself he chuckled. The lad, much admired for his management skills, was a product of his own rigorous training. Here was a lad with exactly the right characteristics, if the Gordon legacy was going to have fresh blood running it. A problem Angus had not counted on was his granddaughter's move to Sydney and a lad who was too much of a gentleman for his own good. A mutual attraction was there, so why did the lad not take advantage of it? The boy had virtually been told he would be a welcome family addition, so what held him back?

'Good manners, blah!' Angus muttered and Shrapnel yawned in agreement.

It was imperative to portray oneself as a gentleman, especially if some deals took a little more enterprise and speculation to achieve . . . But when it came to women . . . Well, he'd taken his own wife Angie at twenty years of age. Employed as a governess on a big station in Western Queensland, Angus spied her only twice before obtaining the help of his half-brother, Luke, to break down the door of the women's quarters (they were locked in every night for protection from the other stockmen) and carry her off on his horse. Admittedly, it was the 1920s, but love was love after all.

Angus looked about him. The sky was an early morning sliver of slate grey. Such a sign meant a brewing dust storm in a couple of days. Since the flood no decent rain had fallen and the earth's surface was loose and dry. With no spring vegetation to curb the brittle top-soil it would not be long before the wind began its ceaseless erosion.

'Memories, Sarah?' he asked as his granddaughter rejoined him beneath a grove of trees.

Sarah could only nod. She recalled rushing down with the wheelbarrow to the woodpile, loading it high with the split logs for the Aga in the kitchen, before stumbling back along the rutted road. Invariably she lost half the contents before making it home, Cameron laughing at the higgledy-piggledy track she made as the barrow swerved from side to side.

'They'll be others.'

'I guess, Grandfather.' The house had been gutted, cleaned and closed up. That was it and all her memories were closed up with that final turning of the key. Part of the contract of sale demanded by her grandfather, the buyer, was to leave the house in a liveable condition. Her grandfather had bought back the property he had gifted to his son on his marriage to Sue, ensuring all of Wangallon remained in Gordon hands and Ronald had money to retire on.

Finally Sarah heard the back door slam shut and her father walked down the cement path. He turned at the end of the path and stared at the house, arms folded, the bunched muscles of his jaw working furiously beneath the tanned skin. Sarah lifted her hand briefly, touched his shoulder. Tears would have come easily if she allowed it. Better to think of something else, she decided. The Gordons never were good at expressing themselves anyway.

Anthony walked towards them and shook Ronald's hand. 'It's been a privilege, sir.'

'Thanks, Anthony,' Ronald replied, staring out at the landscape that he had once loved. Beside him stood Sarah and beyond her, an uncertain future. He thought of his childhood, the years of living and loving his business, his hobby, his life. All gone, but his daughter was saved. He kissed her gently on the forehead. No matter what Sarah thought, she had been saved from Wangallon, as he should have saved Sue, as he should have saved his boy. That was his only regret, the leaving of his son and the rest of their ancestors in the family graveyard. As for his own father, well, old Angus did things his way, as his father before him. They were tough old bastards. The Highlander blood was strong in them both.

'Take care of yourself,' Angus interrupted. He stretched out his arm and father and son grasped each other's hands, staring into similarly creased faces. At last, the large paws parted.

'One day, lad, you'll realise that nothing is more important than land.'

Ronald didn't quite agree with him. They were, after all, merely custodians for the next generation. He hesitated. 'Dad, I wanted to say thanks about Cameron. I . . . well I didn't realise that you knew about –' he searched for the right words – 'Sue's infidelity, until the day of the accident. Thanks for treating him as an equal.'

Angus gave Ronald a quizzical look. 'I did it for Wangallon, Ronald. Not for you and not for Cameron.'

Shocked by his father's blatant admission, Ronald could only say, 'I see.'

'Now don't get me wrong. Cameron was a good boy, even if he was born a bastard.'

Ronald could barely believe what he was hearing. All these years he had mistakenly thought his father loved his grandson so much that he was prepared to forget that he was not of Gordon blood and would not only protect him but anoint him as his successor.

'Clearly for the Gordon name to continue we needed a male heir. Besides, having it known publicly that my own son was cuckolded was not an option. Our reputation would have been ruined forever. I'll say goodbye, then.'

Without another word Ronald watched his father disappear into the trees.

Sarah waited as the car moved off to the strains of barking dogs, then came to an unscheduled halt on the loose gravel. Ronald walked slowly from the stationary vehicle to face the west. She knew what he was thinking, his hands on his hips, his eyes scanning the horizon. Grandparents, great-grandparents, father, mother, brother, gazing outwards, waiting and watching; they'd all stood there. Waiting for the smell of rain, watching flashes of lightning moving closer; watching clouds heralding a storm, or the green glow of disaster that hail could bring to young crops. Searching for frightening streams of smoke, or dust clouds billowing, ready to engulf. The Gordons all stood somewhere on the land that was Wangallon. As the car moved away, Sarah shivered. Their souls still lingered on Gordon land, they always would.

'Your dad will be okay. He'll enjoy his retirement, Sarah.'

Anthony was by her side, smelling freshly of soap and after-shave. Their conversation had been limited to brief snatches over the last two days. Sarah had barely seen him.

'He mentioned he wants to do a bit of travelling, and with the money from the sale of the place, he'll . . .'

'Travelling?' Sarah unclenched her fists, stemming the pain of fingernails biting into her palms. 'Tell me why my family is the one that fell apart. Why, Anthony? Over one hundred and twenty-eight years we've been here; my God, half the time of this continent's British settlement. Now look at us.' She gulped, wiping her nose on the sleeve of her pale blue sweater.

'Sarah, your grandfather is still here,' Anthony said softly. He'd tried to keep his distance from her the last few days. It wasn't his job to placate her, to explain it was not Angus's role to tell Ronald what to do with his life. Surely Sarah knew as much. But then maybe she didn't. She was still annoyed that her father hadn't told her that he was thinking of retiring and now she was acting as if her entire family unit had dissolved. She may only visit Wangallon yearly, but as difficult as her relationship was with her parents it was pretty obvious she relied on them for a semblance of stability. 'Don't worry so much,' he finally said.

'Dad will be dead in five years, Anthony.'

'Sarah, everything will be fine. I'll make sure it is.'

'And how are you going to do that?'

'Well, for starters I can look after Wangallon for you until you come back. I'm the station manager now and . . .'

Sarah gasped. 'The station manager? Geez, you *have* moved fast.' She knew she should have congratulated him. She had no right to behave so poorly towards him. Instead she shoved her hands deep into her jeans pockets and walked towards the Land Cruiser. She slid across the leather seat, revelling in the coldness of it.

'Hey, Sarah. You left all this, remember?' Anthony raised his arms, flinging them wide to encompass the land about them. 'If you want to be part of this place,' his tone softened, 'I would be the first to welcome you home.'

Sarah tightened her grip on the steering wheel. It wasn't his place to welcome her home, even if she did choose to return. 'You could have told me about Dad wanting to leave.'

'Hey, it's not my bloody responsibility to inform you of your family's decisions. Maybe if you came back, acted a bit more interested, then the family –'

Sarah cut him off as the ignition turned smoothly. Anthony had developed an ego and she didn't like it.

'I've had a damn long association with this family, Sarah,' he yelled at her, 'and I don't believe any of your ancestors ever ran away from responsibility. I can see it in your eyes, you know you should be here rather than in Sydney with that wimp. What are you running away from?'

'Nothing,' Sarah yelled as she slammed her foot on the accelerator and left Anthony standing alone.

That night, lying under heavy blankets, Sarah kept vigil. Sleepless, eyes wide, pupils turned towards the two closed and bolted doorways, waiting. She would turn on her side, but what if, unguarded, something were to appear? To do what she didn't know. Maybe chastise, talk, shout, wail, or just plain scare her witless. It was incomprehensible to think that with her dad's departure, a self-inflicted abdication, their forefathers, those who had forged the bush before them, left it for them, would not have something to say.

Eventually she drifted towards sleep and found herself reaching out to follow the contours of the West Wangallon roof, pale fingers gliding along the guttering, her hand dipping to rub her fist over the windowpane. Clearly there were people within. Their silhouettes sprang from the kitchen walls, glancing from table to sink, formless shadows, the faceless apparitions of a subconscious haunting. The voice, when it called, drew her from the house, urging her onwards.

The winding cool of the mountains eased out into the soft

undulations of the slopes, until the sparse flat countryside greeted her. The road was straight, the expanse of sky and stars awesome. The music in her mind serenaded her with soft, lucid tones, a harp perhaps, or the dulcet strings of a quivering violin. Tonight a woman caught her attention. She was pale and finely featured with golden hair; children stood by her side. Then the children disappeared and the woman was walking through a paddock, her long skirts swishing the grass as she moved. She turned to look over her shoulder and Sarah saw the sadness in the woman's eyes.

Sarah woke to the sound of footsteps outside her room. She pushed the covers back, her feet touching the chill of the floorboards beneath. Tentatively she opened the bedroom door, peered into the darkness of the hallway – there was no-one there. Turning on her bedside lamp, she checked the time on her watch. It was a little after 2 a.m. It was then she saw the gold bangle lying on the floor beside her bed. The bangle that her grandfather had given her the night Cameron had been anointed as Wangallon's successor. She picked it up, wondering how it had come to be there when she kept it in her drawer with Anthony's scarf. They were the only two items she'd never taken with her to Sydney. With a sigh Sarah placed the bangle back in the top drawer of the dresser and returned to bed. She was too tired to think.

The next day Sarah rushed to pull on her riding boots, hopping towards the noise of the dogs. They'd spent the morning in the sheep yards, using precious water from the dying dam to settle the dirt in the yards, lest man and animal choke to death in the thick dust. Now as she passed through the back gate, the new jackeroo, Colin, lounged on the galvanised iron fence that had replaced the old one ruined by the flood. Ignoring his sarcastic snort, she called Shrapnel, conscious that Colin had managed to coerce the disobedient cattle dog to his side. One dog was still missing. Sarah ran towards the sheep yards. Although only half a kilometre away, the yards were caught in the midst of a great dust storm. Billowing clouds of dry land were being lifted high into the air. Through the haze, the jet-black coat of Tex, so named after Anthony's favourite US state, was just visible jumping over the yarded sheep.

Taking in great gulps of matted air, Sarah screamed and yelled at the dog terrorising the freshly culled rams. Three hours it had taken to draft the mob, an eternity in the rising heat, and Sarah didn't think she could face the same task again. In the distance, the silhouette of man and horse could be seen in the gusty wind, drought-weary rams in his care. A final choked reprimand was swept away quickly by the noise of Colin on his motorbike. In a swirl of showmanship, he took off after the stray dog with a stockwhip. In a second the sheep had quieted, Tex suitably chastised.

'Nice day for it.'

Sarah nodded, tilting her head upwards to see Anthony's dirt-covered face half-hidden under the akubra hat. If he could pretend their argument hadn't occurred yesterday, so could she.

'I've got some more news,' Anthony offered rather carefully as he pulled on the reins to steady his horse.

'Right.' Sarah wasn't sure if she was up to anything else. She was still digesting Anthony's move up the ladder to the role of station manager.

'I wanted you to hear it from me.' Anthony took a breath. 'I'm moving into West Wangallon.'

She experienced a surge of hurt. Her family home was truly gone. Another door had shut.

'That was quick.'

'Not my idea.'

'Right.' Sarah scowled against flying grit and the glare of the mid-morning sun and imagined the cooling interior of the homestead. She quickened her step. She decided it was easier not to talk than end up in another argument.

Anthony patted the neck of his old horse Warrigal as he followed sedately behind Sarah. Now she probably wouldn't talk to him. Still, this time she wouldn't be able to complain that she didn't know what was going on. 'Is that okay with you, because I can easily stay put in the jackeroo's quarters?'

She looked up at him, the expression on her face clearly registering surprise. She could hardly tell him that she would rather it remained empty. 'Well, no point the house staying vacant. Besides, no doubt Grandfather told you to move.'

'But I won't if it's not okay with you.'

'It's fine,' she finally answered.

Anthony tweaked Warrigal's ear. 'Thanks.' There was no point being on Sarah's bad side. In the future, the distant future, he hoped, he figured he'd be working for her and wouldn't that be interesting?

'I can't believe you still ride that poor animal. He's ancient.'

'Warrigal? My old mate loves it; keeps his joints agile. Did your Dad arrive okay yesterday?' Anthony slowed his horse to a stop near the back gate, searching for conversation. 'How's he enjoying swamp country?'

'Swamp country?'

Shit, he'd done it again. 'Anyway, what about you? How's city life?'

'My parents live on the Gold Coast in a very nice house . . .'

'In a very nice house, along with a lot of other very nice houses, fronting the canal, reclaimed land, water views.' An argument already, Anthony grinned, attempting his dog-hiding-a-huge-bone look. Dismounting, he kicked dry tufts of grass at his feet. 'It's probably a really nice place. Maybe they'll have me

201

to visit. Your mum could cook me some of that mutton stew she was so fond of.'

'Maybe,' Sarah agreed, her earlier annoyance disappearing. 'She was always such a big fan of yours, Anthony.'

'Yeah, I know. I have that effect on people.'

Sarah giggled. He leaned over the fence, his hand flicking the stockwhip in the dirt, his hat cocked back on his head. He had not heard her laugh in quite a while. He twirled the stockwhip in his fingers, the leather handle spinning so deftly that the whip spun out like a gymnast's ribbon.

'It's hard knowing Grandfather is the only family member here now.' She looked at Anthony's sweat-matted hair, his wide-brimmed hat dangling from his fingers. 'I feel I should probably come back a bit more often.'

'Good point. A bit of support would be important to him.'

For a moment Sarah thought of her life in Sydney: trendy coffee shops, sipping a latte on a Saturday morning, relaxing at the beach, nice restaurants; support, albeit mainly long distance, was about as much as she could give. Warrigal began pawing the ground restlessly.

Placing his hat back on his head, Anthony flicked the brim with his fingers. 'See you later.' Swiftly he lifted his body up into the saddle, whistling as he turned old Warrigal's head. As he trotted Warrigal down towards the stables he wondered if the spell of sadness had suddenly broken. Everyone associated with Wangallon had suffered since Cameron's death but he felt a change in the air, like rain after drought. Ronald and Sue were gone, he was now manager and unless he was wrong, Sarah seemed a little more comfortable within herself. That in itself could only be a good thing. Angus deserved to have his granddaughter visit him more than once a year and he needed Sarah to appreciate Wangallon's importance and his importance to Wangallon. With Ronald's departure, Sarah's ongoing commitment to Wangallon, even if it was long distance, was vital to not only Wangallon's future but also his own. Dismounting, Anthony twisted Warrigal's reins around the old hitching post and leant down to undo the girth strap. His hand rested on the hot flank of Warrigal, the horse hair sweaty and dust-coated. If he didn't get a move on he'd be late for his date with young Annie Fields and there was nothing like a backpacker for getting rid of a few cobwebs.

≪ Summer, 1987 ≫

The Rocks – Sydney

'The stench of it!' Jeremy took a sip of champagne. 'You cannot imagine what it was like. Dead animals everywhere.' As Sarah listened to him she realised he'd become quite good at reciting the story of Wangallon's flood. 'They were literally floating past the homestead – and the insects! Well, with water everywhere there was absolutely nowhere for anything to go, so everything headed for high ground and safety. The homestead was built on a ridge that's slightly higher than the surrounding country, so it was like being on an island.'

'It's staggering you and Sarah managed to get out.' Julie smoothed her red taffeta skirt. With its plunging neckline and elongated shoulder pads she felt quite the best dressed in the room. She was rather intrigued with the relationship that existed between her old friend, the upwardly mobile accountant, and the chameleon that was capable of switching from 'cow girl' status to rising photographer. She'd only been abroad for a couple of years, yet had returned recently to find her perennially single Jeremy clearly infatuated.

'Well, Sarah stayed.'

'You didn't?' Julie exclaimed, turning from Jeremy to Sarah.

Sarah felt the expectant eyes of the circle in which she was standing turn to her. 'Wangallon's my home, of course I stayed. I couldn't leave immediately.' Sarah knew Julie was one of Jeremy's oldest friends, but it still hurt to have to revisit the flood of 1985 and she was tired of her nights being caught up in the continual round of parties that Jeremy just had to attend. He kept telling her that the success of his family's practice depended on networking opportunities and Julie, back from London only a fortnight, seemed capable of wangling tickets to every event, including tonight's fundraiser.

'So you weren't actually stranded then?' Julie replied. 'And here was I thinking we had a novel in the making. You know something along the lines of young professionals have horror weekend in outback; barely manage to survive.' She flicked her fingers in an imitation of inverted commas.

Sarah gave her a tight smile. Julie and Jeremy had been 'working' the flood event for the last couple of nights. Julie insisting that the flood was worth rehashing simply from the novelty aspect that would lead to greater recall where Jeremy and a potential client were concerned.

'No, however, one of the workers –'

'Station manager,' Sarah corrected.

'Workers on the property,' Jeremy repeated, 'eager to prove his devotion, literally dropped out of the sky. The helicopter he travelled in returned a couple of days later, so I was airlifted out.'

'Good excuse for a holiday,' Julie's current handbag, Danny, replied. 'Get out there, help our country cousins and all that. You know if you ever have a problem out there, Sarah, we could round up a good ten people to fly out and give you guys a hand.' He ran a pale hand through his gelled hair.

'Thanks.' Sarah took in the *Dynasty*-style cut of Julie's suit and the Chinese red fingernails and tried to imagine her out in the heat and the dust. The solicitor was definitely not the bimbo she portrayed herself to be. She was glamorous, with a syrupy voice and when the occasion demanded it, she always revealed the right enticements. Sarah smoothed her ruched yellow dress, glancing again at Julie's tight short skirt. Her mother, explicit in her description of such lengths, called them fanny pelmets.

'I don't know about the holiday location,' giggled Petra, an advertising executive in pink and white polka dots. 'It's the strapping fellows in flood boats and dropping out of helicopters that appeal to me. Any chance of setting me up with someone?' she whispered shyly.

'Are you happy to go bush?' Sarah asked.

Petra considered the question seriously. 'Maybe I better think about it.'

Sarah smiled. 'I'm going to get a drink.' Resting her empty champagne glass on a damask-covered table she glanced about the room. Behind her, Jeremy was discussing his accountancy business with Petra, while Julie had caught the eye of another guest and was introducing the older woman to their circle. Sarah decided that in future she would ask Julie for some extra tickets to these functions, then she could ask Kate and Shelley to come along as well.

In the powder room a number of impeccably groomed matrons stood preening themselves before the long mirrors. Sarah moved past them to the far end of the room, collapsing tiredly into a large velour armchair. She'd had a five-hour shoot today assisting a photographer with a model's portfolio, and her feet were killing her. Outside, the muted sound of clapping could be heard and with that, the powder room was instantly deserted.

Sarah awoke to Jeremy tapping her on the shoulder. 'Jeremy! What on earth are you doing in here?' Jumping out of her seat, Sarah moved towards the large mirrors, intent on applying lipstick. He moved to stand close behind her, his face concerned. Sarah put her lipstick in her purse.

'I came to look for you. You've been gone for ages.'

'Sorry, I must have fallen asleep,' Sarah answered. 'I was standing for five hours today.'

'You said you wanted to come tonight.'

'Actually, Jeremy, you told me Julie had managed to get tickets for us,' Sarah said briskly.

'So you're annoyed with Julie.'

'We've certainly been seeing a lot of her recently.'

'That's not what has upset you. It's the flood. I'm sorry, I shouldn't have brought it up again, it's just that . . .'

'Don't tell me; great for networking, instant memory recall,' she snapped.

'It's not like it happened yesterday,' Jeremy retaliated. 'You've got to learn not to get so emotional.'

Sarah straightened her back. 'The flood was awful. You knew that, you were there. When did you become so damn insensitive?'

'I'm not,' he looked crestfallen.

'I'm sorry.'

'I love you, Sarah. When I saw everything that made you and your family, I realised I would have to do a whole lot more with my life to keep you in mine. If we're going to be together, we need money and I want enough to be able to care for you in the manner in which you were born. Here, away from Wangallon, it's only you and me, princess, there's no thousands of acres to fall back on, no great machine that just keeps on producing, or carrying you through a bad season. There's only us and if it means I have to go out every night and network with potential clients then I'll do it. And if I choose to talk about my experiences on Wangallon so that people remember me, then I'll do that too.'

Gritting her teeth, Sarah sullenly had to agree with him. Everything Jeremy did was for their mutual benefit. Their conversation was broken by the entry of several females. Startled by a male presence in the powder room, they quickly dissolved into laughter. Jeremy made his excuses and, taking Sarah's hand, led her quickly from the room.

'Ladies and gentlemen. A bra worn, only once I might add, by the very voluptuous . . .'

'And brain dead,' someone in the crowd whispered.

'. . . model of the year, Annabel!'

Amid the fevered clapping, Jeremy held her hand tightly. 'I know things have been difficult for you since your father's retirement and I've stopped myself from commenting on the situation, but this is getting ridiculous. Your father made the right decision when he left. For both him and your mother and whether you're willing to accept it or not it was a move that should have a positive impact on your own life eventually. You'll no longer be tied to that property. You can break free. Besides, the property is still in the family.'

'And our next item is a fine contemporary painting, acrylic on linen, by the formidable Tasker Lewinsky. Do we have a starting bid, ladies and gentlemen?'

It was useless, Sarah thought, trying to explain to Jeremy that it had all happened the wrong way. That it was most certainly not a business decision. Her father had sold out because of Sue's illness, increased his distance from his own daughter and finally cut himself off from his father. 'But Grandfather is by himself now.'

'That's his choice, Sarah.'

'And Cameron has been deserted.'

He placed his hands firmly on her shoulders. 'Apart from the fact that your grandfather is still living on the property, if your brother were in a cemetery down here in Sydney, you wouldn't be living across the road from him, would you?'

Except, Sarah thought, Cameron would never have expected their father to leave. Now with Ronald's departure, the only Gordon left was Angus.

'Sarah, I know you miss Cameron, but he's dead, and once you're dead, that is it.'

'Is it, Jeremy?' She whispered beneath the loud bidding. He looked at her strangely. Sarah couldn't explain it, but Cameron was not just buried on the property, he roamed it, filling the leaves with wind and the creeks with movement. All her family believed in the possibility of life after death, so why was it not possible for a spirit to want to stay near the place he loved? All those buried there still existed in the core of Wangallon. They were its very essence.

'What will be the first bid, ladies and gentlemen?'

'Come and join the others, Sarah. Petra thought she would make a bid on this print.'

Sarah squeezed his hand gently, enough for him to know that they were okay. 'I think I'll go home.'

'I'll drive you.'

Sarah kissed him on the cheek. 'No, you won't. Go and enjoy yourself. I'm too tired.' There was a man walking towards her. She recognised him almost immediately.

'You sure?' Jeremy asked.

Sarah kissed him on the cheek again. 'Absolutely.'

'I'll call you tomorrow.' He turned and winked at her as he walked away, passing the older man who now reached her side.

'Sarah? It is Sarah Gordon, isn't it?'

'Hi, Mr Leach.'

'Call me Matt. I'm past the mister stage, it makes me feel a little too old. How's your dad?'

'Retired to the coast.'

'I heard, and you're down here?'

Sarah nodded. 'How's business?' As a private wool buyer, Matt travelled the eastern states servicing a huge list of clients, most of whom were personal friends. It was strange seeing him in this type of environment.

'Bloody appalling, Sarah. People are starving all over the world and the only method the government could think of in the early eighties to combat falling wool prices was to destroy the very animals that helped to build this country. You know, in my old district alone, in excess of 100,000 sheep were shot in eighteen months. That's a lot of dead sheep. The industry has never really recovered.'

This conversation seemed so distant from the world she presently inhabited. Just before Anthony's arrival on Wangallon, her grandfather and father had contracted a front-end loader to come in and dig deep pits. Then, rifle in hand, they had mustered the sheep. The men stood and fired. Hundreds gone forever; sheep her family had been breeding since the 1860s. Even now the low burial mounds could be spotted, holding the remains of sheep the government had made worthless: a pittance in return for a lifetime's work. The end of the reserve price probably had to come sooner rather than later, but it was handled so incredibly badly. Unfortunately, right or wrong, graziers geared to a reserve price for their wool budgeted accordingly, like any business.

Sarah often rode past the very spot where the sheep were buried and tried to imagine that awful day. The sun rising over the line of belah in the back paddock, the kookaburras calling out in greeting and the green grass springy beneath the men's feet.

Matt Leach shrugged. 'Then the flood and now this bloody drought. Go home much, Sarah?'

'Once or twice a year.'

'And your grandfather is still there. Well, good on him. And I believe no-one could shift young Anthony.'

'No, he's a permanent fixture.'

'You're lucky to have him.'

'I guess.'

'You don't seem so sure about that?'

Sarah accepted a glass of champagne from a passing waiter and wished for something stronger. Matt selected a mineral water, drinking the fizzing water quickly. 'So why Sydney?'

'I'm sorry?'

'Why did you leave the bush?'

'My brother died.' It was her standard answer to the standard, *You never wanted to live in the bush then?* 'You sure do ask a lot of questions, Mr Leach.'

'Guess I just like to know why people leave; especially young people. Sounds like you just needed an excuse to escape.'

'No, I didn't,' Sarah retorted, taking a gulp of champagne. Their conversation was beginning to resemble a one-sided inquisition. She flicked drops of condensation from the stem of her champagne flute and scanned the faces nearby.

'So you're not going back to Wangallon then?' Matt persevered. Had he not owed Angus Gordon a mighty favour dating back ten years he wouldn't have agreed to undertake this once only investigative role.

'Well . . .'

Sarah's mind was obviously not quite made up. That was one thing he could pass on. 'There is only you, isn't there? I mean, you are the last Gordon, aren't you?'

'Yes.'

Two bright pink spots of colour rose in prominence on the girl's face. Matt was beginning to feel decidedly uncomfortable and, obviously, so was Angus's granddaughter. 'So?' he pushed. He promised to deliver a decisive yes or no answer, but at the rate things were progressing Matt was starting to believe that he would have more luck interrogating his pet cockatoo. Maybe it was time to be blunt. 'Don't tell me, you're in love with a city fella?'

'Things changed after Cameron died, Mr Leach. I needed to make a new life for myself.'

Matt crunched ice from his glass and silently thanked God. He had what Angus wanted and the interest owing on the fifty-thousand dollars lent to him following his investment troubles was now repaid.

'I am a girl, Mr Leach. There is a preconceived notion about what people are capable of.'

Matt placed his empty glass on a passing tray and looked at the troubled young face in front of him. The girl carried the unmistakable violet eyes of the Gordons, but there was something else. Then he recognised it. It was the same unbearable desolation that he had seen reflected in the mirror following the death of his own dear wife. Sarah Gordon was lost. 'There are preconceived notions about lots of things, Sarah. Whether you choose to make use of them purely for convenience, well, that's another matter.'

Well, Sarah thought, *here endeth the lesson*. 'Anything else?' she asked cheekily, hoping to direct the conversation back to a more lighthearted tone.

'Give my regards to your grandfather.'

'I will, thanks.' Sarah watched him leave. She looked into the bottom of her glass, swirling the now warm remains. Across the room, Jeremy stood with Julie and Petra. They were all laughing. Nearby Sally Bounds, a former client, was waving at Sarah, trying to catch her attention. Sarah wished she could shake off her doldrums and join Sally for a drink, however all she really wanted at this exact moment was a good glass of cabernet and the solitude of her apartment. She waved at Sally and left the function room.

In the comfort of her small studio apartment, she relaxed against the soft-brushed cotton of her dressing gown. This gift from her grandmother had been her home since her departure from Wangallon. Its tiny balcony had a wonderful view of Centennial Park, enlivening and soothing her spirits. Decorated in shades of white and palest green, the walls were covered with framed photographs. There were old aerial shots of Wangallon and West Wangallon, showing her parents' house in the early stages of construction, while the main homestead's roof was as dominant on the landscape as a mountain.

Black-and-white shots of Scotland, unwanted photographs from her father's collection, were neatly framed. There were ones of lochs and hills, of a small cottage built into a hillside, with smoke curling tightly upwards. The pictures were so bare, their raw beauty incredibly appealing. Sarah liked looking at them; particularly the one of the small cottage. On the reverse of the shot, written in ink were the words *Village of Tongue, 1961*. It was the old country of the Gordons, a land only her father had visited, the same land her grandfather was totally uninterested in.

The collage was completed with shots of prize stud sheep and cattle, Angus' race-horses, and family members, some long since departed, at Christmas and Easter gatherings. Her favourites, those of herself and Cameron, took pride of place. There they were standing chest-deep in wheat, swimming in a river, doubling on the same horse, their faces pressed close together. Dirt-covered scallywags with black-blue icy-pole tongues poking out cheekily.

From the cupboard Sarah took an already open bottle of cabernet and, removing the silver wine stopper, poured a glass. In was then that she noticed the blinking light on her answering machine. Taking a large satisfied gulp of wine, her finger hovered over the play button before finally pressing it.

'Sarah. It's your grandfather. I've booked you a ticket home on Friday night's plane. Humour an old man, will you, lass.'

Topping up her glass, Sarah tried to figure out why she was needed so urgently. What did it matter, Sarah decided as she moved to sit on the floor of the balcony. It was nice to be needed and a weekend away could hardly hurt. A steady wind blew up from the harbour. Profiled by the halo of the sportsground, the trees of the park waved enticingly, the glow of the city forming a crescent shape in a night sky devoid of stars. Beyond lay the jigsaw of the suburbs, each small house protecting its inhabitants and their way of life. Protecting memories of loss and love swirling like willy-willies in a myriad of households. The built-up boxes thinned out as they grew further west, thinned out like the tufts of grass swaying in the heat of Wangallon's forty-degree summers. Taking another large sip of wine Sarah closed her eyes. She huddled into the corner of the balcony, pulling the collar of her dressing gown tighter against her throat, willing herself to sleep. Sleep. It was her one escape, if she didn't dream of the old days.

⊰ *Autumn, 1867* ⊱

Wangallon Station

*P*lacing her spoon on the small dessert plate, Rose patiently
waited while her husband finished his dinner. Her right
hand moved to gently twirl the fine cut-glass water goblet. Then
her forefinger stroked the silver dessert spoon, until finally her
fingers met around the linen napkin resting in her lap. A dozen
of everything, she thought as she mentally began counting the
contents of the large mahogany sideboard to relieve the boredom.
Twelve entree forks and knives, twelve dinner forks and knives,
twelve dessert forks and spoons, twelve soup spoons, twelve cake
forks, twelve bread knifes, twelve teaspoons. Then there were
the linen napkins, tablecloths, glassware, decanters and spirits to
match. Wines, whisky, brandy.

Milly, Boxer's niece, cleared the table slowly and, with a small
curtsy, exited the room.

'Is all arranged for Abdul Faiz Abishara?'

His voice startled Rose. She sucked in her breath automatically, the action lessening the ache of the thick bandages binding

her breasts. She thought numbly of her milk drying up as the heat dried the land about them. Dinner usually passed without conversation and certainly without questions, for there was little to discuss. With one of Boxer's wives now wet nurse, her days stretched wearily ahead with long, unfulfilled hours.

Pushing his chair back noisily over the polished wooden floorboards, Hamish drummed his fingers irritably. Vaguely he recalled an entertaining, well-educated young girl, a creature totally distinct from the woman now forlornly gracing this fine oak table, purchased and transported at considerable expense.

'Howard, Luke and William will sleep with Mrs Cudlow for the duration of the visit,' Rose began slowly, 'baby Samuel with me. Lee has already discussed the menu with Mrs Cudlow, and the new bed linen is finished.'

'Good. I expect Abdul will bring a relation with him and any number of attendants. Still, we will know upon his arrival.'

Hamish glanced contentedly around the room. An arrangement of wild flowers, white and yellow daisies and bluebells, sat in a small glass vase on the mantlepiece over the fireplace, directly above it hung his portrait. The large oil painted by a well known Sydney artist, presented him seated in a high-backed brown leather chair, with both arms resting along the thick armrests. Hamish was particularly pleased with the studious inclination of his head and the dark tan of his face contrasting, as it did, with the crisp white of his shirt. The burgundy smoking jacket added to the overall composition of the piece and he would be pleased when the Abishara brothers could discuss the work's merits. Matching decorative plates hung either side of the gilt frame and a large lacquered fan, vibrant in shades of red and gold, hung above the doorway leading to the drawing room. After some refection, Hamish considered it a bold, yet not unattractive purchase, made by his wife from a travelling Chinese hawker not two years ago.

'The Afghan's business is usually conducted further inland. I anticipated a trip to Bourke. However, Abdul is calling on clients north of us after overseeing the arrival of camels from Karachi.'

Rose smiled encouragingly; rarely did she receive so much information. 'This man, Abdul, is based in Bourke?' she inquired sweetly, her voice dropping in tone.

'The Bourke Carrying Company.' Hamish let his eyes wander over the matching mahogany sideboard with its decanters of sherry and brandy, then the rather ornate bookcase with its delicately carved scrolls and flowers. 'I have ordered wallpaper for this room: red roses on cream and yellow ones for the sitting room. I thought perhaps you would prefer yellow.' Hamish cleared his throat loudly.

Rose fidgeted with the small gold band on her finger, anxious Hamish not see the widening of her eyes at this news. 'Yellow, yes, yes, I like yellow.' Perhaps tomorrow she would remove the bandages from her chest. Check her gowns. Wash her hair. Perhaps tomorrow she would walk to the creek, then later, when the sun grew hot and the countryside still, she would recline on the large rose-coloured settee resting beneath the main window opposite her, where the burgundy velvet drapes cut out the heat of the day.

'Already there is discontent between the bullockies and the Afghans. Still, business is business. Competition, competition is what continues to build this country.' Hamish slammed his fist on the table. Rose flinched at the hard passion in her husband's words.

'I hope you will try to be a little more entertaining when our guests are here. The piano I ordered will arrive shortly and with practice, no doubt, you will do nicely for them.'

'Do nicely for them.' Repeating the words dispassionately, Rose rose from the table, her napkin dropping to the floor. She had not played the piano since their arrival at Wangallon nearly five years ago.

'You never discuss anything with me; not the furniture that fills this home, not the piano, the wallpaper, the glassware, cutlery, none of it.' Not even the advance overheard in Hamish's study some weeks ago, she thought. News Jasperson and Dave were clearly more suited to hearing about. A substantial advance received for their coming consignment of wool, wool grown on sheep amassed through theft and deceit. Perhaps after all it was better she knew nothing of his purchases, for when Rose remembered where the money came from, she did not want any of it.

'Rose, in the past when I've attempted to discuss such things, you have barely listened.'

It was true, she admitted to herself. She drew listless in his company, for Hamish only reminded her of how imperfect her world had become.

'Rose, the piano and wallpaper will arrive in the next fortnight; at least a month before Abdul's arrival.'

'Very well.' Rose stooped to collect the dropped napkin.

'I ordered two dress silks for you, a blue and pink. I thought they would do you very well. I have business this evening. Jasperson and Dave are joining me in my study. Goodnight.'

Little point lay in a reply. He was already gone and with him the harsh male scents of dust, sweat and tobacco smoke. Dropping her napkin on the dining table, Rose listened to the approaching overseers as they scuffed the dirt of the yard, the quick stride of Jasperson, the shuffling gait of Dave. Along the narrow-timbered walkway leading to the kitchen and sleep-out, the scullery maids giggled quietly to themselves; a child mewed in sleep. Rose chose a novel from the bookcase, read the first page, then returned the book to its shelf.

❖

It was late when Dave and Jasperson finally left the homestead. Hamish walked quietly past Rose's room, a lamp lighting his way as he entered his bedroom. He sat tiredly on his bed, sliding the thick leatherbound station ledger he carried between the mattress and bed-springs. Wangallon Station was thriving. There was no mistaking the figures. Fifty-thousand merino sheep ran freely on its plains. With the night thick about the homestead, he pulled a blanket from his bed and, treading stealthily across the cypress floorboards, opened the door leading out onto the verandah. The air was cool, a breeze ruffling the thickness of his hair. At this hour, with no moon and only the stars for company, he could almost believe he had obtained everything he wanted. He sat heavily in the refurbished milk-crate chair, dragging the blanket up high until it reached his chin, and warmth seeped into his body.

Hamish was pleased with his men, pleased with his property and, more than anything, pleased with his sheep. They no longer dotted the land as clouds dotted the sky, they covered it and on their backs grew the most valuable of commodities, wool. Once, having considered the profit margin of buying and selling cattle, their combined advantages, such as ease of movement, grazing and the lack of disease, he had quickly estimated the peak of the animals' demand. He had watched other pastoralists enter the market and make their profits, but it was with sheep that he saw his future, his and the country's. Money was in people; countries were modernising and mankind needed to be clothed.

Matthew Reynolds' comments regarding staff were correct. One had to ensure their loyalty and the only way to accomplish that out here was through money. The loneliness of his distant boundary riders often led to the desertion of their posts, so Hamish tried to only employ married men. He then paid a basic sum to the wives, over and above their husband's wages; in return the women cooked and watched out for their menfolk. A rotation system was also introduced, with the couples moving yearly to different boundary huts. It was a simple strategy, with unreliable men quickly replaced by either whites or blacks. A solution made valuable by Boxer's ability to keep a tight rein on the behaviour of his people.

Wrapping the blanket securely about him, Hamish moved to the floor and lay flat, his back easing itself out against the smooth boards. He understood more than most why they wanted to remain on their tribal ground and they were indispensable with their knowledge of the local country. They could track effortlessly, knew where to find water at all times of the year and where to look for lost stock.

Turning on his side, Hamish propped his head up on his hand and stared into the brightness of the stars. One image shaped like a boiler with a handle caught his attention. The stars forming it were vivid against the blue-black of the night. For the rest of his life, the constellations would remind him of his journey to this great southern land. Although he'd not known at the start of his journey what lay ahead, Wangallon was and would continue to be his life's work. He could thank his beautiful, deceitful Mary and his dead brother for Wangallon. One had given him cause to start anew, the other, the dogged tenacity to succeed. Now he was nearing thirty-one years of age, with four sons under the age of nine. But all this was still not enough. There were over sixty souls under his care and yet his nights were spent either gazing at the expanse of the night sky or with a black girl called Milly. Hamish sighed, his mind recalling the sweet complexion of Claire Whittaker.

❧ *Winter, 1867* ❧

Wangallon Station

*A*bdul, delayed through unexplained circumstances, would arrive at the commencement of shearing, just over a month away. His letter arrived with a gift of boxed dried figs, a badly damaged piano, enough wallpaper to decorate the entire house and two magnificent bolts of dress silk, one the palest blue, the other tea-rose. Upon tasting the fruit, Hamish spat it onto his plate, condemning it immediately.

Rose delightedly filled her days sewing. During her time on Wangallon her daily uniform had been one of white or cream blouses with a skirt scarcely a yard in diameter. There were four to choose from: cream, grey, brown and pale green. A necktie was occasionally added to her other accessories: a slim belt, flat brown lace-up shoes and stockings, yet now she would have new evening dresses with crinolines almost two yards in diameter. Matching blouses with tight, high-necked fitted bodices and leg-o-mutton sleeves finished with eight small white buttons she had removed from some of her children's clothes, completed her new ensemble.

At the thought of her new clothes she felt giddy with excitement. From beneath her bed a pair of bone, lace-up boots were retrieved from their calico holder. The neat heels were only slightly worn from her few walks down the main street of Ridge Gully and, if she did not pull the laces too tightly, they almost fitted her constantly swollen feet. With the remaining blue and pink scraps of silk, she fashioned two neck ribbons, which complemented her better linen blouse, if she chose to wear it with one of her new skirts in the evening. Truly she was quite faint with joy.

Wangallon Station was frantic. Hamish was pleased to leave the occupants of the main house to their preparations. There was much cooking and discussion and sewing and gluing of recently arrived wallpaper. A task that had maids giggling and Rose fuming as she pulled sticky sheets from both their hands and clothes. Hamish enjoyed long days in the saddle with Jasperson and Dave as they inspected the mobs of sheep brought in each week by Boxer and his men. A lot was riding on this clip. Seventy per cent of the advance, amounting to sixty per cent of the total forward price contract, was spent already, the rest being saved for the property's expenses. The remaining forty per cent would not be seen until the wool reached London, its final destination. That forty per cent amounted to the property's entire cash flow for a year, when Hamish would travel to Sydney again to renegotiate the price of his wool for the next season.

Hamish rode back to the homestead, his return greeted with squeals and laughter as Howard and Luke appeared from around the side of the homestead building. Close behind them walked Boxer with three women. Hamish greeted his head stockman amiably, his young sons by his side. Howard stared at the bare-chested older woman and the two younger ones in their formless dresses and bare feet, while Luke sat cross-legged in the dirt, his mouth chewing a pretend wad of tobacco as he copied Boxer's tobacco-chewing rhythm.

'Bring new maid, boss. You choose?'

Hamish hesitated. The house already employed four maids and he wasn't sure they required another. However Boxer had extra mouths to feed at his camp now and although his tribe received monthly rations of flour, sugar and tobacco, the homestead staff received a little more on and above, plus a maid's uniform.

Boxer grinned. 'You choose.'

The girls were the daughters of the melon-breasted woman next to Boxer. She and the newest members of Boxer's camp had walked twenty miles from down south, after having met starvation and whipping at the hands of whites. The girls were equal in height with the same flat noses and broad brows. The dresses showed nothing of their figures, but one's ankles were slimmer than the other and beneath the slack cloth of her dress, her breasts looked bigger. Hamish pointed, nodded at Boxer and walked away. His boys followed, Howard walking sedately like his father, Luke tearing off towards the house to inform the maids that another of 'em was coming. Hamish watched the dust of another mob of sheep hover on the horizon. Tonight the girl would be in his room. He would make sure of it.

The girl waited for him silently in the dark. Hearing the small inhalation as he turned the knob to his bedroom, Hamish glanced towards his wife's room. No light seeped from beneath it. The timber creaked underfoot. Closing the door, he hung his smoking jacket in his wardrobe. A small lamp glowing steadily on his dresser illuminated the white linen and darker quilts of the four-poster bed. The girl, a shadow within a shadow, sat curled tightly, wedged in the far corner of the room and partially obscured by heavy curtains and the large packing-case desk with its cotton reels for handles. The whites of her eyes followed him.

Hamish beckoned, his hand curving in gesture. She moved towards him quietly, carefully, as if she knew instinctively which boards creaked and which offered quieter passage. He gestured to her to remove her dress. The shift fell to the floor softly. He shone the lamp over her naked body, examining her for any cuts or ulcerations. The girl appeared clean. Running his finger down from the hollow of her neck, he rubbed his palm roughly over her nipple. The point of skin rose under his attention. Vacantly he wondered what became of the children, if there were any.

Absently Hamish searched for a name. Sometimes a name came in handy for reprimand, quite often not. No, a name was irrelevant. Carefully he undressed, removing his socks. He slipped his braces from his shoulders, dropping his trousers. The eyes followed each movement, hands quiet by her sides. His habit of taking an Aboriginal girl had begun out of need and he was quick to repay them with extra rations. He prided himself on his rotation system: sleeping with all the maids so as not to incur any problems because of favouritism. Milly he liked though.

Undoing his shirt and folding it neatly along with the rest of his clothes, he moved unhurriedly towards the girl. Her breathing quickened, her breath warm on his face. Lifting a hand, he turned her face from his, turned the wide eyes from his and the warm breath. He allowed his hands to travel freely down the girl's body. He missed Milly. This girl was quiet, afraid while Milly spoke softly, enticing him, stroking, cupping, melding her way on top of him, until quite often he was unable to pinpoint the moment of entry until pleasure came. The girl remained motionless. Roughly Hamish pushed her up against the carved wood of the bedpost, pulling her left thigh clear of her body so that it lay awkwardly on the end of his bed.

Afterwards, out of breath, he pulled free of her, slowly. It had taken some effort to enter her tightness and now tiredness surged through his limbs. The floorboards creaked. Milly entered the room as the girl slid to the floor. Milly's features remained expressionless as she moved to the girl, yanked her hair and whispered fiercely to her. The girl moved slowly at first, and then, as if regaining life, reached for her dress.

Lying down on the cool of his bed, Hamish drifted tiredly. Surely Rose would be able to play something suitable for Abdul and his party once the piano arrived. Yes, a week of practice would be enough for her. Water splashed. Hamish heard the droplets plop into the porcelain bowl from the squeezed washcloth. The mattress sunk as Milly crawled her way towards him and began washing him. Eyes, cheeks, moustache, lips, neck. She smiled, hummed. Hamish crossed his arms behind his neck. The room was cooling now, settling into the long length of night. Slowly Milly lowered herself upon him, lifting her dress clear of her breasts, humming, positioning, pushing her upturned nipples into his face. All the while she hummed, the low voice reminding him distantly of his mother.

Luke was having a bad morning. The maids were curt with him, Mrs Cudlow repeatedly told him to stay out of her way and Howard was reading to William. Even his mother had told him to stay away. Bored with throwing frogs at the shrieking maids in the kitchen, Luke ventured out to Lee's vegetable patch. A shower overnight had made the dirt soft enough to squirm about his toes as he squatted down to poke at a carrot top. The day was not a good one. He had been caught stealing Lee's tobacco, and his Chinese friend would not speak to him. Luke stuck a grimy small fist into his trousers. There, mixed with his pet frog and dirt, were small pieces of tobacco and a shiny coin. Of course he had told his brother it smoked good but, when wrapped in a leaf and lit, it stung his nose and eyes and caught in the back of his throat, like a dose of cod liver oil. At the thought Luke spat into the dirt at his feet, intrigued as the small amount of water surrounded by whiteness dribbled down his chin. He studied the coin in his grubby hand before clambering to his feet and walking across to Lee's bark humpy. An old dog taken up by Lee lay sunning itself, but the Chinaman was not about. Entering the one-room building, he tore a piece of material from his shirt and, having placed it in the middle of a low table, set the coin on top of it. A man needed good loyal people, so his father had told him, and Luke knew he wanted Lee as a friend. Now he owed his brother a week of chores for the coin.

Outside the black maids were talking, leaning against the timber wall of the kitchen. Milly, the thin one, was smoking, refusing to give the other two girls a puff. She walked about in a small circle, her hand on her hip, pointing the cigarette into the air as if she were talking to a whole mob of folks. Luke, crouching down on all fours, scrambled from the humpy across to a wilga tree, quickly hiding behind the trunk. He watched the girls as they giggled and talked, Milly lifting her long grey skirt up to her thighs as she sat barefoot and cross-legged in the dirt. Luke lifted his foot to scratch at the small black ants crawling up his leg. Carefully he picked them off one by one, before moving to the far side of the tree trunk, away from their nest.

On cue Milly reached for the water bag hanging from a hook outside the kitchen. Luke held his breath. She always drank first. Taking a last puff of the cigarette, she stubbed it out in the dirt with her bare foot, before taking a long swig of water. Luke watched as she tilted her head back, greedily drinking as much as she could so that there was never quite enough for the others. Immediately she choked, dropping the bag with a puff of dirt onto the ground as she coughed and carked up water. Luke smiled widely. Baby tadpoles! With a wild screech Milly searched the yard, calling out his name. Luke, his small legs pumping hard beneath him, carried around the side of the house and directly into the path of the new girl, Grace. The girl looked at him blankly and continued past him. Seconds later he heard women's voices, they were arguing.

'What do you mean it cannot be played?' Hamish puffed angrily on his pipe, scuffing the woven Indian rug with its centrepiece of a tiger with boot encased feet. Furious, Rose rushed to the piano and lifting the battered lid, struck a number of keys. The discordant noise quickly disappeared with the slamming of the piano's lid. 'It needs to be tuned.' Rose tucked stray hair from the loose bun at the nape of her neck. 'Until that occurs, it is simply a decorative piece,' she stated archly, removing herself to take up residence on the settee and return to her disturbed sewing. Lifting her darning needle, Rose sighed dramatically, her shoulders slumping with an air of disdain.

'Simply a decorative piece?' Hamish repeated, moving to tap his pipe into the hearth. 'That piano cost a large sum of money, and there was the cost of transportation.' The veins on his neck bulged, gorged with temper. The deepening welts contrasted with the white of his shirt. 'I will not have you behaving in such a, such a . . .'

Rose held the darning needle tightly between her fingers. For three nights she had listened to the creak of door and bed, the pouring of water, the patter of black feet on timbered boards.

'Please accept my apologies if my answer doesn't suit you, Hamish.' She worked quickly at her stitches, mending the small hole in the baby's woollen booties.

'Enough!' His face, contorted with fury, changed from its usual ruddy complexion to deep crimson.

For a moment Rose wondered if he would suffer some form of attack, drop to the floor, dead. She would sell it all, of course. Return to Ridge Gully. Collect her daughter and start anew.

'Mister Hamish, you come, you come quick!' Lee said urgently, barging into the sitting room, hands and pigtail flying, and then scuttling out of the room. Hamish walked quickly after Lee, through the dining room and along the narrow walkway to the kitchen. Pots and pans simmered above the open fire, one of the black maids stirring a blackened boiler nervously. Hamish acknowledged the presence of Howard and William, sitting with untouched plates of mutton and damper before them, and Mrs Cudlow, threatening a wooden spoon in her hand, should they move. The wet nurse sat in a rocker in the corner, suckling Samuel, a knowing grin showing broken yellow teeth.

Out in the dirt of Lee's vegetable patch, Milly hovered about the body of a young girl, a length of bloodied firewood at her feet. She wailed as she encircled her victim, feet shuffling the dirt of the garden. Hamish noted the torn material about the girl's neckline, the darkening spray of blood beginning to dry on the dress, the mad whiteness of her eyes against the black skin.

Stooping to roll the body over, Hamish flinched at the warm skin, almost velvet under its sheen of sweat. Grace lay dead at his feet, the face bashed and raw. Congealed blood matted the dark shoulder-length tangle of hair, clouded the girl's left eye, stuck in the soft curves of her ear, rested in the hollow of her throat. Clearing his throat, Hamish left Milly to her soft moans.

'Very bad,' Lee mumbled.

'Yes, Lee,' Hamish agreed, catching the devastated look on his wife's face as she stood at the rear entrance to the kitchen, 'Very bad.'

'Mr Boss, Mr Boss!' Milly yelled sadly at the sight of Boxer and Jasperson walking towards her from around the corner of the house.

'Sorry, boss. Sorry.' Boxer shook the girl roughly. With his hand gripping hers, he dragged her roughly through the dirt of the yard, the girl kicking and yelling wildly. Jasperson inclined his head towards the body and with a silent look of acknowledgement at Hamish, walked over to the vegetable garden to collect the dead girl. Lee was already down on his knees raking over the blood with his fingers, replanting trampled herbs and vegetables.

At the house boundary, Boxer handed the now sobbing Milly over to two of his tribesman, her legs flailing in the dirt as she was dragged between the two men. Shaking his head sadly, he hitched his slipping braces up over his shoulder, rubbing sleep from his eyes and dust and encrusted snot from around his nose. Pushing a tangle of shoulder-length greasy hair from his face, he re-adjusted his wide-brimmed hat. This was not what Boxer wished for his people, it was not what he wished for himself. He thought the boss was good, but like all whites he thought by conquering the people of this country, the land would easily be his. He would never own it. The land would own the boss, forever.

Perhaps Boxer considered he should have left with the rest of the tribe instead of enticing the thirty to remain with him when Hamish Gordon first arrived as the new owner of this land. Waking early and crawling from his humpy, Boxer had watched as the others gathered their belongings. The boss had offered clothes and food as an enticement for Boxer's people to stay and work for him, but many refused. The white man's clothes were shredded to make head ties and to wrap belongings like small bowls and tools, which were then tied to the end of sticks. The men held hunting sticks and knives in lengths of material wrapped about their waists. Some of the women wore skirts, but most were naked. Children were wrapped tight in pieces of shirt and tied to their mother's backs. In single file the people walked away and

Boxer doubted he would see many of them again. He understood now that they had foreseen something he could not imagine.

❖

That night Hamish dreamed of death. Milly and Grace were buried in the dirt of Wangallon yet, in his mind, overfed crows circled the black women, dark formless shadows circled them. Death, the terrible expanse of it, came to him suddenly. He likened the magnitude of it to a night swallowing him slowly, until his mind wrestled with nothing. Wrestled eternally with nothing, for there was nothing behind it and nothing after it. Milly had been speared.

He awoke late in the evening when the dry plains released a breeze to ease the stifling confinement of his room. He imagined himself and Charlie swooping together as if owls, over Wangallon Station. Their moon shadows hovering over the blacks' camp, down over the river bank to the bark humpy where Dave slept between mother and daughter, across to the woolshed, its yards filled for the next day's shearing. At the picket fence they rested, Charlie smiling as if in encouragement, then he was gone. In the morning, darkness still heavy, Hamish lit the bedside lamp, holding its light high. He waved it about the room, searching for the forms that had been by his side, for the pungent Scottish herbage in his nostrils.

'I will not go near the blacks again,' he murmured. 'I have done wrong.' But nor could he go on the way he had in the past. He desperately needed to make amends for his recent actions. He needed a reason to hope for the future, for didn't he too deserve some semblance of happiness in his life? This morning he would write to the Abishari brothers, he decided. He would owe them a favour, but it would be worth it.

≪ *Autumn, 1987* ≫

Wangallon Station

Screeching birds shattered Sarah's morning dreams. Having arrived at Wangallon the previous afternoon following the request from her grandfather, she was at a loss to explain why she was needed. Angus had picked her up at the airport, and they had eaten Kentucky Fried Chicken straight from the bucket and drunk coffee during the car trip home, her grandfather discussing everything except his out-of-the-ordinary request. From her bed, propped up on pillows, Sarah could see the sun streaking through the doors flung wide onto the gauzed-in verandah. Soon the verandah, littered with ancient tables and chairs and catching the morning breeze, would be the only cool place in the house. A shaft of light stroked her favourite squatter's chair. The half-chair, half-recliner was very old, but the elongated pieces of timber under their armrests could still be extended out to rest weary legs on. Her grandfather reckoned old Hamish Gordon owned it and sometimes, in the still of the early morning, she could imagine him sitting there, smoking his pipe and planning his day.

The grass area in front of the house, rarely soft and green, was now extremely dry. Once it had held a circular driveway for carriages and drays and there had been a hitching post for horses. No wonder, Sarah thought, so many plants struggled to survive during the years. It was almost as if the ground needed to be top dressed every year in order to counteract the years of passing traffic. Odd circular patches, where sprinklers eased the small plants' suffering, highlighted the brittle brown. Year after year, her grandmother, like Sarah's mother, had planted seedlings, tiny plants, bringing the promise of beautiful flowers. So many times it had been a useless exercise. Droughts, birds swooping down to pluck the tasty shoots, dogs, never chained when they should be, rolling and peeing in the turned soil and in the drier seasons, rabbits methodically munching all in their paths.

Now, only trees survived: tall gums, wilgas and belahs waving wildly in the strong autumn wind. Contrasting these were huge cacti. These spiking monstrosities swelled from the ground with such passion that no-one ever had the heart to prune them back. Sarah loved their dull green colour, the angular shapes. They guarded the horizon, reminding her of their cousins in the American west. In the far corner of the garden, old flower tubs held hardy geranium and bougainvillea. As a child, with Granny Angie beside her, fairies had come alive, translucent angels floating on miniature rafts of pink geranium petals. The dark pinks and reds of bougainvillea hid the secret bowers of these invisible princesses. Not that they flowered regularly now. No-one had the same dedication to gardening as her grandmother.

Directly in front of the garden, the red orb of the sun glimmered, its hot rays reaching through bushes and trees, touching all with indifference. Gradually the garden came to life. Small twittering birds darted across the lawn, a rooster sung heartily, the dogs, always anxious to bark, joining in loudly. This had been her grandmother's favourite time of the day. At the memory Sarah thought she saw a figure walking at the end of the garden. Ridiculous, now she was imagining things, just like her mother.

Her grandfather's radio boomed harshly into the morning solitude. Sarah filled a glass with the diminishing rainwater feeding through to the house from the tank outside and joined her grandfather at the large kitchen table.

'Morning.'

'Hi, Grandfather.' She poured a mug of tea from the shiny blue pot and added milk and sugar. 'Um, any particular reason why you needed me up here this weekend?'

'Does there need to be?' her grandfather answered in his usual curt manner.

'Well, of course not.'

'Good.' Angus munched noisily on toast and vegemite. 'Shouldn't really need a reason for a grandfather to want to see his granddaughter.'

Sarah poured muesli into a pale blue ceramic bowl and adding milk, took a mouthful. Maybe age was catching up with her grandfather and he was simply lonely.

'I was thinking about my family.'

'Dad?' Sarah asked.

'No.' Angus took another bite of toast the crunching emphasising her error. 'My half-brother.'

Sarah choked, spitting out the muesli. 'You had a half-brother?' She cupped her hand, wiping the small missiles of chewed grain and fruit from her chin and table.

Her grandfather winked at her. 'You see, you're not so different.'

Sarah deposited the half-chewed remnants of her breakfast back into her cereal bowl. 'I never knew. No-one ever said anything.'

'People don't talk about that type of thing. You know that.'

Sarah pushed her bowl aside. 'Were you upset about it?'

'Why would I be upset? Your great-uncle Luke was a real good fella. He lived here in this house intermittently between droving jobs and would sit at this kitchen table, tin mug in hand, talking of the stars. I was near forty years his junior.'

'Wow.' Sarah thought of all the conversations from over the years, nestling in the ancient timber, stoking the old fuel stove in winter, stirring a breeze in the long heat of summer. 'But how does he fit into the family tree?'

'Just like Cameron. Nicely.'

'Why doesn't anyone talk about this family-tree stuff?'

Angus hunched his shoulders. 'Anyway the point is, girl, no-one deceived anyone with regards to Cameron, they just didn't know how to handle it.'

'So it wasn't that no-one wanted me to know?' Sarah asked, needing a final confirmation.

Her grandfather inclined his head to one side and gave an exaggerated scowl. 'It didn't change the way you felt about him, did it?'

'No.' Sarah poured herself more tea, her eyes moistening. 'Thanks, Grandfather.'

He waved her words aside. The water carrier, due today to fill the homestead's tanks, reminded him of Anthony's garden at West Wangallon. It too was starting to suffer from the prolonged dry spell.

'Sarah, why don't you go and visit your old house? Anthony is just caretaking it after all, and I'm sure that –'

'No, thanks. I better wait for an invite.'

Angus scratched his scraggy neck. 'Stubborn, eh? Well, it will be a hot one today, Sarah.' There were four hundred head of cattle to be moved to another paddock. Yesterday, a mob of sheep had escaped through the fence on the west boundary, and the stock inspector impounded them.

'I don't want another debacle like the one we had with the sheep yesterday. You know that bastard could have called.'

'You wouldn't have spoken to him anyway.'

'Well, with everything starving, it wouldn't matter if you had a brick wall, the animals would still manage to see what's on the other side. What's the bloody point of inspecting the routes now? If an animal strays onto any of the stock routes around here at the moment, the only thing he's going to be getting is a mouthful of dirt.'

'You should tell him that,' Sarah agreed, sipping her tea. 'How's the new jackeroo going?'

'Well, if you're asking me if he is as good as Anthony was at the same age, you know the answer to that one. I hand-picked Anthony myself. You get what you research.'

'Right. You didn't choose Colin then?'

'Nope. Thought I'd try out Anthony's managerial skills. The kid's from the territory. An orphan or something like that.'

'Is he worth paying?' Sarah asked, using a favourite line of his.

'I'm reserving judgement. Well, what are you waiting for? Time to clock-on, lass.'

Sarah looked at the brass-rimmed clock hanging above the now rarely used Aga wood stove, which electricity and bottled gas had long since relegated to only the coldest of days. It was 6.20 a.m. It didn't matter what time she got out of bed in the morning, she was never up early enough to finish breakfast.

'Day's half gone, lass. You're the Gordon, so get out there and give some orders.'

⬥

Anthony waited patiently at the stables. Colin, having already saddled Warrigal and his own mare, Bette, rolled himself a cigarette and inhaled deeply.

'Thought you were going to give those up?' Anthony said as a Land Cruiser came into view, haloed by dust.

'Next year.'

Anthony patted Warrigal's neck. 'Sorry about your day off being buggered up.'

Taking another drag of his roll-your-own, Colin shrugged. 'Guess no-one can do much when the head honcho steps in.'

'Yeah, well, I think Mr Gordon delayed this job so Sarah could get out and do a bit on the place.'

'When do you reckon he'll retire?'

'Retire?' Anthony laughed. 'Never. He'll stay here until the next generation is ready to come home and even then he'll still be steering the ship.'

'What? You mean her?' Colin questioned, finishing his statement with a sour spit of flem into the dirt at his feet. 'I thought youse would get the place.'

Anthony clapped Colin on the back. 'Last time I checked my surname wasn't Gordon.' He watched as the vehicle pulled up and Sarah appeared.

'A woman.' Colin drew the word out slowly.

'Yes,' Anthony said, 'a woman.'

Colin narrowed his eyes in annoyance.

'Hi Anthony.'

Anthony allowed himself a quick admiring glance at the slim form hidden within a long-sleeved pale blue cotton shirt and dark blue jeans. 'Good to see you, Sarah. You remember Colin?'

'Sure. Hi Colin.'

Colin barely grunted. 'Which horse?'

'Blaze,' Sarah answered, 'thanks, Colin.'

Anthony shook his head. 'He's a bit testy, Sarah. I'd take Oscar.'

'My riding hasn't deteriorated that much, Anthony.'

'I think old Oscar would be better,' Anthony persisted.

Sarah shook her head. 'And I think we had better stop quibbling and go.'

'Day's half gone already,' Colin said pointedly.

'In that case, Colin, the sooner you get Blaze for me the sooner we can be on our way.' Sarah watched Colin as he walked around to the horse yard to fetch Blaze. 'I think your new jackeroo has a bit of an attitude.'

'He's not the only one,' Anthony replied with a bemused expression.

'Keep a firm hand on those reins,' Anthony yelled after Sarah as Blaze took off. 'And no stockwhips near him. You hear that, Colin?'

Colin gave a brief nod of his head.

'Whatever,' Sarah yelled back. After all, Blaze was her horse. Well, officially he was her grandfather's, but he was the last colt out of the old mare Charlotte, Cameron's last horse.

The cattle were scattered in varying-sized mobs along the stock route. The familiar red and white of the Hereford breed was strikingly prominent against the pale of the grass. Sarah twitched her heels lightly against Blaze's flanks and headed towards cows and calves sheltering beneath a tall belah tree. The mothers, annoyed at being disturbed, stood their ground for several seconds before stalking off to join the ever-growing mob, their young racing behind. Every so often the old cows would slow to ensure their babies followed, often turning to walk back through the mob to check on their progress. Sarah kept Blaze at a steady walk, picking up more cows and calves as she neared the boundary fence. What undoubtedly started as a broken barb wire was now a trampled mess of broken wires extending about eighteen metres. It would take a good hour to repair, she concluded, a good job for Colin. No-one liked fencing.

Ahead, Anthony was walking up about forty head. To Sarah's right Colin chased a steer who was leading horse and rider a merry chase, refusing to join the main herd. She turned the mob towards the fence and waited as they crossed over the damaged section back into Wangallon. Six kilometres lay ahead of them, a good half day's travelling with cows and calves, but the animals needed to be moved down to the creek and onto some wheat stubble. Here with a supplement of molasses they would retain some condition, at least until they began feeding out hay if rain didn't come soon.

Colin appeared from the tree-line, galloping after the steer that was finally heading towards the main herd. He rode hard on the beast's flank, his horse shadowing every turn the steer tried to make, both animals rubbing against the other at full speed. With a final surge he manoeuvred the beast into the herd and, with a satisfied smirk, rode past Sarah.

'Get 'em moving, will yah. We don't wanna be 'ere all day,' he called out to her as he broke into a trot, cracking his stockwhip pointedly beside her as he rode past.

Blaze reared at the sound of the whip and took off at a gallop. Unable to look back, with the noise of the muster fast disappearing, Sarah gripped the muscled flanks harder with her legs. Adrenalin surging, she held her body low, arms aching with the strain.

Anthony saw Blaze moments before the horse hit the tree-line. It was all he could do to bash through the moving cattle and call out her name. Reaching the timberline, he heard the crashing of sticks ahead and without hesitation held fast to Warrigal's neck and galloped in after Sarah.

As the terrain grew rougher, Blaze stumbled into one of many potholes. Sarah's hat caught in the branches of a dead sapling, her hair tumbling loose from its ribbon. Blaze sprang over the cracked ground and Sarah hung on grimly, knowing that Blaze would tire eventually.

Anthony saw the cloud of dust before he caught sight of Sarah. He reached the road leading to the boundary gate between Wangallon and West Wangallon, cursing under his breath. Ahead, he could see Blaze tiring.

Lifting her eyes away from the sweat-woven hair of Blaze's neck, Sarah saw with dread that the high boundary gate was closed. 'Whoa, fella, steady down!' But Blaze kept charging, the foam from his mouth flying back to splatter her cheeks. 'Shit, Blaze!'

'Sarah, pull him up. Now! You won't make it!' Warrigal was almost level with Blaze. Anthony stretched his arm towards her.

The gate was only metres away and Blaze was no jumper. Sarah sat up, leaned backwards, and pulled tight on the reins, her stirrups digging hard into the horse's flank. Blaze swerved violently, but the movement was too late. Unable to hold on, a rush of air hit her face and body as Sarah was flung out of the saddle, straight over the horse and onto hard-baked earth. A sickening crunch sounded.

Anthony was beside her in seconds, talking to her, his hands on her face and torso examining her for injuries. Raising a hand, Sarah touched the side of her jaw. Anthony's hand covered hers immediately, his fingers probing the injured tissue.

'Ouch!'

She looked past him where he squatted, his hair plastered to his head from sweat, his hat gripped tightly in his hand.

'Sarah, are you okay?'

Staggering in circles, Blaze glared in pain. The right nostril was hidden beneath a bulbous mass of bleeding flesh. The sweat-encrusted shoulder was crisscrossed with deep gashes. Blood streamed from the lacerations. In some places, the thick hide was torn so deeply that the contour of white muscle protruded clearly. As the horse whinnied in pain, Sarah dropped her eyes to its right leg. It was broken. She looked straight through the pained expression on Anthony's face to the death mask of the horse, which should have belonged to Cameron, and screamed.

'Sarah, get a hold of yourself,' Anthony murmured. 'Anything broken?'

'No.' Struggling into a sitting position, she shook her head, ridding herself of an image of her brother being dragged through the scrub, his arms and legs thrashing hopelessly amidst grass and fallen timber. It had taken Anthony two days to find Cameron's injured horse all those years ago. No-one else thought about the horse, but Anthony had been determined to find the poor animal and put him down.

'Bloody hell, Sarah, you could have really hurt yourself!' Anthony placed both his hands under her armpits, pulling her to her feet. She looked scared and it was possible there were a few ribs broken, but otherwise she appeared all right. 'Gawd, you've gotta learn to be more careful.' He brushed dirt from her shoulders and back, pushed strands of sweaty hair back from her forehead. 'When you're here, I'm responsible for you.'

'Responsible!' Sarah squinted at him. 'I didn't ask for a watchdog.'

'Not that a watchdog would make any difference. Why did you persist in riding Blaze when I told you not to?'

Sarah hung her head.

'Look, all I'm saying is that your grandfather doesn't get out as much as he used to. So if something happens to you, I'm responsible.'

She would have rather kicked him in the ankle than agree. From the scrub, the crackle of undergrowth sounded sharply. Blaze was hobbling away from them. She watched Anthony call Warrigal, his friend standing in the hoof marks of Blaze, snorting the air at the side of the dirt road. Once in the saddle, Anthony pulled his rifle from its holster and loaded it, before riding off.

Two kilometres from the homestead, with the temperature creeping up steadily, Sarah walked to the nearest belah tree and, having checked for snakes and goannas, collapsed. Her hair, plastered with sweat to the back of her neck, stuck with the same persistence as her pale blue cotton shirt. From the corner of her eye she was able to make out the pieces of horseflesh caught in the rough wood of the gatepost. If she walked towards the fence, she would see blood drying on the ground. Already clusters of flies could be seen buzzing around the spot.

Leaning back against the bark, willing her body to cool down, Sarah tried not to recall words spoken by her father years ago. One of the jackeroos had carelessly run over a favourite dog, and the animal, suffering from severe internal injuries, had no chance of making the hour trip to the closest vet. While listening to her parents arguing in the kitchen of West Wangallon, Sarah and her brother had stared out the window to where old Joe lay collapsed in pain, only his mournful eyes suggesting life, as he waited for his master to appear.

'I'll have to put him down, Sue. If I leave it to that boy, I couldn't be satisfied he would do the job properly.'

Sarah had watched Cameron take the rifle, following their father who carried the wounded dog. Even now she still heard the soft murmurings of a hard man, heard the whimpering responses of his dog. Within minutes, Cameron was striding up the cement path and rounding the corner of the house as a lone shot echoed.

Sarah closed her eyes, sucking in the sounds of a settling bush, the heat forming a blue haze. Pain throbbed in her hip, ribs and ankle, and there was a burning sensation in her cheek. Her ears picked up small rustles, a movement in the foliage. In her mind she relived the wild gallop through the scrub, saw herself falling and Blaze's proud neck swerving violently to sideswipe the boundary gate. She vomited into the dirt.

Colin. It was Colin that cracked the whip, Sarah suddenly remembered. He'd been with them at the stables listening to Anthony's advice, not to ride Blaze, not to use a whip near him as the young colt was definitely flighty.

A rifle shot sounded. Birds scrambled frantically from branches. Sarah stood and walked stiffly to the boundary gate, trying not to stare at the flesh and hair on the fence post. The road swam ahead. Blaze, the last horse associated with Cameron she thought sadly as she opened the gate. She should have listened to Anthony. She should not have ridden her brother's horse. It was just like the day of the accident when she had pushed her brother to go for a ride, except this time it hadn't been her fault.

Behind her the familiar clip-clop of Warrigal carried across the hard-packed earth of the road.

'Hop up.' Anthony pulled Warrigal to a halt and held out his arm.

'Colin did it. He cracked the whip on purpose.'

'He hardly would have done it on purpose. Now hop up.'

'But he did.'

'Sarah, hop up.'

'I'll walk.'

'What, two kilometres?'

'It'll do me good.'

'Sarah, please don't argue with me. There's four hundred head of your cattle that still have to be walked to the corner paddock and it's nearing mid-morning already. It's a slow enough journey with calves but once it starts to get hot, you know how hard they are to move.'

Sarah looked ahead down the dirt road, already a blur of heat shimmering across the country. Her face stung and her ribs ached.

'All right.' Wincing as Anthony helped her onto Warrigal, she gave a weak thank you. Gradually Anthony increased Warrigal's pace, his voice urging his horse onwards. Too tired to grasp the flanks without stirrups, Sarah slipped from side to side.

'Sarah you're moving around back there so much, old Warrigal doesn't know if he's at a rodeo or a disco.' His hand reached around, pulling her tight to his back, ensuring she was safe. She gasped at the jolt. 'Put your arms around my waist. It'll be more comfortable.'

Quietly obedient she slipped her arms about him and turned her head so that the side of her face rested against his shoulder blade. He was right, the position eased her aches.

'Tell you what, Sarah, you did a good job with the cattle this morning. We had a mad steer that came in from the back paddock on the eastern boundary last year and he chased your grandfather and me around the yards like a demon. I was ready to shoot the bugger, but your grandfather wouldn't have a bar of it. By the time we scrambled out of the yards, I was pleased to see the last of him. Maybe one of our lucky neighbours has him now. I should have branded an H on him for homeless.'

'You don't have to talk for my benefit,' Sarah said quietly.

It was difficult having Sarah so close to him; with every step old Warrigal took he could feel her slight body against his, the soft curves of her body melding into him. He shook his head to clear his thoughts.

'It was Colin's fault. He did it on purpose. It was no accident he came straight past me and cracked his whip.'

'I'll have a word to him.'

By the time they reached the main house, Colin was leaning nonchalantly on the bonnet of his four-wheel drive, a gangly leg cocked up on the front tyre. Anthony gave him a brief nod. The boy should have stayed with the cattle instead of returning to wait for them.

'Have a buster then?' Colin drawled, flipping a box of matches between the fingers of his right hand. 'Well, Anthony tried to tell you Blaze was too fresh. What happened then? Is he lame?'

'Dead. He's down near the box trees we poisoned a few months ago.'

'Pity.' He pulled a match free from the pack, chewing softly on the end of it. 'Horse just needed someone with a bit of ability. Waste of a good horse.'

Anthony gave Colin a frown of disapproval. 'You'll have to get a rope and drag the old fella to the tip after we've finished moving the cattle.'

'Well, I thought I should come back, you know, just in case there was a problem, which there was.'

Swinging her leg over Warrigal's back, Sarah reluctantly slid down to the ground, her ribs jarring as she touched earth again. 'That was pretty helpful of you cracking that whip, Colin.'

'What ya talking about?'

'You rode past and cracked the whip right near Blaze. No wonder he bolted.'

'Is that right?' Anthony intervened.

'Not that I'm aware of, boss. Sure didn't do it intentional like.'

'Fair enough.'

'Fair enough,' Sarah retorted. That'd be right, she thought angrily. Now he was taking the word of this scruffy-looking kid.

'Real pity about Blaze. He was your brother's horse, wasn't he?'

Anthony looked from Colin to Sarah. He could feel the tension radiating from her.

'You coming, boss?' Colin grinned, walking to his beat-up Land Cruiser. 'Want me to hook up the horse float so ya nag doesn't have to walk all the way back to the mob?'

'Sounds good. I'll meet you down at the stables in five and, Colin . . .'

'Yeah, boss?'

'Don't leave a mustering job like that again. The cattle will be camped by now and it will take us another hour to get them moving.'

'Yes, boss.' *Bloody city slickers,* he mumbled.

'You be okay?' Anthony asked Sarah. The gravel rash on the side of her face was an angry red.

'Sure,' Sarah called over her shoulder as she walked up the back path. Next on her list of great things to do today was informing her grandfather that Blaze was dead.

'Don't be pissed off, please, Sarah. Colin means well.'

'Right, so he scares Blaze, I fall off and now the horse is dead. Oh he means well all right, just not in the way you think,' she called out before slamming the back door.

'Shit! Looks like I'm in the doghouse.'

Warrigal whinnied as if in agreement.

Sarah applied a disinfectant cream to her badly grazed face and pretended her ribs were fine. Three times she agreed with her grandfather about her good fortune that Anthony was present when she fell. Yes, he was a fine man, she agreed for the sake of peace. Yes, they were extremely fortunate to have him. A small jenny wren came to rest on the awning of the kitchen blind as Sarah emptied the small bowl of warm water and Pine-O-Cleen.

'Stations like Wangallon need men like Anthony. In the years to come you'll appreciate his talents, girl. I've taught him a lot.'

'What if he leaves?'

'Leave Wangallon?' Angus scoffed. 'He won't leave and even the ones that do,' he pointedly implied, 'come back.'

Only for visits, Sarah thought. Strangely enough though, she was beginning to feel a little more settled. Perhaps it was due to her parents' absence. With their departure, her visits to Wangallon were more peaceful, less filled with angst and feelings of guilt.

'Good man, Anthony.'

She supposed it was natural that Anthony benefited from her grandfather's knowledge. Although sometimes she wondered if she would have been taught half as much if she'd stayed and her brother was still alive. She doubted it. Still, it didn't matter much anymore. Anthony allowed Wangallon to survive, allowed her grandfather to live his days out on the blood soil that cradled the souls of their family. If Anthony left, Wangallon's future would be insecure.

It was fairly plain that the girl's ribs were bruised. Angus could tell by the way she favoured her side as she moved. Leaning back into his old high-backed chair, he listened to the comforting squeak of old leather as he manoeuvred his bum amongst the unruly springs beneath. The old girl really needed to be re-upholstered but he just couldn't bear to part with her, even for a couple of weeks.

His granddaughter hovered in the doorway.

'And you're waiting for?' Angus asked gruffly.

'My plane leaves at –'

'Yes, yes,' he waved a hand at her in annoyance, 'back to the big smoke tomorrow, eh?' And lover-boy he supposed. 'Well I'll drive you to the airport on condition that you return to Wangallon for the annual picnic races.'

'So soon?' Sarah asked tiredly. She figured she would need at least a month in Sydney to recover from this visit.

Angus gave his best old-man smile. 'Please.'

'All right.'

'Excellent.' Angus already had his report from Matt Leach, now all he needed was to get the girl back as soon as possible. Money and love, those two things, he decided, would win anyone over, including his difficult granddaughter.

It was late afternoon. Sarah wandered through Wangallon homestead. It had been built to capture and direct as much cool air as possible. In its interconnecting rooms, curtains fragile with age billowed in the morning breeze; heavier damask, in faded golden hues, hung sedately in darkened formal rooms. Rich timbers of oak and mahogany rested under a fine layer of dust, while last century's novels and encyclopaedias were shuttered within cedar bookcases. Its pisè-walled rooms, a nineteenth-century concoction of baked straw and mud, were smooth and covered with plaster and Sarah ran her hand over the cool surface, enjoying the touch. Behind her she heard footsteps on the polished cypress floorboards. Expecting to see her grandfather, she waited. The sound vanished. Sarah walked back through the drawing room and then crossed another hallway.

She was in the oldest part of the homestead now, where age and the earth's movement had cracked walls and upset foundations. The wooden floor was uneven and the long hall that had once led out to the covered walkway to the cook house was now sealed up, a tapestry hanging on the wall where a door use to be. Again the footsteps sounded, this time only briefly. Sarah turned. Diagonally opposite were two bedroom doors: one room once belonged to her great-grandfather, Hamish, the other to his first wife, Rose. This area of the house was never used now. Her grandmother Angie had used Rose's room as a sewing room when she was alive and Sarah's mother had made Rose's room her own after their forced move from West Wangallon after the flood.

It was strange then that Rose's bedroom door was open. Sarah walked towards the partly open door and pushed at it tentatively. The door swung open. Inside was a washstand with a matching ceramic bowl and water jug, an old wardrobe and a bed. Sarah laughed at her nervousness. Yet she could smell lavender and the slightly creased pale pink bed cover looked as if someone had been sitting there only moments before.

'What are you doing in this part of the house?'

Sarah started at her grandfather's voice. 'I thought I heard something.'

He cocked an eyebrow. 'You probably did. Your grandmother often heard the odd thing, although I put it down to an old house having a bit of a stretch now and then.'

'What was Rose like?' Sarah asked.

'Who knows, girl. She was gone way before my time.'

'But there are no pictures of her or anything.'

'Wasn't a lot of photographic stuff back then. Now why don't you go out and get a bit of air.' Angus waited until Sarah's footsteps could be heard echoing through the house, then he entered Rose's bedroom, smoothed the bed cover and opened the curtains so that the afternoon light filled the room. When he left he closed the bedroom door securely behind him.

Dusk was falling. Having slithered through the concave of dirt under the back gate, Shrapnel wandered slowly up the cement path. He sat down beside Sarah on the back step, resting his head on her leg. With a yawn, he stretched out and slept quietly under the rhythmic stroking of Sarah's hand, a hind leg twitching from the chase of his dreams, occasional soft yelps coming from him. Spiky hairs stuck out from his nose, and he limped slightly from a wound received last year. Out one day with his master, he'd baled up a wild boar at the base of a wilga tree. Barking and yelping, Shrapnel had charged continuously, rushing in to nip at the squat body well fed on young, weak lambs it had devoured over the course of a week. Eventually Angus, managing to keep Shrapnel clear, unloaded a round into the old boar, not however, before the pig made one last assault on Shrapnel, ripping the dog's hind leg with its tusks. Sarah ran her fingers along the scar.

Earlier in the day, Sarah had walked down to the line of trees sheltering the dog cages. These large wire compounds with their kennels and self-feeding water trough held the black-and-white sheep dogs and cattle dogs so crucial to the working of Wangallon. With Shrapnel, Sarah watched Colin pull the still warm kangaroo carcass off the Toyota's tray, the animal hitting the ground with a heavy thud. It was usual practice to supplement dog biscuits with fresh meat and Sarah observed as the jackeroo deftly used a long blade to slice through the coarse brown hair, pulling the hide smoothly away. As he did so, he pointed out the most efficient cutting procedures, explaining which joints to crack and the direction they twisted in most easily.

Sarah squatted on the ground, listening carefully to his detail, surprised at the way he turned a basic task into a skilled abattoir procedure. Within ten minutes the operation was completed and each dog was content with a large slab of fresh meat.

'Why did you crack the whip this morning?' She finally ventured to ask.

'I didn't.'

'There's not much point denying it.'

'Believe what you like.'

Sarah couldn't see the point in arguing. It was clear Colin wasn't going to admit to his part in her accident. It was only as she turned to leave that she noticed the pouch.

'Colin, you killed a mother. What happened to the joey?'

The jackeroo speared the dry ground with his butchering knife and casually wiped bloody hands on an already filthy shirt. They both knew the rules: never kill a roo with a joey in its pouch. Colin took a cigarette from his top pocket. Dried blood and fur stuck to his fingers as he brought the cigarette to his mouth.

'Dead. Chased her down and ran over the bugger.'

'You did *what*?' Grandfather had always been explicit: look after the bush and it'll look after you. To this end he maintained the roos might well bugger his crops and the dogs had to be fed, but shooting mothers with joeys was not his idea of natural selection.

'Look, Sarah,' Colin dragged heavily on his cigarette, 'if you don't like it . . .'

'It is not a matter of not liking it. There is a right and a wrong way.'

Colin took another drag. Snorting contemptuously, he leaned down slowly and pulled his knife from the dirt, wiping it again before securing it in its sheath. Sarah crossed her arms.

'Your boss is my grandfather. He would expect . . .'

Colin dropped his cigarette in the dust and ground it dead with the heel of his Cuban boot. 'My boss is Anthony. I do the jobs I'm meant to.' He reached down and grasped the hind leg of the mutilated carcass. 'I don't reckon you'd have any idea what that involves. If you were meant to be in the bush, you'd be here. Instead you're causing problems and killing horses.' He began hauling the carcass towards the Toyota.

Sarah walked after him, kicking the dirt angrily. 'Just remember who you're talking to, Colin. I know you caused my accident. Don't think you're so indispensable. I can quite easily tell Grandfather to fire you.'

He didn't answer immediately. He would've liked to say something to get her real stirred up, stupid bitch that she was. Wasn't much point losing his hair over it, though, wouldn't help Anthony none. Besides, Anthony ran Wangallon, not the old fella. Sure it wasn't his place, but the old bloke had to leave it to someone, and he couldn't very well leave it to a sheila. His job was safe.

'Expecting people to watch out for ya. This is a station you know, not a –' Colin heaved the roo carcass onto the back of the Toyota – 'a camp.' She called out something, but he revved the vehicle, easily drowning out her whining as he drove away.

The dry air hung about Sarah's body. Shrapnel, scratching furiously, bit into the stillness, attempting to rid his face of small insects. The noise of crickets intensified as daytime creatures quieted. Even the feeding dogs were settling, their growls quietening as they retired to their kennels or found a hollowed cool place to sleep. A horse whinnied, the sound so far off it was possible it had carried for miles. This was her favourite time, just after sunset, with the animals fed and the cries of birds dulling. Inside, her grandfather was showering before settling down to the ABC news. A breeze stirred as she headed towards the recently delved house dam where accumulated silt had been choking their water supply. Normally water was pumped from the dam to a large underground tank. Here the water settled before being piped into the house. With the dam finally dried up, the tank attracted everything from small mice to snakes. It was better not to look in it before you showered; just the smell of drowned animals was enough.

The warm evening breeze caressed Sarah as she circumnavigated the rough dam bank and moved to a spot on its far side. Beneath a belah tree, the last of the day's light disappearing, she watched five kangaroos and their young scratching for grass. The joeys sniffed their mothers, hopping a short distance away to stare hopelessly about them. The older roos, their grey fur ragged and coarse, maintained their hungry search, claws seeking out hidden roots, ears twitching in constant surveillance. Edging nearer to the dredged silt, Sarah pursed her lips, whistling loudly to scare them away. They could smell the water dredged up with the silt, but would be bogged down as soon as they got near it, too weak to escape. They hopped away quickly in the direction of a trough filled with water for other stock in the house paddock.

'How are your war wounds?'

Sarah, lost in her thoughts as she sat on a log near the dam, barely heard Anthony as he hunched down beside her. Instinctively she raised a hand to carefully touch the embedded particles of dirt covering the left side of her face from cheekbone to jaw. 'Sore,' she replied truthfully, debating how she was going to bring up Colin's attitude towards her.

'I just came over to collect some papers. Saw you sitting here.'

Sarah found herself examining the fine golden hairs on the deep tan of his forearms. She glanced at the men's quarters, the lights of which could be seen clearly through the tall trees about a kilometre away. She opened her mouth to speak.

'Yes?'

'Nothing.' The last thing she wanted was for them to argue. 'Well, it's about Colin.'

'You do know that we've only got two full-time station hands left? The other two were laid off six months ago.'

'Yes.'

'We're using contractors for the fencing, but if we need anyone else it's almost impossible to get help now. Heaps of blokes have either headed up north or they've moved to the coast to get work.'

'I was talking about Colin.'

'So am I. There is a drought on, Sarah. It's hard to get staff.'

'I know but –'

'Let's not talk about Colin. Let me take care of it. That's why you employ me, right?'

It was the first time Anthony had ever spoken of his position on Wangallon in that way. It seemed strange, like there was a wall between them. 'Okay.'

Anthony rested his back against the tree trunk. For every two paces forward with Sarah, there were three in reverse. First the accident, now Colin complaining Sarah wanted him fired. He watched her staring at the stars clustering in the darkening sky. They were always brighter out here away from the deflecting city lights, a ceiling of suspended crystals.

'Not as clear as it usually is. The dust really clouds the atmosphere.' Anthony spoke quietly, pleased that at last they could at least sit and talk. They only had Wangallon in common, he realised, that and an emotional past. Someone told him once people were drawn together for only two reasons: common interest and/or common passion. Maybe Wangallon wasn't enough. 'My dad's just purchased an adjoining property,' Anthony offered. 'I could return home if I wanted. There would be enough land for me and my brother.' He waited for a response. Now that the opportunity to return home had presented itself after all these years, it held no interest for him. His life was at Wangallon. Sarah was right all those years ago when she'd told him that the place got into your blood. It had. Anthony stared at the wide-eyed girl opposite him, wishing, not for the first time, he knew her thoughts.

'Would you leave?' Wangallon without Anthony was an unimaginable future. Sarah shivered slightly, struggling with the implications of a yes or no answer.

'Probably not.'

The tingling of relief caused Sarah to smile, to touch his arm slightly, wordlessly.

'You're going tomorrow?'

'Yes. But I've promised Grandfather I'll come back up for the picnic races.'

'Excellent. You'll save me a dance?'

'Sure.' She thought of Jeremy, wishing she could ask him to join her, knowing that he wouldn't come. 'Absolutely.'

Anthony grinned. 'I'll keep in touch, let you know how old Angus is going.'

'Yeah, well he is getting on, but his mind is still as sharp as a tack.'

He was running out of inane things to talk about. 'I'll start looking for another horse for you.' He left her sitting at the base of the tree.

'That would be good, thanks Anthony.' A tinge of sadness placed an edge of regret in her voice. She was sorry to be leaving this time. It was the first time she'd experienced that emotion since Cameron's death.

❧ *Autumn*, 1987 ❧

Centennial Park, Sydney

Sarah poured herself another glass of merlot and sat back in the canvas deck chair on her balcony. The sun was just setting as she sipped, listening as Jeremy proposed a short getaway for the weekend. Down below the shouts of teenagers leaving the park carried up to them on the warm breeze.

Smiling encouragingly, Jeremy squeezed her hand. 'I've booked everything,' he said excitedly, 'and rearranged my schedule especially.' From the small wrought-iron table, he opened a folder and retrieved a brochure with a picture of a cute cottage in the Blue Mountains. 'You'll love it.'

Sarah looked at the picture of the quaint cottage hugged by trees and pots of flowering plants. It did look enticing.

'Well?'

Sarah knew that this was Jeremy's way of apologising for the way he talked about the flood at the charity auction a fortnight ago. And considering they had barely spent any time together recently, she knew a trip together was just what they needed. 'I'd love to go, but –'

'Excellent,' Jeremy smiled, bunching up the sleeves of his baggy blazer.

'Unfortunately I have a shoot tomorrow.'

'Can't you change it?'

Sarah shook her head slowly. She could hardly tell him she had already brought the shoot forward so that she could keep her promise to her grandfather and fly up for the picnic races the following weekend. 'I'm sorry, I really would have liked to have gone.' He was frowning in annoyance. 'You should have discussed it with me first,' she finished, feeling guilty.

'Then it wouldn't have been a surprise,' Jeremy commented, tucking the brochure back in the folder. Picking up his empty wine glass, Jeremy walked back inside the apartment and deposited it on the kitchen bench beside the beautiful bunch of flowers he had arrived with.

Sarah decided it was definitely not the time to tell him about her trip north for the picnic races. As if on cue, the telephone rang, breaking the awkward silence.

'Sarah, it's Anthony. How you doing, kiddo?'

'Good, Anthony.' She looked hesitantly at Jeremy who rolled his eyes in response before slamming a kitchen cupboard. She sat down on her pale pink couch, pushing a stack of photography magazines to one side.

'Thought you'd like to know that I've found you a horse.'

'Really? That's great,' she answered less than enthusiastically as Jeremy stacked their coffee mugs in the dishwasher.

'A nice little mare, ex-hacker actually. Only cost five thousand.'

'Is that good?'

'Absolutely. Old Angus said it was a bargain. He's fit by the way and looking forward to your next visit.'

'Right.'

'Picnic races?'

'Yep,' Sarah said trying to make the conversation brief.

'Good. I'll be speaking to you then.'

'Thanks, Anthony.' She replaced the receiver, 'Anthony's got me a new horse.'

'They just can't leave you alone, can they?'

'Hey,' Sarah walked into the kitchen. 'I asked him to call. I like to know how Grandfather's doing.' She placed her hand on Jeremy's arm, only to be shrugged off.

'You know he's in love with you.'

'In love with me?' Sarah blew out a puff of air. 'Now that is a good one.'

Jeremy looked at her carefully. 'Whether or not you see it, Sarah, is immaterial. It's plain to me he cares for you and that Angus would welcome him into the family.'

'Look, Grandfather loves Anthony. I know that, after all, Anthony is the one helping to keep the place going.' That much was true, Sarah thought as she walked back to the couch. Jeremy followed her. 'As for Anthony, he's just looking out for me.' Sitting closely beside her, Jeremy took both her hands in his.

'They both want you back there and I guess I can understand it. There aren't too many properties as large as Wangallon that are still privately owned in New South Wales and you are the sole heir.'

'I'm here, aren't I?' The statement hung between them awkwardly. Patting his thigh reassuringly, Sarah tried to ignore the feeling of unease in her stomach. Since her last visit home she'd dreamed of the brown swirl of creek water, of long-legged grey cranes stalking at the water's edge and of birds dive-bombing each other as they refreshed themselves in the water. It was a dream that woke her with the crisp, dry air of a fragile landscape. 'So can we postpone the trip?' Eager to divert the topic away from Wangallon and Anthony, Sarah suggested another date.

'That date doesn't suit,' he scratched his head in annoyance. 'Besides, I've paid for everything up front and money's too hard to make to blow it. I think I'll go anyway.'

'Really? By yourself?' This was definitely at odds with Jeremy's character.

'What am I meant to do?' his voice tightened, 'I'm taking your lead, Sarah. You're the one that's usually going away. In between your job at the studio and your own landscape shoots, you're barely around. Shelley and Kate see you on a more regular basis than I do.'

'You're right,' Sarah agreed.

'I'll use the time to do some business planning,' he said slowly as if thinking aloud. 'The accountancy practice is short of funds and I have to think of something to keep the business liquid. You know Dad left it to me and I have to try to turn things around.'

'I'm sorry, I didn't realise.'

'Well I haven't been dragging you all around Sydney attending functions for the hell of it. I did tell you I needed some new clients.'

'I'm sorry, Jeremy.'

'Yeah well, the firm is my inheritance. If you think about it in the same terms as Wangallon, you'll get a pretty good idea about what it means to me.'

'Of course.' Heavens, Sarah couldn't believe that she had been so self-absorbed. 'How much trouble is it in?'

'Enough,' Jeremy stated in an I-don't-wish-to-discuss-this tone. 'Things wouldn't seem so bad if we had more time together. I love you Sarah,' he laid the palm of his hand against her face, softly cupping her chin. 'I want us to be together but sometimes I feel like your old life is dragging you away. Look, I have to go. I have to meet up with a prospective new client and I promised Julie I wouldn't be late. He's her old boss.'

'Julie?' Sarah tried not to sound annoyed. 'On a Friday night?' Sarah almost wanted to say that she would go to, but of course it was a business meeting and Julie was only trying to be helpful.

'Every day's the same, Sarah.' He kissed her softly on the forehead.

Perhaps that was the problem between them, Sarah considered as the apartment door clicked shut. Every day was the same. Sometimes she felt her life was no longer her own. It was controlled by work, by deadlines, by the bus schedule and the state of her bank balance, by Jeremy and Wangallon and her grandfather and her emotional responses. There was never any time for her dreams. Out on the balcony she watched Jeremy drive away. Nearly three years seemed a long time to be devoted to someone. He was an attentive partner; thoughtful, sensitive to her needs and a great lover. Perfect, Jeremy was the perfect partner, and he admired the loyalty she felt towards her family, even if he had told her on more than one occasion that it was a little skewed. Perhaps she had just not given enough serious consideration to a life with Jeremy.

Saturday's shoot, headshots for a young actor, was completed within two hours and by lunchtime Sarah was back in her apartment. It was a beautiful day and there was nothing to stop her from jumping on a train and heading up to Katoomba to join Jeremy. Sarah tapped her nails impatiently and glanced at the silver-rimmed clock hanging above the kitchen cupboard. It was a little after 1 p.m. By the time she had a shower, threw a few things in an overnight bag and booked a taxi to Central railway station, she would probably arrive late afternoon. She dialled the number on the brochure Jeremy had left behind the night before.

'Blue Gum Cottage.'

'I was wanting to speak to Jeremy Barnett please.'

'They've gone out for the afternoon, dear.'

'They?' Sarah queried.

'Yes, dear, I expect them back before dinner though. Would you like to leave a message?'

A ripple of nervousness stirred in the pit of Sarah's stomach. 'No, that's okay. Thanks,' Sarah replied as politely as she could. With great control she replaced the receiver. Who on earth was Jeremy with? She looked at the brochure, read the description of the bed and breakfast carefully.

A delightful B&B in tranquil garden surroundings. Perfect for couples seeking a romantic weekend or a mid-week break. Our large double bedroom with on-suite provides the ultimate privacy . . .

Sarah thought of the meeting last night, of Julie Miller once again doing all she could to support Jeremy in his business, and burst into tears.

≫ PART THREE ≫

≪ *Winter, 1867* ≫

Paddington, Sydney

*C*laire Whittaker glanced with pride at her new oyster-grey
gloves as she twitched the two dappled mares with a short
riding crop. The horses increased their pace at her touch, the
wooden wheels bouncing the open dray down the dirt road. A
small trickle of perspiration ran down her spine, the wetness
also gathering at the nape of her neck. She patted a few stray
tendrils of hair flat, glancing at the feathery occupant confined
in a rickety wooden crate in the tray behind her. Some bargain-
ing had been required to obtain tonight's evening meal. Indeed
at one stage Claire considered sausages to be a more modest
choice. Her favourite butcher in George Street certainly would
have rescued her if her patient yet persistent haggling had
failed.

A number of carriages passed her by. Two small sedans and
a larger ebony-coloured coach that was packed high with suit-
cases, parcels and large bags stuffed with mail. Inside, a female
passenger held a white handkerchief to her nose. Claire smiled at

the driver cursing in the late morning heat then, with practised efficiency, manoeuvred between a cart stacked with coal and another larger dray hauling lengths of timber. With a flick of the reins she directed the horses into a small rutted street.

Within moments the bustle of the main thoroughfare was far behind her and her horses trotted quietly along the tree-lined dirt road. Claire passed a child, a stray dog and an olive-skinned white-turbaned man. At this last figure she looked over her shoulder. He was seated in an open carriage, dressed in a grey suit and accompanied by a burly driver of similar heritage. This unusual sight drew her attention until she stopped outside a small wooden terrace house. Tying the horses to the hitching post, she lifted the beige wool of her skirt, clasped her rattan basket and jumped down, landing with a light thud. By then, the turbaned man had gone, however the housekeeper, Mrs Cole, was already out the door of the terrace, and frowning.

'Where have you been, Miss Whittaker? Your father has been asking for you this past hour.'

Claire gave Mrs Cole a consoling glance as she latched the small gate behind her. Since their recently changed circumstances, her father had become both demanding and more inactive, as if no longer having to worry about money and food had rendered him useless. 'I am sorry, Mrs Cole, however I have purchased fresh lemons and oranges at the market and I have duck for dinner.'

'Duck, well good heavens.' The woman rubbed her hands together as if in anticipation.

'You do know how to prepare it, Mrs Cole?' Having finally managed to buy one she dearly hoped Mrs Cole could manage the slaying of the poor creature.

Mrs Cole gave her best imitation of annoyance by lifting her dimple-marked chin skywards. Bustling past Claire she hurried her wiry frame out to the dray and collected the wooden crate under her arm. 'He's a mite scraggly.' She pointed a crooked finger through the wooden slates. 'Ouch, and a biter.'

The duck began squawking loudly. 'I think you've offended him, Mrs Cole.'

'The next time you're wanting a duck, do tell me, Miss, and I'll fetch one myself for you on my usual rounds. There's no need for you to be doing the housekeeping now.' Mrs Cole looked grimly at dinner. 'This will be my pleasure,' she assured Claire. 'I'll send Humphries to bed the horses for the day.'

'Thank you, Mrs Cole.'

'He'll be making some find lard for my cakes and, oh, I can taste him on a bit of bread already.'

In the small musty parlour, Claire drew the new rose red curtains against the midday heat and turned up the kerosene lamp on the mantlepiece. The light flickered before settling down to a strong glow and the familiar acrid scent strung out across the room. Removing her bonnet and gloves, Claire paused to check her reflection in the mirror. An oval, flushed face, framed by a thick mane of black hair tied back with a bold scarlet ribbon, stared back at her. With a minimum of fuss Claire shook her hair free before retying it and turning her attention to her father.

He lay dozing in his favourite chair, an old, unstable contraption that had barely managed the trip from their small holding on the outskirts of Parramatta to their new home. On a round hardwood table by his side sat a copy of the Bible and a number of unopened letters. Claire settled the worn travelling rug over his knees, carefully prising his reading glasses from his hand.

'So you've managed to wake me then?'

'Sorry, Father.' Removing the fawn crocheted cover from the water pitcher, Claire poured two glasses, passing one to her father.

'Your mother made that.' He held out his fingers for the small cover, his fingers feeling the weight of the miniature green beads, which, sown in myriad strands along its circular edge, helped to keep the small piece of material in place. His fingers held onto the material tightly and then he passed it back to Claire.

'I miss her too, Father.'

He took a sip of water, ignoring her sentimental tones. 'You've been out?'

'To the markets. I purchased a duck for dinner. Mrs Cole is seeing to it now.'

'An extravagance.' Her father admonished with his customary raised eyebrow.

'One which we can now occasionally afford,' Claire chided gently. Months ago they had ventured into George Street, she in search of a position with her father as chaperone. Unable to handle the upkeep of their small holding on the banks of the Parramatta River and with her father's fading health, Claire had considered it their only option. They had sold their allotted acre with its two-bedroom house and rather formidable vegetable garden and moved into town. With hard work Claire hoped their circumstances would improve, especially when she became companion to a widowed lady of means. It was after the move to their current address that Claire learned by letter that she had somehow managed to gain a benefactor.

'It seems you are to have an education, my dear.'

Claire spluttered. 'An education?' She took the letter retrieved from her father's breast pocket, pausing to study the letterhead: Wilkinson & Cross – Solicitors. Under her father's impatient gaze she scanned the contents written on the fine parchment.

Our client wishes to offer Miss Claire Whittaker the advantages of a private tutor to be made available at the beginning of the next month. This arrangement is to consist of five mornings a week. Subjects to be studied include English, Latin, geography and history.

'Heavens.'

'There is more, my dear. Have you not got to the part referring to the piano?'

'A piano?'

Furthermore our client advises us of his wish that you study the pianoforte. One will be delivered to your address over the coming weeks. A tutor will call on the morning to make your acquaintance.

Yours in good faith . . .

'Father, I don't believe it.'

'I myself feel the same for I have no idea where the instrument should be placed.'

'Father,' Claire laughed, 'a piano.'

'I did in fact venture out this morning . . .'

'By yourself?'

He gave an impatient cough. 'I ventured to Messers Wilkinson & Cross in order to establish the name of . . .'

'And,' Claire asked with feigned patience, 'who is it?'

'They told me nothing more than before. You, my dear, made an impression on a wealthy personage, whom it would appear has decided to make you his project.'

'His project!' Claire objected indignantly to the word. She was most certainly not anyone's project.

'Mr Wilkinson's words, Claire, not mine. As for me, it appears I am simply along for the ride.'

Claire patted her father's hand. Mrs Cole had pointed out only recently that Claire's patron had to some extent made her own father redundant. 'It is a ride we shall be taking together, Father.' He fashioned a smile of sorts, one of stubby, ground teeth.

It seemed most peculiar to Claire that a person would chose to be her benefactor, yet keep their identity secret. What was to be gained from such a venture when the very grateful recipient remained unable to thank the person who had changed her life? Claire no longer needed to retain her position as companion to the aged Mrs Medway, nor clean or cook. These facts alone were sufficient enough to render her days blissfully free of obligations, a thought that at once worried and intrigued her, for how would she fill her days? Evidently her benefactor thought likewise, for now she was to be educated.

'Tea, Mr Whittaker?' Mrs Cole arrived with a tray of biscuits to accompany the steaming beverage.

'I'm to be educated,' Claire announced brightly. 'A private tutor.'

Mrs Cole gave a nod indicative of approval. 'A fine life you're leading now, Miss.'

'Thank you,' Claire's father accepted the tea and reciprocated with a letter. 'For you, Mrs Cole.'

Mrs Cole examined the handwriting. 'It's from my sister. I've not heard from her since . . .'

Claire waited expectantly for the rest of the sentence, which was not forthcoming. Her father rested his teacup and saucer on his knee.

'I'll be seeing to dinner then.'

With Mrs Cole's departure, Claire strung her fine eyebrows together in thought. 'That was a little strange, Father.'

'Indeed. Still we can only trust your benefactor in his judgement of our new housekeeper.'

Having appeared with her baggage and a letter of employment courtesy of Wilkinson & Cross, Mrs Cole could hardly be turned away. Within a day she had firmly ensconced herself in the small maid's room behind the kitchen. Two months later Claire was left wondering how she had ever managed the house, the cooking, the buying of foodstuffs and the caring of her father. 'The fact remains we know little about her, Father.'

'On the contrary, my dear Claire, we know she can cook.'

After the excitement of the day Claire found the stringy richness of the duck strangely dissatisfying. Having not tasted the flesh before she was surprised how quickly she found herself wishing for some of her mother's vegetable broth and a hunk of doughy bread to accompany it. She settled herself in her small room on the second floor of the terrace. A window opened out onto their cramped rear yard and Mrs Cole's fledging vegetable garden. Beyond was a laneway which ran between the rear of their house and their neighbours'. During the day she would sometimes come up to her room to look down upon the happenings in the lane: young scallywag children playing in the dirt, couples arguing, and the coal vender wending his way through the laneway maze. In the distance she could hear the night-carts rattling as they travelled through the streets, emptying the buckets of refuse from the outside toilets. Next door her father snored loudly, his nose making an intermittent humming noise between gasps of laboured breathing.

Climbing from her bed Claire knelt beside the small window, her eyes drawn to the stars hanging above her on a stretch of black velvet. No matter how she tried she could not recall a kind deed which could have manifested itself into their current good fortune. There were any number of friends and acquaintances, whom, in the course of a week, she would run into, and on occasion she may have run an errand or assisted someone in some manner, but none was wealthy enough to be the client that Wilkinson & Cross referred to so mysteriously.

'And now I am to be educated,' she whispered, remembering her dear mother with her readers and chalk board and the limited education she herself had to work with. Claire pinched her arm firmly, biting her lip at the pain. None of it was a dream, especially the weekly money for food and rent. Yet it was the thought of playing the piano that delighted her, for truly it was a talent that belonged to the upper classes.

'The upper class,' Claire repeated. If only her father had accepted the offer of better accommodation, but on that subject he would not be moved.

'I am capable of providing a roof for my daughter,' he announced firmly to her ceaseless pleading.

Claire said a quick prayer and returned to her bed. She would work hard for both her father and her patron, as her future was still unknown.

❦ Winter, 1867 ❧

Wangallon Station

Abdul Faiz Abishara arrived in a fine carriage accompanied by his younger brother, Abdullah. Their head man, Mahomet, followed in a covered wagon with four armed men on horseback bringing up the rear. Waiting on the homestead verandah Rose experienced a rush of excitement; her stomach tightened as the entourage stopped amidst a creak of wheels and the neighing of horses. Two men descended from the carriage. They were of medium height, attired in dark suits and turbans. Pinching her cheeks to heighten their colour, Rose smiled a number of times in quick succession, as Hamish walked with enthusiasm towards his guests.

'Heavens above!' Mrs Cudlow exclaimed, wiping her clean hands repeatedly on her stiff apron. 'They look like savages.'

'The children, Mrs Cudlow.' Rose refused to allow this morning to be ruined. Even as she voiced her disapproval, Luke was escaping from the confines of the house and rushing past both of them to join his father, Howard and William close behind. 'Leave them,' Rose ordered. The last thing she needed was a scene between Mrs Cudlow and her wayward sons. Mrs Cudlow sighed indignantly and, collecting the folds of her skirt in her fleshy hands, disappeared inside the homestead.

The three men shook hands, laughed, and gestured around at the countryside. The visitors bowed formally to Howard, William and Luke. Rose intended on serving a cooling punch before the luncheon hour was upon them. Indeed, she looked forward to fresh conversation and animated dinners. Five minutes passed. Rose dabbed at the perspiration on her brow, lifted her arms slightly to ease the dampness forming in her armpits. The air carried the stench of manure, the acrid smell of wool and urine. If she turned her head to peer past the timber support of the verandah, a halo of light and heat haze would be resting over the woolshed, where shearing was now in its tenth day. A small rivulet of moisture traced her backbone. Her feet began to ache.

Still the men remained where they had alighted from their carriages. Behind them their attendants unpacked a number of trunks, large and small, and three wooden packing cases. The three boys followed each movement like hungry birds watching lizards. The men scrambled atop and inside the carriages. Once an item was on the ground, the boys inspected it, careful to keep clear of the dark, wiry men, but anxious to prise open the heavy, padlocked lids, to see what curious things they had brought. Luke took two paces back, scratching his small chin thoughtfully. The trunks were very large, large enough for an animal, or for the dead Milly.

Rose lifted each foot in turn, tilting her ankles to relieve the blood that seemed to gather whenever she stood for longer than necessary in the heat. Finally the men began to move. She tucked her handkerchief into the sleeve of her blouse and clasped her hands together again. But the small group walked to the nearest carriage and examined the rear wheel, talking all the while. With

a deep sigh, she shifted the weight on her feet, her thighs damp
beneath her long skirt.

⬥

The merchants appeared well behaved, spoke English, although
their words were funny-sounding, and seemed good friends with
his father. Luke liked that. 'A nice carriage, solid and serviceable,'
he advised his two older brothers.

Howard agreed. 'And many men to protect them on their
journey.'

The head man, Mahomet, carried a shiny leather briefcase,
did not speak unless spoken to and glared ahead at nothing in
particular. Luke observed the man's swarthy skin. Obviously it
was important to have a black as the head of your staff. Well, they
had one too, they had Boxer, but best of all they also had Lee.
Luke waited with his hands behind his back, copying Howard
and William, who in turn copied their father's stance as the men
continued their discussion.

They had travelled from Melbourne, the one with the moustache said in a quiet voice as he smoked a very long, dark
cigarette; then to Sydney, where cargo bound for London was
checked and arrangements made for Wangallon's wool consignment. Luke sniffed the air. The smoke from the cigarette smelled
like crushed flowers.

The younger of the two Afghans passed his father an
envelope.

'I am pleased to be of service in this matter, Mr Hamish.'

Luke noted the slight widening of his father's violet eyes,
before the cream paper disappeared into the inside breast pocket
of his suit jacket. 'Thank you.'

The younger man grinned. Luke liked him with the clean-
shaven face and paler skin. He would make a point of behaving

properly around him, especially since this visitor seemed to have pleased his father.

Rose noted the exchange of the envelope and muttered angrily to herself. Surely they could discuss their business inside, not out in the sun. Three weeks she expected these visitors to stay, and in three weeks, there was time enough for business. Still the men talked near the carriage. Straightening her shoulders, she walked the length of the verandah slowly, twice, then returned to the doorway of the house. A tall dark man led his men forward towards the verandah, their bodies bowed as they carried trunks and three packing cases. They were a rough-looking team of men, all turbaned, very dark-skinned and dirty to look at. The smell of perspiration and strange scents loitered in the breeze. Taking a step backwards, Rose brought her handkerchief to her nose and mouth as the items were deposited with a heavy thud not five feet from where she stood. Alone on the verandah again, she watched her husband give directions to the head man, after which the Afghan's men left the dirt of the homestead yard and walked out towards some hastily erected humpies. Bored and tired, Rose waited a few more minutes before retiring inside.

Abdul and his brother charmed their hosts at once. Their English, though peppered with a heavy accent, was perfect, thanks to an English minister, and they dressed and acted like lords. Soon Mrs Cudlow was forced to re-evaluate her initial impressions. Perhaps, she explained to Rose a few days following their arrival, they were not heathens after all. Merely wealthy merchants, Afghans, yes, but not the money-grabbing, inferior, dirty men she'd supposed. Their hands were evidence of this, she concluded: the soft, unmarked hands of men unaccustomed to manual labour. Indeed, she was grateful also for their gifts. The packing cases revealed small jars of preserved oranges and lemons, carrots and cabbages, dried meats and other exotics, such as dried prunes and figs.

Seated at the oak dining table, with the fire glowing to keep the chill of winter at bay, they were really quite acceptable. Both brothers were attired in fine suits, with starched white shirts beneath fine waistcoats, and double gold watch chains. The head of the company, Abdul, had a bushy moustache, which emphasised the almond of his eyes, low eyebrows and dark face. Abdullah, however, was paler in skin colour, clean shaven, with large bright eyes and generous lips. Rose thought him quite the most exotic thing she'd ever seen. Even his simple turban agreed with him.

'You see, Mrs Gordon, there are some who would prefer to do business with their own kind. However, as your husband will agree, our carrying company provides the most reliable, efficient and cost-effective service.' Abdul spoke with an easy charm, managed his knife and fork most proficiently, never once touched the food with his hands and appeared highly intelligent.

'Indeed,' Hamish nodded as he bit into a small damper roll. 'Cost and service – these are the main considerations for all land-owners in these remoter areas. Abdul convinced many at the club during my last visit to Sydney.'

'And for your introductions,' the younger brother Abdullah replied, bowing his head gravely in Hamish's direction, 'our company thanks you.'

Rose felt an almost imperceptible undercurrent pass between the three men. Had she not known better she would have been convinced of some secret between the three.

Highly seasoned boiled potatoes, fried fish from the river, baked mutton-and-parrot pie and boiled cabbage were all consumed as if these two men were seated before the greatest feast imagin-able. A fluffy cake served with treacle and cream completed the meal. Rose, satisfied at this first of many dinners, wondered at the kind treatment Hamish afforded them. Their visit, though important considering the size of the coming wool consignment, was suggestive of great expectations on the part of her husband. By all accounts Hamish had introduced the two brothers to the inner circle of squatter aristocracy and he never put himself out for anyone unless he received a favourable return.

Following dinner, when Abdul and Hamish withdrew to talk, Abdullah escorted Rose outside for an evening stroll. It became a nightly occurrence, after which Abdullah would leave her in order to rejoin the men. Abdullah, eight years his brother's junior and born to his father's fourth wife, not his first as Abdul had been, was not interested in business. Thank heavens, Rose thought silently, as they began their evening walk. It was Abdullah's very reticence towards his family's transportation business which rendered their time together possible. Indeed, he held such disdain for the search for clients, for the general travelling involved, that he had informed his mother at age eighteen he would not remain in Australia. Instead, with his early years spent in the company of women – his father's wives and their daughters, his half-sisters – he rather delighted in the presence of women, although never before, he explained to Rose, had he been granted the opportunity to spend so much time with a lady such as herself.

Abdullah's presence was a welcome distraction and Hamish appeared content to let Rose be escorted unchaperoned by him. Rose could only surmise that Abdullah's offer of a nightly stroll freed Hamish from the social convention of retiring to the drawing room after dinner to continue with polite conversation in his wife's company. Instead Abdul and her husband could discuss the issues of the day without female distraction.

It seemed to Rose, as she and Abdullah walked slowly about the yard perimeter, that each evening their walks became a little longer, a little slower, or perhaps it was merely the wishing of it on her part. They talked little, observed the clear night sky, she pointing out the Southern Cross and the brightness of the stars, he listening intently, asking questions about Wangallon, about her life here.

At first the monotony of her existence silenced her, yet by the third evening small incidents seemed worth telling. He laughed at her description of the Chinese hawker, congratulated her eventual selection of the Chinese fan hanging in the dining room. The arguments between Lee and Mrs Cudlow over the running of the kitchen provided a whole evening of conversation, while her account of the murder of the serving girl softened the chip of stone lying deep within Rose's soul. At Abdullah's gentle questioning about her family, she found herself describing her life before marriage. She told him about Sir Malcolm, his beautiful gift, and her life at Ridge Gully.

'And your mother?'

'Lorna resides in a large brick residence in Ridge Gully with my only daughter, Elizabeth. She turned nine this year.'

Abdullah lit a long cigarette and rested his back on the timber fence. Over a hundred feet away, the main homestead stood forlornly on a bare patch of dirt. Light glowed through the windows, the silhouette of his brother clear in the sitting room. 'You visit her regularly?'

'No.' Rose turned away from the glow of the house towards the expanse of the bush. Red streaks smeared across the horizon. 'No, I've not seen my daughter these five years now.' She wondered at the changes within her girl child. Were her eyes still a wondrous brown? Did they shine with curiosity? Was her hair longer? Did Elizabeth think of her mama or had time and distance relegated Rose to a distant memory?

'Why do you not visit?' Abdullah asked.

Surprised at the directness of his questioning, Rose began to walk back towards the house. She imagined she sounded uncaring, or worse, disinterested. By her side his footsteps, sure and heavy in the dirt, were the only reminders of his presence as blackness deepened. The twittering of dusk birdsong faded and the melancholy weight of a windless night entered the homestead yard.

'I lost a child two years ago,' Rose began, the night freeing her thoughts. 'Matthew is buried by the river's edge. A small white fence surrounds him, although there is space enough for others to follow.' At the verandah Rose hesitated. How positively impolite of her. Her husband's guests deserved entertainment. Witty and engaging conversation such as she'd once shared in Sir Malcolm's household. She could not bear these precious evenings to cease on account of her own dreary ramblings. Yet she could not think of one amusing story to share.

With Abdullah's hand delicately under her elbow, they mounted the two small steps onto the verandah. 'I think your husband must always be away,' Abdullah said gently as they walked the length of the verandah.

Rose slowed her pace and they sat silently in the verandah chairs. Hamish, returning at the death of his son, immediately set about the construction of a white fence to surround the family graveyard. How could she explain to anyone, Rose wondered, that as a mother she had resigned herself to the fact that more of her children would likely die, whether by disease or accident or attack? Though God forbid their blacks should ever rise up against them. The construction of the graveyard, during which Jasperson whispered carelessly to Dave, *with room for more*, only emphasised the futility she felt in this bleak world.

'I do not visit my daughter, as she is safe in such a town as Ridge Gully.' Rose folded her hands gently in her lap. 'The travelling would be too arduous and dangerous and of course I cannot leave my children here alone.' Rose's throat constricted with dryness at this last statement. She did not agree with one word of what she had just said, but what was she to do? One didn't share marital difficulties with a house guest.

Abdullah sat forward in his chair. He wanted to speak plainly, to tell her to take her children with her. Life was indeed harsh in this wild country and with death so prevalent he believed it vital to enjoy every precious moment one had with one's children. He himself had lost two sisters in infancy and was not immune to grief. Besides, he knew of many women who travelled with their young ones, but it was not his place to say anything. Indeed, each conversation between them straddled the boundaries of what men and women could discuss in polite society. Their light discussions regularly turned to deeper subjects, ones commonly shared between women.

Afterwards Abdullah lingered on the verandah, watching the pale blue silk of Rose's dress fade into the doorway of the house. The faint scent of lavender water trailed her progress and he was keenly aware of a sense of disappointment at her leaving. He imagined all women who lived on these remote stations were as lonely as Mrs Rose Gordon. Did they rush for the mail when it came, hopeful for a letter or parcel from a friend or relative? Did they push their own desires into the deepest recesses of their beings, concentrating instead on their children and the running of their households? He had seen her on the day of their arrival, a petite figure waiting patiently on the verandah, one hand support-ing her on a timber pillar. He wondered how many years ago Wangallon's last visitors looked up into the cooling welcome of this verandah. Looked up into those deep eyes, with smudges of darkness muting the fine lines at the corners, crisscrossing the bridge of her nose when a smile graced the egg-shell porcelain of her features.

❧

On the sixth day Abdullah presented his hostess with a rich bolt of moss-green silk and a selection of exquisite laces. Delighted with the laces, of which there were cuts for cuffs, necklines and more formal collars, Rose immediately planned the completion of a new evening dress prior to Abdullah's departure. To Mrs Cudlow he presented two bolts of fine cream linen, enough for a dress for herself and clothing for the children.

'Abdullah, you are too generous.'

They had retired to the sitting room to take tea. Mrs Cudlow placed a large bone china platter of scones, treacle and cream on the small table between Rose and Abdullah and departed with a warm smile.

'It is you who is generous, Rose.' Abdullah spoke her name in the same caressing way in which he had spread the moss-green silk before her, cautious of becoming too familiar with it, of addressing her by her Christian name in front of her husband and Abdul. 'Opening your home to my brother and me, spending your precious time entertaining me when you have a busy household to manage.' Abdullah sipped his tea slowly, his little finger curling slightly out from the base of the cup. She was wearing a white linen blouse today, complemented by a darker skirt. It suited her well.

Rose rested back against the firm lounge chair. Only a few feet away, Abdullah reclined also, his eyes half-closed, his breathing slow, comfortable. She felt wonderfully languorous. Every fibre of her being oozed goodwill, in fact even Hamish had been the wary recipient of a warm smile at breakfast. Her appetite, meagre in the years since her arrival at Wangallon, also appeared to be growing daily and she felt stronger for it. She made an effort to spend time with her children once a day, ensured the day's menu was suitable much to the surprise of both Lee and Mrs Cudlow, and slept a full eight hours every night. Overnight, her life was suddenly filled with the minute happenings of station life never previously noticed.

Rose gazed across to where Abdullah dozed. His long black eyelashes curved against the light tan of his skin, his lips partially open trembled slightly with every second or third breath. Rose watched mesmerised for a few moments before turning her eyes to the yellow rose wallpaper. It added to the serenity of the room, the room in which months before Rose had spoken her last words to Hamish in private. The day Milly murdered her young cousin. The matter discreetly forgotten by the occupants of the household lay in the back of Rose's mind. An eternal reminder of her sadness at the life she'd so foolishly chosen. Abdullah woke and gave her a caressing smile.

'I feel I will need to walk four times around the perimeter of your garden, Mrs Gordon, so I am not forced to visit my tailor on my return to Sydney.'

'Do call me Rose, Abdullah.'

'In private only,' he relented. It was the third request.

'In private then,' she repeated, their eyes meeting for just a few scant seconds.

He talked softly, his fingers rising to rub his clean-shaven cheek, to brush a fly from his face. All the while Rose savoured every moment; his words, his accent, his dress, his habit of inclining his head upon joining her, his musk-scented clothes, the stray hair escaping from his turban at the nape of his neck. It was an opportunity that few white women of her status had the privilege of enjoying, spending idle time with an exotic young man, alone, without a chaperone.

'Would you care for me to read to you?' Rose walked to the mahogany bookshelf and selecting a book of verse, settled herself once more in her chair.

'Indeed,' Abdullah extended his hand graciously in approval, 'I should be delighted.'

As she read she became conscious of Abdullah walking about the room, examining various knick-knacks arranged artfully on the mantlepiece. Her concentration faltered as he moved to stand behind her, his hands coming to rest on her shoulders. Rose's breath quickened.

'Do keep reading, Rose.'

His lips touched the nape of her neck, a single extraordinary kiss. Then Abdullah returned to his seat, folded his arms and closed his eyes.

Rose kept reading, though her breath quickened and her heart sped uncontrollably, unaware of Mrs Cudlow silently closing the door.

Hamish was looking forward to the next five years, for if the Abishara brothers brought with them the recognition of his success as a wool grower, they also brought hope. He had lived in turmoil for the last months since his return from Sydney. The dull days bore witness only to his wife's ill humour and the most unfortunate business with Milly. Now he glimpsed something tangible, similar to a sodden cloud in the west, hanging like hope on the horizon.

In return for a number of major introductions, which could only increase the Bourke Carrying Company's clientele, Hamish had sought one favour. It had been done, and now Claire Whittaker was lodged safely away from the dangers of the Sydney fringes. The fact that Hamish knew little of Claire was irrelevant. He placed great faith in that one moment on George Street. There, standing in the dirt under a butcher's awning, the fine cloth of his dark suit splattered with mud, he had seen a girl with possibilities. They exchanged only a few brief words, however he recalled the lass's tender gestures towards her father and her face so full of the expectation of life that she looked as though she would fight her way towards it.

It was quite an improper exercise no doubt, but harmless, Hamish had decided. He had seen her, admired her and was in a position to be of assistance to her and, of course, the girl's father benefited as well. It was a splendid arrangement and the monthly reports he received as to her progress in her studies were a most enjoyable diversion; until he found himself thinking more of her than polite society would have deemed correct.

Hamish's conscience argued this was his chance to help a woman. To study her progress, to ensure her happiness and in doing so not only was he rescuing the young woman, but he was also proving by his very actions that some women were special and deserving of admiration, even if it was from afar. However, as the weeks passed, Hamish acknowledged his interest in Claire went beyond the purely altruistic motives he'd convinced himself of. In fact he found himself wanting the girl. He doubted Claire would be bored or indifferent like his wife and he was certain she'd not betray a loved one as his Mary had. His dilemma lay in the distance between himself and the young Claire, and in the singular, sad fact that he was already married. For the time being he decided he would content himself with reports of Claire's progress. The girl certainly wasn't going anywhere and neither was Rose; whereas he would make a trip to Sydney in the New Year.

❧ *Autumn, 1987* ❧

Centennial Park, Sydney

'*H*ow was the shoot?' Jeremy asked as he passed Sarah a bunch of Australian natives and kissed her cheek. He moved to the small kitchen in her apartment and, pulling out a glass, helped himself to a beer, draining it immediately. 'What a day.' Loosening his tie, he undid the top button of his starched collar. His cheeks, slightly flushed, contrasted sharply with the whiteness of his shirt. 'Ah, Miss Gordon is unhappy.'

Dropping the flowers into the kitchen rubbish bin, Sarah pushed the banksia and wattle roughly inside until the flip lid slid back into place. Jeremy leaned against the laminate bench, a stunned look on his face. 'Hey, what did you do that for?'

'You're drunk,' Sarah said tightly, taking in his red face and slightly dishevelled appearance that was so at odds with his usually pristine appearance.

Jeremy sighed. 'There is a difference between being drunk and absolutely buggered, Sarah.' He went to the bin and retrieved the flowers. Turning on the tap over the kitchen sink, he filled the tub with water and plonked the flowers into the cool liquid. 'I brought these back from the mountains for you. If you had bothered to return my telephone calls you would have had them before this.'

And what exactly was she meant to say to him? Sarah wondered. Gee, come right over, I've missed you and by the way how did the weekend go in the double bedroom at the B&B with your mystery guest?

'You know I tried to call you early Sunday morning,' Jeremy wiped his hands dry on a tea towel. 'I thought you could have come up for the day.'

'I was busy.' It was easier to lie, Sarah decided, than reveal that she had sat and listened to his voice on her answering machine before deleting his message.

'Come on, Sarah, this isn't like you. What's the matter?' he asked, sitting on the couch beside her.

'How was your weekend?' She waited for a reaction, but the expression on his face never altered.

'You weren't the only one doing the telephoning. I rang you. Well I tried to. I was going to come up on Saturday after my shoot finished early; that is until I learned that you were already ensconced up there in the nice private bedroom with a *friend*.'

Jeremy laughed. 'What?'

Sarah took a deep breath. 'It's Julie Miller, isn't it?'

'What are you talking about?' Jeremy looked at her, confusion obvious, then he sank back into the couch. Slowly, he straightened his tie, shaking his head thoughtfully. 'I have always loved you. Ever since the day I met you at the gallery. You were like a broken flower, fragile and closed off from everyone around you. But I waited and I persevered. Here's a girl I could love for the rest of my life, I told myself. Here's a woman worth fighting for and helping. And I did help you, didn't I, Sarah?'

'Yes,' Sarah replied softly, confused by the sudden change in topic.

'When you cried for your brother, I held you. When you deliberated over your mother's accusations regarding your part in Cameron's accident, I listened.'

'I know.' Sarah didn't want to hear any of this.

'Your family didn't see what they did to you, what you did to yourself through your tortured memories and then I met your mother and I prayed to God that you weren't going to end up like her in the years ahead, disorientated and out of touch with reality.'

Tears now spilled down her cheeks. 'I won't be like her. I won't.'

'And here you are accusing me of having an affair with Julie. Yes, we shared a room for a day. Yes, I could have slept with her. Shit, part of me wanted to sleep with her to get you out of my mind. But I didn't. Julie was only there on Saturday. We discussed business and then she drove back to Sydney. Before dark.'

'Oh.'

He lifted his hand to stop her from speaking. 'I've told you that Julie is just a friend; a very old friend, but you still don't trust me, or want to trust me or perhaps you just don't love me enough.' He walked towards the door of the apartment. 'Look I've had a big day. I signed on two new clients,' he smiled briefly at the thought. 'I would have liked to have shared that with you, Sarah.'

Sarah walked towards him as he opened the door. 'Don't go, Jeremy.'

'I've an early start. But we should try and get together over the weekend, I think we need to sit down and –'

'I can't,' Sarah bit her lower lip. 'I'm going away for the weekend.' She hurried on, 'Grandfather asked me if –'

He shook his head, 'So you're going back to Wangallon again.' Sadness ringed his eyes. 'The morning we drove through the boundary gate when we arrived for Christmas, I saw that look in your eyes. You've never looked at me the way your eyes caressed that bloody bit of dirt, Sarah. And then I saw it again the morning Anthony arrived during the flood.'

'Jeremy you're wrong. He's a friend.'

'And it's the same look when he calls you on the telephone. Maybe you can't accept your feelings, like you can't accept your life had to change after your brother died.'

'How can you say that?'

'You know, I figured that if I never doubted your commitment you would stay with me. Well this time I want you to go back to Wangallon. I dare you to go and face your feelings. Decide whether you love him or me and then put one of us out of our misery.'

The apartment door slammed.

Sarah, her eyes fixed on the closed door, crumpled to the floor. Did she love Anthony? How could she when everything Jeremy spoke of was true? Jeremy was the one who had cared for her, talked through her problems, reminding her constantly that she was a good person, both capable and deserving of a happy life. Gathering herself together she poured herself a glass of merlot and sat on the kitchen bench. Jeremy was right about one thing though. She loved Wangallon and regardless of whether Jeremy wanted her to return to Wangallon or not, she was going home. She had made her grandfather a promise.

✠ *Autumn, 1987* ✠

Wangallon Station

*T*he plane began its descent. Sarah looked down at the neat paddocks devoid of movement. Stock hung in groups, shaded by trees, grazing on remnants of fodder. An occasional vehicle crossed the land, heaving balls of dust into the air. The fields closer to town showed small irrigation systems watering a variety of crops, the slight difference in colour providing a vibrant contrast to the brown desolation.

The Dash 8 aircraft and its thirty or so passengers landed with a shudder and the plane taxied slowly across to the small terminal building. There were only six flights a week making Friday's early morning flight very popular, especially the day before a picnic race meeting.

'Hello, Sarah.'

'Hi,' Sarah replied quietly to Anthony's welcoming voice as she walked into the one-room terminal. He looked good, tanned and lean. 'Where's Grandfather?' she blurted out, aware that her suddenly heightened senses made her guiltily aware of Jeremy's recent accusations.

The dark eyes dulled before narrowing into a frown. Swinging Sarah's travel bag over his shoulder, Anthony strode off in the direction of his utility. He walked quickly. 'Well, it *is* a 300-kilometre round trip, Sarah,' Anthony said over his shoulder. 'It's a fair drive when he has to come in again tomorrow for the races.'

At the vehicle her bag bounced onto an old mattress in the tray as the driver's side door slammed. Instantly Sarah wished she had not been so damn unfriendly. She was, after all, pleased to see him. It was just that she was torn between Jeremy and the obvious distress she had caused him and the hum of nervous anticipation she was currently experiencing.

'Sorry.' Sarah's own door closed as the vehicle accelerated out of the car park. 'I just didn't expect to see you.'

'So I gathered.' His fingers clenched the steering wheel as the utility sped in and out of a dismal flow of traffic. Within seconds they were parking, and Anthony left Sarah to follow him into an antique shop. 'Just have to pick something up.'

Inside the shop Sarah scanned the interior. Coffee tables and sideboards bustled for room alongside ornately carved chairs, lamps and an assortment of silver, crystal and porcelain all displayed in tall glass cabinets. Anthony, in quiet discussion with an elfish-looking gentleman with a contagious smile, ran his hand along the edge of a small dining room table that appeared to be oak, although it was in the process of being wrapped securely for transportation.

'Nice piece,' she commented, running her fingers along the smooth surface. 'It's yours?' She vaguely recalled a pair of high-backed Australiana chairs and matching hardwood sideboard that his mother had sent up to him along with some other items during his first year at Wangallon.

'Yes, it's mine.' He smiled easily, locking his eyes onto hers until she smiled back.

'Good taste, love. That's what your young man has. From the moment he walked into my shop I thought to myself, now here's a bushie who is used to more than the average. On all counts, if you don't mind me saying,' the shop owner finished with an exaggerated wink.

'Well, I'll let you finish packing.' Outside the shop Sarah dawdled in the main street. She loved the fact that he'd wanted to make Wangallon his home from the beginning. He'd been a jackeroo, bunking down with the other staff in the men's huts, occasionally having to share his room during branding and shearing when extra men came in to help during the busy times on the property, however he still had his precious bits of furniture that made the place home to him and he always accepted the contractors' taunts about his *stuff* with a smile. In his progression from jackeroo to station hand, little had changed, but now he was the manager of Wangallon. Sarah thought of the lovely oak table inside and of her old home, West Wangallon, which was now his home. It was almost as if Anthony was living the life meant for her brother.

Thirty minutes later the table was resting top down on the mattress, the extension leaves secured inside the frame. The vehicle moved at a steady pace over the bitumen. Leaving the town they slowed to pass through a herd of cattle, Anthony lifting his hand in salute to the three drovers travelling steadily behind their charges. The cattle were road-weary, their bones protruding at sharp angles through a thin covering of skin. Some of them looked ready to drop at any moment.

'There's another two thousand head only a day's walk behind them. They'll lose a few, but they're better off picking up what feed they can here than dying up north where they've come from.' Anthony caught the expression of interest in Sarah's eyes and settled a little more comfortably in the driver's seat. 'You'll like your new horse, she's a beauty.'

'I can't wait to ride her.'

When they arrived at West Wangallon, Sarah and Anthony carried the table up the cement path, resting it near the back door. Sarah was loath to enter after managing to stay away for so long, but how could she not help Anthony without feeling foolish?

'Better call someone to help,' she suggested.

'Why? It's not too heavy for you, is it? All the extension leaves are out of it and . . .'

He stopped, as he realised his mistake. 'I'm sorry, Sarah.'

'I suppose it shouldn't bother me.'

'Look, it's my fault. I forgot you haven't been inside since –' Anthony stopped. None of the Gordons had lived there after the flood, and Sarah had not been back since the day her father had left. At the other end of the table, Sarah took hold and gestured to him to keep going. This was not the time to be sentimental, she chided herself as she gritted her teeth.

They manoeuvred the table through the kitchen and living room, only just managing not to bump fingers and arms on doorways.

'What do you think of the place?' Anthony asked when they had finally placed the table in the dining room.

'It's so different.' Gone were the memories of that last Christmas. The dining room was a golden yellow. A gilt mirror hung over a low old-fashioned sideboard empty except for a tray holding two bottles of rum. The table, taking pride of place, was surrounded by six tapestry-backed chairs.

'Your grandfather gave me the chairs. They're fairly ancient.'

A colourful rug lay over the polished floorboards. Old black-and-white portraits covered a wall.

The entire house, altered substantially, exuded a warm friendly feeling. They moved from the dining room to the lounge room, where Sarah studied the suitably sombre early-twentieth-century portraits.

'Grandparents in here and parents in the dining room. Keeps everyone happy,' Anthony offered.

'The perfect family?' Sarah asked, raising her eyebrows at a series of framed movie posters depicting western actors from the fifties.

'Exactly,' Anthony agreed chuckling. 'I'll make us some tea.'

After boiling the kettle, Anthony and Sarah moved into Sarah's old bedroom, which had been transformed into the sitting room. Anthony passed white tea and a shortbread biscuit from the packet and settled back in his chair. 'Sorry, didn't have time to bake.'

'My favourite,' Sarah grinned taking a bite of the crumbling mixture. Breakfast, consisting of thick bitter coffee and what appeared to be an excuse for a muffin on the plane, had left her ravenous.

'What do you think?'

'It's good.' Similar to her room at Wangallon, the view from her old bedroom took in the entire garden, except her mother's beloved flowers no longer existed. Only the mature trees survived, the grass thinning out towards the rear of the garden. Through the windows the midday sun warmed the soft-coloured room. Dried bulrushes rested in a large terracotta urn in one corner, a smaller dining table and TV filled another. Rows of books lined one wall, while the two comfy armchairs they were seated in were uphol-stered in kangaroo hide, while a cattle hide sat squarely in the middle of the room. A particularly fine fox pelt mounted directly on the wall opposite caught the sun's rays. She walked towards it.

'Cameron tanned this, didn't he?' Sarah asked.

'Yes.'

Touching the silken pelt, Sarah brushed the fur upwards. 'I miss him,' she said simply. It was years since they had spoken of him. 'You and he were great friends.' If she closed her eyes, she could see Cameron lounging in the chair next to Anthony's, staring with amusement from beneath ruffled light brown hair, a lopsided grin widening into a full-throated laugh.

'Yes, we were.' Anthony put his cup down and rubbed his hands on his jeans. 'The three of us were once, Sarah. Why do you keep staying away? Why don't you come home?'

The question hit her like a bucket of water, dissolving the image of her brother instantly. Sarah tried to answer, the words dissipating even as they formed.

'You can't let go of Wangallon as I couldn't let go that last day by the creek when I asked you to stay. It took me a while, but eventually I understood your decision. But now it's different. I think you're still deciding.'

'Deciding?' Sarah heard him get quietly to his feet, and immediately she thought of the squeaky floorboard he would hit if he made his way across to her. She glanced at the remains of her mother's garden through the windows, shuffling her feet on the boards beneath.

Anthony crossed the floor between them to stand slightly to one side of her. Her thick hair fell back over her shoulder to reveal well known contours. He watched a small vein throb beneath the soft skin of her temple, studied the high cheek bones. Tentatively he lifted his hand.

Sarah swallowed, the noise sounding inordinately loud. Why did she feel so troubled about giving him an answer?

Anthony stared at the soft skin and lowered his arm. He could sense her nervousness.

'I have to go.' Turning, Sarah brushed past him, the momentary closeness causing her to take a deep intake of breath. It was then that he kissed her, his hands firmly grasping her shoulders. Sarah didn't respond immediately, but she soon found herself lifting her hands to the side of his face, her fingers tracing the outline of the scar that had entranced her since her teenage years. His kiss was deep and pure and Sarah let herself be engulfed by a surge of passion. Then Jeremy's image came to her and she was untangling herself from Anthony's embrace and racing through the rooms, past her brother's old bedroom and outside into the safety of fresh air and space.

Back at the relative safety of Wangallon homestead, Sarah sat on the end of the path, boots scraping the dirt, watching numerous ants march relentlessly back and forth. Three fought fearlessly with an upturned beetle, small legs clambering over thrashing parts, before once more joining their comrades. She followed the ants' progress, likening them to herself, Anthony and Jeremy, wondering who was chasing who. Noises of dogs and machinery dwindled with the rustle of brittle grasses. *Anthony*. He was part of the landscape of Wangallon, like the tall trees hanging thirstily over creek banks, a reminder of her youth, of Cameron. She had successfully managed to keep the past where it belonged – behind her – yet suddenly, irretrievably, it was altered and images from their shared times together were flooding her mind: the night at the stables, out riding, swimming in the creek. And with the memories came those of Cameron. Sarah began to sob quietly.

Her tears splattered on the cement path. Wiping her eyes, she rubbed her nose on her shirt sleeve. What was she doing? Did she really want to open herself up to allow something to happen with Anthony? She didn't really know how she felt about him and she had already decided how difficult it would be to return to Wangallon. And what if things didn't work out with Anthony and he resigned? What would happen to Wangallon then? Sniffing loudly, Sarah wiped her cheeks with determination. She was being a melodramatic fool. At least with Jeremy she always knew where she stood. Most importantly, he couldn't break her heart, not like her brother did with his death and not like Anthony might if she allowed herself to get close to him. In truth, she couldn't bear any more loss.

That night while her grandfather showered, Sarah dialled Jeremy's number. 'Jeremy, it's me.' She could imagine him sitting on his pristine white sofa refusing to pick up the telephone.

'I just wanted to say that I'm sorry. I've made a real mess of things. Anyway, I promised Grandfather that I'd go to the picnic races with him tomorrow, that's why I'm back up here. I'll be staying at The Overlander motel tomorrow night if you need to call me. Thanks. Bye.'

◈

'Goddamn that jockey, he is about as useful as tits on a bull. Sorry, girl.'

'Don't apologise, Grandfather, I think you're probably right.' They smiled at each other, tearing up their third consecutive losing betting tickets. Behind them the horses entered the enclosure, the place-getters lining up to receive congratulations from owners and trainers to the cheers of the few lucky onlookers.

'Bad luck, Angus,' a jovial-faced man called out.

'Hmm. Bloody bookmakers.'

Dust swirled across the racetrack, hitting the crowds dispersing from the trophy presentation. Women clutched frantically at their hats as their partners walked swiftly to escape the wind. Buffeted by gusts of air and dirt, Sarah and her grandfather battled the remnants of the luncheon throng gathered around the boots of cars and retreated to one of forty vehicles lined up, noses to the railing.

Sipping chilled white wine from their eskies, safe from the sting of the drought, the crowd only left the calm confines of their vehicles to place bets and watch each race. It had been a long day, the racegoers appearing more exhausted than the horses. Sarah knew the organisers would be disappointed. The meeting was not a success. Entries were down, as were the crowds and the jovial atmosphere present last year.

Angus, his hands slightly shaky, poured coffee from a thermos. He sipped slowly, his forehead creased with age, deepening as he thought. He was still strong enough to survive a few years yet, but Wangallon's future needed to be cemented, just in case. His family, the spiritual custodians of Wangallon, relied on him to ensure that the land continued to be guarded. It was providence then that the picnic races had presented themselves as his excuse to get the girl back up from Sydney relatively quickly. It was just a matter of logistics and the timing was perfect, coming as it did following Matt Leach's interesting snippets.

'You have got to make your mind up where you want to be, lass. Here in the bush or in the city.'

Sarah glanced at him quickly, the clear eyes composed, the hands still. Angus watched the brightly coloured riders enter the track for the next race, their mounts prancing and pawing the ground in the flying gravel. He wished they were discussing commodity prices, the purchasing of a new tractor, anything than trying to force the girl's hand. The announcer called out the name of each horse as they entered the starting gate.

'Girl, I know you better than your parents, better than Anthony.'

'I'm sure the grey will win this time, Grandfather.'

'Listen to me, girl, being defensive won't help. Your father sits in the sun, staring out at the water, dwelling on his old life while Sue potters in the garden, absently growing roses. Don't throw away your life. I'm sure you don't want to end up like them.'

The race began in a flurry of muted yells. In the car next door, five adults were cheering wildly, hats knocked askew, spilt champagne dribbling down the inside rear window. Angus pretended to concentrate on the race, watching the knuckles of his granddaughter's fingers grow white as they tightened around the stem of her wine glass. Well, he decided, at least the girl's attention was back on Wangallon. The horses screamed around the turn, and in disbelief he watched the grey pound past the winning post; yells of abuse streamed out of the car next to theirs.

'Shall I repeat myself then?'

'I'm not throwing away anything.'

Angus stared beyond the peeling paint of the fence, past the garish colours of the apprentice jockeys. Out there lay the only thing valuable – dirt. It was just part of the cycle: once you learned not to try to control it, just to accept it, it was easier. The droughts couldn't hurt Wangallon, nor the floods; it was far too big an enterprise for God to destroy. Only stupidity could destroy Wangallon and in the bush that usually lay with the next generation.

'Sarah, I think you feel there is some sort of competition between you and Anthony. There isn't. You'll always be just as important to me as he is, more so because you're my girl, the only one with any guts, the same as your great-grandfather Hamish. Still, Anthony is also vital to Wangallon.' He had her attention now. 'I have my preferences, you have your own priorities, somewhere in between the two I think we agree the current situation needs little alteration. As long as you and Anthony get on, Wangallon and the two of you will be safe and the future secure.'

'What are you trying to tell me, Grandfather?'

'God damn it, he's in love with you, girl, and if you would stop and smell the roses as the saying goes, you would probably realise you love him too. Damn and blast it, the world's gone mad when two young people can't see they are made for each other. I've been waiting for bloody years for you two to come to your senses. Once you do, everything will fall into place.'

'You-you have?' Sarah stammered.

'Didn't I just say that?' This gentle politeness took some working at. 'Look, I'm sorry to hurry you, but I'm not getting any younger, and it's important you understand the future.'

His stare was hard, a thousand-yard stare, her brother used to call it.

'The future?' Sarah queried.

'A lot of our ancestors died for Wangallon and, between you and me, girl, there were shifty deals a-plenty in its acquisition. Still, the Gordons have held property in New South Wales since the late 1850s, and I know you'll agree when I say it has to be protected at all costs.'

'At all costs?' Sarah repeated. What on earth did that mean?

'Good! Now that I know you understand, we'll get down to basics in the morning.'

The town hall was decorated with bright streamers and balloons, while the local jazz band, its members resplendent in an assortment of black garments, played and sang with great enthusiasm on the slightly raised platform serving as a stage. The hall was filled to capacity, and laughter echoed off the high wooden ceilings and peeling walls, as wine flowed and a fragrant curry was consumed ravenously. Caught between two graziers, Sarah ate her own dinner in silence with a bottle of wine for company, as they spent forty minutes arguing good-naturedly about the economy.

'Twenty-eight per cent, I tell you. Australia contributes around twenty-eight per cent of the world's wool production and over half of the world's wool trade.'

'But not now, Alec. We've flogged too many prime merino rams to places like Argentina and the like.'

'Well, I don't know, but I'll tell you one thing, you can sell as many rams as you like over there. They're not being grown in Australia, and that makes all the difference.'

To interrupt them seemed pointless, so Sarah leaned across the paper tablecloth and, pushing aside a collection of unused plastic knives and forks, helped herself again to the rough red wine. At least it was alcohol, something to dull her grandfather's cryptic words. Love, inheritance, pride, Anthony – it was all too much. Was her grandfather insinuating that he intended to leave the property to Anthony, or to both of them to be shared equally? Or did it depend on the type of relationship she and Anthony had in the future? Sarah shook her head and took a large gulp of wine.

'The European community is still our largest market for wool.'

'No it's not.'

'It is when it's real cold.'

'Don't expect things to pick up for a while price-wise, mate. The Chinese aren't rushing to buy.'

The wine tasted much better. Still, as much as Sarah tried to numb her mind, it wasn't working. She scraped her chair back noisily, standing with equal clumsiness. Her companions looked up, gave brief farewells and resumed their disagreement. The band, now relieved of their ties and jackets, played loudly to their followers, a dedicated collection of varying age and ability, most of whom appeared to be struggling to remain upright. The men's lapels held small flowers, and the hall's decimated flower arrangements bore mute testimony to the scavengers' work.

Sarah wandered outside. A long trestle table erected beneath two stately lemon-scented gum trees lit with floodlights served as the bar. A number of forty-gallon drums stocked with wood burned brightly, and it was here that the racing crowd gathered together, jostling for both heat and alcohol. Sarah struggled through the mass of tobacco and alcohol fumes and finally, a rum and coke in hand, took a long drink. It would be her last for the night, she decided.

'Dance?' Colin's voice was rude and demanding.

'No thanks, Colin.' A corner of his shirt was untucked and torn, dirt stains coloured his pale trousers and his red tie was askew.

'Come on.' He yanked her roughly by the hand, causing her drink to spill as he pulled her through the crowd of partygoers.

'Stop it. You're hurting my hand.' Managing to extricate herself, Sarah took a step backwards.

'You'd say yes if I was Anthony,' Colin slurred.

Sarah ignored the jibe, screwing her nose up at his breath, a potent mix of rum and cigarette smoke.

'You continually coming up from Sydney. Woman like you. Anthony's got a great opportunity coming to him. Don't ruin it just because there is no other way for you to get hold of a piece of land your family didn't want you to have.'

Instinctively Sarah raised her hand to slap him, but he caught her wrist, squeezing it hard, a sneer spreading across his concave face. Tugging her arm back quickly, Sarah took an unsteady step backwards.

'How dare you comment on my life? It is none of your bloody business!'

Colin's flushed face contorted, his drooling caterpillar lips drawing tightly together. 'All of a sudden the old fella starts to get a bit of age about him and the granddaughter begins to fly in real regular, like a vulture.'

Sarah felt a surge of bile rise in her throat. 'Colin, you're fired!' He stared back at her for a moment, his eyes disbelieving. Then he was gone, disappearing into the crowd.

Sarah left the area quickly. Groping her way through the trees bordering the edge of the Town Hall garden, at the fence she hitched her skirt up and slipped effortlessly between the wires. A voice trailed her escape, smothered by the crunch of gravel underfoot as she ran across the council car park and finally reached the road and her car. Head pounding, she rested one hand on the bonnet of the car as she fumbled for the keys. It was all too much, Colin's accusations, her grandfather's words, the insinuations.

Anthony's hands touched the woollen shoulders of her jacket at the exact moment Sarah sensed him. Automatically she clutched the jacket to her body, wondering how much he heard, wishing her head felt clearer. Then she felt his fingers on her forehead, following the line of her cheekbone tenderly. Her breath tightened as he caressed her neck. His body was close, so close she could see the sparse blonde hairs at the base of his neck. Gently he lifted her chin upwards.

'What did he say to you?'

The breath escaped briefly from her throat in relief. He'd not heard. 'Nothing.' She waited for Anthony to speak as the moon, bright and unforgiving, highlighted his tired face, touching the fine lines, shadowing the strong bone structure.

'I'm sorry I was late coming in tonight. We had a breakdown with the feed truck and –'

Anthony edged forward with incredible slowness, his breath touching her lips. She could smell alcohol. 'We never planned anything.' She placed her hand lightly against the firmness of his chest, recalling her less than graceful exit from his embrace only yesterday. 'We can't do this, Anthony.'

'Do what?'

'Jeremy.' Sarah said his name slowly.

'He's not here.' Anthony kissed her gently on her lips.

She was confused and tired. She knew she should be backing away from Anthony, but the memory of their kiss yesterday overshadowed right and wrong. A light breeze rustled leaves as they twirled down the road as the rise and fall of music, laughter and shouts carried from the Town Hall.

'I thought about you yesterday after you left.' He held her face between the palms of his hands. 'I thought I'd scared you off.'

He kissed her once, softly and gently on her lips. His hand trailed inside her half-open jacket until his fingers rested against lace. He lifted her onto the bonnet of the car, his arm encircling her hips. The smell of him, the musky scent of his aftershave, the pressure of his body against hers sent Sarah's mind spinning. He traced the length of her spine before settling his hand on the small of her back. A distant sound of tearing came to her as he pulled her body towards him, her skirt riding to her thighs. Her skin tingled as his fingers grasped the nape of her neck and, finally, his mouth was on hers.

Sarah drew her arms tightly around Anthony, feeling the exquisite pressure of their bodies touching, leaning forward into his embrace. Then the sensual pleasure changed to one of urgency. Sarah placed her hands over Anthony's as he caressed her thighs before pressing his hand on the small of her back so that his groin was hard against her. In response she automatically wrapped her legs about his body. She felt the cold metal of the car beneath her back, and was conscious of the moon through the tree canopy above her as her hands stroked the muscles of his broad back. She kissed him back fiercely.

'God, I'm sorry, Sarah,' Anthony gasped. Having anticipated this moment for so long, he knew if he didn't stop immediately, he would not be able to contain himself. No, he was not taking her out here in a damn council car park.

Sarah slipped off the car as Anthony, his supporting arms gone, retreated. Her heart was beating so rapidly she could barely think. She ran her fingers through her hair to steady herself.

'I'm sorry, Sarah, I didn't want things to get out of hand. At least not out here. Come home with me.'

'I can't.' Flustered, she adjusted her skirt.

'Of course you can.' He was beside her again, his arm encircling her shoulders. 'I'll drive. We can come back in the morning and pick up your car.'

'But I'm meant to be staying in town. Grandfather booked a room and . . .'

'Better still,' he grinned.

'What about Jeremy?'

Anthony swore under his breath. 'What about bloody Jeremy?'

'He's my boyfriend.'

'And what am I meant to do about that?' Anthony asked.

Her face coloured with embarrassment.

'Are you coming home with me or not?' His face, briefly illuminated by a ray of moonlight through the overhead foliage, looked angry.

Dreading his answer, Sarah asked, 'Is this about Wangallon?'

Anthony gave a sour laugh. 'I'm not even going to dignify that question by replying.'

My God, Sarah thought, was that what her grandfather was alluding to? He had hinted about the two of them being in love, about safeguarding Wangallon. Sarah could see it now. It was the perfect solution to her grandfather's inheritance quandary. If they married, a Gordon would still be on Wangallon and Anthony would run the property and there would be heirs with Gordon blood. Did Anthony actually think she felt the same? That she was prepared to do anything for her inheritance? 'We've obviously both had a little too much to drink,' she managed to say.

'And I can't do this psychoanalysing bullshit at the moment, Sarah. I'm sorry.' Anthony walked into the darkness, intent only on reaching the bar and downing a couple of rum and cokes quickly. He liked her, but she was hard work, difficult and stubborn, and how the hell did Wangallon come into the conversation? He stalked back towards the growing noise of partygoers, aware the few beers he had consumed earlier probably hadn't helped. If he'd been sober he doubted he would have kissed her again. He reached the bar and jostled among the drinkers to place his order. Yesterday's kiss had been a spur of the moment thing. It seemed right at the time, even if he probably shouldn't have done it. But hell, it made up for not kissing her all those years ago when Cameron was still around. Shit, now he had to go and find Colin and drag the kid home, but not before he'd had a couple more drinks. He caught the bartender's eye. 'A double, thanks.'

Sarah ate her fried bacon and eggs quietly as she tried to block out thoughts she could not unravel. The earth seemed to have swallowed her up unawares and exhaustion gnawed at her bones.

'You're looking a bit pale today, girl.'

Sarah gave her grandfather a weak smile and took a sip of water.

'Big night?'

An understatement, considering she spent the later hours of it staring at the light bulb above her bed in the motel room.

'The ravages of alcohol, hey? I thought you would have been in practice, what with all the swanning about you do in Sydney.'

'I don't swan.'

'Right. Save me the petulant outbursts, girlie.' Angus tapped his teaspoon on the edge of his teacup. 'What is all this about, Sarah? Is there something you're not telling me?' He asked gruffly. Then, more kindly, 'Did you and Anthony have a fight?'

'Yes.'

'What is it with you two?'

'I'd rather not talk about it.' Sarah pushed her plate of half-eaten breakfast to one side.

Angus rubbed his eyes tiredly. 'Well you better. I've already received a telephone call from Colin this morning.'

'Colin?'

'Yes, Colin. If you and Anthony have to argue, I would have thought you would be able to find something a little more interesting to argue about.'

'What is that meant to mean?' Sarah asked defensively. 'I fired Colin. He was drunk last night. He was rude to me in front of a large group of people. Not only that, but he caused my accident with Blaze.'

Angus studied his granddaughter carefully. 'Do you have any proof?'

'Why? Do I need it, Grandfather?' Sarah retorted.

'No. But, you can't fire Colin, lass. Only Anthony can do that.'

'Why? You're the boss, I'm your granddaughter,' Sarah said hotly.

Draining his teacup, Angus leaned back in his chair. 'Oh, Colin will go, lass. Make no mistake about that. I myself never took to the boy. He has a streak of the feral in him. However, the timing is critical. You know how difficult it is to get people to work in the bush these days. Anthony will give him a talking to, and set about finding a replacement before he leaves. I always thought the boy was missing something in the top paddock.' Angus tapped his own head. 'As for you firing him, well, you should know better, Sarah.'

Sarah slouched back in her chair, crossing her arms.

'Now don't go getting all petulant. I guess you and Anthony didn't get to talking about life, love or Wangallon?' he queried carefully.

Sarah sighed. It was better that the truth came out immediately. 'Anthony wants Wangallon, doesn't he?'

'Is the Pope a Catholic?' he asked incredulously. 'Sarah, near everyone in the bush would like a slice of Wangallon. It's a historic, top-producing bit of dirt and there's a bloody lot of it. Now what's bothering you?'

'Wangallon's always been there for me. But I had to leave it.'

305

'I know that. But you've thought of coming back for good.'

'I miss the country.' Sarah looked out the window next to their breakfast table. 'I miss the land and the feeling of continuity, but it's cost me a lot personally.' The wind stirred the leaves in the tree across the road, an empty plastic bottle rolled randomly in the gutter. 'I have all these memories, Grandfather, but they seem to have been swallowed up by a hundred different things.' And now the cherished image she'd always held of Anthony was disintegrating as well. 'Anthony's not the person I thought he was.'

'No-one ever is. But you do care for him, don't you?'

A fleeting picture of Anthony's lips on hers came to her. But it was useless, she thought sadly. She had made a terrible mistake in assuming the past could be rekindled. If Anthony wasn't at Wangallon, she couldn't live there and if he was there, well, she would feel the same devastation at her misjudgement of him, at her loss, every time she saw him. How was it possible to have misread him so? It never entered her mind that he would do anything for a chance of being left Wangallon.

Angus smiled. 'I was about to relegate you to the useless bin. I'm sorry if you felt threatened by Anthony's role in the running of the place, but let's face it, someone needed to be trained while you fluffed about down in the city. Wangallon is yours. It's always been yours. You're a Gordon, like I said yesterday. You're blood, it has to be yours. You have to understand it needs strong management though. We have that already, of course, but provisions have to be made. My will is contingent on Anthony staying on as manager. After all, he is indispensable. I firmly believe the two of you will do a fine job together.'

'But –'

'For the first five years you have to defer to him.' He winked. 'I can't imagine you'll find that too difficult. The two of you have always had such a special bond and I'm aware, my girl, that your all-too-frequent visits have not been for a doddering old grazier.

Now that you suddenly seem to be seeing Anthony in a new light I'm hopeful that you'll be moving back up here shortly.' Angus slurped the remainder of his tea.

'Moving back?' A sickness seeped through her bones. The conversation was moving at the speed of light.

'Well, what did you think? You'll hardly be able to make a go of things in Sydney.'

'But Grandfather –'

'My terms include you living on the property for five years, with Anthony as manager.'

Sarah looked blankly at her grandfather. 'I need to see Dad,' she finally blurted out. There was no-one else for her to speak to. 'I'll ask reception to book a seat on the coach across to the coast.'

'What's the matter with you? This is a momentous occasion. Not to mention a major milestone in your life. I expect you to say something along the lines of "Thank you, Grandfather", or "I'll do you proud, Grandfather", or "You'll never regret this, Grandfather".'

'That's the problem,' Sarah said, aware of how angry he was. 'I might.'

❧ *Autumn, 1987* ❧

The Gold Coast, Queensland

Sarah gave her father a hug and followed him down the marble-floored interior into the open-plan kitchen. Dropping her leather overnight bag on the couch, she walked through the pale green living room and out onto the patio. Never would she get used to seeing her father here. He was like some type of bush creature in captivity, surviving because he had decided to do so, for the moment. At the back of the house, surrounded by palm trees on gently sloping lawn leading to the river, her mother sat at a small wrought-iron table, arranging roses. They walked across the cosy wooden sundeck, passing bags of fertiliser, potting mix and a variety of rose-filled terracotta pots.

'Sarah, darling, what a fabulous surprise,' the voice cooed.

She located her mother's cheek beneath an oversized hat and saucer-shaped sunglasses. Ronald said she was fine and Sarah supposed she was, in her own way. Alone with her mother while her father went to make tea, Sarah waited for her to speak. She knew her mother preferred it that way. The hands continued to fuss with the assortment of roses standing proud in a tall vase. Sarah cleared her throat, carefully and quietly. Sighing deeply, her mother pulled all the long-stemmed roses from her arrangement and tossed them on the table. Removing her gardening gloves, she turned to face her daughter.

'Everything's great,' Sarah said, in response to the silence. She watched the corner of her mother's mouth flicker. 'I came to visit from Wangallon.'

Her mother removed her sunglasses, cleaned them with her shirttail, and rested them on the table. 'You're pregnant?'

A powerboat dashed past them along the river, pulling a skier behind. Sarah looked on in embarrassment as her mother yelled out loudly, stamping her gumboot-encased feet and raising her fist in the air. The boat vanished at the next bend, and she sat down abruptly as if their conversation had never been interrupted. 'Jeremy's asked you to get married?' She replaced her sunglasses, and now she was smiling. 'You've broken up with him?' She frowned at her hands, then lifted her chin to resume her stare at her daughter.

'It is nothing like that, Mum.' Sarah stretched her hand out to touch the pale softness of her mother's cheek. 'Mum, everything is fine, really.'

Her mother sniffed. 'I don't see how everything can be fine, as you put it. You have been going out with that young man for what, fifteen years?'

Sarah hunched her shoulders and sat back in her chair. 'Nearly three, actually.' Beyond the sloping grass lay the canal, wide and brown, rippling with the wake of the recent speed boat. Her mother removed her sunglasses, wiping the lenses on her floral jumper before placing them with great control on the tabletop.

'Remember who you are talking to, girl. Cameron never talks to me like that.'

'Cameron?'

'Perhaps we should see how Ron is getting along with the tea. It's really getting a little too cool to be sitting out here, you know. Still, it's so pleasant and so nice to watch the boats on the river. Such nice people on the river, don't you think?' Her mother plonked the cut stems into the vase and, gathering the roses, threw them, along with her sunglasses, into a row of palms bordering the garden wall. 'Let's have tea.'

The three of them sat at the cane table next to the kitchen. They talked aimlessly, non-political chitchat that passed between them and touched no-one. Then her mother announced she was going to water the roses.

'She is comfortable here,' Ronald assured Sarah, rising to gather the dinner plates and place them on the bench in the kitchen. 'So what happened at Wangallon to make you come running up here?'

'Nothing.'

Ronald poured more wine into both their glasses. 'How's Jeremy?'

'Good.' Guilty as charged, she thought. Jeremy could never know what happened, never. 'Anyway, Mum would be comfortable, as you call it, anywhere, Dad. Ever thought of going back to the bush? To Wangallon?' Sarah joined her father on one of the tall stools at the kitchen bench. He looked uncomfortable, like an emu on a budgie's perch. 'I sort of figured this move to the coast was for Mum's benefit and having seen how she is . . . well, it seems to me that you'd be better off at home. You and Grand-father could . . .'

Ronald slammed his fist on the bench, the impact rattling the collection of seashells sitting loosely at the base of a small lamp. Sarah spread her hands on the granite bench top, using the surface to steady herself. It had been stupid to mention her grandfather, she knew they barely spoke. And, having seen her mother, she now appreciated the strain her father was under.

'Sarah, I've made my share of mistakes, and my father knows that.' The large hands were steady, folded across his chest. 'Leave my life to me.'

'But Dad, you don't owe Mum anything. If anything . . .'

'If anything, what?'

The years melted away and it was as if they were all back in the kitchen again at Wangallon; the radio playing in the background, Cameron rolling his eyes and her mother threatening to pack her off to Sydney until she'd finished her final exams.

'Dad, don't you think it's time to recognise the wrong Mum did to you and me?'

The old tightness rose in Ronald's chest before sinking into resignation. He felt his shoulder's slump and the weariness that invariably accompanied his early evening hours since moving to the coast made him rub irritably at his eyes. He didn't want to be having this discussion with Sarah. There was clearly little possibility that his daughter would feel any respect for Sue.

'It was hard for me, you know.' She bit back her tears, surprised her father's face showed so little emotion. 'Would you ever have told me?' she asked.

Ronald considered the question carefully. 'No. I couldn't see the point. Well, it's in the past now.'

'That's all you have to say?'

'Geez, Sarah what the hell do you want me to say? Was I shocked and shattered? Did I know Cameron wasn't mine? Yes, immediately. Did I blame your mother? No. We never should have married. She was like this delicate flower that arrived at Wangallon in full bloom and then started to fade from day one. I couldn't give her what she wanted and within six months we both knew we shouldn't have rushed into the relationship. Your grandfather warned me, but I wasn't perfect either, Sarah, so I accepted your brother as my son.'

'Who was he?' For years Sarah's imagination wavered between a Valentino-like figure, someone worthy of a woman losing her heart to, to the nasty intruder whose stealthy methods succeeded in stealing both her mother and brother.

'A wool buyer,' he shrugged. 'Sue said she was in love and I would have let her go, but a few weeks later he was dead; killed in a bungled robbery apparently.'

'So you stayed together.'

'It was 1961, Sarah. Besides, it seemed the right thing to do and, as I said, my life was far from perfect.'

'I don't understand. After everything that you've told me, why would you leave Wangallon for Mum? Why would you not consider coming back and becoming involved again. You could advise. Manage.' Sarah slumped back on her stool. 'Why would you want to be *here*?'

His eyes were steely. 'The place has taken too much from me. Wangallon's time is over.'

After a quiet dinner of grilled steak and green salad with coriander and parsley, Sarah told her father about the conditions of inheriting Wangallon. Ronald kept his face expressionless, glancing only once into the next room to check on Sue, who was watching television with the sound off.

'You declined, I hope. Really, Angus is a bloody old fool.' He poured a generous glass of shiraz. 'You live and work in Sydney and you're in a serious relationship. It's a most irresponsible suggestion. All this –' he emphasised with a huff of disgust – 'is in addition to the fact that you are a young, single woman. He expects you to live on an isolated property?' Ronald laughed.

'Dad, listen to me, I didn't decline.' Or accept, Sarah thought. She knew she had to give her grandfather an answer, if only because he had probably taken it as a foregone conclusion she would accept his terms. But this was something different. Her father did not want her to inherit Wangallon.

When he finally stopped laughing, Ronald spoke with great amusement. The thing he loved the best about his father's cock-amamie idea was that the will was contingent on Anthony staying on as manager. That, he said, was truly remarkable. 'So reading between the fine print it would seem that Dad expects you to marry Anthony eventually.' Splashing shiraz into his daughter's glass, he took a sip of his own drink. 'So it's quite simple: if you want Wangallon, you must eventually marry Anthony. Bloodline secured, inheritance secured and Wangallon continues.' He slapped the table for emphasis.

'Bloody hell, Dad, why are you being so flippant? Why does there have to be conditions. Why Anthony? It's impossible.'

'Don't agree with my father for the sake of Wangallon. Nothing is worse than not following your . . .' Ronald lifted his glass and took two long sips before emptying the remains of the wine bottle into his glass. 'My advice to you is to accept the terms of the inheritance. Just say yes. A will is a will after all, Sarah, it's not open to discussion.' He paused, replacing the cork in the bottle. 'Sell it when the time comes. If need be you could contest it. You're the sole heir after all; you would have a legal entitlement. There is no place for sentimentality in business, and the days of arranged marriages are over. Wangallon's time is over.'

Sarah's mouth gaped. 'Dad, I can't do that. How can you ask me to sell Wangallon?'

'You haven't lived in the bush for ages.'

'But it's wrong. I'd be lying to Grandfather and what about Cameron? We can't sell the land he's buried in. And what about all the others buried there? Our forefathers?'

'Cameron's gone, Sarah, and the Gordons' time is over.'

'But, Dad –'

'Don't be so bloody melodramatic, girl. If the place meant that much to you, you would have stayed.'

'That's really unfair, Dad.' Sarah couldn't believe her own father could so easily forget the hurts of the past, specifically what she'd endured.

Ronald shrugged his shoulders. 'You're my girl and I know enough to understand your initial reasons for leaving. Sometimes life gets in the way of our best intentions, Sarah. And sometimes it's for the better. You have a good life now and you have a good man by your side. Don't ruin that happiness by following some romantic notion involving obligation and ancestors.'

'But –'

'Go to bed,' Ronald insisted. 'Get some perspective.'

❈ Late winter, 1867 ❈

Wangallon Station

Rose sat quietly on a three-legged stool near her bedroom window, her slim fingers working nimbly. Having managed to prick herself three times already she willed herself to stop imaging Abdullah's beautiful face, to stop reliving the moment his moist lips touched her skin. She sucked at the bead of blood welling on her index finger and, carefully wrapping a piece of cloth around the wound, continued in her task. Having unpicked the neckline of her rose pink gown and inserted a length of delicate cream lace, she found the effect perfect. It framed the luminous sheen of the silk perfectly and, Rose thought with a small blush, would compliment her complexion. Her fingers touched the slight indentation on her neck and once again she imagined Abdullah's lips on her skin. Deftly she turned the dress over and with two neat stitches, bit the cotton with her teeth. The gown now featured a deeper neckline with a new cream lace edge. Rose admired her handiwork one more time before resting the garment over a high-backed chair to air.

Having instructed a rather moody Mrs Cudlow on the household's meal requirements, the day was filled with a series of small duties. Rose checked her wardrobe and continued the sewing of the moss-green silk gown. With barely three hours a day free, the completion of the gown became both crucial and a major task. The skirt, over two and a half yards in diameter, took quite some cutting and sewing, while the tight-waisted bodice, scooped neckline rounding to the shoulders and small cap sleeves, were of a design Rose never previously thought of attempting. Even now she could not help but giggle at the thought of Abdullah flicking through the pages of a two-month-old Sydney department store catalogue. His long, tapering forefinger tracing each page until, abruptly stopping at a particular design, he had cried aloud as if making a miraculous discovery.

'This is it, Rose. This gown would be markedly fine.'

'Markedly fine,' Rose repeated, fingering the green silk lying on her bed. His fingers had reached out to touch her hand, moving effortlessly to the soft tender skin of her elbow. The closeness of his body affected her thoughts and she'd found it difficult to concentrate for the rest of the morning. Indeed she found herself hoping for a more intimate embrace. Even now, four days on, she still felt his lips on her. Surely Abdullah knew he was driving her to distraction.

With only an hour before dinner there was no time to spend daydreaming. Pouring water from the porcelain jug into a matching bowl, Rose added a few discreet drops of lavender water and began to undress. Surely it was her good fortune Abdullah's interests lay only in the transportation of Wangallon's wool and not in the growing of it. Wringing the linen washcloth free of excess water she rubbed soap into the soft cloth before wiping her face, neck and underarms. Heaven forbid if he developed a liking for sheep, horses or the interior of their woolshed, she thought, such as his older brother, for then their time together would be limited indeed. She swirled the cloth through the soapy water, wringing it again before washing her breasts and torso. With a critical eye Rose examined her reflection in the small oval mirror above the mahogany wash stand. If only she had a little of her mother's rouge, she contemplated, turning her face first to the left and then the right. Certainly her face would be agreeable to a little colour, especially when she was wearing the rose silk gown tonight.

'Oh well.' With a sigh, Rose unpinned her hair. Freshly washed only a few days prior, it fell past her shoulders in a veil of brown. Lifting her silver-backed hair brush she began her customary hundred strokes.

Later that night, over a dinner of kangaroo tail soup, stuffed roast mutton, potatoes and green peas, Hamish and Abdul began a heated debate on the virtues of cattle and sheep. As a transport company, Abdul's livelihood depended on the carrying of wool, yet Hamish cautioned his friend about the growing importance of cattle.

'Diversification is vital to any landholder, Abdul, and so, by extension, any business.' Hamish sipped his wine appreciatively. 'To that end, your company would do well to consider investigating other modes of business. Sheep will not always be the mainstay of the country.'

'I believe, Mr Hamish,' Abdul inclined his head politely, 'that you indeed understand your business, but as for mine,' he lifted his wine glass to his mouth and sipped, 'well, there are certain aspects that I believe I am the more experienced in.' Reaching for his napkin he patted his moustache and beard with a birdlike pecking motion.

'Business is business, Abdul. Take my advice and thoroughly investigate your options.'

Hoping to break their argumentative conversation, Rose broke the short silence. 'And whose opinion do you share, Abdullah? That of your brother or my husband?'

'Neither,' Abdullah answered shortly, his face a mask. 'I do not argue over which commodity may succeed over the next years in Australia, for such a question is unanswerable. Each commodity has its time and place, and one can either follow or lead by seeking new avenues and ensuring continued livelihood.'

'Here, here!' Hamish slammed his fist on the table, the silver cutlery rattling loudly on their empty dinner plates.

Frowning in irritation, Rose reached to stabilise her own fork, perched as it was on the very edge of her plate.

'I can only hope the path my brother and Mr Hamish choose is correct, for I do not wish to starve on account of bad management.'

'Agreed, brother,' Abdul answered good-naturedly. 'As always he is the diplomat. And our loss at your leaving will surely be the reward of those in Karachi.'

'You are leaving?' Twisting the napkin between her fingers, Rose waited for confirmation of what in her heart she knew to be true. 'Leaving New South Wales?' She searched Abdullah's unblinking gaze.

Hamish coughed. 'Congratulations, Abdullah. Abdul informs me you are to take charge of the business in Karachi. And Rose, my dear, he is to marry. Is that not wonderful news?'

'Wonderful,' Rose agreed quietly.

Hamish poured himself more wine. Rose felt her chest constrict, her breathing became rapid.

'Yes, a very welcome addition to our business in Karachi.' Abdul raised his glass. 'To you, brother.'

'To Abdullah,' Hamish repeated.

Hamish was nodding in her direction now. His glass held high, his full lips curling into a semblance of a smile. Rose willed her own lips to turn upwards. Did Hamish know of her feelings, she wondered?

'I shall leave you, gentlemen, to your cigars and port.' Excusing herself from the table, Rose inclined her head towards her dining companions as she laid her napkin by her place setting. Avoiding Abdullah as he stood at her departure, she walked slowly across the rug in front of the fireplace and out through the sitting room to the verandah, her low heels click-clacking quietly on the wooden boards beneath.

Outside, she rested her hands on the cool timber of the wooden fence. Tears did not come naturally to her; not since Hamish's revelation of the theft of Sir Malcolm's gift had she allowed herself the luxury of regret. Bitterness was her comfort; envy and loss when she thought of her daughter; disgust when she thought of her husband's black lovers. Over the years the small pool of sadness within her, untouched by summer's scant rain, managed to shelter her dead sons and protect the small memories held dear by her. A life like hers was survived in such a way. Why then should she be so surprised that this man from another world would not live his life in New South Wales? What had she expected?

'Your husband knows, I fear,' Abdullah said softly as he joined her.

Rose turned to him. Her heart ached for what she couldn't have. 'You should not have kissed me. It has changed everything.'

'Yes,' he answered. 'That is why I should like to kiss you now.' He took her hands in his.

Rose looked warily towards the homestead.

'They are arguing over the future of wool prices.' He turned her face towards him, his fingers strong and sure. 'Rose, I must kiss you.'

Later, when she thought of this moment, Rose knew she would be unable to tell who moved first. His strong arms encircled her body and she experienced the blissful crush of her breasts against the broadness of his chest. The fragrant scent of unknown herbs wafted from his clothes and the taste of wine mingled with the sweetness of treacle. His lips pushed down upon hers and as the breath began to leave her body, Rose felt herself go limp. His arms gathered her up, carrying her swiftly away from the verandah and to the seclusion of a clump of trees in the garden. He set her down lightly. Rose clung to him for long minutes, her cheek squeezed close to his chest. She felt his hand stroking her hair, the beat of his heart. Slowly, calmly, he let go of her.

'I do not wish you to be sad, my Rose.'

Rose allowed her arm to be taken and together they walked the perimeter of the yard in a semblance of normality. In the distance sheep could be heard calling to their young, a horse whinnied from the direction of the blacks' camp and closer to the homestead, small creatures scuttled through the tall grasses beyond.

'Loneliness makes us sad,' she answered truthfully. The dream of the last two weeks broke irretrievably as they walked arm in arm up the steps to the verandah. Once Abdullah left, life would resume with the regular monotony endured for the years already lived here. She would rise as the sun did, complete her day's journey regardless of inclination and slip into darkness with the last rays.

'Not sad for my leaving, I hope, for I would not wish to be responsible for that.'

'You ask me not to be sad, Abdullah?' She sat heavily on one of the packing-case chairs, gathering her thoughts as she spread the rose silk of her gown smoothly across her knees. 'I never thought beyond each day we shared. I thought only of the sweetness of each moment together.'

'The fault is mine.' He spoke softly, each word strewn with longing. 'I allowed myself to be entranced. Perhaps if we'd not spent so much time together, Rose.'

'Perhaps.' But she knew better. Passion did not come lightly to her. There was a deep connection between them.

'I know from how you spoke when I first arrived, how quickly the words rushed from your mouth, any words; then as the days continued, your gentle speech slowed until we could just sit in silence and yet still talk.'

'Yes,' Rose agreed. 'It was good.'

'Very good.' Abdullah reached over to touch her hand softly. Her look made him feel as if he were a young child again, a child within reach of a precious gift. 'A present of friendship, for tomorrow I leave.' From within his coat pocket, Abdullah retrieved a gold bangle. He slipped the beaten metal over Rose's wrist and took a number of paces backwards from her.

Rose fingered the bangle gently, her slender forefinger and thumb touching its surface as she pulled it around her wrist. 'Tomorrow?' She thought foolishly of the moss-green silk dress he would never see her wear. 'I thought perhaps a few more weeks?' The maids were giggling quietly in the lean-to behind the kitchen, their voices carrying on the wind. In the kitchen, Mrs Cudlow was speaking in angry tones, Lee's agitated voice talking over hers.

'In four days the camel train arrives, Abdul will depart, and your wool clip, one of the largest in New South Wales, will be en route to Sydney to be shipped to London.'

Rose shook her head as if the action would erase his words. 'I know all this, Abdullah. I just thought that, well –' She looked into her empty hands.

'Your husband knows there is something between us. At dinner tonight . . . his reactions, well, he knows. I do not wish to cause unnecessary trouble.'

Then you should not have kissed me, Rose thought.

'It is best I leave.'

'For whom?' She couldn't help but ask the question.

'I hate Australia, Rose, and the whites that populate this country, claiming it as theirs. They have no more hold over this new land than the Chinese or the Afghans. All searched for a new beginning, a chance for money, so how could the whites declare themselves sovereign over a land that belonged to all? A convict settlement no less.'

'I can't answer that.' She wanted to tell him that she didn't care about any of those things.

'I don't wish you to. Few are like you, Rose, yet if we were in a town or city, Sydney perhaps, would you cross the street so as not to pass me by; me a dirty Afghan?'

'Abdullah!'

'Were it not for your feelings of desolation, for the fact your husband has forsaken you . . .'

'Abdullah,' she strained to keep her voice low, 'why are you making excuses for how I feel about you?' Rose felt her heart increase its beat.

'So you see the real world. There will be many battles in the future, Rose, between whites, blacks, Chinese, Afghans. They go on now but few hear the truth. Already there is resentment towards us. You employ us, the Bourke Carrying Company. Our camels travel for many days without water or a rest day and flourish on saltbush, bluebush, mulga and continual work. Yet your bullock teams complain we steal their business. Men are sent to attack our trains, kill our cameleers and ruin our business. It is not only us that lose in the end, but your people are too ignorant to see that. Then there are those like your husband, important, respected men, who –' Abdullah stopped midsentence to sit in the chair beside her. 'I apologise. I should not speak such words to you.' It was an unsought attraction and an impossible one. 'I am not happy in this country.'

'Have they stolen, cheated or murdered to get to the position they are in today? I think these are the things you are asking me, Abdullah, asking indirectly of my husband. I see your anger. We are, or some of us whites, as you call us, are like that, but then I think all races of the world have such people.' A stray tear stole silently down her cheek. She was both lucky and unlucky to have met such a man. 'Do you wish me to agree with you, Abdullah, convict my race for the sins of the few?' Rose could feel the perspiration building at the backs of her knees, between her breasts and on her forehead, even as the air grew colder. 'Why do we argue,' she whispered, 'when tomorrow you will be gone?'

'I sold my twenty per cent share in the Bourke Carrying Company to Abdul. This is why I now depart for Karachi to my new life.' He swallowed, turning his body in his chair to face her. 'I am to marry my cousin.'

'I see.'

'I have a fine house and a number of servants, yet it is a jail to me, Rose.'

'There are many jails, Abdullah,' Rose answered wearily. Surely he realised that she was uninterested in his fiancée or his future. There were only a few significant moments left for them; a brief caress, the aching promise of a kiss. Rose wept inwardly. Why were the fates against them when in another lifetime their fledging relationship would be fluttering with anticipation?

'Our cameleers rest between consignments in small corrugated huts. Ghan towns, the whites call them. Here my people arrive for a short term only to stay forever, their blood intermingling with the low whites through need, with the mixed blood of the town blacks through desire. And the whites think them dirty heathens! My people will never truly be welcome here, Rose. I will never truly be welcome.'

'But why do you tell me this?' Rose asked quietly. Tomorrow he would leave and the desolation, a devastating hollowness, already wound its hand tight about her waist. Once he left she would be alone again: a woman without love, a woman without his company, his soft words, his look of pleasure when she entered a room. How could she tell him of the enjoyment she experienced in his presence, let him know of her lifted spirits, her sense of value, of being needed. How could she stand the empty years ahead?

Abdullah moved to kneel by her chair. In Karachi, as a senior partner in the company, he would be wealthy, happy and safe among his own people, with a wife thought quite beautiful, though he was yet to meet her. Placing Rose's slim hands between his, he squeezed them gently before twirling the bangle slowly about her wrist. He studied her rose silk gown, the insert of lace purchased by his own hand in Sydney, the way the fine weave of the material pulled across her breasts. 'I tell you these things because I love you.'

Rose gasped. Immediately his warm fingers were on her lips, soothing her and then, gently, slowly, he leaned forward, his hand resting on the nape of her neck, his lips touching hers for a second, a fleeting brush of two lives. The aroma of sweet cigarette smoke and the taste of rich wine hovered in the air and then he withdrew.

Abdullah wondered at the existence of such a fragile creature out here in a land he himself disdained. Her delicate neck, endowed with the graceful sweep of a swan, the fanning out of those finer bones to meld with the faintly blue veins beneath the skin of her chest, the generous swell of her breasts. He stemmed his thoughts for already the signs of his yearning were beginning to stir. Yet her breath, sweet and untouched, reminded him of his youth; the gentle, insistent pressure he felt as he withdrew from those soft, yielding lips proved her affection. Abdullah looked out over the darkening forms in the garden, aware the woman's husband sat only a wall's thickness away from him, conscious of the four young boys asleep inside. The leaving of Wangallon without her troubled him deeply, yet there was more to his heartache for his departure was laced with guilt. Nothing would expel the blame Abdullah carried within his heart. It was true Rose was unknown to him at the time of Hamish's request, yet the bitter truth of his betrayal could not be undone.

Rose waited, wanting him to kiss her again, needing to feel his warmth about her body, aware of the pounding of blood deep in her chest. At one point his hand, warm and sticky with perspiration, caressed her neck, cupping her head and carefully pinned hair with such tenderness she believed she would swoon as she had earlier in the garden. It seemed such a little thing. He was leaving in the morning and she would never see him again. One kiss. One more, she pleaded silently, imagining his dark face next to hers, picturing the long length of his lashes flickering against her cheek. Yet he remained immoveable, her thoughts undetected. She prayed for him to sense her longing. 'Abdullah, why do you tell me of your love?' His figure remained rooted to the edge of the verandah, to the edge of her world. The desperate longing within her turned to fading hope.

'I tell you these things, Mrs Rose Gordon, so that you will understand my affection. So you will know my heart. I leave you with sorrow.'

'Why, why must you leave?' Even as she spoke the desperate pleading in her low, plaintive voice reminded her of how dependent on this man she had become.

'Because you are white and I am Afghan.'

He stepped out into the blackness of the bush night. Oblivious to propriety Rose walked swiftly along the wooden boards of the verandah. She would run away with him. She would sail to this place Karachi and she and Abdullah would lead a new life. By noon tomorrow Wangallon would be a distant memory. With only the slightest hesitation Rose reached the verandah steps and lifted the pale silk skirt of her gown. Abdullah's footsteps crunched dirt and fragile grasses. Behind her familiar footsteps sounded on the verandah.

'Come inside, Rose.'

Hamish extended his hand to her. Rose listened to Abdullah's passage, his movements growing faint.

'Rose.'

If she didn't follow Abdullah, it would be over.

'Have you forgotten your children?'

She took the first step tentatively. Perspiration stained the silk of her gown where she clutched it.

'He didn't ask you to go with him, did he?'

Rose took another step. Her legs were beginning to shake slightly.

'You are making a fool of yourself, my dear. And worse, you would desert your own children and become what you detest in me, an adulterer.'

Rose faltered. 'An adulterer?'

'And a hypocrite,' Hamish emphasised.

He had taken her arm and, childlike, Rose allowed herself to be led indoors. 'How did you know?' she asked faintly.

'You have become a schoolgirl again these past days. Initially I found it amusing until Mrs Cudlow informed me of your impropriety. The good woman seemed torn in her revelations. It appears you have a friend in the woman, but eventually her concern for our children outweighed any obligation she felt towards you.'

'What about –' She hated to say Abdullah's name aloud. She was suddenly scared of the consequences.

'Abdullah?' His hand tightened on her arm. Rose flinched. 'You will not see that heathen again.'

Abdullah left early the next morning. He awoke to a trace of fear circulating in his blood and he hurried to make space between himself and the husband of the woman he coveted. Hamish Gordon was a powerful man and it was best he decided not to rest or linger through the heat of the day. He would keep moving until nightfall. At Wangallon's boundary fence he drew the dray to a stop to take a sip from his water bag. Dawn was approaching, the first rays of another day stretching its fingers over country cooled by the fleeting hours of night. Behind him the dirt track was empty. It wound back desolately through a sand ridge awash with lizards and small birds, disturbed by his passage. Bird calls and warning screeches had shattered the pre-dawn silence causing Abdullah to spend long anxious minutes looking over his shoulder. Now there was only silence, punctuated occasionally by morning birdsong. He was safe. No-one followed.

Abdullah's knowledge of the girl in Sydney gnawed at him. Even as he'd kissed the sweetness of Rose's lips last night he fought his desire to warn her of the young girl being educated and cared for. After all, he cautioned himself, he didn't know what Hamish's intentions were. Perhaps Miss Whittaker was a project of sorts. Perhaps Hamish knew of the girl's family and, knowing their pride prevented them from accepting any kindness, chose instead to remain an anonymous benefactor. Besides, what was the point in telling Rose of the girl's existence? He certainly couldn't have taken Rose with him to Karachi. Apart from her being completely ill-suited to that world, the effect of his actions on the family business would be catastrophic.

Even so, telling Rose about Claire Whittaker was the right thing to do. Whatever the repercussions, he owed Rose the truth and in some minute way he believed the sharing of such knowledge would help eradicate some of the shame he felt.

Re-positioning himself on a cushion, the only padding between him and the splintery seatboards of the dray, Abdullah flicked the reins. The horses jolted to a slow start. Immediately he felt the unpleasant sensation of his bones jarring in a discordant rhythm over the rough ground. In three hours he would reach the staging post for the Cobb & Co coach and in four he would have managed some food and perhaps a nip or two of rum and water. He swatted at the flies crawling over his hands and face, glanced once over his shoulder at the empty

327

road and settled back patiently for the first leg of his long journey.

Abdullah decided that, when he finally reached Sydney, he would make one last call on Mrs Cole. Write one more report on the girl's progress as a gentle reminder to her benefactor of his continued presence. What Hamish Gordon needed to remember was that it was he, Abdullah Abishari, who held the cards at the moment. He only needed to alert the newspapers to the whiff of a scandal and Miss Whittaker and her secret benefactor would no longer be anonymous. And he need only send a telegraph to Rose and she would have her own evidence of her husband's betrayal. Abdullah smiled to himself, pleased with the sudden improvement in his circumstances. Knowledge was a wonderful commodity and Karachi was a long way from Wangallon Station and Hamish Gordon.

❦ *Autumn*, 1987 ❧

The Gold Coast, Queensland

*R*onald smiled. It was a soft warm smile of love. 'Jeremy called while you were out walking on the beach this morning, Sarah. He's on his way up from Sydney. He's booked an apartment for the weekend at Main Beach. Here –' he passed a leaf from a small notepad – 'the address is there.'

'But how did he know where I was?' Sarah queried.

'You called him and left a message about staying at The Overlander. Supposedly the receptionist told him that she'd booked a seat on the coach for you.'

'Oh.'

'Why don't the both of you come by tonight for dinner?'

❖

Late that afternoon after a perfectly wonderful day of walking on the beach and wandering the busy streets, they drove to a small park leading to the water's edge. Jeremy spread a blanket over freshly mown grass protected by a hedge of bougainvillea. A gentle sea breeze washed over them. Seated, another blanket spread over their legs, he pulled smoked salmon, pâté and champagne from a bag and then lit a candle protected by a glass funnel.

'When did you manage this?' Sarah asked.

'The receptionist in the lobby helped me out. Before you say anything,' he began, 'I just want to apologise for everything that's happened recently. We've been through a lot. You've been through a lot, Sarah.'

'Don't apologise. You're right about what you said in Sydney. You did care for me and help me through a really tough period in my life when I had no-one else.'

Jeremy draped his arm over her shoulders. 'Sometimes I think if it was just you and me we wouldn't have any of these problems.'

'I know.'

'I didn't sleep with Julie, you know. We were working.'

Sarah knew she was the last person who should be passing judgement on other people. 'Guess I jumped to conclusions.'

'Well, I can't blame you for being annoyed with me. It was a bit inappropriate from your point of view.' He poured her a glass of wine. 'We're going to have to trust each other.'

Sarah thought of the kisses she and Anthony shared, two in two days, and drained her glass.

'You okay?' Jeremy asked.

Lulled by the reflection of the streetlights illuminating the expanse of white beach and the noisy unfurling of foamy waves, Sarah nibbled on some pâté. 'Sure, just thinking.'

'Good things I hope.'

'I feel like I've been manipulated by everyone. Anthony, Grandfather, even my dad. Everyone feels the need to tell me what to do.'

Jeremy pulled her closer. 'They all care about you, Sarah. I have no doubt in my mind about that.'

'I suppose.'

'You know things started to get tangled between us when you started returning to Wangallon on a more regular basis.'

'I know, but I feel torn between my Sydney life and the pressures of being the only Gordon who can inherit.'

Jeremy's hug tightened.

'Now I realise how much you care for me to have put up with all the crap in my life. And I'm pleased you're here. Everything just seems to be a lot simpler when it's just us.' Sarah hugged him back.

'That's how relationships should be, Sarah.' His grip loosened. 'Especially if you love each other. You do love me, don't you?' He ran his finger down her cheek. 'It's okay. I know after everything you've been through it's hard for you to voice your feelings. Just know that I love you.'

'I know.'

Sarah sniffed the salty embrace of the ocean, her neck resting securely in the crook of Jeremy's arm, his warm breath hovering like a soft summer breeze against her forehead.

'This is how our relationship should be,' Jeremy said quietly. 'Not filled with arguments.'

If she imagined at some point in her life that she would ultimately be able to repair the damage coursing through her fractured family, Sarah knew now that she was almost too exhausted by it all to try.

'Your dad told me about your quandary with Wangallon.'

'Quandary? That's an interesting choice of words.'

'Your father is a businessman, Sarah. Family attachment aside, you should listen to his advice. I'm not really in a position to tell you what to do. But I personally believe, and I don't think I'm alone in my thoughts, that the days of the old bush are numbered. You have to look at ways of ensuring not only your future happiness, but security as well, and you are still in a prime position to ensure the work of your forefathers is kept alive.'

'How?'

'Your dad says the property is worth millions of dollars. You could sell it and the money could be invested in real estate and shares. Perhaps a small portion could go to form an endowment scheme established to entice young people to work in rural and regional Australia. That would be a fine use of the Wangallon legacy, don't you think?'

'Or,' she countered, 'I could sell a part of it and retain the rest. Anthony could stay on as manager.'

Jeremy wasn't convinced. 'If you keep it, Sarah, you'll never truly be free. You'll always be going back to visit. Don't you think you need, *we* need, a clean break? From everyone?'

The insinuation was clear. 'Hey, weren't you the one just talking about trust?'

'Okay, you've got me there. Just think about it though.'

'I will,' she agreed.

'I love you, Sarah.' Jeremy's arm tightened around her as he twisted towards her, his warm lips resting briefly on hers.

She nosed him gently in the cheek like a small puppy, guilt flooding through her. 'Let's drink to new beginnings,' she said, extricating herself from his grasp, sitting upright. The cooling air hit her beach-flushed skin like a splash of water.

'Absolutely.'

She watched him fondly as he opened a bottle of champagne and filled their glasses.

'To new beginnings,' he repeated, as he dropped something into her long stemmed glass.

Sarah followed the soft plopping sound to its final clink as it reached the bottom of the glass. Lifting the vessel to eye level, the many facets of the stone glittered brilliantly. Astounded, she took a large gulp of champagne before tilting the glass to prise the diamond ring from within. The stone glittered in the palm of her hand as a small pool of champagne fizzed against her warm skin.

'Will you marry me?'

Sarah stared at the stone.

'When I discovered you'd left Wangallon so abruptly I figured that maybe you had finally let go.'

'I –' The wind rose, the sand scattering itself in her hair and the soft whorls of her ears. 'I'm sorry, Jeremy, I wasn't prepared for this.'

'It's a wedding proposal. You're not meant to be prepared. You're meant to say yes.'

'I can't. At least –'

Jeremy took the ring from the palm of her hand and placed it in his trouser pocket then began packing up the remnants of their picnic. 'I think we better leave.'

'Hang on, please, Jeremy.' Sarah stood up.

'I'm listening,' he said but he continued to pack up, standing to shake the sand out of the blanket they'd been sitting on.

'Look, I'm willing to sit down and discuss our future, as long as you're willing to listen to my thoughts on Wangallon. Any decisions regarding Wangallon have to be mine alone.'

Jeremy looked at her. 'How can that be, Sarah? You're suggesting we do have a future together while telling me that I have no say in something that continues to affect our relationship. You have to be a bit fair. Shit!' He rubbed his face roughly. 'I asked your father for permission to marry you. Don't I look like a right git!'

Sarah looked at the man who loved her unconditionally, who cared for her and was trying to build a secure future for them as a couple. Had she really been so silly trying to keep their relationship in a holding pattern? Her dad was right. People like Jeremy didn't come along every day. 'We could use the money if I eventually sold part of Wangallon. Buy ourselves a house, even put some funds into your business.'

He looked at her. Sarah held out her left hand and extended her ring finger.

'I would love to marry you, Jeremy.'

He slipped the ring onto her finger, kissed her quickly and then, taking her by the shoulders, looked her in the eyes. 'You're sure?'

'I'm sure. As long as you understand that I don't think I could ever sell all of Wangallon.'

'And Anthony?'

Anthony, Sarah thought, is a damn good manager and if he is happy to stay on in that capacity then that would suit everybody. 'As my mother says,' she said firmly, 'he's staff.' Sarah kissed Jeremy, hugged him and glanced repeatedly at the ring on her finger. 'Let's go tell Dad.'

'Excellent news. Well done. Congratulations.' Ronald pumped Jeremy's hand enthusiastically and passed brimming glasses of champagne to Sue and his daughter. For once his wife appeared attuned to the occasion and capable of conducting a reasonable conversation. 'Congratulations, my darling girl.'

Ronald had an irresistible urge to call his own father and tell him of the impending marriage. He felt so damn pleased to be saving Sarah from a life at Wangallon and even more bloody pleased that the old bastard wasn't going to be able to put his foot on his daughter's neck.

'The ring. Show me the ring.'

Sarah proudly displayed the glittering stone to her mother.

'A spring bride,' Sue said happily. 'A morning wedding, glorious hats, lobster and champagne. How wonderful!'

Jeremy wrapped his arm around Sarah's shoulders. 'I have another surprise for Sarah.'

'You do?' Sarah beamed.

'What now?' Ronald asked. 'Don't go spoiling her too much.'

'A holiday,' Jeremy announced, taking a sip of champagne. 'Just thought of it actually; only a couple of weeks.' He squeezed Sarah's shoulders. 'We could both do with a break.'

'Excellent idea,' Ronald enthused, sitting heavily on a stool at the kitchen bench and reaching for the bottle of champagne.

Sarah was immediately concerned. 'What about your practice?'

'I have those two new clients; big ones actually. They aren't coming on board till next month.'

Ronald topped up everyone's glasses and raised his own in salute. 'Well done. So where are you going?'

'Scotland,' Jeremy answered.

'Fantastic!' Sarah yelled.

The bottle landed with a crash on the pale green terracotta tiles and smashed. 'Shit!'

'Here, Dad, I'll do it,' Sarah offered, bending to pick up the large shards.

'No, you sit down. Jeremy and I will clean up.'

The men busied themselves with paper towels, dish cloths, quickly sweeping up the mess.

'How about we head out for dinner now?' Jeremy suggested, noticing Ronald looked a little rattled.

'I'll go get my coat,' said Sue as she walked slowly through the kitchen towards her bedroom.

'Why on earth would you want to go to Scotland?' Ronald asked his daughter.

Sarah looked directly at Jeremy.

'Plenty of other places to visit – Italy, France, Egypt,' Ronald continued.

'It just seemed like a good choice, considering the Gordons are from there. And Sarah's got all those old photos of Tongue hanging in her apartment.'

Sarah kissed Jeremy on the cheek. 'Sounds like a great idea to me.'

Ronald scratched his head. If he told her not to go, she would question his reasoning and go anyway. The last thing he needed was the opening of another unsavoury episode in the history of Clan Gordon. 'No. I just thought that having made your decision about Wangallon it would be good to break all ties.'

'I guess the decision has been made,' Sarah thought aloud. Suddenly everything was rushing forward at a tremendous speed. 'Scotland it is.' She smiled at Jeremy.

'Bed and breakfasts and a hire car sounds like the go.' Jeremy felt now that he finally had Sarah.

'I'll call the studio and ask for some leave. Actually I've been thinking of going freelance.'

Jeremy waved his hand. 'Hey, don't leave them yet, we all still have to eat. Wait until we get back from our trip and then we can look at getting a bigger place to share,' he suggested.

'With a dark room,' Sarah added.

'Sarah, you'll have to go back and tell Angus personally, you know.' Ronald didn't want to dampen the moment, however the fact remained that Sarah owed her grandfather a response in person.

Sarah looked at her father. Slight jowls gathered at his chin and sagged downwards to flesh out his neck. He hadn't yet developed the sunken look about his eyes that aged his own father, but the beginnings of disrepair were evident – more emotional than physical, Sarah decided. This was a mental ageing that she knew he could control if he wanted to; if he only had the strength to pull himself into the future.

'Why can't you just telephone him?' Jeremy asked. He didn't want her back there. Father and daughter exchanged long knowing looks. He may as well have not been in the room.

'I'll go in the morning, Dad,' She looked down at the gorgeous ring on her finger, determined to block out tomorrow. 'Can I just ring Shelley and Kate before we go out for dinner? They'll be so thrilled.'

'Two bridesmaids.' Sue clapped her hands in delight. 'How wonderful.'

✑ Winter, 1987 ✑

Wangallon Station

The radio crackled loudly as the Toyota jarred along the dirt road. 'Two thirds of the state has been drought declared.' Seated between Sarah and Angus, Shrapnel tried to rest his muzzle on the dash, his cold nose repeatedly striking empty air. Finally he growled in annoyance before resting his muzzle back on Angus's thigh. Through the closed window of the vehicle, Sarah watched as a steady wind carried the topsoil of country hundreds of kilometres from the west across the road in sheets. Having arrived on the coach from Brisbane at 10 p.m. the night before, Sarah had read the accounts in the newspaper of the pall of red dust hanging over Sydney. Now the choking dust, lifted high into the atmosphere by the arid conditions of Australia's red centre, dropped over their vehicle, the gloomy pall shrouding everything in sight.

Her grandfather worked down through the gears as they approached a stock ramp. She knew he would never have considered the possibility of a negative answer and she felt the unforgiving stare of his violet eyes before they flickered back to the dirt track they had turned down.

'Problem, girl?'

Sarah shook her head as they turned towards the cattle yards, her right hand moving to softly stroke her bare ring finger. It seemed easier to take the ring off until she was ready to tell him her news.

Four horses stood motionless under a clump of belah trees as they drove up and parked beside two bull-bar-engulfed utilities. The horses munched laconically in the heat, a row of saddles resting along a length of fallen timber only metres from where the animals grazed. A couple of motorbikes and three horse floats were parked a little further away while the metallic sheen of a helicopter made the whole picture look like a trade show. They walked to where the men lay camped under a shady tree, the smell of both horse and human sweat greeting Sarah as the camp stirred. The wind blew steadily in her face, grit and dust clawing its way into her clothes, up her nose and down her throat. She coughed, squinting against both glare and grit. Anthony, clad in filthy jeans and a faded green shirt, jumped to his feet as they approached, his grubby hand extending quickly to shake Angus'. She felt rather than saw Anthony touch the brim of his hat in her direction. She barely nodded, staring instead at the jackeroo, Colin, trying her best to give him a look of pure disdain, grateful for the six contract stock-workers calling out cheery hellos to her as they shook Angus's hand.

'Boys,' Angus greeted them one by one. 'Well, Mick, how did you go?'

'Good. Some of the cattle were weak, but otherwise good,' Mick answered. 'Couldn't find that mickey bull that went for you last year, Mr Gordon.' Mick heaped fresh tobacco into white paper and rolled the cigarette, his fingers leaving smears of dirt on the thin white paper as he lit it and took a deep drag. 'Dead, no doubt.

Probably ran what little fat he had off himself and dropped dead. Stupid bastard.' Mick stopped abruptly and looked apologetically at Sarah. 'Sorry. Mad bugger though, wasn't he, Anthony?'

Anthony agreed. 'We were delayed, Angus. A lot of the steers were caught up in the far corner and we could only use the horses,' Anthony reported, though it seemed to him that his words sounded strained and not at all authoritative. 'Luckily the dust storm didn't get really bad until about an hour ago.' He willed himself not to look in Sarah's direction, moving instead to stand by her side.

'Be seeing you, boss,' Mick announced with a jaunty tip of his hat in Sarah's direction.

Anthony rolled his eyes.

'Visibility okay?' Angus asked.

'Yeah. No problems. Gotta get a move on. I'm due back in the Territory in five days.' Mick left the group with claps on his back from the surrounding men and walked quickly to what he called his 'bird'. Everyone watched, admiring the smooth swirl of the blades as the neat two-seater flew straight up. It hovered for a minute, then, with technical precision, the nose of the helicopter dropped in salute, before disappearing over the line of trees and into a blur of dust.

'Good trip, Sarah?' Anthony took a long look sideways at her, his mind returning to the passionate kiss so recently shared and Sarah's sudden outburst that night.

Sarah kept her eyes straight ahead. 'Fine.'

'Okay, you two. Save the bonding for later,' Angus huffed. 'Who is knocking off and who is staying?'

Sarah listened half-heartedly as Anthony and her grandfather chose the men for the afternoon. Colin and another stationhand were sent back to Wangallon, having commenced the muster at 5 a.m. on horseback with Anthony. An unknown worker, employed only for the muster, also left.

'Right. Anthony, that's five. Including me as supervisor,' Angus winked. 'Let's get to it.'

Sarah sighed as she pulled off her heavy jumper and did up the buttons on her shirtsleeves. She had rather hoped for two quiet days at Wangallon, giving her time to talk to her grandfather and keeping as far away from Anthony as possible. It was after two. Trucks were coming at six o'clock to collect six hundred head. These had been drafted and separated into another yard, so at least that task was already accomplished.

'There's only three hundred to be branded,' Anthony instructed as he crawled through the timber railings of the yard.

'What?' Sarah followed him, her back scraping on the rough hewn timber above her. 'In one afternoon?'

'And the non-sale cattle have to be taken back to their paddocks before nightfall, so they can forage for food and water.'

'Not by me,' Sarah said sullenly, suddenly suspicious of the grin on her grandfather's face.

'He's pulling your leg, kiddo. There's only one hundred and thirty left to be branded by the looks of things. We can thank the drought for throwing the cow cycles out of whack!'

'Great.'

Sarah stood halfway down the drafting race with a three-foot length of polythene pipe. Anthony was at the neck of the race and her grandfather at the swinging gate that would separate the cows from their calves. At the signal, Sarah took a step back to allow the race to fill. Out in the main body of the yards, the two remaining contractors herded the not-for-sale cattle into the deepest yard so they could begin walking them back to their paddock.

The majority of the animals were exhausted from the morning's long walk. But there were always a few waiting to cause havoc, reversing down the narrow drafting race, crashing into the railings and stirring those others weak from the drought. Within forty minutes the calves had been drafted off and were in the pound yard ready to be forced back up the race in single file.

Sarah's legs were heavy as she drank thirstily from the large water container sitting atop a yard post.

'You have lunch in town?' Anthony pointed to his esky. 'If not there's some food in there.'

Angus grumbled as he accepted leftover sandwiches from Anthony's esky, biting into a corned beef and raw onion roll. Sarah settled for half a corned beef and pickle, scooping some of the thick layer of the relish out with her finger and flicking it to her feet. A dog was there instantly to sniff at the offering in the dirt.

They battled it out for another two hours. Sarah stood at the side of the crush. The bellowing calves, frantic to be reunited with their mothers, were pushed from the narrow race into the steel tray that positioned the kicking and shitting animals on their sides. It was an efficient process. Anthony tagged the struggling youngsters in one ear with large plastic ownership tags, then earmarked the other ear with a quick snip of the flesh. This first job done, the young bull calves were then castrated.

Sarah grasped the intertwined 'G' branding iron. The iron, glowing red hot from a nearby fire, left a clear symbol of ownership in singed hair and skin. Sarah hated the stench, but it was the most efficient and least painful method. She lifted the iron in her right hand, placed her left boot on the animal's rump while Anthony held onto its tail. The job was over and the animal released before he knew what had happened.

Every so often, her grandfather stepped in to give her a break, but it was clear that he, too, was exhausted. She was debating what excuse she could use to get him to go back to the homestead, when Anthony spoke.

'Angus, another hour and we'll be done. I'm quite happy to

finish up if you want to take the boys back.' He gestured to where two riders were appearing from the scrub, having taken a couple of hundred head back to their paddock. Anthony spoke with concern. 'They're buggered, you know. Don't want to put them off the bush for good.'

'Good point,' Sarah agreed. 'I'll drive.'

'Not a bad idea. Sarah, you'll have to stay and help Anthony.'

Sarah didn't bother to argue. She was tired and hungry, but somehow she didn't think her complaining would change much. 'I'm not exactly accustomed to manual labour anymore. Bit out of condition, you know.'

Her grandfather gave her the same look he used when he hit a fly with his ancient swat in the kitchen at Wangallon.

Angus left the yards, Shrapnel nudging his right leg as he walked. He lit a cigarette, inhaling reverently. He knew every bird call, every nesting season, could sniff out a subtle weather change, the lair of a fox, discover where wild pigs nestled during the daylight hours and, when younger, get close enough to shine a light into a joey's eyes while it cocooned within its mother's pouch. And he knew young Sarah's mind was turning. Oh, he knew of Colin's behaviour, of the scene in the car park. A man needed someone to report on the gallivanting around the place, after all. What he didn't know, what he couldn't discover was what the argument consisted of. Lovers' quarrel? No. He shook his head. Well, as he'd often remarked to himself, you can lead a horse to water, but you can't make him drink, especially if the trough is as consistently unclear as Sarah. This was a situation he couldn't control, despite the years of planning, of selecting Anthony specifically. Oh, he knew he couldn't make young people fall in love, but they had always got on so damn well. Shit! Perhaps he should have attempted some of his father's tactics, done a bit of culling, got rid of the stray Jeremy, that ever-present boil, as persistent as a bad case of haemorrhoids.

'Lucky for you, old mate,' he said as his gnarled hand patted Shrapnel roughly on the head. 'A man needs some sensible people about him.'

Shrapnel wagged his tail in agreement.

By dusk, the calves and cows were reunited, and the yard gate had been opened to let them escape into the cooling night. Sarah leaned against the wooden railings of the yard. The steel bucket at her feet held ear markers and a pocketknife in bloodied disinfectant. Removing the implements, she lifted the bucket, tossing the contents onto the still-glowing branding fire, making it sizzle loudly. Anthony was checking the cattle for transportation before tying the remaining dogs up in the back of his utility.

At the touch of a cattle dog, Sarah squatted down to pat the dusty animal, letting his wet snout rest on her filthy jeans. Suddenly darkness descended, and with it the noise and bustle of the day dwindled to nothingness. She was conscious of cold air biting through the cotton sleeves of her shirt. The night encroached eerily. For the first time she felt alien to the land, as if it did not want her. She shivered. Whatever lay out in the paddock knew she intended to sell part of Wangallon, Sarah felt it in her bones.

'Sarah, I wanted to speak to you about . . .' Anthony had walked over to her.

Sarah busied herself with the steel bucket. She had managed to work beside him and not think. If only the trucks would come, then it would all be over. 'Nothing to talk about, really.' She brushed her hands on her jeans. 'I'm pleased we can still work together.' She walked to the utility, leaning into the back to lift the water container up and perch it precariously on the side. Family interference aside, Wangallon still needed good management.

'Let me help you.'

His skin touched hers momentarily as he tipped the container and he looked at her. Sarah cupped her hands and waited for him to pour water into them. She splashed the cold water on her face, shivering as it washed away some of the day's grime, then she drank heavily again. When she finished, she took a step back. Anthony was staring at her. Under his gaze, Sarah wiped the streaming water off her face and walked around the Toyota. She opened the vehicle door.

'I want to talk to you. Sarah, bloody hell, can't we talk?' He touched her shoulder.

'What's done is done.'

'What's done?' Anthony shoved his hands in his pockets. 'Do you think you could talk a bit less cryptically?'

An air horn sounded. 'The trucks are here,' Sarah replied. She could not bear his pretence any longer. Clearly Anthony and her grandfather had everything mapped out neatly between them. Anthony gets a lifelong management position on Wangallon, her grandfather ensures the Gordon name remains associated with the property.

'Damn.' Anthony lingered only a second before climbing into his vehicle. He turned the ute towards the main road, leaving his headlights on high beam so the trucks could see the yards clearly.

Two hours later they were driving back to Wangallon. Anthony, exhausted, fiddled with the radio before finally turning it off. Somehow, something of huge significance had happened to Sarah since the night of the races. It was as if the earth dragged at her, as if she had lost interest. Oh, she had worked in the yards, however it was more like she was just going through the motions. The vital, argumentative girl appeared to have been transformed over the past few days into a remote woman, one he barely knew. Anthony didn't know what to think or say. All he knew was that kissing her had been the single most stupid thing he'd ever done and it made things pretty damn awkward. He had to clear the air.

'I want to speak to you,' he hesitated, 'about the future.' He gritted his teeth. Talking to Sarah was akin to poking at a beehive to get at the honey.

She cared for him. She could admit that now. But he had let her down. He had let her down by misunderstanding the type of person she was, by assuming she would agree to their union for the sake of Wangallon.

'I'd like us to be friends,' he said cautiously.

'I'm sorry about the races, I was drunk,' she answered flatly, her fingers gripping the edge of her seat.

'Me too,' he answered, almost too quickly. He breathed a sigh of relief, yet his stomach felt hollow. At least they were halfway through their forty-minute trip home. The headlights haloed trees and kangaroos on the side of the road. Anthony slowed a number of times to avoid hitting the kangaroos that raced across the road in a kamikaze style attack on their progress. The remainder of the journey back to Wangallon was spent in silence, Anthony trying to think of something light-hearted to say – he couldn't even think of a decent joke.

'When I marry I want it to be for love. I want to know that the man beside me loves me for my sake only and not as a chance to get his hands on a piece of dirt.'

Anthony waited until their vehicle pulled up outside Wangallon homestead. It had been a very long twenty minutes. 'What?'

'You can deny it, but Grandfather's told me the conditions of my inheritance and I'm turning him down.'

'Do you know how ludicrous that sounds? A will is not something that you accept or turn down. Anyway, your inheritance is none of my business.'

She was looking at him with an expression of total disbelief.

'I guess with me coming home more frequently this year you figured it was worth a shot. After all we have a shared past and –'

Leaving the vehicle Anthony walked around and opened Sarah's car door. 'I think you better go inside, Sarah.'

'Why? Aren't you interested in what I have to say?'

He waited for her to get out of the vehicle. It was late and they were both tired.

'Anthony . . .'

'Don't.' He put up his hand to silence her. He just couldn't go through another argument with her.

'Just thought you should know,' she said as he got back in the driver's seat, 'I'm engaged to be married.' There it was. She had actually said the words.

Anthony opened his mouth to speak, however his mind was a blank. 'Congratulations,' he finally said, before shifting the vehicle into first gear and driving away.

Not even the heavy tea her grandfather drank lifted Sarah at breakfast. He rose, walking to the kitchen window. 'Your grandmother planted a passionfruit vine out here thirty years ago. The bees came and went, but somehow they couldn't get close enough to the flowers. There was hardly any fruit. Oh, it wanted to grow, wanted to live out here where so many things give up and die, but it wouldn't let itself.' His tone was defiant, his facial muscles taut. 'Couldn't let those little bees get close enough. Eventually the life just went out of it. First it was the flowers, then the entire vine withered and died.' His hands, sun-spotted with age, gripped the edge of the sink where he leaned. His eyes, slithers of violet, pierced the growing brightness of the room as the sun rose.

Sarah pushed her mug of tea aside. She couldn't do what her father suggested, she couldn't lie. Besides, she had Jeremy to consider now. 'Grandfather, I wanted to let you know that when the time comes, in the future, I intend to sell at least half of Wangallon.'

'That vine was stubborn and probably a little afraid: afraid like you, Sarah. You see your destiny but question your ability. And you place too much faith in others' opinions.'

'My ability was questioned the day you left Wangallon to Cameron.' Sarah could have almost hit herself for voicing something that was irrelevant now.

'You weren't the eldest.'

'And I was a girl.'

'That's bullshit!'

'Is it? You would have left Wangallon to me had I been a boy. After all I'm all Gordon, not fifty per cent diluted.' It was the first time she'd talked about how unfair she considered her grandfather's succession plan.

'So then what's stopping you now?'

'You're about four years too late. And your reasoning *now* isn't necessarily due to the regard in which you hold me.'

His eyes blazed. He paused, swallowing twice, to encase the anger welling within him. 'I've protected Wangallon all my life; seen a lot of stupidity, lost faith in my own boy. No-one will live comfortably on the blood of this family. Remember what I've said and remember your brother when you do.'

'I am. I'm second choice, Grandfather. I was when Cameron was alive and I still am.' Sarah waited, her hands trembling where they rested, sweating, in her lap. Her grandfather cleared his throat, folded his arms across his chest and drew himself upwards. His near-white hair framed his head like a halo. Sarah wished she were anywhere but in this room. His gaze was like a probe, hard and unforgiving. Sarah's spine felt as if it would melt into the kitchen chair.

'Your marriage choice is up to you. And yes, your father did ring and gloat about it. But if that is truly what you intend to do, if you really intend to sell Wangallon, then I won't leave it to you. On my death you'll receive one hundred thousand dollars, that's all. The property will be sold along with the members of our family buried here and the entire proceeds will go to charity.'

Shocked, Sarah quickly weighed the implications of his words. 'I would have to sell though. Can't you see how hard you're making it for me, Grandfather? I can't fulfil your requirements and live here for five years.' The words spluttered out of her parched throat.

Angus rubbed his chin thoughtfully. 'Very good, lass.'

'Why?' she whispered dazed. 'Because of Jeremy?'

'Hah!' Angus allowed himself the pleasure of a deep snort through his nostrils. 'Christ, girl, outta the entire population there's always a good ten per cent not worth feeding. It's like a line of fine Hereford cattle. Jeremy would be the first to go to the butcher.' His granddaughter's face paled. Angus shrugged. He was beyond conforming to the niceties of society anymore. It was a privilege of age. 'Sarah, my father lost too much in select-ing Wangallon. Christ, girl, your own brother's blood stains this ground. Don't kid yourself into thinking your forefathers can be forgotten. This is Gordon land, lass, solid, dependable, lucrative. I would sooner give it to the dogs' home than hand it over to be sold up and wasted. If there is no Wangallon, there is no family, Sarah. You once had enough brains to see that. Let's hope you find them again before it's too late.'

'But, Grandfather –'

'No buts, you've stuffed about in the city long enough.' He raised a hand to stop her questioning. 'You make the decision, girl, and stop bloody whinging. I know things have been difficult for you but it's about time you accepted your responsibilities. Being born a girl doesn't mean you can run away from them. The world might demand testicles when it comes to succession but I don't.

Basically you were next in line. Take it or leave it. But remember one thing. I want a Gordon and if you don't want it, well then, the dogs can have it.' His fist slammed down on the wooden table top, the force of the blow knocking over mugs and splashing the contents of the small jug of milk across the aged wood.

Stunned, Sarah could only watch as her grandfather stomped out of the kitchen.

≼ *Winter, 1987* ≽

Castlereagh Street, Sydney

'One hundred thousand dollars?' Jeremy paced the confines of his office like an angry terrier. 'Geez, you're all obsessed. Do they really think the place will go on forever? Good years, bad years, blah, blah, blah. Damn them all. Every couple of years there's a death and they all sit back and say "Shit, this is hard!" then it's back to the flies and the bloody heat. Bloody hell.'

Tired and dirty, Sarah stood silently in the centre of Jeremy's office. Having come straight from the airport expecting advice and support, she found herself grasping her brown leather handbag as her feet shifted uncomfortably on the thick beige pile beneath her.

'Your brother was probably the lucky one, Sarah. He got out early. Didn't hang round to watch you controlled by heritage or your mother go mad by it. Shit!' He sat heavily in his leather chair, then rose to swing it roughly around on its pedestal base, a stack of loose papers blowing off the desk in the ensuing draft. 'I should have known something like this would happen. Shit!

351

Well, just take the hundred thousand and get out. Sure the money would have been great, but we'll survive. It's not like I was counting on you for your inheritance.' He began shuffling cream manila folders, stacking and restacking them, moving the foot-high edifice from one side of his long desk to the other. 'The old bastard still thinks he's living in the early nineteen hundreds.'

A crystal water jug lay to right of the desk, a large glass paper weight to the left. For the first time Sarah noticed how incredibly large Jeremy's office and desk were and how incredibly bare.

'Jeremy, please. I know you're upset. So am I. I told Grand-father no. I told him to give the place to the bloody dogs but I'm trying to be rational about this. I can't throw away Wangallon, which is effectively what you're asking me to do.'

Jeremy looked as if someone had just thrown a bucket of icy water over him. 'It's for your benefit, Sarah.'

'Is it?'

'What kind of question is that?'

The dark brown panelled walls of the office swam around her. Sarah tried to calm herself. 'I understand that the bush isn't your scene, but you have to realise that I just can't throw away a multi-million dollar property; a property that has been in my family's hands for years.'

He stacked and re-stacked the files once again, the move-ment becoming slower, more controlled. 'If you accepted your Grandfather's conditions you would still have to move back to Wangallon with Anthony as manager until your grandfather's terms were fulfilled. Is that what you have in mind?'

'I could come down to Sydney every couple of weeks and you could come up and see me,' she offered hopefully.

'What? For five years? That's not exactly how I planned to spend my engagement, Sarah.'

'You don't really want me to throw away all that money, do you?'

Jeremy laughed. 'Oh, Sarah, I love how you can delude yourself into believing almost anything. You and I both know that this isn't about the money. It's about Wangallon. You don't want to lose it. You don't want anybody else to have it. If you don't go back and take up your responsibilities, you'll never be happy, Sarah. I can see that now. Even if you fail, which I sincerely doubt, you won't be happy unless you give it a go.'

'Jeremy, listen to me . . .'

'I need structure in my life, Sarah. I need someone who needs me as much or more than I need them. I can't play second best to a piece of dirt in bloody whoop-whoop.' He laughed again, running his hands through his blonde hair. 'I was a fool. Here I was thinking that poor old bloody Anthony was my main competition. But he's not, it's Wangallon.' Slumping down into the plush leather of his chair, he poured ice water from the crystal water jug. The water rushed down his throat in loud gulping swallows.

Sarah desperately wanted to say that she wanted to be with him more than her need to keep Wangallon, but she couldn't. Jeremy was right. She couldn't let go of Wangallon. She looked down at the lush carpet, at her dirty riding boots, the dry dirt of Wangallon already settling in the long strands of fine wool beneath her feet.

'I will never live in the bush, I can't, and you'll never be able to leave it.' He walked towards her, hugged and then kissed her: one long, painful brushing of his lips against her forehead. Then he was opening the door as if she were an unwanted client.

Words formed in her mouth, words of hope and encouragement, but she found she couldn't speak.

'I love you, but I need you to go, Sarah.'

Hooking her handbag over her shoulder, Sarah walked past him through the cool cream interior of the reception area towards the elevator, which, once entered, would take her away from him forever. She straightened her shoulders as Lucy,

Jeremy's receptionist and personal assistant, sauntered back to her half-moon shaped desk, her black patent leather stilettos click-clacking loudly on the tiled office floor.

'Sarah, hi there. How are things up north?'

'Good thanks, Lucy,' she answered automatically.

'Wait.' At the elevator door Jeremy pushed a large manila envelope into her hands. 'It's all booked; non-refundable. So please make use of it.' Touching her cheek lightly he gave her a fleeting kiss on the lips. 'If you change your mind . . .' He kissed her again, his eyes moist.

Barely registering her actions, Sarah stepped into the empty elevator, the silver doors closing firmly in her face.

❦ *Spring, 1867* ❧

Wangallon Station

Rose toyed with the watery soup before her, her silver spoon partially disappearing into the grey green of the vegetable broth.

'Are you ill?' Hamish's voice echoed down the length of the table.

'Take this away, please.' Rose waited for the maid Colleen to clear her bowl. 'Can you bring me something edible?' Colleen looked to Hamish for confirmation, her thick bottom lip trembling. 'Do it,' Rose said firmly. Colleen finally did as she was bidden, reappearing with dinner plates and two more black maids in tow. One carried a platter of vegetables, the other a large covered tureen. With little ceremony Colleen arranged a plate before Rose and within minutes was dishing up vegetables and a watery stew with shaking hands. Then the girl began to cough. Rose poked at the large chunks of meat, unrecognisable vegetables and shooed the girl away. With a cautionary stab at a piece of meat, she smelled the food before chewing thoughtfully.

She pushed the plate away again, dabbed at her dry lips with her napkin and folded the fine lawn in half.

'I ask again, are you ill?'

Rose could see her husband was becoming angry. His fingers twirled the fine cut-glass stem of his wine glass.

'I am not hungry.' She sipped from a glass of water, the moisture barely quenching her dry throat. How she longed for something cool.

'It would appear,' he countered, 'that the food is not to your liking.'

Rose was about to explain that in her opinion their menu had deteriorated significantly since the departure of the Abishari brothers, however she was loath to even mention the surname. Footsteps sounded from the cypress wood hallway leading to the kitchen. Rose knew immediately who the owner of the unmistakeable clomp was.

'There is a problem with dinner, Mr Gordon?' Mrs Cudlow's concern showed itself in the twisting of her apron.

'Must you sneak about, Mrs Cudlow?' asked Rose. 'It would be more appropriate if you knocked and then announced yourself.'

The older woman started in surprise. 'I apologise, Mrs Gordon. Colleen said you did not like the soup.'

'Apart from my having said no such thing, your question should be addressed to me, should it not, Mrs Cudlow?'

The nanny turned puce. 'My apologies.'

Since Abdullah's departure last week Rose found Mrs Cudlow's behaviour much changed. Only yesterday on returning to her bedroom to collect her sewing Rose disturbed the woman, her sure grip on her bedroom doorknob. Then this morning she had peered over her shoulder while Rose was immersed in a long letter to her daughter, Elizabeth.

'Wait.' Hamish took a large mouthful of stew and rolled it

around his mouth appraisingly. 'It is excellent. My wife is merely not hungry. Thank you, Mrs Cudlow.'

'Thank you, sir.'

'Must you disenfranchise yourself from everybody?' Hamish began when Mrs Cudlow departed. He took a mouthful of stew, chewed, swallowed and took another mouthful. 'It is bad enough that you paraded your affections with Abdul's brother in front of the poor woman. Now I find you behaving in a rude and condescending manner towards her and the rest of the staff under this roof. I will not tolerate it, Rose. Why should they suffer because you are unhappy? They are not the cause of your discontent. Nor may I add, am I in this particular instance.' Hamish took a sip of wine and recommenced eating.

'I am not altogether inexperienced at how certain affairs can affect a household,' Rose replied bitterly. It was as if all the sadness she'd experienced in her life were piling together into an insurmountable barrier. And now her domain, the household that she'd so recently come to play a satisfying part in, was treating her as one might treat an unwieldy child.

'You have not eaten properly for the last three days.' Hamish shovelled the remains of the stew into his mouth and then rang the sterling silver bell resting on the table. Colleen entered the room almost immediately.

'Some of Mrs Cudlow's apple pie, Colleen.'

'Yes, sir.' The girl coughed again, the exhaustion weakening her.

'I had not realised my diet was important,' Rose continued as the girl bobbed a tight curtsey. 'You are ill, Colleen. Leave the homestead until you are well and send someone else in with the dessert.'

'Won't you at least eat for the children?'

Rose thought of how willing she'd been to leave them behind and join Abdullah. 'I would eat if I was hungry,' she answered wearily. 'And Hamish . . .'

He drew his concentration up from where he mopped his gravy with a wedge of bread.

'I would appreciate it if you would cease Mrs Cudlow's invasion of my privacy. There will be no further contact between myself and Abdullah Abishari.'

Hamish inclined his head in agreement. 'He is to be married, you know.' He wondered if Jasperson had been in contact with Tootles. It was one thing for his wife to have an infatuation, quite another for a business acquaintance to take advantage of his wife's delicate nature.

'I am very much aware of that fact. Excuse me.'

Moments later, in the privacy of her bedroom, the remnants of food lying in Rose's stomach rose up. There was barely enough moisture to wet the base of the porcelain bowl.

⋘ Spring, 1867 ⋙

Paddington, Sydney

Mrs Cole signed her name at the bottom of the letter to her sister and sealed it safely within the envelope. Whilst instructed not to discuss any detail of her current employment with the Whittakers, Mrs Cole felt it was only polite to let her dear sister know how she was progressing. After all it was upon her sister's recommendation that she had the good fortune of being selected for the Whittaker's housekeeping position and it was fine employment. The terrace was a little damp and drab and the neighbourhood definitely middle class, but Mrs Cole could hardly fault her wages. The extra money allowed her to save a little each week and she took great delight in placing the coinage in the toe of her stocking and tucking it between her bed and mattress.

No, she doubted the contents of her letter flaunted the strict rules regarding her new charges. Talking of Mr Whittaker's failing health and of Claire's improving progress with her lessons was hardly exciting news. Of more interest to Mrs Cole was the household's benefactor. She guessed him to be wealthy and a widower, aged, perhaps, with no dependents. The fact that he was only one of these things made him and his interest in the Whittaker family all the more intriguing, especially when her duties required ad hoc reporting as to young Claire's progress, to a foreign gentleman no less.

Placing the letter in her basket with the days' shopping requirements listed in her neat writing, Mrs Cole opened the back door of the terrace. It was early. The sun's rays were only just visible in the dawn sky. Resting her basket on the ground she checked quickly for rodents and other pests in the oblong vegetable garden. Tufts of greenery marked out carrots and potatoes while three pale cabbages, the last of the season, bore the mute passing of grubs. Mrs Cole squatted down on her haunches. Pulling two fat caterpillars from one cabbage, she squashed them beneath the soles of her leather shoes, grinding them into the dirt of the backyard.

'Mrs Cole?'

The familiar accent startled her and she rose to her feet. She walked to the back gate and peered down the laneway. Pressed flat against the wooden palings of the next door fence stood a swarthy man dressed in an expensive dove grey suit, his hair hidden beneath a turban. Mrs Cole stole a glance nervously behind her before joining the man in the laneway.

'I was not expecting you,' she cautioned, lifting her skirts to step over a pile of horse manure.

'How is the girl?' He lit a long cigarette, coughing at the first intake of tobacco.

'Her lessons are improving.' Mrs Cole looked back towards the terrace. The upstairs window remained shut, the curtains drawn.

'And the father's health?'

'Fair to poor.'

'So you don't expect him to last the year?'

Mrs Cole shrugged. 'Who is to know these things?' The wind blew up about them sending leaves and litter hurtling down the street.

The man drew his collar up about his neck. 'Thank you.'

He was gone before Mrs Cole could say another word. She watched him walk down the laneway before disappearing around a corner. Turning back towards the terrace, she walked across the dirt of the backyard to where she left her basket. It was empty. 'Blast.' The shopping list she found between the carrots and cabbages, but the letter had disappeared. 'Blast and blast.' It was then that she noticed Claire's window. It was wide open.

❧ Part Four ❧

≪ *Summer, 1987* ≫

Tongue, Northern Scotland

*T*he air carried unknown scents, a wisp of moisture from both loch and sea. Sarah's vehicle travelled comfortably on the dirt road as she passed sparsely located buildings. A tiny crofter's cottage with a B&B sign emitted thin curls of smoke into the pungent air, smells intensifying as she passed close to stagnant pools of water. Only now did she see the world she had entered. A dog sat patiently near a wrecked car while a mother pushed an ancient pram as scattering birds soared low. It could have been any place in the world, but it was like no place ever imagined. It was as though in the forty kilometres she had travelled yesterday, she had crossed into a vast moonscape. Rocks lay everywhere: at the side of roads, by the varying-sized lochs she passed, in the form of fences, up hillsides, scattered in mounds on fields. And in the fields themselves; many were cut away, great hunks of earth removed with systematic adeptness. The large slices had been left to dry, mutilating the scenery. Sarah slowed her car, wondering how much more peat the soil could give up, in this treeless land ravaged by weather and centuries of habitation.

It was summer. Yet it was not hot. There were no trees, no flowers, and no gardens, except the barest kind. Exasperated, longing for a break from the monotonous scenery, Sarah turned left onto the bitumen. The small car instantly shuddered in a gust of wind. On her right, the North Sea pounded below. Above, a hill staggered under a carpet of heather blowing in torrents of purple and green. Arriving in the village of Tongue, a narrow road led her to a parking spot outside the freshly white-washed façade of an otherwise uninspiring pub. Turning the ignition off and pulling on the handbrake, Sarah let out a slow breath. In the days since leaving Australia, she replayed her final moments with Jeremy as if she were caught in some kind of time warp. That moment, the last she would ever spend with him, continued to flick through her mind, yet in the last couple of hours many thoughts began to combine and crowd her head. Anthony, her parents and grandfather and her beloved dead brother pushed and pulled at her subconscious like unwanted children; yet underlining her every thought lay Wangallon. Shaking her head, as if the motion would eradicate her thoughts, Sarah flipped through her itinerary, her finger coming to rest on the address of her next B&B. It was on the outskirts of the village, giving her just enough time for an afternoon walk before it got dark.

Gathering her backpack, she headed for a signposted trail. The track sloped downhill through tall wet grasses and mud, and her feet, awkward in boots already pinching her heels, slid in the soft vegetation. In the distance, across the sea entrance, Sarah glimpsed mist swirling on far mountains, then she was sliding downhill again to the bottom of the small valley, where a wooden stile marked the presence of a small stream. On the soaking banks the freezing water stung her fingers as it ran rapidly over worn pebbles. Flies rose in a dense mass, invading her eyes and nose so that she quickly navigated the stream and its slippery rocks, and rejoined the overgrown track leading uphill on the other side. The woods she passed through were dense and, having climbed two higher stiles, she was about to give up on ever finding anything of interest when a clearing appeared on the other side. There, perched atop a steep hill, stood a castle. Silhouetted by sun and cloud, the ruin rose prominently above the surrounding countryside.

Judging it would be a good ten minutes uphill once she breached the thick clumps of thistle-type vegetation before her, Sarah hitched her backpack and slipped through another fence. Her boots, for all the sales jargon, still slipped on the moist hillside that was virtually bare of any growth, yet by keeping her head down, her eyes clear of the increasing wind and measuring her breath, finally she reached the summit and the ruined castle. Closing her eyes briefly, she took a deep breath. Beyond the ruin lay an incredible view. The distant inlet was suffering from the effects of a low tide and was bordered by ridges of exposed sand, while further down towards the chilling North Sea, a long low bridge carried two cars.

Wiping flying hair from watering eyes, Sarah gazed at the village. Around it, fields were dotted with tiny cottages and curling smoke, the mountains still shrouded in cloud. Circumnavigating the tall tower and its fallen slabs, a small entrance, dark and unwelcoming, finally came into view beyond a jumble of rocks. Clambering over the ruins to stand on the threshold, Sarah waited until her eyes adjusted to the dim interior. A trace of light seeped through a crack. Checking her footing, she jumped down to the submerged floor, not realising the drop was one of two feet. 'Shit!'

'Better to investigate first before you go jumping here. It's a long way down with a broken ankle to wear.' The heavy accent belonged to a male outline.

Sarah stepped back quickly at the voice, suddenly aware of their isolation. 'Who are you?'

'And I could be asking the same of you?'

'A visitor.' Sarah turned to leave.

'Don't go on my account, lass.'

Sight now accustomed to the light, Sarah watched as her companion returned to sit on a small ledge. He looked tall, taller than her five-foot-ten inches. His hair was a golden red, forming a halo in the refracted light. Heading for the crack of light creeping through the old stones, Sarah nervously pulled out her water bottle.

'Well, at least you are prepared.' The figure reclined, book in hand, on the opposite side of the circular building. 'You're Australian. You've travelled a long way.'

'Yes.'

'You don't say much.'

'Well, you know, strangers and all that stuff,' she answered abruptly.

'We don't have strangers here, lass.'

Based on the size of Tongue, Sarah figured it was a bit like Wangallon town; if people didn't know your business they'd make something up. 'This is a great lookout,' she announced, deciding it wouldn't kill her to be friendly.

'Exactly what it was built for, the inhabitants could see everything. Attack from the land, from the sea. Steep defensive position. One small doorway.'

Taking another sip of water Sarah touched the cold crumbling walls. 'When was it built?'

'Hundreds of years ago, I'd say. Initially to watch for Vikings, or built by them. Then rebuilt, renovated, who knows?' His voice deep and lilting echoed slightly in the cavernous space above them.

'Why isn't it listed? You know, preserved? Most of the ruins I've passed are run by trust organisations.'

'Too many. Besides, there's more money to be made down south. Up here, this far north, not many people travel through, and there aren't many monuments. Weren't too many invaders either. Not too much in the way of spoils to make off with and, well, look at the land, lass: it's not exactly fertile.'

The rich wealth of Wangallon sprang up in her mind. 'So what do you do?'

'I'm a farmer, of course.'

'Really? We have something in common. So am I. Well, a grazier is what we call it.'

'You own your land? Yes?'

'Of course,' Sarah answered, aware of a slightly imperious tone creeping into her voice. 'My family has been there for years.'

'Of course they have.'

Unsure of whether she was being mocked, Sarah screwed the lid back onto her water bottle. 'Strange name, Tongue.' It was a little disconcerting talking in the half-light like this.

'It's Norse,' he explained to her. 'In the Gaelic it's known as Kintail Mackay, being the heart of Mackay country.'

'I think I had better go.' A mist of rain seeped in through the ancient entrance and Sarah didn't relish being stuck in some drafty monolithic structure with a total stranger.

'The weather changes frequently. Keep your bearings and tell someone where you're going. Once the mist creeps up, that'll be it. It's possible to die of exposure.'

'Great.' *Tell me something welcoming*, she thought, escaping from the smell of damp soil and worn stone. Outside she zipped her wet coat firmly up to her chin and began to make her way painstakingly down the hillside. She looked back only once to check her progress, but the rain had obliterated the ruined fortress from view.

Back in her hire car, Sarah continued with her sightseeing. Below the narrow road, the North Sea ate away at the cliff face. Masses of bulbous seaweed reached in and out at a beach that at low tide stretched a healthy kilometre back to the tiny houses nestled together at the base of a small hill. It was as if a slice of the land had been cut away, leaving a great semi-circular gouge at one end. An end filled with mouldering weed. Winding the window up, Sarah leaned back into the cracked upholstery of the car. Cold seeped through her bones. Distance made Sarah regret her many arguments. Maybe it was purely because she was miles away from the pressures of her life, or the knowledge that she cared enough about everybody to feel upset about her last conversations with Jeremy and her grandfather. Then there was Anthony. She shouldn't have kissed him and she was embarrassed it had happened. He was a friend and they should have known better. The fault lay with both of them, however, and in apportioning the blame equally, she considered it was possible that Anthony could have been unwittingly led into her grandfather's future plans for Wangallon.

What Sarah had not reckoned upon during the long flight from the southern hemisphere was her increasing frustration at the possibility of Wangallon being left entirely to Anthony. After all she had left Australia without informing her grandfather immediately of her broken engagement to Jeremy and considering how furious he'd been with her when she had last seen him, anything was possible. Her pride had stopped her from telling him, although by the time she landed in Edinburgh commonsense told her that her father would have probably shared the news by now. Her grandfather's reaction would be the opposite to her father's initial shock and then disappointment, of that Sarah could be certain.

Seagulls stalked the sand below, while beyond only smoke suggested habitation in the windswept hills. Tearing her eyes from the great shivering expanse of water, Sarah studied her road map. Tongue lay to her left while the ruin and its resident stranger hung soundlessly to the north. The ignition turned over smoothly, and soon the car was running easily back to the main road. Within a short space of time, she was heading towards a signpost pointing to the left. Sarah hesitated only slightly before turning the car down the dirt road in the direction of the B&B.

As she increased her speed, the heather-covered hills blurred as the road narrowed to a mere track, her small car bumping alarmingly as she cut through desolate countryside. Sarah gripped the steering wheel tightly. The road was too narrow to turn back. Slowing down to a mere crawl, she twisted the radio dial and was rewarded with static as the noise of a car horn jolted her. Glancing in her rear-view mirror, she saw a large black four-wheel drive.

'Okay, okay.' The vehicle remained hot on her heels, the outline of two men just visible beneath two long fishing poles strapped to the roof. Sarah slowed as she rounded a bend, instantly the car behind her pulled out to overtake her, Sarah felt her vehicle spin out instantly as she was pushed to the side of the road.

A number of voices were talking loudly in unfamiliar accents. Sarah lifted her forehead from the steering wheel. Touching her face instinctively, she checked her hands. 'No blood,' she mumbled. Cautiously she peered down, feeling her ribs. It hurt to move. With shaking hands she undid her seatbelt and shifted her legs from their position squashed hard against the door. It was only then that she looked out her window. Horrified, she burst into tears as she stared at a sea of water.

'You all right in there?'

'She was travelling very quickly!'

'Do you know where the doc is, Jim?'

'No, Dad.'

'Hmm.'

A red-bearded face appeared in Sarah's window. 'Are you all right, lass?'

'Yes, yes, I think so.'

The door opened and Sarah found herself lifted up and out of her vehicle. After a few unbalanced moments, they reached dry ground and she was released from the grasp of the burly red-beard.

'I'm Robert, and this is my son, Jim.'

'Dad, I met her this morning.'

Beginning to shake, Sarah gave a broken thank-you. 'Can we get my car out?' Her white sedan, having slid down the embankment appeared to be stuck fast, right on the water's edge.

'I think we should find the doc for you first, lass,' the red-beard announced gruffly.

'At the old ruin. She's from Australia.'

'Australia,' Sarah mumbled before collapsing.

Sarah woke in a double bed, light streaming in from a narrow window. She looked about the room, saw her suitcase and handbag and gingerly got out of bed. Someone had rummaged through her belongings to find the T-shirt she was dressed in, her clothes were resting over the back of a wooden chair. On the bedside table she saw some brochures on items of local interest in the area and realised she was in the B&B she had booked. She dressed slowly, tied back her hair and walked slowly down the narrow staircase outside her bedroom.

'Did you sleep well, then?'

A grey-haired woman bustled her through a doorway.

'Yes, thank you.'

'Good. There's porridge ready.'

Squeezing through the partially opened doorway, wedged in place by a protruding bookcase, Sarah entered the small, cluttered sitting room, managing to slip down between a solid pine table into a high-backed wooden chair. The pain hit her sharply.

'Doctor says you've a fractured rib. I'm Mrs Jamieson. You were booked in here so,' she hunched her shoulders as if to suggest the entire situation was out of her control. 'Nothing too serious that a good few days' rest won't cure.'

'Oh.' Sarah looked around the small, cluttered room.

'The publican will be here soon to take your statement.'

'Statement?' Sarah breathed in, holding her ribs, until she managed to wriggle into a more comfortable position. 'My car!' Water appeared in front of her eyes. 'Do you know —?'

'Lass, the Mackens brought you here. Didn't talk to them any more than that. Suffering from shock, the doctor said. You've been asleep since four o'clock.'

'Oh,' Sarah replied weakly. The space in front of her was laid with a single vinyl place mat, cutlery and an assortment of jams.

'The fish man will be here today. Dinner's at seven. How will you have your haddock? Creamed? Steamed? Baked? Breaded? There you are.' She placed a bowl of porridge down and flicked a tea towel over her shoulder. 'Now would you like one or two eggs with your bacon, sausages and beans?'

Beneath Sarah's nose, steam from the porridge rose in huge bursts, almost matching the size of the serving. 'Just one, thank you, Mrs Jamieson,' she sighed.

'Just one? Dear, you're not used to our weather up here.'

'Well I . . .' She hated to offend, especially when she was a guest.

'You people always do so much walking about, and it's a long time before dinner. Changes every minute, you know. Look out there.'

Sarah rose awkwardly, leaning over her cooling porridge to peer through a small window set back in two-foot-thick walls. The house, situated on the side of a low hill, gazed down over a valley where creeping mist was only just beginning to recede from the paddocks. On the opposite side, a slightly larger hill was doing its best to block out the struggling summer sun. Sitting, Sarah pulled the sleeves down on her cotton shirt, thinking instantly of Wangallon's long, hot summers.

Discovering she was starving, Sarah quickly shoved five spoon-fuls of watery meal into her mouth, her gaze straying to the crack of the kitchen door barely four feet away. She noted the bashed-looking two-seater and large armchair. A bookcase, crammed with wedding and christening photographs in cheap plastic frames, filled one wall. Shots of what could only be the woman's children and grandchildren intermingled with men in military-type jackets and kilts.

'It was really very nice.' Sarah held up her bowl, as her hostess re-entered the room, 'but I really can't eat anymore.'

A slight crinkle appeared between the older women's eyes. 'It's a staple, you know, lass.'

'Really?' Sarah gasped at the plate of eggs, bacon and sausages placed before her.

'It makes oatcakes, scones, pudding, gruel and porridge. My personal favourites are "brose", which is hot, and "crowdie", which is cold, lass.' She fetched a pot of tea and four large slices of toast. Sarah gulped at the huge mound of food and ground a sprinkling of pepper over a dietician's disaster.

'Anything else you need, just let me know.'

'I will, but I'm sure I'll be fine, thanks.'

As Mrs Jamieson crossed the few steps to the kitchen, Sarah

took two large forkfuls of burnt bacon and overcooked sausage and poured herself a cup of tea.

'Anything you need?' Mrs Jamieson enquired as she continued to hover in the kitchen doorway.

'No, no, thank you,' Sarah replied.

The woman started scrubbing the woodwork surrounding the kitchen door. 'With brose lass, you pour boiling water over a handful of meal and add a pinch of salt. Although butter, vegetable or bone-stock work just as well as variations.'

Sarah took another mouthful. 'Call me, Sarah, Mrs Jamieson.'

'Aye, lass.' The scrubbing continued. 'Crowdie is my favourite, though. Some go for buttermilk or cream, but myself, I like whisky. Poured straight over. So, you're a Gordon?'

'Well, yes.'

'When did they emigrate?'

'The 1850s.'

'Hmm.' The reply sounded faintly disapproving. 'Is your allegiance to Clan Gordon?'

Sarah shrugged, 'Well, we have the same surname, so I assumed . . .'

'No doubt you've got your piece of tartan, bought from a store in Edinburgh.'

'Well, yes actually I do.' Sarcasm wasn't something Sarah was expecting to be dished up at a B&B. She placed her knife and fork down on her plate with emphasis. 'My great-grandfather Hamish Gordon lost nearly everything he owned crossing a flooded river in New South Wales in the mid 1800s. It was my grandfather who showed me a picture of the Gordon colours. So yes, I purchased a woollen scarf.'

The scrubbing stopped. 'It was him that emigrated then? This great-grandfather Hamish?'

Sarah nodded before resuming her meal. Clearly this snippet of information immediately gave her a modicum of respect.

Mrs Jamieson drew her eyes together, peering at her closely. The woman's creamy-skinned hands rose to her face, as if in recognition, but just as quickly she resumed her scrubbing. 'You know, lass, just because you hold the same surname, doesn't mean you belong to the clan.' The dishcloth, scrunched and shoved into the pocket of a flowery apron, spread its wetness through the material. 'Are you visiting relatives up here, lass?'

'No.'

'Looking up your forebears?'

'No. Just interested to see where my family came from.'

'Well, never mind. I expect you won't be staying long. You can wait here for Mike O'Reily and dinner's at seven.' The kitchen door shut firmly.

So much for Scottish hospitality, Sarah sniffed, pushing her half-eaten breakfast away from her. She could only assume that this O'Reily fellow was the publican. With a sigh she carefully manoeuvred her aching ribs away from the small table as the noise of a vehicle carried through the walls of the cottage.

'How are you feeling?' A small weedy man, almost jockey height and dressed in dark trousers and braces walked into the cluttered room.

'Much better, thank you. You are?' Sarah asked, a little affronted as three more men crowded into the room. Clearly they didn't stand on ceremony here.

'The doctor. It's Sarah, isn't it?'

'Yes. Sarah Gordon.' At her name, an obvious glance passed between the doctor and an amiable-looking man beside him.

'Well, I'll check you, Sarah Gordon.' The doctor rose.

Unsure if he intended to examine her then and there, Sarah held her palm out. 'If you don't mind, Doctor, I'd prefer not to have an audience. Besides, I'm fine.'

'Well, with a name and temper like that, she must be Scottish.'

Sarah turned slowly at the familiar voice. 'Do I know you?' she asked.

Piercing violet eyes struck her. 'My name's Jim.' He smiled.

They were the same as hers and her grandfather's . . .

'We met in the ruin. She didn't talk much then, either. It was my father and I that nearly hit you yesterday.'

'I think she may still be suffering from shock.' The doctor was kneeling beside her, studying her face.

'Your, your eyes?' Sarah finally spoke, conscious of the room watching her. 'I'm all right, Doctor, please sit down. I'm sorry, Jim just reminded me of someone.'

Mrs Jamieson cleared her throat and introduced the room. 'Lass, that's Jim and his father Robert Macken, the doctor of course, and Mike O'Reily, the publican. And this came for you.'

Sarah accepted the envelope and then thanked the Mackens for rescuing her. In return they all commented politely that it was no problem at all. Sarah had the distinct feeling her accident provided them with some entertainment, for although they no doubt all had reason for being there, she doubted she warranted such attention. 'You obviously don't have too many accidents,' Sarah said lightly.

'Well, Sarah . . .'

She tried not to stare at Jim but it was difficult. He was almost six feet, about as tall as her father, dressed in heavy cord trousers, grey bulky jumper and a tweed cap.

'Mike's here to take down the details of the accident. He'll also inform the hire car company for you. So you don't have to worry. And, of course, you have your luggage.'

'Yes, thank you,' Sarah answered quickly. 'How soon before we get my car out?'

'Ah, Sarah.' The strong accent came from Jim's father, Robert Macken. 'Your car is gone, lass. The edge of the Middling Loch is pretty boggy.' He finished stuffing his pipe and lit it.

Sarah grasped the armrest of the chair and pulled herself forward into his circle of smoke. 'What do you mean, gone?'

Robert Macken puffed heavily on his pipe and blew the smoke out noisily. Sarah momentarily envisioned herself stuck in Tongue for the rest of her life. Somehow, the idea did not bother her as much as it should have.

'It sunk, Sarah,' Jim answered.

'Sunk?' Sarah echoed. 'It can't have sunk. It only went to the edge of the loch, not into the bloody thing.' Her ribs pulled painfully as she rose. 'Will someone please take me out there?' she asked through gritted teeth.

'Settle down now, lass,' suggested Robert Macken.

Sarah stomped to the front door, trying not to hurt her ribs as she struggled to pull her boots on.

Sardined between the Mackens, they reached the loch in silence. Sarah walked carefully down the embankment. Horrified, she felt her feet sinking deeper into the silty ground until she reached her car. She stopped at the tracks leading down through the soft, boggy ground. Surrounded by oozing mud and water, only the hire car's roof showed. Shaking her head disbelievingly, she took a few steps backwards before sitting with a thud on the ground, her ribs paining at the impact. 'Shit!'

'It's the ground around here, you see.' Jim squatted beside her. 'You can get these peaty bogs anywhere in Scotland.'

Sarah turned to look at him. 'But it's so dangerous.'

'Not really. You saw yourself how boggy it was. You didn't go any further.'

'That means no stock can use it, though.'

'Stock?' Jim laughed, placing his hands behind her back to gently ease her upwards.

Reaching the top of the road, Sarah grimaced at the waiting men. 'Sorry, I had no idea.'

Robert Macken lifted his eyes to the sky.

Sarah set off at a slow pace, her ribs aching with each breath as she trekked upwards behind the house whose back wall was dug well into the hill's soil. The green and purple vegetation blew in ripples. Here and there clumps of purple swelled, sprigs of violet appearing to dart towards her, gleaming with life amid the prevailing sombre browns. Navigating a crumbling stone fence, Sarah continued her ascent up the steep hill, her hand crumpling the now opened envelope shoved deep into the pocket of her coat. The memory of her submerged car made her swear quietly under her breath as she acknowledged that for the time being, she was stuck in one of the most northerly parts of Scotland.

On the hilltop she made out the outline of a cairn. The pile of rocks, statue-like in appearance, was in line with another cairn on a hill further into the distance. Standing on top of a boulder, Sarah turned slowly in a full circle. There was nothing behind her except hills and lochs, the cairns on each substantial rise silhouetted against the horizon. It was all so endless. She crossed the gully separating Mrs Jamieson's mound from the taller one with the cairn. She was not far from the ocean, yet there was only the musty odour of soil and dampness seeping upwards from the green–brown ground. The tussocky vegetation was deceptive. Twice Sarah found her heavy boots breaking through soil and grass to hidden streams below. They were only tiny trickles at this time of year, yet they were enough to twist an ankle if you weren't looking. By the time she reached the top of the next steep hill, where the cairn stood proudly, Sarah was exhausted. She touched the mound of stones; many had rolled down and were lying at the base. Stooping to pick up a rock, Sarah added it to the pile.

Finally, her left hand closed around the crumpled telegram in the pocket of her canvas jacket.

Sorry to hear of your accident. Will inform parents/grandfather of your delay in Tongue. Keep the ring.

It would seem that the doctor had taken it upon himself to contact Jeremy, whose booking details were included with the hire car paperwork. In her right hand she weighed a smooth rock, feeling its curved surface, squeezing her palm against it as if she could release its strength. It didn't matter where she was in the world, someone always had to stick their nose into her business.

The next morning Sarah felt much better, except that she only had one more night booked at the B&B, a slight problem considering she had no vehicle. She finished her coffee and scooped up the last piece of egg with her fork. Immediately Mrs Jamieson was out of the kitchen and clearing the table.

'So lass, when are you leaving?'

'I was hoping I could stay a few more days, if you aren't expecting more guests. I have to wait until I get a car.'

Mrs Jamieson paused in her clearing of the table as if considering her request. 'I'll manage.' She peered through the narrow window. 'You expecting anyone?'

Sarah walked outside.

'Need some company?' Jim Macken pulled up in a screech of old tyres and spurting gravel with a broad smile. 'How are the ribs?'

'Oh, heaps better, thanks,' Sarah smiled warmly, standing cautiously to lessen the slight pain from her ribs as she zipped up the front of her jacket.

'Good, then you'll be up for an adventure. Firstly though I hear you're to get a new car. A week, they tell me.'

'A week.' Sarah looked out towards the mountains. 'Damn.'

'Tongue isn't that bad, Sarah Gordon. Unless there's something you need to be hurrying off to?'

Mrs Jamieson called out from the cottage door, her hands wiping the rumpled floral apron about her waist as if they were separate from her body. 'The lass is still suffering from her recent accident, Jim,' she declared, crossing her arms and giving a stiff nod that caused a lock of grey hair to fall down over her forehead.

Jumping into Jim's old truck, Sarah slammed the door, trying not to wince at the pain the action caused. 'I'm fine.'

'Cranky,' Jim rolled his eyes as he accelerated. 'She always has been, at least towards my family. Though I have often wondered why; people speak highly enough of her in Tongue.'

Sarah pulled the fraying seat belt across her shoulder and settled back into the lumpy seat of Jim's old truck. Ignoring Mrs Jamieson probably wasn't conducive to a happy holiday, but then she wasn't exactly in the mood for interference.

'Holidaying?' Jim was asking. 'Or have you come to look up ancestors?'

'Not either, really.' Sarah noticed the strong hands grasping the ancient steering wheel and searched for an explanation. An easy one eluded her. She gave a wan smile imagining how uninterested he would be to hear about her ex-fiancé and her grandfather's manipulations. Besides, Jim was quite cute actually, in a freckled skin, reddish hair sort of way and it felt good to be with someone who knew nothing about her baggage and, more importantly, didn't have an agenda where she was concerned.

They followed the bitumen for ten minutes, before turning off down a narrow road and into weather that became progressively worse as they continued. For the age of the vehicle, it handled the road well, and soon they were passing through a heavily wooded area, over two ramps and towards a small shed. Light rain fell as they drew up next to the building. Sarah wound her window down.

'Ah, Jim lad, you've brought us a visitor.'

Sarah smiled, noticing the money belt and dog trial sign. 'Hi! How much to get in?'

The man, aged somewhere in his fifties, wore a kilt, perky cap and a mischievous grin. 'For you, lassie? Nothing.' Then he added, winking at Jim, 'You'll excuse me if I return to my position and warm myself with a few drams.'

Driving up a steep incline, they parked at the end of a row of cars, Jim pulling at the park brake twice before giving Sarah a lopsided grin. He was about Cameron's age if he'd still been alive, Sarah decided. It was the first time a memory of her brother was not accompanied by an overwhelming sense of loss.

'Now it's time to meet the family.'

Mrs Macken was a slim woman with a beautiful complexion. Her green–blue eyes positively glimmered when she smiled, managing to soften her husband's face immediately.

'Jim told us about your predicament, Sarah. We hope you'll let us look after you while you're stranded,' she offered.

'Oh, thank you. Actually everyone's been very kind since I arrived in Tongue.'

Robert Macken nodded and passed her steaming coffee and a hard barley biscuit. A whistle blew shrilly and Sarah found herself following the Mackens to the front of the old truck, the three of them leaning against the bonnet. The spectators, of whom Sarah saw there were few women, were ringed around a large paddock. At the far end, the top of a hill, two men, who looked more like stick figures, were standing near a gap in a stone wall. Halfway down was a freestanding gateway; a little further on, a post. Barely fifty yards away, close to where Sarah sat with the Mackens, was a small sheep pen. Sarah turned her collar up against the mizzling rain, as Robert Macken sat a cap on her head. His grey eyes stood out prominently. He was short-necked and nuggety-looking. His sombre dress, combined with the pipe clenched between his teeth, reminded Sarah of a bad-tempered cattle dog.

'So,' Sarah asked. 'Do you always have dog trials on a weekday?'

Mr Macken looked at her with an expression of forced patience. 'Sheepdogs are a ritual part of our way of life, lass. The day of an event is unimportant.'

The mist curled and eddied on the distant rise, giving everything an eerie quality. While the spectators circled the paddock, the thick mist circled them. Sarah thought of Jim's words that day in the ruin. It would be horrible to be captured in the folds of the mist, left to die on the exposed rocks and heather, with only the biting wind from the lochs as company.

'Where's Jim?'

Robert Macken nodded out towards the field.

At the top of the rise, sheep appeared, smallish specs thrown into relief by the stone wall and the dense mist. A man, dressed head to foot in tweed and shiny black gumboots, patted the large black-and-white sheepdog sitting at his feet. The dog scratched and yawned, then lay down beside his master. Sarah thought they were spectators, but when the whistle sounded a second time, the dog was gone.

Then she saw the dog racing directly uphill towards the sheep and, gathering them, brought them smartly down the hillside. The dog's master used a series of whistles and commands, as the four sheep ran towards the open gate.

'He's got to drive them fair through the middle, first go,' Robert Macken chewed the end of his pipe.

The sheep stopped halfway through and reversed, causing the owner to increase his verbal commands and the dog to work harder. The second time, the mob was through and headed for the post. Only now did the dog's barks drift over to where Sarah sat.

'They have to veer to the right of it, lass,' Robert Macken explained in a flat voice, a stubby thumb and forefinger scraping contemplatively at the light stubble on his chin.

The dog turned the sheep smartly, shouldered them around the pole and headed for the pen. The rain increased. Sarah held her breath as the owner rushed to the pen gate and opened it. Unfortunately, the dog lost control and the sheep flew in all directions. Three times he reeled them to the gate and just as often, they broke free. Eventually, he ran out of time and the whistle blew. The dog wandered back to his master, head and tail dragging, drenched by the rain. He was rewarded with a gentle pat on his head.

'So what do you think, Sarah?' Mr Macken asked.

'It was great. The owners have so much control and that dog, wow, could he move!'

Mr Macken's mouth twitched up in one corner. 'The next one should interest you, lass.'

A few feet away, Jim squatted, ruffling the neck of a small sheepdog. In one hand he held a long wooden staff, the top of which was curved, almost like the staff in Sarah's old nursery-rhyme book. He looked up and winked at Sarah. She winked back. The dog turned towards her instinctively and she winked at him too. Jim burst out laughing as the whistle blew.

The dog came to attention immediately. His tail moved furiously, his neat black face turning continuously from the direction of the sheep to Jim. Then Jim leaned down and appeared to whisper in his dog's ear. The dog stilled. The second whistle blew, and he was gone. Sarah could never remember having seen an animal run so fast. Even her grandfather's dog, old Shrapnel, had never moved the way this dog could. The black body streaked uphill to reach the sheep in one smooth arc, the running circle was then completed as he directed the sheep downhill at a hurtling pace. Sarah looked in awe at the Mackens on either side of her, and by the time she looked back to where the dog was, the sheep were through the gate and just rounding the post.

Jim was already at the pen, gate wide open, when the rain poured down in such torrents that Sarah lost sight of the field. Robert Macken moved around to the side of the vehicle, while Mrs Macken made clicking noises. Sarah stood waiting, peering through the sheet of water. Then, as suddenly as it had started, the rain stopped. Jim was squatting again, talking to his dog. The sheep were penned. Sarah clapped loudly.

Mrs Macken fiddled nervously with her gloves as Jim rose to speak to a bespectacled man dressed in a brown suit with matching waistcoat, his baggy trousers tucked into knee-high dark brown leather boots.

'Well? What's the result?' Sarah leaned down to pat the bedraggled animal at Jim's side when the twosome arrived back at the old truck minutes later. 'You're a great dog. Fantastic! Hey, aren't you fantastic?'

'Easy, Sarah,' Jim laughed. 'He'll get enthusiastic about himself if you keep on at him like that.'

'He deserves it. How would you like to come back to Australia and work for me?'

The dog looked up at her then walked to the truck.

Jim chuckled. 'Well, there's your answer.'

'Worth a try,' Sarah grinned. 'Besides, we do have better weather. Now what happens?'

'Nothing. I'm disqualified.'

'What? Why?'

'The judges couldn't see my dog, sheep or the pen. They can't judge what they can't see.'

'That is ridiculous! Where's the judge? I'll go and speak to him.'

'M'am?'

Sarah turned to find a well dressed man standing behind her.

'Eliot, Eliot Andrews.'

Sarah clasped his offered hand.

He was balding and moustached, in his mid-sixties. 'So you're Sarah Gordon. I met your father once. Ronald, isn't it? Heard of your misfortune. If there's anything I can do, please call.' He inclined his head to one side.

Stunned, Sarah found herself stammering hello. 'You know my father?'

'You didn't tell me he'd been over here as well,' Jim interrupted.

Mr Andrews cleared his throat. 'Barely. Met him many years ago. We had dinner on a number of occasions. Swapped stories, that type of thing. You had a query, Sarah?'

'Right, yes, well, I was wondering why Jim's dog was disqualified?'

'Of course. The dog must be in clear view at all times. We can't possibly predict the weather, that's Scotland you know. Still, rules are rules. Is that not correct, lad?'

'Mr Andrews is correct,' Jim answered curtly, before excusing himself.

'I hope you enjoy your visit, Sarah. But don't waste your time in one place with this rough lot.' He studied her carefully, then with a slight bow, left her standing in a muddy puddle. As the whistle blew, she walked back to the old truck where Mrs Macken greeted her with a mug of coffee and a warm smile.

≪ *Summer, 1867* ≫

Sydney Cove, Wharf District

*A*bdullah closed the lid on his trunk. His lodging was now empty of all traces of his presence. The single bed, writing desk, chair and wardrobe suggested he'd not inhabited the room for the past three weeks. Only his letters remained on the cracked wooden desk, his suit jacket resting on the end of the lumpy narrow bed. Walking into the boarding house's hallway, Abdullah threw some coins at the young lad lounging against the timber walls. The boy, thin and ragged in appearance, took the money willingly enough, his thin lips twitching in response to the coin in his hand. With a heave, the boy carried the trunk down the stairs to the landing below.

His ship was due to depart on the night's tide and Abdullah was eager to be gone. He scanned the room, then, picking up the letters he'd written, called again to the youth below. The boy scrambled up the stairs and with letters and coin in hand, disappeared into the night. The first, penned to Hamish Gordon, reported favourable progress as to Claire Whittaker. Abdullah also tactfully apologised for any misunderstandings while cautiously reminding Hamish of his desire to see Rose both happy and safe. If Hamish Gordon wished to take this inference as a veiled threat, well, Abdullah grinned, so be it.

As for the second letter, he could recall every sentence written, word for word.

My Rose,

I am hardly able to imagine the suffering you may have endured since my departure. I can only tell you that the last thing I wish for you is unhappiness. I now write to tell you of something shocking, although I have scant information and would not dare to presume your husband's intentions.

Your husband has become the secret benefactor of a Miss Claire Whittaker and her aged father. They are lodged in a terrace in Sydney and your husband provides for all that such a household might require.

I say 'secret', for the Whittakers are unaware of their benefactor's identity and to all intents are good honest people.

I tell you this as an offering of goodwill between us. May you use this information as you see fit.

May you live in Allah's care,

A. Abishari

As he turned to leave his room, the knife blade cut deeply into Abdullah's chest. For a moment he was unsure of where he was then his hand clutched at the bed cover as he fell, the worn brown material sliding down to partially obscure his fading vision. He felt his breath catch, heard a gurgling in his ears. Two men talked in muted tones and then his world spun into oblivion.

'Tell Mr Reynolds the job's done.' The taller of the two wiped the knife on his trousers. Leaning down he pulled Abdullah's gold fob watch and chain from the pocket of his waistcoat. He flipped the lid open, noting the fine engraving on the inside. 'Give him this. It carries his name.'

≪ Summer, 1867 ≫

Wangallon Station

Rose was not in the habit of searching her husband's mail. It was just that her Elizabeth had grown tardy in her correspondence. Regular monthly letters had remained the norm between them for the last two years. In fact her young daughter's increasingly maturing hand represented a lifeline to Rose. Elizabeth was now able to converse on subjects beyond schoolroom antics and was fond of describing a new dress, a scrap of lace, or her grandmother's reprimands. It was a life far removed from the obscure frontier Rose inhabited and she envied her daughter's life in Ridge Gully. It was with some dismay then that Elizabeth's letters began to grow less frequent. It was as if distance had rendered Rose redundant and she felt the ostracism keenly.

Forever dutiful, Colleen left the fortnightly mail on the hall table, ready to be distributed by Mrs Cudlow at dusk. It had become something of an event, this apportioning of correspondence, rather like last rites, Rose thought. So much anticipation was present at least on Rose's behalf, so the disappointment was that much greater when no catalogue arrived from the department store in Sydney or Elizabeth did not reply immediately to her mother's missive.

Today Rose was in no mood to wait for Hamish's regulated mail hour. Her continuing disinterest in food had rendered her patience non-existent. She slunk from her room and sorted the mail efficiently. Statements of accounts and three-week-old newspapers comprised the bundle. There was no letter from Elizabeth. With a tight frown Rose was about to return to the sanctity of her bedroom when she noticed a cream envelope addressed to her. She snatched up the mysterious letter hurriedly, tearing it open to read the contents. Perhaps a former Ridge Gully matron was the author. Such letters arrived randomly and usually included a discreet snippet of scandal that once would have been delicately discussed over morning tea. A brief moment of unbridled exhilaration sped through Rose's bones when she realised the identity of the author.

'We found her in the hallway, Mr Gordon.'

Mrs Cudlow followed him into Rose's bedroom.

His wife's face was a sheen of perspiration, yet the room was cool and dark, scented with the lavender water she so loved.

'Rose, what ails you?' He sat carefully on her bed, careful not to disturb her. 'Will you answer, please?' It occurred to him that he'd not been in this room except to visit a newborn or perform his husbandly duties. They'd never simply sat and talked of the day's events, or discussed their children or laughed at the shared follies of the past. They seemed to share no happy memories at all, at least not enough to blank out the bad ones.

Mrs Cudlow looked meaningfully at a folded piece of paper on the bedside table and left the room.

Rose coughed quietly in the darkness. 'I know of the woman, of this Miss Whittaker. I take it our marriage is over.'

'Claire. You know of Claire?' He reached for the letter, read it and frowned. He had never thought of the possibility of Rose discovering Claire's existence.

'A pretty name. You wish her to be your wife.'

He should have known better than to give such a task to one outside his most trusted circle. 'I have never met her and she knows not who I am,' he replied honestly.

'That,' Rose said sharply, 'is surely the most wicked of lies.'

Hamish tore Abdullah's letter in half and sat it back on the bedside table. 'You're not really in a position to pass judgement, Rose. Goodnight.' He turned down the lamp so that only a dull circle of light remained and left her in the semi-darkness.

In the middle of the night, Rose awoke to the hurrying of footsteps and the slamming of doors. She reached lethargically for her shawl, fearing the worst, a fire perhaps or an attack from the Aboriginals. She must move, she told herself, willing her starving body to obey her command.

'Mrs Gordon. Mrs Gordon?' A series of taps on the bedroom door followed the voice, then Mrs Cudlow flung the door open to Rose's bedroom.

'What is it, Mrs Cudlow? It's the middle of the night.'

The nanny held a candle, the pale light drawing streaks of flickering shadows across her lined faced. 'It's the children. They are ill.'

❦ Summer, 1987 ❧

Tongue, Northern Scotland

*T*hey had been climbing steadily, time passing quickly as Jim spoke of his great-grandfather who had disappeared on his last droving trip. Sarah listened intently, fascinated by both the history of his family and the lilting beauty of his Scottish accent. It was a voice at once deep and penetrating, yet with the highs and lows of the hills and lochs they passed.

'No-one knew if he made it to the sales or not. I say he was killed on the road somewhere.'

'That's dreadful,' Sarah exclaimed.

'He was a crofter, Sarah Gordon, with no money and nothing to lose. Still, he allowed my father's family to remain on their land.' As he spoke, they passed a group of shaggy-haired Highland cattle. Deep red in colour, their appearance reminded Sarah of water buffalo.

'My great-uncle Luke, my grandfather's half-brother, was a drover too. He died on the stock route doing what he loved. It would have been the same for your great-grandfather.'

'I guess. Not far to go now.' Jim ran ahead, pulling her upwards. Sarah winced at the pain in her ribs as she pulled her hand free. The blackface sheep munching at the low covering of heather did not stir as she passed them. 'Ugly-looking buggers,' Sarah commented.

'Do you always say what ye think then?' he called after her.

'Usually,' she admitted playfully, as he joined her. 'What does your family grow?'

'Oats and potatoes. We sell the excess to the market, and my mother has a fine vegetable garden.' The crinkles at his eyes smoothed as he spoke, the light beige of his freckles highlighted by the pale skin beneath and the thick weave of his olive green jumper. 'Each year we're increasing the numbers of cattle and sheep for sale.' Jim's voice tapered off.

They had been climbing gradually for the last twenty minutes, yet their ascent was so unnoticeable that Sarah was surprised when the view below her stretched out spectacularly for miles.

'This is amazing.' The sun warmed her back as she gazed across at the numerous lochs that crept out between small hills. It was as if they had climbed a thousand feet.

'It's just the positioning of this rise. If it were a few feet either side, you would never be able to see all this.' He appeared to be talking to himself, as if he was not used to company.

Sarah counted the lochs under her breath. The last one, curling like the top end of a question mark, lay many miles away. At the sight of it her thoughts were drawn to a similar pattern, the scar etched on Anthony's cheekbone.

'There's no mist this morning. I can see out to Shannon, number twelve. See how that shaft of sunlight dances on her?' He caressed each word as if talking to a lover. 'I can remember seeing fourteen with my grandfather when I was very young. Never seen it since.'

Sarah sat cross-legged on the heather. It felt springy beneath her, like soft rubber coils.

'Tell me how long your family's been in Australia, Sarah. Why did they leave Scotland?'

'My great-grandfather, Hamish,' she began, 'emigrated with his only brother in the 1850s. Charlie died in a mining accident soon after. Hamish blamed himself for the boy's death and spent his life trying to achieve his dream.'

'What was the dream?' Jim asked. He was leaning back on the springy heath, his hands burrowing into the vegetation by his sides.

'To become huge landowners. He did it too. He selected the family property, Wangallon, in the early 1860s, and we still live there.'

'That's impressive, lass.'

Sarah began tugging at the vegetation in her hand, pulling green growth free of its soil.

'You don't agree?'

'There just seems to have been a lot of death associated with Wangallon's history.' Sarah gave a half-laugh, brushing her hands free of dirt. 'Sorry. That sounds a bit morbid.'

'Who died?' Genuinely intrigued, Jim moved forward, crossing his long legs in front of him into a semi-lotus position.

Sarah hesitated. It was such a nice day and here she was dredging up the past. 'I guess you have to have a few deaths when there is a long history in one place.'

'It sounds pretty terrible. Do all your family live on this place, Wangallon?' He pronounced the word with difficulty, his tongue twisting to sound out each vowel.

'My parents sold out to my grandfather after a big flood some years ago.'

'And you?' Jim asked. 'You obviously live there.'

Sarah shook her head, getting to her feet. They began the long descent to the valley below.

'Why don't you live there if you love it so much?'

'You know you remind me of Cameron,' she replied, ignoring a question she couldn't answer.

'Cameron?'

'My brother. He died in a horse-riding accident years ago,' she said quietly. 'Not a day goes by when I don't think of him.'

'And I remind you of him? Then I can't be complaining if it's a good thought.'

He stopped and Sarah found herself looking into the deepness of his violet eyes. 'It's because of your eyes – they're violet.'

'Not uncommon up in these parts. No doubt there's been a bit of interbreeding over the centuries. That would be how you got your violet eyes.'

'Yeah, right,' she laughed, pulling away from his intense gaze.

Jim shoved his hands deep into his trouser pockets. 'Guess you'll be wanting a coffee or something now?'

'You guessed right.' She walked on ahead, agilely missing rocks, sidestepping the uneven ground, surprised by the sulky expression curling the lips of the man she barely knew.

The fax from Anthony arrived in the late afternoon via the post office, then via the publican. Sarah took it delightedly, noting Anthony's scrawled signature at the bottom of the page. The letter explained that her grandfather was in Sydney for a regular check-up. Just in case she telephoned.

Heard about your accident and the break-up. Hope all okay.

Having read the last line Sarah folded the piece of paper carefully. For some reason Anthony knowing of her broken engagement made her feel awkward.

'Problem?' Mrs Jamieson asked from the kitchen door. 'I don't care to know about the other young man, lass. But your face lit up reading that, the way young Jim's does when he sees you.'

Tucking the note into the pocket of her jeans, Sarah shook her head, 'Oh, Anthony's just a friend from home, Mrs Jamieson.'

'And Jim?'

Sarah wanted to tell the woman to mind her own business. Instead, she said honestly, 'He's just a friend too. Besides I've only known Jim four days.'

'Four days is enough.' Mrs Jamieson nodded pointedly at the paper sticking out of Sarah's jeans pocket. 'Hmm, have you thought about how you feel about that young man and the way Jim Macken feels about you? Hearts are difficult things to mend, lass. Don't use another's in the hope it will help yours.'

Sarah found herself blinking in reply. How did the receipt of a telegram lead to the discussion of her personal life with a woman she barely knew? Mrs Jamieson was glaring at her as if she expected an answer, her forehead creasing further as each second passed. When the telephone rang, interrupting the brief stand-off, Sarah let out a burst of air subconsciously held in her throat.

Mrs Jamieson held the receiver abruptly towards her. 'The operator's putting a call through to you now. And by the way, I expect some decorum in my house.'

Sarah accepted the telephone receiver feeling like a naughty child. She was at a loss as to what she had done to provoke Mrs Jamieson.

'Sarah, how are you? Where are you?'

'Hi, Dad. I'm fine. I'll be stuck here in Tongue for at least a few more days. Here's my number . . .' Sarah repeated the digits stiffly.

'Tongue? Tell me, Sarah, is . . .' There was a questioning edge in his normally monotone voice.

'What, Dad? Is everything okay?'

'Fine, fine. Been there a couple of times myself.'

'I know, well, I met a friend of yours. Well, an acquaintance really. Eliot Andrews.'

Nicole Alexander

Sarah heard a gasp behind her only to find Mrs Jamieson rubbing the small dining table as if her life depended on the shine factor.

'You still there? Anyway, I'm not sure I share your enthusiasm for the place, Dad. Still, most of the people here are friendly.' Sarah looked directly at Mrs Jamieson now shadowing the kitchen doorway.

'When are you moving on?' her father asked. 'There are a lot of interesting things to see in Scotland.'

'I'm waiting for my replacement hire car,' answered Sarah.

Through the thick walls the wind whistled around the cottage.

'You spoken to Jeremy yet?'

'No, Dad, and I won't be. It's over.' Above the whine of the wind, Sarah picked up the rattle of Jim's old truck. 'I'll call soon. Bye, Dad.' Sarah placed the receiver down softly.

Mrs Jamieson had gone.

Sarah agreed to dinner with Jim and his parents partly to escape another evening with Mrs Jamieson, although to be honest she was looking forward to seeing the Mackens – they were nice people. On approach their cottage was much like Mrs Jamieson's in appearance. It, too, was set into the side of a hill, with smoke curling from the chimney. But there, all similarities ended. The neat grass in front of the building flowed down a few hundred yards to a large loch, beyond which the flat land extended for almost a mile, until the start of a gradual incline of a hill. The house also faced east, but instead of crumbling fences and buildings, the Macken's cottage was in good order. As the truck pulled up, Sarah noted the stone wall running past the house, up the side of the hill.

'I hope you like haggis,' Jim said, as they walked to the front door.

Sarah slowed her pace. 'What?' The thought of stuffed sheep's stomach for dinner was not something she had reckoned on.

Jim grabbed her arm and pulled her forward. 'With neeps and tatties.'

'Neeps?' Sarah repeated, smiling weakly. It wasn't just the food. His excitement flowed through him like one of the hot-wires they used to keep out cattle that pushed through fences.

After a quick welcome, the four of them sat around a sturdy wooden table, eating soup. The room served as a kitchen, living and dining area. It was cosy, small and sparsely decorated, with only two round rugs, books and photographs on the mantlepiece relieving the whiteness of the walls and the darkness of the furniture.

'We knocked the wall down when Jim was a young lad,' Mr Macken said between mouthfuls of barley soup.

'We're all together. Just the three of us,' Mrs Macken added.

'How is the haggis progressing, Mum?'

Sarah caught the look that passed between mother and son. There was an undercurrent she could not quite pick up on. Mrs Macken wiped her hands on her apron several times and, collecting the soup bowls, went to the large oven.

'So, Sarah, Jim tells me your family were pioneers?'

'Is that so?' Mr Macken interrupted. 'Hmm, my family's been in this same cottage for about one hundred and fifty years. Not sure of the exact dates. No records, you know. It's been rebuilt, re-roofed, burnt out, you name it, but we're still here.' He sounded defensive. 'We'll keep going for a bit longer. There are about eighteen thousand or so crofts, you know, lass, each averaging around four acres.'

'Four acres!' Sarah's mouth dropped open.

'When the English moved in, they cleared wooded areas for cultivation, moved clan members off land they owned, or rented out cottages to the same families that had lived there for years. Everyone, well, near everyone is a tenant farmer, Sarah. Crofters.'

'Sarah wouldn't understand,' Mrs Macken interrupted.

Jim gave Sarah a look that begged forgiveness. Sarah was beginning to feel a little uncomfortable. The friendly Mrs Macken of the dog trials seemed to have been replaced by a woman far less welcoming.

'Tell us about Australia,' Jim finally asked, breaking the difficult silence.

'Umm, a bad drought every ten years on average. The current one has been going for a couple of years.'

'Don't forget the bushfires.' Mrs Macken placed laden white plates on the table. 'They're a form of regeneration for the trees.'

'I never realised you knew so much about Australia, Mum,' Jim said with interest.

'Hope you like haggis, Sarah.' Mrs Macken poured water from a tall plastic jug and passed everyone a glass.

'Yes, it's a specialty, you know,' Mr Macken said.

Sarah brought her knife down tentatively to cut across the brown, rubbery surface. She knew all eyes were on her, so she took a quick mouthful, followed by a forkful of potatoes and turnips. 'Interesting.' She smiled, not sure whether she should say thank you. The flavour was like roast chicken stuffing, almost gamey.

'Well, a small drop won't go astray.' Mr Macken had risen and returned to the table with a bottle and four dram glasses. 'Goes particularly well with haggis.' He poured and passed the squat cut glass tumblers.

Sarah sniffed the straight whisky, as the other three drank theirs down.

'Drink, Sarah, it won't hurt you,' Jim coaxed. 'In the Gaelic, whisky means the water of life.'

Sarah swallowed the bitterness and ate a mouthful of haggis.

'You had better give Sarah here the details,' Jim said to his mother.

'Well, Sarah, you take one sheep's stomach, wash and clean thoroughly . . .'

Sarah scraped the soft food onto her fork.

'Most important, lass,' Mr Macken interrupted, 'most important.'

'. . . then stuff.' Mrs Macken continued.

In Sarah's mouth, the contents squashed easily. She chewed lightly on the meat.

'The recipe's a secret, Sarah,' Jim said in a mock serious tone, 'but maybe, if Mother likes you, she'll share it with you later.'

Mrs Macken rolled her eyes.

Sarah automatically thought of the Colonel's secret recipe of herbs and spices and wished she was eating Kentucky Fried Chicken.

When dinner was finally finished, Sarah thanked God silently and passed her plate.

Selecting an old book from a cluttered shelf, Mr Macken sat down on the floral two-seater sofa. They had moved from the dining table and, having pushed it back against the wall, the four of them now sat before a softly glowing fire. Gliding loving fingers over yellowing pages, Robert Macken pointed to the Clan Gordon tartan, a faded picture of blue, black, green and yellow, with the motto, *Abiding*. 'Loyalty, the essence of being a clansman, bind the Scots together, hold them fast,' he said. At his father's words, Jim left Sarah's side to warm himself by the fire.

Mrs Macken watched her husband as he spoke, her eyes never leaving his face. Behind them, Jim gazed into the air above their heads. The Mackens were very close, Sarah realised, which would no doubt make Jim feel like an outsider occasionally, living as they did in such a small house.

Robert Macken drained his whisky and settled back in his chair. 'It was the late 1840s – my family immigrated to America after the potato famine,' he explained. 'Nothing to live on here, no way to pay rents.' He continued, 'Jim wants to carve out a huge area, grow sheep and cattle in great numbers,' he shook his head. 'The ground is no good. It is a waste of good money and effort. A man should be happy to have a roof over his head and live on the land he loves.'

'I never said Tongue was the place to be doing it,' Jim retorted angrily. 'South, now that's where the good soil is.'

'Not a week goes by, Sarah,' Mr Macken continued, ignoring his son, 'when our talks don't disintegrate into arguments.'

'Differences of opinion, dear,' Mrs Macken said, correcting her husband carefully. 'Jim has lots of suggestions when it comes to improvements,' she added, directing her comments to Sarah. 'And he's smart enough to handle things by himself.'

Sarah had the most unpleasant feeling that this last comment was directed at her.

'We were like slaves when the English first came, and not much has changed.' Jim drained his whisky. 'Working the land is hereditary for us, Sarah, communal. In the old days we gave military service in return and perhaps a share of the staple crop. But the landowners moved many of us off to improve their lands, to make way for large-scale sheep and cattle production.'

'And you want to do it again, lad.' Robert glared at his son.

Jim didn't seem to hear him. 'I want equality. I want a chance to expand our business. Here we are on impoverished lots. Some of us are still trying to eke out a living from fishing and kelping, but there wasn't much of that left a hundred years ago.'

'But surely the government must be –' Sarah tried to speak.

'Oh sure, Sarah, there have been a number of Acts. At least now it's easier for tenants to purchase their crofts, and we have security of tenure as well as the right to bequeath tenancies.' Jim's voice was sarcastic. 'Some crofts are agriculturally viable, but some can't even provide their owners with a subsistence living, so they have to diversify.'

'Like B&Bs?' Sarah asked. She thought of the numerous cottages passed on the long road north.

'Exactly.' Jim turned to his father. 'I don't want that life. I want to buy more land. Look around you: people barely subsisting, surrounded by rusting machinery, derelict vehicles, stray dogs and goats tied up at fences.'

'Oh, but Jim,' Mrs Macken said, 'what of the sleek cattle and stacked peat?'

'The simple life,' Jim said sarcastically. 'I don't want to be poor, and I'm sure as hell not ready to retire.' He stared at each of them, wild-eyed and defiant. 'My idea, Sarah,' he said, swallowing hard, 'is to sell to Lord Andrews, and move south or buy from him to increase our portion.'

'I will never sell,' Mr Macken announced with an air of finality. 'And I'm not buying either. You're a little boy with mighty large ideas. Goodnight, lass,' he called to Sarah as he walked across to the narrow staircase leading to the bedrooms upstairs.

'I thought you loved Tongue.' Sarah spoke quietly to Jim.

Jim waited for his father to leave the room, the heavy thud of his steps carrying noisily through the cottage. 'Oh I do love the north, Sarah, but being poor, never amounting to anything, well, that's not being patriotic, that is just stupid.'

'Well, it's time for bed, I think,' said Mrs Macken as she rose.

'Mum, I thought Sarah and I might stay and talk a while.' Jim moved to sit next to Sarah on the couch.

'I'm sure Sarah would like to get back to her B&B. After all, Jim, she is only visiting.'

Mrs Macken was already walking towards the door. Sarah took the hint. 'Absolutely. It was a lovely dinner.'

'Have a safe trip home.'

Somehow Sarah didn't think Jim's mother was referring to Mrs Jamieson's home.

'Had enough already?' Jim said, his tone one of disappointment as he followed her to the door, his mother smiling and waving behind them.

'I guess I'm tired.' Sarah tried to sound casual, but clearly Mrs Macken didn't have a high opinion of her.

They drove back the short distance to Mrs Jamieson's B&B in silence.

'So, Sarah –' Jim began, his voice sounding strained as he parked in front of the B&B, 'what's going to happen? Are you just going to leave?'

His words came unexpectedly. 'Jim, we've only known each other for a few days.'

'I know, I know. It's just that I feel like I have known you all my life.'

Sarah looked directly into his violet eyes, feeling the pull of her past against an unknown future. 'I'm not looking for a relationship, Jim. I'm sorry.' She got out of the truck and closed the door gently.

That night, Sarah slept fitfully. Her mind drifted, returning to the Gordons and to a time she never knew. Soaring above Wangallon she followed the lines of fences crisscrossing the expanse of country purchased by theft and christened with blood. The air was dry, the lack of moisture making it difficult to breathe. She awoke anxious and uncertain, her eyes flickering across the semi-gloom of Mrs Jamieson's scantily furnished guest room. The land was far more sacred than any of them realised, the Aborigines knew that. They had lived in and around Wangallon for many years. Their mark could be seen in the carvings on the old trees;

food carriers for women, canoes for the men, shields for ancient battles. Perhaps Wangallon was wound up in some huge spell of regeneration, with each successive family compelled to follow in the steps of those before them. Then there were the great-uncles and half-uncles, young children, teenagers, men who, over the century, had died during the foundation and life of Wangallon: her great-grandfather's brother, her grandfather's half-brother, Luke, and her own brother. Only her father's generation had survived unscathed, or had it? Her dad was an only child. Was it Wangallon's way of protecting itself? The property would never be split up as there was only one heir in every generation. If she stayed there, if she had children, would only one survive?

Downstairs, Sarah made coffee and sat quietly in the pre-dawn gloom of the sitting room. It was almost disconcerting to be in an environment that was so quiet. She half expected a dog to howl, and she ached to hear the scatterings of some small creature on a corrugated iron roof. Even the old owl, perhaps the descendent of one from years past, the one present at the settlement of Wangallon, was silent in her mind. Sarah could see him sitting, peering into his domain, searching for the tiny mice and small lizards that inhabited Wangallon's garden. Sarah knew it was time to leave Tongue. Her dreams of Wangallon had reinforced the importance of the land and made one thing clear to her. Her family's association with Wangallon could not end with words said in anger. Nor could she deny the important role Anthony played in the property's future. Regardless of whether he had ulterior motives, they needed to be friends.

≪ Winter, 1987 ≫

Wangallon Station

Angus shrugged his shoulders deep inside his oil-skin jacket. The only warm patches on his entire body came from the tin mug of coffee clasped firmly in his hands and the spot on his thigh claimed by Shrapnel's head. His backside had lost all feeling, perched as he was on a fallen bough that, reincarnated as a log, provided a sturdy if not damn uncomfortable seat. Anthony, sitting opposite him on an upside-down twenty-litre oil drum, tossed the dregs of his black tea onto the camp fire, the splats of moisture sizzling on the dying embers. The boy looked exhausted, in fact they all were. There was nothing more debilitating than working in cold conditions with a southerly wind biting all day long, after a freezing night in a swag. Resting his hand protectively on the soft down of Shrapnel's head, Angus inclined his own towards his young station manager.

'Let Dave and Lyle go when they've gathered in the last of the steers, they can take the horses back and unpack the gear.'

'You want to go too?' Anthony asked, stretching his legs out to ease the ache of coldness needling at his bones.

'What, and leave you and Pete to enjoy this beautiful day all by yourselves?'

They were miles away from Wangallon homestead on the southern boundary. Expediency remained Angus's prime motivation for camping out last night, but even with the hours of travelling saved, the job of trucking eight hundred prime steers to market was a two-day exercise and Angus had been frozen for every minute of it.

'There's only one more road train to load. So if you're up to it?'

Angus scowled into the wind. He'd been up to it forty years before this young lad had even been born. From the pocket of his jacket he pulled a small chocolate-chip biscuit and, ignoring Anthony's disbelieving shake of the head, he fed the morsel to Shrapnel, the dog crunching up the choc-bits like a kid. Pity, he thought, they used to be his favourite but age had relegated his dentures to the soft variety. At the thought of it he prodded the outside of his jaw where it hinged top to bottom. Things hadn't quite been mechanising properly in that department since dawn when his pocketknife had been required to crack the ice holding his dentures in a tin mug of water.

'She'll be on her way back soon, you know.' He was telling Anthony of his granddaughter's hoped-for imminent return, in part because the whole bloody episode continued to drag out like some midday soap opera. If Sarah didn't agree to his terms when next they spoke, he intended to disinherit her. Yet he still needed to keep the boy's interest peaked. Surely the news of her broken engagement had done that. 'You two are really going to have to put your bloody differences behind you. I'm sick and tired of it all.' Out on the horizon, a cloud of dust rose high into the atmosphere. Pete, Lyle and Dave, three experienced cattle musterers from the top end, were bringing in the last two hundred head from over the river. Angus nodded approvingly. At least some people knew how to keep to schedule. Soon the bellowing of over a hundred years of breeding would carry through the slate-grey afternoon, stirring the bush creatures into wakefulness with their dirt-shuddering gait. 'I'm getting too old, Anthony, and final decisions have to be made. You know I want you to stay on as manager, but I've another offer. If you marry Sarah you'll inherit thirty per cent of Wangallon.'

Anthony looked across to where Angus's hands brushed the thick pelt of his old dog. The old fella certainly knew how to get a man's attention and the carrot he'd been dangling for the last three years was now finally a solid gold one. Thirty per cent of Wangallon. He'd dreamed of the possibility, never daring to believe it would happen. He'd *almost* accepted the probability of being life-long manager. The problem was . . . well, the problem was Sarah and he was damned if he knew why he was even thinking about her. 'Does Sarah know that?' A small grain of concern was beginning to form in his gut.

Angus picked at a small brown tick, which, having settled itself proprietarily behind Shrapnel's floppy left ear, was proving diffi-cult to budge. Finally he prised the pest free, squashing the tough body between a stockyard-filthy thumbnail and index finger. 'Sarah's opinion is irrelevant.'

'It seems pretty relevant to me,' Anthony perservered. 'Does she know?'

'I told her of the conditions.' Flicking the remains of the tick towards the dying fire, Angus wondered, and not for the first time, how the hell he'd managed to choose a boy with a conscience. 'If you don't marry within the next five years, Wangallon is to be sold. She'll get zilch. Well, actually I think I said something about marriage sealing the deal. She has to move back and live on the property for five years.'

'What?' Anthony looked at the old man opposite him, a man

hardwired by sun and rain, a man whom he knew would do anything to protect his beloved property. But it wasn't about protection anymore, it was about total control until the very end. 'You can't force people to marry, Angus.'

'I know every bend in the creeks and rivers that flow through this rich fertile land. I can follow the trails used by my ancestors when they first selected Wangallon and I can take you to corroboree grounds even the local Aboriginal elders are unaware of. This land is mine and I will do with it as I see fit.'

'Even take away your own granddaughter's inheritance?' Anthony didn't want to be a part of this mess. This whole business was seriously screwed up. Shit, Angus was seriously screwed up.

'I can hardly leave it to an inexperienced single woman. That's where you come in.'

'This isn't the 1900s, Angus.'

'I have a buyer already. A Yank actually, but he's a good operator and he knows what he's doing. He wants it, he loves cattle and he has a son to inherit. I'm looking for a strong custodian, Anthony. Someone who wants Wangallon, someone who deserves Wangallon. I expected more from you.'

'What do you mean you expected more? I've worked my arse off here, delivered year after year, kept within budget, ensured profits grew –'

'Blah, blah, blah,' Angus lifted his arms briefly into the air. 'Of course you did all that. You would have been out the bloody door years ago otherwise. No, I chose you. Out of all the would-be-jackeroos I chose you. Anyway, you had a good pedigree. I knew your grandfather. Fleeced him once in a card game down in Melbourne actually,' Angus chuckled. 'With the financial situation on your own property, there was little chance that you would ever be given the option of returning home, so you were perfect. Your mother's Scottish on her maternal side and both you and your brother were big, strapping, good-looking boys. Perfect.'

'Perfect?' Anthony began kicking dirt onto the embers of the fire, his riding boots grinding in the soil and smouldering wood. Satisfied it no longer posed a hazard, he dropped his empty mug into the top of his esky before replacing the lid firmly. 'Perfect,' he repeated slowly, the ramifications of Angus's words burning him like a red hot branding iron. His fist curled automatically and for a fleeting second he imagined himself crossing the few feet between them, his knuckles crunching bone on bone, the old fella tumbling backwards over the log. His fist dropped to his side. 'It won't work,' he said simply. Dogs were barking loudly, the lead of the cattle were only five hundred metres away from the yards, Anthony listened to the loud bellowing and heard the sound of a whip cracking. 'It won't work because Sarah already thinks I want to get my hands on Wangallon.' Now finally he understood why the night at the races had turned sour. Sarah, he and innocent old Jeremy were only pawns in a game that most probably had been played for generations.

'And?'

'Well, that's what you've bloody well insinuated to her.' He thought back to their last conversation. No wonder Sarah didn't want to talk to him. Down the wide dirt road the unmistakeable rumble of a road train reverberated in the air. The chrome expanse of the truck glittered in the weak mid-afternoon sun, the driver working slowly down the gears as he neared the loading ramp.

'You can fix things,' Angus stated firmly with an exaggerated wink.

'These are peoples' lives you are messing with. Jesus, I can't believe this shit. You chose me as a fucking breeder.'

'Get over yourself, Anthony. Business is business and there is no place in the world for second best.'

'Yeah, well you certainly illustrated that with your own son.'

Angus stood up. Shrapnel, jumping up quickly onto the log

beside his master, began to growl softly. 'Don't presume to dictate to me, boy.'

'Isn't that exactly what you have been doing all your life?' The cattle were at the yards, streaming in in a rush of red and white, filling the pens with dust, dogs and the yells of the men as they forced the cattle onwards. 'You're not the man I thought you were,' Anthony finished simply. The truck, already reversing, gave a great exhalation of breath as the air-brakes came on and the long vehicle became stationary.

Angus joined him as they walked towards the yards, his knees paining with effort as he fought to keep up. 'I'm exactly the man you thought I was, Anthony. That's why you're still here.'

At the cattle yards Anthony scaled the high timber fence, jumping down into the yard below.

'I'm giving you two months' notice, Angus,' Anthony called back. 'I've had enough.'

Angus rested his arms on the timber railings, his gnarled fingers playing with the rough splinters beneath his hands. 'I won't accept it.' He'll get over it, Angus decided. Maybe now things were out in the open some kind of reconciliation would be possible between Sarah and Anthony. At least that is what he wished for, that and wishing Cameron had been a better horseman. With difficulty Angus climbed the timber railings, his face distorting as his knees suffered under the twisting motion of lifting one leg over the top railing to begin the climb down the other side. Years ago he would have flown over the bloody thing in a flash, made a mockery of these new breed of lads who called themselves stockmen. God, how he hated old age, especially when there was still so much to accomplish. Walking through the first empty yard, he lifted the chain on the large gate to enter the next, which held about fifty head of steers. They were in forward-store condition, a long way off being fat but certainly a handy enough weight to consider selling them, a far better option than trying to feed them as the bite of winter exaggerated an already debilitating drought.

'Angus, get out of the way!'

It was the lad Anthony, screaming and running towards him from the left. To his right, old Shrapnel barked and straight ahead a steer was charging directly at him.

≪ Summer, 1987 ≫

Tongue, Northern Scotland

'You don't strike me as the kind of lass who would rush into something.'

Sarah looked up slowly from the untouched water glass twirling in her fingers. Leaning back into the two-seater couch, she rubbed the bridge of her nose tiredly. Last night's dream of the settlement of Wangallon still haunted her thoughts. She listened to Mrs Jamieson's deep sigh as she joined her on the couch. Great, Sarah thought as she made room for the older woman.

'Sarah Gordon, times were when things didn't matter so much. The clans did inter-marry. That was then.' Mrs Jamieson pulled herself upright. 'Not now.' She cleared her throat carefully. 'You can't have a relationship with Jim.'

'What? Who's talking about a relationship?'

'Who do you think? Mrs Robert Macken.' Mrs Jamieson got to her feet, smoothing her plain cotton dress and gathering her worn cardigan about her. 'Besides, you love someone else.'

413

The conversation seemed to be moving very randomly. Sarah shook her head vehemently.

Mrs Jamieson inclined her head knowingly. 'Aye, you run from your heritage, as lost within your own life as Jim is. Half of him is missing, lass. An important part he's unaware of: his father.'

'His father?' Sarah repeated, screwing her eyes up in confusion.

'Lass, I look at you and see myself. I look at you and . . . Sarah Gordon, lass, your land is far more important to you than anything else. You love your country, the land. As I love mine. I don't believe you would forsake your home, even if you did care for Jim.' Mrs Jamieson reached reluctantly into her dress pocket, her hand quivering as she withdrew an old black-and-white photograph. 'I can see it in your eyes as sure as I saw it in your father's.'

Sarah accepted the photograph. 'My God, it's Dad!'

'Drink this.'

Sarah threw back the dram of whisky accompanying the fresh coffee and thought of the many photographs salvaged from her father's office in West Wangallon. Then there were the discarded ones, images Sarah found so entrancing that they hung in her Sydney apartment. The cottage in one of those photographs was the very same she now inhabited. Why hadn't she seen the resemblance sooner?

'Pride, lass, pride stops a great deal from being accomplished in the world. It stops people from sharing the truth with the very ones they care most about.' Mrs Jamieson took a fortifying gulp of her whisky. 'Maggie Macken knows who you are now, Sarah, yet how could she acknowledge you? By doing so she would break her boy's heart. She hopes you will leave. She only ever wanted her son's happiness, but even if a romance were possible between you two young people we both know you would not leave Wangallon for anyone, let alone Jim. Maggie and I, well we have never seen eye to eye, thanks to your father, but in this case we have agreed it is for the best.'

'For the best?' Sarah moved to stand opposite Mrs Jamieson. Her head pounded with the strain of this bizarre conversation. Perspiration collected at the waistband of her jeans, her palms were sweaty. 'I don't understand any of this. How did you come to have a photo of my father and why on earth would you think that there is something between Jim and me? That *is* what you're insinuating, isn't it?'

'Maggie loves her son. She's always loved him, you know, as much as I have. Who is to blame her for wanting everything for him? Those who know the story would keep their mouths shut all right. But there are others who would not. This is a small community, Sarah Gordon. It is too small for your dreams and even if you both left, those of us who remain would suffer the gossip for years.'

'Gossip? What are you talking about?' Sarah asked, her voice rising uneasily.

'This place is in our blood, as yours is in you. And if you truly listen to your heart, you will understand the truth. Jim is your half-brother.'

Sarah saw the faces of the men in her family, saw their piercing violet eyes, heard Maggie Macken's descriptions of a country she had never seen.

'Robert Macken is not Jim's father.'

Sarah experienced a pain in her abdomen, a feeling of being physically hit.

'Jim doesn't know you are his half-sister, Sarah, lass, and it is better that way. You must break off your friendship, if that is what it is.'

Much later, after Sarah managed to consume a couple of spoonfuls of thick barley soup, her head cleared a little. Now she knew why her father had been less than thrilled with the idea of this trip.

'I lost my only brother, Cameron, in a horse-riding accident. Every day of my life I –'

'Your pain lingers like a shroud, but none can bring him back; nor should they.'

'I see so much of him in Jim. It's the way he looks at the world, joking, caring about everything as if, as if –'

'It were his last?' Mrs Jamieson finished. 'It is easy to love the reckless, for those are the ones we fail to truly understand. But you love Jim for your brother's sake. You want to see those things in him, but he is not reckless, he is his own person, steady, responsible, serious and strong; no doubt, lass, a good counterpart for a brother.' Mrs Jamieson pushed the soup closer to Sarah, nodding towards the bowl. 'Be content to know there is another like you in the world, Sarah Gordon. Most of us are never fortunate enough to have more than one gift bestowed on us in a lifetime.'

'But Jim, surely he has a right to know?'

'At some time. We all have to be ready. Maybe the time has passed, maybe it will come again in the future.'

'And my father?'

Mrs Jamieson leaned back and smiled.

'He arrived from nowhere with stories of his home and his family. At the ceilidhs he entranced us with his tales of settlement, told us of how his forefathers set out from the Gordon Highlands and carved a country such as Australia until they had a portion of their own. I loved him then and there. We all did. He was the embodiment of so many of those who left, of so many forefathers never seen again. In him he carried a sister, brother, aunt or great-grandfather. He had the passion of a hundred lifetimes in his eyes, and he loved his people and place as much as I loved mine. I adored him.'

'You?' Sarah could not believe the grey-haired woman sitting opposite her.

'I wasn't always old, Sarah,' Mrs Jamieson replied, her feathery eyebrows lifting in amusement. 'I thought of marriage, but then I believed I could no sooner leave the North Country than he could leave his blue haze. We spent many a day together and then on the last, at a time of my choosing, I turned away from him. He left without a word and returned, oh, months later. When I saw him, I knew then and there that if he asked me, I would go with him. He stayed part of the winter here. There were many days he spent in the company of Lord Andrews and his father. They were a gentleman family then. We saw each other and I waited, but he never asked me again. He was too proud and I said nothing. Before he left, I heard young Maggie was outing with him. I saw the flare in both their eyes one night and knew he would not visit me again, as sure as I knew he would not stay for Maggie, nor would he ever return to Tongue.

'In the summer, Jim was born and Maggie married Robert. I did not need to see the boy to know who the father was. And I had heard of the violet eyes of one line of the Clan Gordon. Young Jim had those eyes like his father and –' she nodded pointedly at Sarah – 'his sister. I spoke to Maggie many years later, told her I had written to Ronald, your father, telling him of his boy. She's not spoken to me since, until this morning. She believed young Jim's birthright should remain a secret. But it was too late. I told your father because it was only right he should know.'

'Dad never said anything.'

'And you would be expecting him to? He didn't know about Jim until the year your own dear brother turned five.'

Sarah couldn't stop her eyes filling with tears as she recalled the gradual disintegration of their family.

'I'm sorry, lass. Things have been hard for you.'

'Hard!' Sarah gave a weary sigh. 'My mother virtually ignored me. Her life revolved around my brother. She adored him, I guess, because Cameron was the son of her lover, while I was the daughter she didn't want.' Wiping tears from her cheek, Sarah blew her nose loudly.

'I'm sorry, Sarah.' Mrs Jamieson patted Sarah's hand, the roughness of her calloused palms pulling the soft skin beneath.

'Well, it's done now,' Sarah replied sadly, removing her hand from the table top to place it protectively in her lap. 'I guess after Mum learned Dad had been unfaithful she just found it difficult to love me. Ironic, isn't it? She was also unfaithful, yet there was no room in her heart for me.' She wondered if the revelation of Jim's existence caused the wedge between her grandfather and father. 'Grandfather must have found out about Dad's affair and been disgusted.'

'Or supremely disappointed young Jim wasn't shipped out to Australia. Look, Sarah, I gave no thought to how the news of Jim's existence would affect your family. No doubt your father believed your mother would be able to handle the situation, otherwise he never would have told her. But, you see, you can't tell how people will react, that is why it is so important for you to keep this to yourself. You met a soul on the other side of the world, lass. You know a part of your father few would. What's done is for a reason. Don't destroy a family you may never see again.'

'But doesn't Jim deserve to know about his father and his family? Don't you want to know . . .'

'What? Tell us what in our hearts we know, lass? Tell us he married a woman who didn't share his love for his beloved home, but at least bore him two strong children? All a man can ask for is strong young 'uns. I see the sadness and know you, Sarah Gordon. Go back to Wangallon, it's what made your family. Go back and live. Don't wonder for the rest of your life what might have been.'

❖

Sarah was sitting on the cracked cement step outside the cottage when the familiar rattle of the ancient green pick-up slowed on approach. Swallowing involuntarily, her hands grew clammy as Jim appeared from the vehicle's interior. Dressed in dark jeans and a round-necked jumper in a mottle of green and grey hues, Sarah noted that although tall, it was his barrel chest and thick arms that marked him as a Gordon. And, violet eyes aside, he only needed a pipe and a dog by his side to replicate the yellowing photograph of her great-grandfather, Hamish. He walked steadily towards her and, as Sarah's eyes traversed the length of his body, she studied this man who was blood related, and caught her first glimpse of the steadfast, sensitive boy Mrs Jamieson spoke of. As he sat next to her, spreading his legs out before him, crossing his ankles carefully, Sarah sensed the weight of responsibility that rested comfortably on his broad shoulders. How wrong she had been. Jim Macken was a Gordon all right.

'You won't stay, will you, Sarah? Mother said so.'

Preferring to have been given a day to gather her swirling thoughts instead of the few hours granted to her, Sarah touched his forearm, her fingers resting there, feeling the deep curve of his bicep. 'I have to go home.' She watched the bunching of his facial muscles, poring over the features of this man who was her half-brother, rendering his image forever in her brain. She wanted to run upstairs and grab her camera, take heaps of photos, jump, leap and wail, cry out to the world she was not alone anymore. 'Leaving you will be like leaving my best friend.' It was the most she could say. 'But I can't stay here, Jim, it's not my life, it's yours.' Already her tears were rising unbidden.

'Answer me, lass. Do you really love your land so much you would never leave it? For that is what Mrs Jamieson says.'

Her silence answered him. He wiped his hands roughly on his jeans, 'I should go then.' He stood slowly, straightening his back as if finishing a long day of manual labour. With the slightest incline of his head he began to walk away.

'Jim . . .' There were so many things she wanted to share with him; so many inconsequential things that she realised only he could fathom, for they were alike; he was her half-brother. 'You know that out of everyone in the living world, you are the essence of me?' Running to the door of the truck, her hands caught his.

Jim raised an eyebrow, the action turning his quizzical scowl at what he considered an overly melodramatic outburst into genuine concern. Something wasn't right here, but it was beyond his control. He turned the ignition, comforted by the familiar rattle of the engine. He cared for her, but he would not ask her to stay. 'You cannot pass through someone's life, Sarah, without leaving a little of yourself behind.' He accelerated sharply and did not look back.

Mrs Jamieson waited patiently by her side, her arms folded in the pose Sarah would come to remember her by; the pocket on her flowery apron bulging with dust rags and tissues, the perpetual scowl of dissatisfaction and shock of grey hair at odds with the youthful gleam in her eyes. Agreeing to disagree on the subject of revealing Jim's true birthright, they had finally reached a truce that allowed this last moment of companionable silence as Sarah waited for a taxi outside the cottage.

'One day Ronald Gordon will meet his son and glad he will be to know that the bond between his daughter and young Jim will not be broken by distance or time.'

Sarah hugged the older woman tightly. 'Tell me one thing, Mrs Jamieson,' she asked, breaking free of her friend's protective arms. 'How can you decide someone's life for them?'

'How can you not give your young man in Australia a chance?'

They had only discussed Anthony twice. Once on the arrival of his telegram some days ago and this morning when Mrs Jamieson asked his name. Within seconds Sarah found herself discussing her broken engagement to Jeremy and her grandfather's will. As for Anthony, Sarah knew her friend meant well but Mrs Jamieson was really off-base. The taxi drew up in a shower of gravel.

'Thank you for everything.' Sarah's mouth stretched flat in thought, 'Geez, I've made such a mess of things.'

'Nonsense.'

'And Anthony changed. I don't think he is the same anymore. And there are so many stipulations and options and –'

'Rubbish, lass. It is strength of belief that is required. You think you have to make choices, but you don't. Your life is waiting for you. Now let's pop that bag in the boot and send you on your way.' Mrs Jamieson opened the boot of the dark sedan into which Sarah placed her luggage, 'If you think you leave a part of yourself behind, well, remember you take a part with you. In the end, it will make a whole.'

'I'll telephone.'

'And I'll expect it,' Mrs Jamieson replied.

❧ *Summer, 1867* ❧

Wangallon Station

The eastern sun shadowed the country. It took her an hour to walk to the cemetery, during which Rose stopped to pick the small paper daisies managing to cling to life. She drew breathless, her feet dragging on the narrow track that wound onwards through the spring herbage, her long skirt trailing twigs, soil and leaf litter. There was rain last night. A brief cooling shower that washed clogging dust from leaves and petals and it was this fleeting glimmer of freshness that propelled Rose onwards.

The clearing resembled a still pool of water. About its edges, aged trees formed a cooling canopy overhead while grasses swayed in a calming ripple. There was a low paling fence surrounding the wooden marker, the face of it lying in the sun's path until mid-morning, when the sheltering trees protected it for the rest of the day: protected the sleeping place of her dead children.

The fever came in the dark of night and spread its tentacles outwards from the nursery to also claim three of the servants. William and baby Samuel succumbed first. Then her beloved firstborn, Howard, having survived the worst of it, was bitten by a snake while convalescing in the garden. Snakebite, fever, no matter the malady the resultant end remained death and within two months of Abdullah's leaving only young Luke remained as the heir to Wangallon.

'Have pity on those that come after,' Rose whispered to a God now firmly entrenched in her soul. Separating the small clutch of flowers, she brushed leaves and twigs from the dirt mounds to place a dried offering at the base of each marker. Breathless, Rose sat heavily at the base of the only large tree within the enclosure. Any remnant of strength that once remained had surely drained out of her during the walk to the cemetery. Food had become unwelcome in her body. What little nourishment she managed to consume was for one purpose; to enable her to walk to this place and lie down with her children. There was nowhere left to go. Tilting her head back against the knobbly bark, she observed a flock of multicoloured lorikeets as they flew overhead. In their beauty, Rose thought of Abdullah.

She awoke to feel the sun burning through her thin blouse, prickling the wasted, sallow skin beneath. Rustling foliage revealed an owl. The bird lifted his head from the soft feathers of his breast, stretched his wings slowly and arched his delicately feathered neck. Large oval eyes, dark with intelligence, blinked sagely at her. Rose remembered the owl from Howard's funeral and she found herself smiling. With a swift flutter, the bird lifted itself clear of the old gum's branches and, having breached the canopy overhead, flew clear of the gravesite and out into the morning. Rose followed the bird's progress until it disappeared from view.

It was better this way. Since Abdullah's leaving nothing was at it should be. Rose woke from ravaged dreams to the scent of his body, to the silken touch of his skin on hers and she knew she could not endure the future. Her heart had been blessed and it was enough. She thought of the owl leading the way to freedom and she accepted the glorious knowledge of release. It was good and proper, for clearly Hamish Gordon had little need of her in the future. And this was one decision in her life her husband could not control. It took so little to free oneself of the binds of this life, one merely had to cease eating and drinking; one merely needed to decide they wanted to be free.

Minutes later her right hand, encased by the gold bangle, dropped to the dirt by her side. Her slight chest rose and fell, then stilled.

⋘ *Summer, 1867* ⋙

Paddington, Sydney

Claire tucked the bed quilt beneath her father's chin and followed the doctor down to the parlour. It was warm tonight. A small fire in the hearth added to the heat, however it kept the flies from seeking refuge in the cooler confines of their home. A green wreath of eucalyptus leaves sat fragrantly on the mantlepiece between two candles. Claire touched the simple decoration. It was Christmas Eve.

'He is simply tired, Claire.'

The doctor stood opposite her, his black suit and leather bag making him appear rather like a forbidding crow. Claire knew she should offer him sherry or some of the watery wine her father had recently taken to drinking, but the day had already lasted far too long. She wished Mrs Cole would appear with her bustling energy and whisk the doctor out of their home, but she was long asleep, having sat with Claire's father through the previous night.

'Will he recover?' It was a question that needed to be addressed, although she hated asking. Over the previous weeks

Claire attempted to prepare herself for what Mrs Cole called the inevitability of life, but the fortitude she had depended on in the past was failing her.

'Now, my dear, there is a stage a person reaches when they've endured enough of this world.' The doctor patted her arm reassuringly. His face, having being drawn downwards with life's disappointments, found a smile almost impossible. 'At least you are well provided for. That must be a great comfort to your father.'

Claire desperately wanted to hear more than this. She wanted to know that her father would be down sitting in his favourite chair within days. How she longed to sit beside him and share her lessons, to play one of the musical pieces that many hours of practice had finally rewarded her with.

'Your father would wish you to be strong, my dear.'

'Of course,' Claire answered soberly. Already the safe and familiar appeared to be sliding into obscurity.

'It is the finite quality of our lives that makes life itself so precious. Remember that, my dear. Now, what plans have been made for your future?'

'My future?' Claire gave a small frown. She did not want to discuss her future with anyone. For one thing it was hers, not some commodity that could be secured by brown paper and string. However, she supposed her kindly doctor had already reported back to Wilkinson & Cross, making her father's fading health common knowledge. Taking a candle from the mantlepiece, Claire lit the doctor's passage to the front door. 'I am tired, Doctor. I do thank you for coming.'

He patted her arm. 'You know where I am should you need me.'

Claire bade the doctor goodnight and closed the front door, turning the key securely in the lock. The question of her future suddenly seemed to have taken on a matter of urgency, for Mrs Cole had quizzed her on the exact same subject. Claire naively assumed that she would go on living in this house when the time came for her father to leave this world. Here, surrounded by the familiar, she hoped at least that her studies and music lessons would help ease the loss of her father. Yet having attempted to explain to Mrs Cole of her expectation of continuing on in the present manner, her housekeeper had proceeded to kindly but firmly remind her that her current life existed because of the good grace of another. It was with shocking clarity that Claire realised that at this point in her life anything might happen to her. Her benefactor might lose interest, the money could cease and her marvellous chance at an education would disappear. What would happen to her she had asked of Mrs Cole, if her worst fears were realised? Mrs Cole, having neatly avoided her concerns, suggested what she considered to be Claire's best and only option – an arranged marriage.

Settled in her father's chair before the fireplace, Claire pulled a folded letter from her pocket and with a wary glance in the direction of Mrs Cole's sleeping quarters, opened it. She had carried the letter on her person for the last few months. Guilt following its theft led to the initial concealment, then a plan of sorts began to formulate itself in her mind.

It had been early morning in September when Claire noticed Mrs Cole in the laneway talking to the stranger. Having thrown open her bedroom window in anticipation of the arrival of the pianoforte, her recognition of the man had been instantaneous. He was the same turbaned gentleman she passed driving the dray down their quiet street the morning she had returned with the duck. Such a liaison was intriguing in itself, more so when Claire enquired as to who the man was. Mrs Cole had denied knowing him. The letter had appeared that same afternoon. Blown about by the gusty wind Claire accidently trod on it in the vegetable patch. After the morning's events it had taken little decision as to whether she should open it.

The letter, written to Mrs Cole's sister, talked of the usual minute details of running a household. The buying of food-stuffs featured prominently, as did the price of produce and the quality. What was most intriguing however, was the paragraph referring to Mrs Cole's gratefulness, for it seemed her sister had found her the housekeeping position with the Whittakers. This, Claire decided, was the pearl of knowledge required to begin tracking down her benefactor. Yet Mrs Cudlow's address, some remote property many miles from Sydney, provided no further clues. Certainly Claire could not simply write and announce herself requesting further information. There had to be more, but there wasn't, at least not until today. Claire flicked through the newspaper purchased by Mrs Cole earlier until she came to the page that had captured her attention just prior to the doctor's arrival.

News has reached our shores of the sinking of the Southern Star last month en route from Sydney to London.

Claire ran her finger down the column as the reporter detailed the incident.

All hands lost . . . well known vessel . . . shocking tragedy . . .
The cargo included the largest single shipment of wool to sail from Australia. Belonging to the wealthy Scottish pastoralist Mr Hamish Gordon of Wangallon Station in north-western New South Wales . . .

Claire checked the property name on Mrs Cole's letter. It was exactly the same. Wangallon.

With a flutter of excitement she tore the article from the paper and folded it along with the letter. This Mr Gordon had to be her benefactor. It had to be him. Mrs Cole and Mrs

Cudlow's relationship, a wealthy Scottish gentleman, these were facts surely too great to be coincidences.

Tomorrow, after she had seen to her father's comfort, Claire decided to pay Wilkinson & Cross a visit. She could not sit and wait for an uncertain future. True, she may well be presuming the worst, but in the future she would most certainly be alone and it was vital that she knew what awaited her.

❧ *Winter, 1987* ❧

Wangallon Station

*T*he storm gathered in the west. Far out on the horizon, the cloud billowed savagely, moving ominously towards them. The wind lifted as Sarah and Anthony locked the garage and untied the dogs at their kennels. The animals cowered in the dust beneath proud trees, now bending like rubber bands. Inside, they closed every door and window, blocking any openings with towels. When the storm hit, it carried with it the red heart of Australia, the grainy particles bashing at the house, forcing their way through cracks and crevices, the badly eroded topsoil dropping like a blanket of ash before being collected by the wind and scattered. By nightfall, dirt from Ayers Rock would be mixing with the dry dust of Wangallon over the Pacific. By nightfall, the international news would show Sydney surrounded by a thick pall, office workers choking in the dust of the bush.

'Will you be okay?' Anthony asked. The kitchen was just as Angus left it a week ago. Dried toast crumbs sat on a plate at the sink, a half-drunk mug of tea on the table. He watched Sarah staring out the kitchen window. All he wanted to do was comfort her, yet only the minimum of words had passed between them since he'd told her briefly of Angus' accident.

'Will you tell me now?' She clasped her hands together tightly, trying to stem their shaking as she sat at the kitchen table. Tiredness seeped through her body, the hazy otherworldly feeling of jetlag dragging at her thoughts.

'He was horned by a rogue steer,' Anthony began. 'We were nearly finished loading them to fulfil a contract at the feedlot when this mad terror broke free and . . . well, your grandfather just didn't have time to move.'

'Where were you? Couldn't you do anything?'

Anthony cleared his throat, concentrating on controlling his facial muscles. In truth, distracted as he was following Angus's staggering revelations that afternoon, the accident was beyond anyone's control. 'As I said, it happened so quickly. He was pretty badly off.'

Sarah visualised the picture: the blood, her grandfather lying in the dust of the yards, the chaos of assessing his injuries and the desolation of the property.

'I contacted the police and that travelling nurse on the two-way radio.' Anthony broke off, clearing his throat again. 'Anyway, Pete went to direct the ambulance and I don't think your grandfather thought he was going to make it.' Moving to sit next to Sarah, he laid his hand over hers, imploring her to understand the magnitude of that day, that he would have bloodied himself if it would have helped. 'We built up a campfire when it got cool and carried him closer. He never complained, never said one bloody word. It was a beautiful night, Sarah. The stars were so close you could have touched them. He shook my hand.' Anthony's voice dropped to a whisper. 'The ambulance was taking so long. I put Shrapnel beside him. Funny thing is, Sarah, and I couldn't say this to anyone else, but I think he wanted to be left out there by the campfire.'

The scent of gum leaves washed over Sarah as a steady stream of tears began to fall silently down her cheeks.

'It was as though the night was full. As . . . as if there were other people around. He said, "It's a good death, for both of us"'.

'But he didn't die,' Sarah said, full of hope. 'He didn't die.' She swiped roughly at tears she believed she could no longer keep producing. Outside the wind rattled the faded green and white awnings sheltering the homestead, their aluminium stays creaking in complaint.

'No, he didn't.' He couldn't go, Anthony thought wryly, not when his life's work remained unfinished.

The warmth of Anthony's hand finally began to seep into the chill of her own. Sarah's shoulders slumped as she stretched her neck from side to side trying to ease weeks of tension in one unconvincing movement. 'S-Shrapnel?' she questioned, waiting as Anthony dropped his eyes to the table-top.

'The dog went to his rescue,' he mumbled before lifting his head. 'Never seen anything like it in my life.' Anthony took a breath, his voice filled with pride. 'I never would have believed it. Shrapnel must be over six years old. When he saw that steer attack Angus, he didn't hesitate.'

'Shrapnel's gone?' Even as she asked, she knew it was true.

'The steer charged, knocked your grandfather over, Shrapnel rushed up and held onto the animal's neck for dear life. Three times he was shaken loose, and three times he rushed back. It all happened so quickly. By the time I got the rifle, your grandfather had been gouged pretty badly in the side. He was still standing though; tough old bugger, trying to pull himself up the fence. Pete was on the railings above, trying to heave him upwards. Shrapnel knew what was going to happen. I let out a round of bullets, but the steer had already made his charge. Shrapnel flew into the air, and was caught between your grandfather and the animal's horns. He was ripped pretty badly, I reckon he died instantly. The steer dropped dead about two feet from your grandfather.'

'And?' Sarah knew there was more.

'Angus staggered towards Shrapnel, patting him once before collapsing himself.'

The last thing she wanted was to continue crying, for once started she doubted her ability to stop. It was as if there was a vast untapped well inside her.

Wordlessly, Anthony left Sarah sitting at the kitchen table and began walking through the old homestead, turning on the lights. If anything could make them friends again, only this tragedy could. So why did he find it so difficult to reach out to her? At the airport they had hugged once in a kind of nod to solidarity, but at the hospital she had been uncommunicative, so after listening to the doctor explain Angus' critical condition, he chose to leave her alone to spend time by the old fella's bedside. Little time passed before her reappearance in the hospital waiting room, where she had kicked fiercely at the drink-vending machine, before slurping down a can of soft drink and eating a chocolate bar.

Leaving the kitchen table Sarah wandered through the musty rooms, running a finger along the oak dining table and making a deep line in the thick sheen of dust. Even the silverware, scattered as it was on sideboards, inlaid tables and display cabinets, appeared tarnished. Her fingers marked where Cameron had rested all those years ago. There was the scar from his spurs. A small pen mark was etched at the head of the table from a letter once written there, next to it a crack was forming from the dry heat of the outback. More cracks showed in the skirting boards of the rooms she passed through and some walls were also affected by the shifting foundations. Rooms creaked with the memories of family, of a grandmother, of love, of death, of joy. So much more time seemed to have elapsed, more than the weeks since she had last seen Anthony, left her home country, found a brother she never knew existed and then lost him again. And now her grandfather lay in hospital. He was nearing eighty-seven years of age and she doubted his body's ability to fully recover.

In her bedroom, the old packing-case desk with its cut-off cotton reels for handles, greeted her. She stared at the ancient piece. The wood, though cracked across the top, remained in remarkable condition, the right edge worn smooth by the movement of arm and wrist. The pale blue paint was almost faded, but the small drawers mounted on the top of the desk still opened and the twin cupboards beneath revealed two shelves stuffed with letters, photos, dried flowers, stones; precious oddments from the life she had known before the death of her brother. It was an old desk, rather ugly in its handmade form, unwanted, except perhaps by collectors of the rough-hewn furniture of this country's early pioneers. Once used by her great-grandfather Hamish, then by her grandfather, she had claimed it following her parents' departure from West Wangallon. Where now was the family to which she could pass it on?

The wind was dying and with it, the consuming dust of the drought. Sarah did not need daylight to see the decaying world awaiting her: struggling dams, caking mud, creeping skeletons where once animals could be recognised. In darkness as in daylight the endless struggle to survive surrounded her and her home. Yet with her grandfather's accident it had moved beyond the bearable and struck deeply at the core of what she could only describe as her soul.

Anthony found her sitting on the edge of her bed. He knocked on her door, placed her suitcase down, then ensured the doors leading onto the verandah were locked tightly against the wind and dust.

'We start shearing tomorrow.'

'Everything under control?' Sarah answered automatically. Why couldn't she say something? Tell him how desperately sad and worried she was. He leaned heavily against the doorframe, one hand shoved into the pocket of his jeans, his brown arm looking dark next to the cream of his jumper, where the rolled material ended at his elbow.

'Your father was here last week, then he returned to the coast. He is trying to organise Sue at some type of hospice. He hopes to be here by Saturday. Well, I'll let you get some sleep.' Still she sat on the bed, her eyes listless. 'Your grandfather treated me as one of the family. I didn't expect it, but he did. And it meant a lot.' He hesitated. 'I just wanted to let you know that I appreciated it.'

'I know.'

Well at least she was listening, that was something Anthony thought. 'Anything I can get you?'

'No, thanks.' There was something that needed to be said. 'Anthony?'

'Yes.'

'Thank you for everything.'

He smiled slowly.

Sarah searched for some way of prolonging the conversation.

'I, um, wanted to let you know that I gave Angus two months' notice just before the accident, but obviously I'll hang around until he's up and about and I've found a replacement.'

'Why on earth would you go and do that?' Sarah asked, pulling herself up from the bed. 'I thought you loved it here.' She took a step towards him. 'I know things have been a bit difficult, I know things have been awkward, but . . .' Sarah didn't know what else to say without opening up the angst between them. 'Business should come first,' she finished lamely.

Anthony looked at her, remembering she was the grand-daughter of Angus Gordon. 'It's never been about business, Sarah, I realise that now. Wangallon gets a hold of you. She gets into your blood and damn she's hard to rid. Sure I love her, sure I wanted to be a fixture here, but things have changed for me. Angus basically showed me the difference between the right way and the wrong way to live your life and I guess in the end, I'd rather be friends than enemies.'

'But you can't go, Anthony.'

'No one's indispensable, Sarah.' He looked away from her as if he was eager to leave. 'I'll see you at the shed later on.'

'Anthony?'

He shut the door softly.

Sarah stared at the closed door. What on earth was she going to do if Angus didn't make it and Anthony left Wangallon? Outside the wind howled around the homestead. She drew the curtains on the verandah doors and unzipped her suitcase, intent on pushing her problems away. She would think about it tomorrow. Removing a couple of shirts and a jumper, she opened the top drawer of her dresser. There, resting on top of Anthony's blue scarf, was the gold bangle. She couldn't remember having left it there. She picked it up, examined the fine workmanship of the piece, noting slight marks and scratches, wondering why it had never appealed to her when it was so beautiful in its simplic-ity. About to slip it onto her wrist, a creaking floorboard distracted her and she dropped it back into the drawer. She thought she heard footsteps.

At the closed door she leaned against the cedar wood, her ear almost touching, her hand hovering above the ceramic doorknob. This is silly, she chided. The house was stretching, wasn't that how her grandfather termed it? She shivered nonetheless and climbed under the bedcovers fully dressed, pulling the blanket to her chin. The wind howled and bashed against the homestead, the house groaned in response. Anthony was leaving and her grandfather was in hospital. It seemed nothing was as it should be; no-one was happy, least of all her. As she closed her eyes, the sound of footsteps followed her into her dreams.

The life of the woolshed reached out to Sarah in an engulfing sweep of wool and manure. It was early, men were bellowing out in the yards, penning the sheep for the day's work. The smell of chemicals filled the soft breeze with an acrid odour. It was a cold morning, cold enough for the sheep to shiver under the icy breath of winter when once, freshly shorn, they were moved from small pens directly outside the shearing shed to a larger yard that fed into a long race. Pushed along the race in single file, they were coaxed with the aid of the dogs to proceed up a steel-reinforced ramp, part of the mobile plunge dipper hired for the duration of shearing. At the top of the ramp, the sheep would halt, before a quick push by hand sent them stepping off and down into a trough filled with a mixture of water and dip used for lice preven- tion. Immersed, they swam forwards, emerging to clamber out the other end, shaking and shivering before being let out to graze in a nearby paddock. Sarah remembered the old days, when a dug-out cement-lined trench was used for this very job. The dip had been filled in for years now. She vaguely recalled a visitor to the shed losing sight of their toddler and managing to catch the child before he fell in.

Renovated by her great-grandfather Hamish, the woolshed was a cavernous building. It rested on five-foot-tall foundations, allowing sheep to be yarded underneath, as well as in adjoining yards, spreading out around it like an intricately designed spider web. A large beam ran the length of the long board from which kerosene lamps once hung; today electric lighting and fans were secured to it. Beneath, on the lanolin-smoothed board, twenty-six stands for twenty-six shearers lay ready for action, ready to remove the soft rolling wool from the animals that continued to be Wangallon's life blood.

A long fluorescent light hung next to a skylight. How her great-grandfather would marvel if he could see the changes of this century, Sarah thought. The wool press was now electric, a shiny metal monster that was at odds with the age of the shed. Gone was the timber press of the old days, gone the need to stand in the red bin treading the wool down as if treading grapes. Even the hessian wool packs were part of history, replaced with a synthetic substitute. The risk of contamination, however, had not altered. Sarah glanced around the shed and saw that the old place was spotless. With the tests they did these days, cigarette butts, packets, discarded food wrappings and plain dirt were the last things you wanted an inspector to find. A clean clip was essential. The animals themselves had enough to contend with, what with the dust and burrs of a succession of bad seasons matting their wool and dulling fibre strength and quality.

'Here already?' Colin took a battered red notebook from the classer's table, looking her up and down as if surveying some alien creature.

'And you're still here,' Sarah replied stiffly, hands on hips.

'Actually, thanks to you, I've lost my job. Managed to hook up with the team for shearing though.'

'How surprising.' Her condescending tone succeeded for once in getting rid of him. A grim smile formed on her lips as he walked away. Knowing Colin, he would have spun the shearing team a few stories about her so she would have to make sure she didn't do or say anything to give anyone ammunition.

Anthony touched the brim of his hat as he walked past her to the engine room. Twenty-six shearers of varying ages followed him. Some nodded, some ignored her, and some grinned. Sarah smiled at them all evenly. At the rear of the blue-singleted procession, one of the men elbowed another in the ribs, glancing briefly over his shoulder towards her. She knew what they were thinking. She was the last Gordon left on the place, and they wouldn't expect her to stay.

'Didn't think we'd see you back here.' Colin had reappeared, and spoke slowly into her ear, lingering over the words as he casually rolled a cigarette.

'Likewise.'

'They reckon the old fella will kick it. What a way to go. No family around either when it happened, well, apart from Anthony.'

Sarah kept her hands shoved in the pockets of her moleskins. What he wanted was a reaction, any reaction, to gain the admiration of men he would never equal.

He pulled a half-squashed box of matches from the pocket of his jeans and lit his cigarette.

The hum of the electric engine carried across loudly to where they faced each other. The shearers walked in unison to their respective pens and, each dragging out a sheep, began the day almost simultaneously. Colin took a long drag, blowing the smoke directly into her face, before dropping it on the boards and putting it out with a prolonged twisting movement of his heel. Then he carefully used the toe of his boot to push it through the floorboards. 'They say Anthony will be left the lot.' The electric shears bashed out each word. 'Well, it's the only thing the old fella could've done. He can't leave it to a female.' He spat the last word from his mouth as if it was a fly, pulling the red tally book from his shirt pocket. 'Besides, your family doesn't exactly have a track record of sticking it out. Tell you what,' he said with a lopsided grin, opening the small book and chewing on the stub of a pencil, 'we could have a bet on this . . .'

'Bet on something you can win, Colin,' Sarah found herself answering.

He shrugged, tobacco smoke hugging his face like a fog. He watched the girl walk away. One thing was for sure: if she did stay Anthony was going to have his work cut out if she was ever boss.

❖

At smoko Sarah drove back to the homestead. She felt the need to talk to Mrs Jamieson and with Australia eleven hours in front she hoped it was not too late to telephone her.

'Lass, it is good to hear from you.'

As they talked, Sarah could imagine Mrs Jamieson sitting on her worn sofa, a cardigan pulled around her shoulders, one hand smoothing the apron over her knees. Briefly Sarah described her grandfather's accident as she sat at the kitchen table, her hand gripping a mug of coffee. Though he was off the critical list and talking there was a long road ahead of him.

'I am sorry, dear. Your father spoke very highly of him. Still, he's not beaten and I warrant there are a few years left in him yet. Tell me, have you spoken to your young man? Anthony, wasn't it?'

'How is Jim? Have you seen him?' It was easier to ignore Mrs Jamieson's questions. 'Do you think I could ring him?' How she would love to talk to him now. She stirred her coffee absently, resting the spoon on the table.

'He's gone to Edinburgh, lass.'

'He knows. Does he know, Mrs Jamieson?' Sarah asked breathlessly, almost forgetting to swallow the mouthful of coffee as a feeling of exhilaration surged through her body.

Mrs Jamieson pursed her lips together. 'No lass, he doesn't.'

'Oh.'

The girl's voice was flat. Quite frankly Mrs Jamieson thought it was for the better. 'Now, how's Anthony?'

Swallowing the lump rising in her throat, Sarah took another gulp of coffee, the hot beverage burning her throat. 'Things are a bit different now I'm back at Wangallon. He's resigned.'

'And you've told him not to?' Mrs Jamieson clucked hopefully into the telephone.

'Of course. It's just that things are difficult, what with Grandfather's will.'

'I'm not surprised. I would imagine his plans will be buggered up somewhat if Anthony leaves.'

'I hadn't thought of that.' Sarah pushed her coffee aside, giving the conversation her full attention. 'I figure Anthony has decided that this inheritance thing just won't work; especially the bit about me having to live here for five years and –'

'If he leaves it will solve all your problems, lass.'

That's right, Wangallon would be hers if she stayed. 'There would be no conditions, no . . .'

Mrs Jamieson cleared her throat. 'No Anthony,' she reminded her. 'Do you care for him?'

'That's not really the issue, Mrs Jamieson.'

'Well, Sarah, why don't you enlighten me?'

Sarah thought back to the day by the creek following Cameron's death. 'It was after Cameron's funeral. I knew there was something between us, however he never asked me out. Then suddenly, when I told him I was leaving Wangallon, he asked me to stay. And much later, at the races, I turned him down again.'

'So you believe his feelings must have changed towards you because of that one incident?'

'That and pressure from my grandfather and Wangallon.' Sarah rubbed her face tiredly. 'I think Anthony was pretending to care for me at one stage because he knew of Grandfather's plans, and thought it would make things a whole lot easier.'

'You know what you're saying? That you do care for him but you're scared that your feelings won't be reciprocated.'

'No, I'm not.'

Mrs Jamieson almost laughed aloud. It sounded like that Anthony boy had morals and if her intuition was correct, affection for Sarah. 'So, he must be leaving the property because he can't stand being there a moment longer and can't bear the thought of being in close proximity to you because he dislikes you so much.' Mrs Jamieson could almost hear Sarah's mind ticking over across the miles of telephone line. 'Don't you think you have known Anthony long enough to know where his mind is at? It seems to me the only person who doesn't know what they want is you. Now listen, I have to go, I have guests arriving. Just consider one thing for me. How would you feel if you never saw Anthony again? Think about that, and take care of yourself, lass.'

Hanging up the telephone, she patted down her hair and exchanged her stained apron for a fresh one. There was an American couple arriving shortly and there was dinner to prepare and fresh produce to be ordered. Yet she hovered between the immediate concerns of her daily life and the burdened young lass on the other side of the world. It was time for the Gordon men to take responsibility for their actions, she decided, picking up the telephone. She had done it once before and there was nothing to stop her from doing it again. 'I'm after a telephone number. In Australia, it's a hospital.'

Working on one side of a wool table, Sarah kept her thoughts to herself as she skirted the burry ends off each fleece spread out over the table's surface. As each fleece was thrown high in the air to land perfectly in a spray of grit and dust, she grasped the edge of the fleece, tearing at the soft wool, removing burr, manure, urine stain and any other vegetable matter caught down the underside of the sheep. These pieces she threw into a large wire cage to be baled later. With each fleece skirted, the sides and corners were then thrown inwards so it could be gathered and rolled over to expose its creamy underside. With the soft white staple exposed she then assisted a grinning, flannel-shirted Pete with the classing. Each fleece was examined and then categorised according to staple length, colour and fineness before being carried to the respective bins lining one wall of the shed.

At smoko, Anthony appeared from bringing in another mob of sheep and assumed his position with the rest of the men, sprawled on the wooden floor of the shed, their backs propped up by the shed wall. The cook, having provided egg sandwiches and tack-hard Anzac biscuits, returned to collect what was left before their break finished.

'Finished with the tea?' he grunted, waving the large white enamel teapot at no-one in particular.

'I'll have another,' Anthony lifted his battered tin mug, waiting for the teapot to be walked the five steps in his direction. He should really have got off his arse and helped himself but Corker the cook was such a drama queen when he wasn't swilling rum, that Anthony rather liked the idea of being waited on by him.

'Sugar?' Corker asked politely, after depositing the almost tar-black contents into Anthony's mug. Anthony caught his sly grin, made more ominous by two missing front teeth and an unsavoury wave of onion breath. 'Thanks, but I'm sweet enough.'

'Rissoles and toast, and it was burnt,' one of the team called out from where he lay prone on the floor. 'Not much of a cook if you ask me.'

Corker gathered up the mugs, teapot and empty sandwich plate. With a hairy arm he brushed the plate clean before wedging it securely under his armpit, long hairs bushing out from between flesh, singlet and crockery. He'd had enough of their rissole sniggers. One day he *would* make them under his arm. 'Eat it all though, don't you? Bloody ingrates!'

'Food's shit, boss,' a young fella called.

Anthony chuckled, 'Well, get rid of the toaster then the toast won't be burnt.'

'Hmp!' Corker rubbed a bulging belly unable to be concealed by his faded blue singlet or bum-hugging jeans.

'Who called the cook a bastard? Who called the bastard a cook?'

'Righto,' Anthony called. It was all too easy to get Corker riled up. 'Ignore them, Corker. This lot wouldn't know what good food was.' His efforts received a weak smile, but at least the beginnings of any tension were abated and at his word the men were on their feet, moving back to the board.

Sarah, sitting on a wool bail removed from the men, caught his attention. Quiet for the duration of their allotted half-hour break, she remained sitting, her legs crossed, both hands gripping her tin mug. At least one of Corker's egg sandwiches had been consumed. He was pleased her appetite was better. She certainly hadn't looked that great the first day back at Wangallon.

'Anthony, can I talk to you at lunch?'

'Sure, Sarah. See you at the house.'

Sarah was sitting at the kitchen table, exhausted from another long morning standing at the wool table, when the Toyota pulled up. Luckily her father was due tomorrow night after he'd visited Angus in hospital. It would be good to see him.

'How's it going?' Anthony strolled into Wangallon homestead as if he had lived there all his life and opening a kitchen cupboard, selected a tall glass before pouring some water and sitting down. 'Lunch for one, hey?'

She pushed across a corned beef sandwich and they ate silently. She had been waiting for him to check on her work for the last three days, but he had barely shown any interest in her job. The task and responsibility of examining the staple, checking length and fineness and placing each fleece in the matching appropriate pile was damn difficult. Sure Pete, the head classer double-checked, but she still felt uneasy.

'Everything going okay?' Anthony said good-naturedly, picking at a piece of fat caught between his teeth.

'This clip obviously isn't very important to you,' she countered. 'Otherwise you would be checking on me. After all, I'm not qualified. There's no two-year technical course certificate in wool-classing hanging on my wall.'

'Didn't know you were a fan of corned meat, tastes good though.' Anthony finished his share in two bites.

'It takes years of growing sheep, of knowing your flock. You have to be born and bred to it. If there's no consistency in every bail, how can we expect a good price come sale time?'

Anthony poured another glass of water for himself, drank thirstily, and glanced at the clock on the wall. There was only an hour for lunch and the woman was doing a damn good job of ruining his break, belittling her own abilities and pissing him off.

'I know you understand wool and the characteristics the family has been trying to breed into it for the last hundred and thirty years or so. You're a Gordon, Sarah, and the Gordons have been here from the very beginning. I can't think of anyone better qualified to be in the shed. So live up to your name, stop bloody whinging, take some responsibility and do it.'

Sarah opened her mouth.

'Besides, as I'm the one who's leaving, you are going to have to become a lot more involved in the day-to-day running of the place. You'll have to be capable of asserting authority so the new manager treats you with respect, and ensure you know enough so the men on the place know you're not only a worthy successor but a contributing team member as well.'

She waited for the flinty taste of anger to settle in her mouth, for her fists to clench. Instead, the opposite occurred. She finished her sandwich, cleared the plates, and told Anthony she would be back at the shed on time. After the back door slammed shut she considered his words. It was a revelation to realise that Anthony had every faith in her and he was leaving. At the thought she burst into tears.

❧ *Summer, 1868* ❧

Wangallon Station

hrough the carriage window, wavering grasses heralded a westerly wind. Here and there clumps of tall trees almost obscured Claire's view while a white haze blanketed the country-side in the late afternoon heat. Dabbing at the ceaseless moisture on her brow, Claire slumped back in the cracked leather uphol-stery, her slight figure moving in time with the rutted dirt track. Wet weather two days prior was the cause of their delay. Instead of arriving in the relative cool of late mid-morning as planned, she would appear at Wangallon exhausted and dishevelled. If first impressions counted for anything, Claire doubted her ability to create even a modicum of interest. Suddenly the carriage shud-dered to a stop. Momentarily startled by the absence of movement, Claire found herself looking out at a large homestead.

The long white-washed building was low set with a deep verandah. Three wide steps invited weary travellers to the cool expanse of timbered boards, a scattering of chairs and occasional tables. A porcelain jug and squat glasses sat invitingly on a round table and Claire could almost taste the cooling liquid. A covered walkway at one end of the building led to another small house; by the billowing smoke emanating from its chimney, Claire assumed this to be the cookhouse. An attempt at establishing lawn had been made to average effect. Irregular shapes of olive green were interspersed with tufts of brown and patches of dirt, while a long hitching post spoke of horses, unknown journeys and great distances.

A wiry, anaemic-looking man approached and assisted her from the carriage.

'Miss Whittaker, I'm Jasperson, welcome.'

The Englishman swiftly removed her trunk from where it was tightly secured to the rear of the carriage and dropped it unceremoniously in the dirt. Claire felt like a sailor as her body familiarised itself with a stationary position.

'Thank you,' she answered. Her politeness unacknowledged, she tugged at her skirt and smoothed the jacket of her travelling gown as Jasperson walked away. 'Now what?' she murmured as the carriage moved off in a scattering of tiny stones and a whirl of dirt. A few seconds later she was alone. Her short-brimmed straw hat did little to shade her face from the late afternoon heat and perspiration had begun to saturate her stockings. This was certainly not the welcome she expected. Her part at least had been accomplished. In agreeing to remain in Sydney after her father's passing this past year she had studied diligently, become most proficient on the piano and learned the art of good house-keeping from an ever-hovering Mrs Cole. In return she expected to be greeted cordially, if not enthusiastically. Especially after three days travelling.

'Are you going to stand out in the heat all afternoon?'

A silhouette, tall and lean, appeared from within the cooling recesses of the verandah. As if materialising from another world he stepped out from the shadows of his domain.

'Mr Gordon?' Claire enquired. 'Mr Hamish Gordon?'

He wore pale beige trousers, a white shirt and waistcoat and a jacket clearly cut by a notable tailor. Behind him two Aboriginal girls appeared. They walked towards her, and picking up her trunk, carried it back to the house.

'Good afternoon, Mr Gordon.' With a deep breath of firm intent Claire walked directly across to where he waited at the top of the three wide stairs. 'It has been a long trip.' She saw his eyes now. Remarkable violet eyes lit by pleasure and shadowed by lines of labour. Claire could smell cigar smoke and musk and the earthy scent of animals.

'I never intended for us to meet,' he said without softening his expression.

She took his offered hand, wondering at the response expected of her. His grip was firm, yet a tinge of wary expectation shadowed the strong contours of his face. 'It is lucky then that I have the characteristic of stubbornness,' she replied, not prepared to be considered weak of mind. Claire took both his hands in hers. 'Thank you for all that you did for my father and for me. Such generosity I'm sure is rarely to be found.'

'It gave me great pleasure.'

'And I believe that you did intend us to meet, Mr Gordon; at some stage and after a suitable period.' Although she doubted his widower status was the reason. It was more likely, she decided, taking in the strength of his face and the proud stance, a question of control. A characteristic that she had, through her own investigations, managed to wrench out of his hands and into her own. She could tell he was amused by her and that, Claire decided, was as good as any place to start. She wanted Hamish Gordon to grow acquainted with her as a person, not as a distant object of interest. She wanted him to let her be free, without expectation or desire.

'Welcome to Wangallon.'

At his words the sun dipped to the horizon, lacing the countryside in red and yellow. The breeze dropped and then directly opposite her, in a large gum tree, an owl called once, twice as if announcing his presence. She could feel it now, the warm welcoming breath of the heart of this country, of his heart. And another more poignant feeling, relief.

'You must be tired.'

Claire removed her straw hat, shaking her black hair free of the day's grime as she breathed in the remarkable beauty of her new surroundings. 'Not anymore.'

⊰ Winter, 1987 ⊱

Wangallon Station

*T*he day was slipping over the edge of Wangallon's horizon. Sarah almost expected to hear the long sigh of the earth as she waited for rest. The track she followed was almost indistinguishable from the grassless dirt spreading many kilometres in all directions and for a moment she was pleased Angus couldn't see the destruction caused by the drought. The rising wind carried the sounds of sheep crying across the paddocks, calling for the early-born lambs separated from their mothers during the day, while the smells from the woolshed, the acrid combination of urine and dung, mingled with the baked earth. Sarah found the odour comforting. It reminded her of the old days, before life got in the way of everything once hoped for.

By the time the sheltered clearing came into view, birds were already settled for the night, their feathers fluffed up warmly about their bodies. Only the wind followed Sarah's progress, lifting her hair, rustling the leaves about her. She stared at the headstones, at the ageing monuments appearing to guard each other. Whether grouped together against the dark of night or cradling each other in the shadow of the sun they were, in their collective masonry, sentinels. Above her the sky darkened and the wind stilled as she breathed in the night air. If they could speak, she wondered if they would try to explain to her the cycle of continuity, as strong as the pull of the moon to the ocean.

The furthest headstones were darkening, their outlines beginning to merge in the gathering shadows. Rust-coloured leaves blew across the granite slab marking her brother's final resting place, as tears left salty trails across her cheeks. Sarah knew in her heart she couldn't leave him or this great expanse of country. Jeremy had been right.

The great guardians of the cemetery stirred about her. Immediately the breath of life, that intangible thread, the essence of what protected and nurtured her, threw its arms about her soul. She was home.

◈

'It's past nine o'clock.'

Ignoring Anthony waiting for her in the kitchen, Sarah wearily pushed past him to slump down in a chair. She was still trying to comprehend the decision so recently made and the ramifications it would have on everyone's lives. Rubbing tired eyes, she gradually noticed the old fuel stove crackling warmly and the smell of a beef stew wafting enticingly towards her. The tension eased a little from between her shoulder blades as she sipped from the glass of red wine that appeared before her, took the warm washcloth offered and obediently wiped her face and hands. The day's grime streaked the pale green material. Only then, when her body began to warm a little, did she notice that Anthony was showered and warmly dressed. The white of his shirt suited him, as did the heavy cable knit of his beige jumper. Placing the bowl of warmed stew in front of her, he sat opposite. Sarah stared at him. The size of his hands intrigued her. They were like the bear paws of her father. She had always thought they were the hands of someone she could rely on.

'I just went for a walk. Lost track of the time,' she said in answer to his gaze. She took a mouthful and chewed slowly, recalling Mrs Jamieson's recent words on the telephone. How the hell was she going to approach him with her news and, most importantly, open her heart to him? It was important to eat. As she took a mouthful of the stew, the flavour of pumpkin, potato and beans soothed her stomach, the tender meat and rich gravy warming her body.

Anthony uncrossed his legs to lean forward. Pale, tired, worn out, she looked all those things, but she also looked content. It was not a word he'd ever used in the same breath as Sarah Gordon; at least not for a very long time. Her violet eyes were shining and he admitted that he still found her beauty almost overwhelming. Immediately he chastised himself inwardly for being too hard on her. He thought of the two kisses shared in the four long years since Cameron's death and imagined his body next to hers, not one tiny space between them. He stared across the table at her. Maybe leaving was going to be harder than he realised, especially when after all this time there was a strong chance she was coming home.

Sarah felt him watching her. She could smell the faint scent of him in the warmth of the room. Finishing her meal, Sarah placed her plate on the sink and stared out the window into the night. 'I don't want you to leave. It's not right.' The world outside was black, empty. His strong arms were reflected in the window. Little conjuring was required to remind herself of the faint hairs on his neck kissed golden brown by the sun, of his weather-streaked hair and the attractive face of a youth now grown striking with age. Suddenly it seemed unbelievable to her that she had been prepared to lose Anthony for Wangallon or Wangallon for

Anthony. She took a breath, steeling herself. There was another problem before her life could begin. Jim Macken.

'I met someone in Scotland,' she found herself explaining, now desperate to tell him about Jim's existence. Only he would understand. Only he had known Cameron as she had, loved him as she had. He would share her sadness and joy. He would keep her secret until the time was right for Jim to learn about his family. 'His name is Jim Macken and he's my half-brother.'

'What?'

'I know with everything that has gone on with this family and between us it seems surreal. But Dad had an affair over there. He's definitely my half-brother. This woman Mrs Jamieson wrote to Dad and told him about Jim,' her voice slowed.

'Bloody hell. What a mess!' Anthony scratched his head. 'It sure explains a lot of things.' But he wasn't sure if the news changed anything for him. 'I'm glad for you, Sarah,' he smiled briefly, his dark eyes lighting up. It was time they discussed the crux of their problems, the damn conditions of the will, the reason for his leaving. 'Sarah, I know how much you love this place. The will doesn't matter. Not anymore. You're the Gordon. You should be here.'

'I know.'

The simplicity of her agreement after her years away came as a surprise to him. 'This land means more to you than anything or anyone?' He thought of Jeremy. 'More than anyone's love?'

Sarah wondered how to articulate something so inexplicable. Her grandfather told her once: 'The land and the family are as one, you can't have one without the other.' Now Sarah believed it. 'Grandfather talks of an all encompassing love for the land and the creatures on it; an understanding much like that of the Aborigines for the sacredness of the earth; a belief in life after death, of a guardianship, both of the living and the dead. The spirits roam the world that is Wangallon because their love is so deep they cannot leave. That is why I believe Cameron is still with us. That is why I keep returning and why you have stayed. You too love Wangallon as I do, she's in your blood, but she is nothing without your careful management.'

'She is nothing without you.' His arm encircled her waist as he pulled her towards him.

Sarah placed the palm of her free hand flat against his chest. Even with the layer of wool and cotton she sensed his skin, smooth and warm beneath her touch. 'Wangallon has been between us. I believed you only wanted me for Wangallon's sake and . . .' Sarah closed her eyes, opened them, 'I didn't realise how much I cared for you until you said you were leaving.'

Anthony shook his head in disbelief. 'Sarah, you are wrong. Firstly, I only learned of the conditions of Angus's will on the day of his accident and secondly, I love Wangallon, but –' had he really been so good at self-deception? – 'it could never equal my love for you.' Revealing the truth of how he felt fairly winded him.

'What are you talking about?' Sarah whispered.

'I've only known about Angus's intentions for ten days. I love you, Sarah. Sure I wanted to be a permanent fixture at Wangallon, I even had a screwball daydream about old Angus leaving me some of the property, but it was only a dream. Besides, I made a promise to your brother, a promise to look after you. But, your brother didn't need to hear those words from me, Sarah. He knew then that I loved you.'

'You do?' She was looking up into his eyes. His hand cupped her face. His lips brushed her forehead, lingering momentarily next to the warmth of her skin.

'Sorry, guess with your leaving and living in Sydney and then Jeremy . . .' He screwed his nose up.

Sarah pinched his forearm lightly. 'Be nice.'

'I pushed you out of my mind.'

'Stay with me, Anthony: not because of Wangallon, not because of Grandfather or Cameron, but because I need you.'

Beneath her touch, his jaw quivered. 'Say it. Say that you love me.'

'I love you tonight,' she said quietly, squeezing his hand, 'and tomorrow. Always.' Slowly they edged together until Sarah felt a soft pressure on her mouth as she leaned into his embrace.

Did he carry her to the bed? Anthony could only remember the soft murmurings of love as their lips touched again and again. Their embraces were gentle at first, her mouth soft and pliant beneath his, their hands tentatively resting on shoulders, waists and backs. When he could wait no longer he pulled at her jumper, lifting it high over her head, removing his own with a one-handed shrug that caused Sarah to giggle a little. He paused then, kissing her lightly before undoing the buttons of her shirt and twisting the material off her shoulders to run his hands down her bare arms. His own shirt was unbuttoned as her bra fell away and he shivered at the touch of her hands on his chest, even as her warm skin moved smoothly beneath his. He traced the fineness of her neck, the soft swell of her breasts and the delicate whorl of her ears, his head light and fuzzy as if he were a teenager again. He burrowed his chin into her shoulder, tipping her back onto the bed, the scent of sandalwood drifting from her hair, engulfing him as her legs entwined themselves about his body.

A late-rising moon shone brightly through foliage into a small corner of Sarah's bedroom. She watched the patterns dancing prettily on her wall, hanging like Christmas baubles. They were like bright flashes of hope hanging down from heaven, their brilliant designs like streams of ribbons linking an old day to the hope of a new one. Linking loved ones past with those of the present. Starlight filtered through the trees of the garden to dance across her bare body, her fingers tracing the invisible painting on her skin, mimicking the flutter of light as it skipped deftly around, slowly gathering momentum as a midnight breeze shifted the leaves on the trees beyond. She had dreamed of that last day with her brother, but within the agony of remembrance now lay understanding, for Anthony had been there with her. It was Anthony who had wondered at their long absence, Anthony who had set out to track them and finally found them some two hours later. Sarah dimly recalled looking up from where her brother lay in her arms, at the shape of a galloping horseman.

It was as if Wangallon herself sent him to her, knowing how much he would be needed, knowing one day she would feel alone in the world. Both Wangallon and Sarah needed his love and protection. Perhaps the old ones had a hand in his employment as well, for although gone in body, their spirits melted into the heart of Wangallon. Rising from bed Sarah tiptoed across to her dresser. No thought entered her head, yet she found herself opening the top drawer, locating the aged gold bangle and slipping it onto her wrist. In the moonlight it looked like the most beautiful piece of jewellery she'd ever seen. For the first time in her many visits back to Wangallon she realised how peaceful the old homestead was. Everything was quiet. She climbed back into bed. Tomorrow she was going to take lots of photographs.

'I need you,' she whispered to the sleeping form beside her. Having spent her life trying to hear a word never uttered to her by her mother; to replace the same word lost with the death of her brother, only now did Sarah realise that *love* was far too limiting a word for her world, for if Anthony was her love,

Wangallon represented her soul. Anthony turned towards her, his arms encircling her body, pulling her close to his heart.

An owl, its large eyes blinking studiously, glanced in the direction of the dimly lit room. Hours before daybreak, the frogmouth left the tall gum tree to soar above the homestead, its wings lengthening until realising their full span. The night air rushed. Ahead, a canopy of trees waited, their branches wrapping protectively about each other, their energy glowing aura-like in the blackness. The owl swooped, wings outstretched, gliding through the tightly packed leaves that wept the scent of eucalyptus. It landed lightly, its anxious head swivelling slowly from left to right, its claws grappling the crumbling headstone of Hamish Gordon. Finally, as light rain began to fall and the earth opened its throat to quench a long thirst, the owl slept, contented.

❈ Spring, 1905 ❈

Wangallon Station

*H*amish Gordon lay in his hammock on the verandah, one leg slung over the side with his foot touching the timber floorboards beneath. He pushed himself occasionally, the gentle rise and fall giving glimpses of blue sky and green lawn, between which masses of deep pink flowers from the bougainvillea hedge enclosing the garden assaulted his afternoon tranquillity. Towards the rear of the garden, Claire's stringy barks grew tall amongst native leopardwood and wilga trees, while the lawn, the scene of many weekend luncheons and summer strolls, was lush and green. It took some imagining for him to recall the sparse wooden perimeter that contained Wangallon's excuse for a garden in the 1860s. Nor would one recognise the homestead now, for under his direction the home had been enlarged and redecorated to its current splendid form of plaster ceilings, rambling verandahs, chandelier-lit living areas and fine brocade soft furnishings.

It was a fine spring day, the type of day that had rushed past him during his life and that he had never managed to enjoy.

Today, however, was different. It was his birthday, or he believed it was. No matter as long as he had one every year and 1905 was as good as any time to be alive.

'Hell, a day out, a few months? Who cares?'

'I care, my darling.'

Claire Whittaker Gordon strolled along the verandah with regal elegance. From a tray of iced tea, she poured a tall glass for her husband before settling herself in a large wicker chair, white muslin flowing about her. Around her throat she wore a fine strand of pearls and on her wrist a beaten gold bangle, a trinket she had found only this morning.

'You have been keeping things from me, my dear.' Claire held up her wrist, displaying the bangle.

Hamish stared at her, a number of concocted stories coming to mind. Instead he said, 'It was Rose's. Where did you find it?'

'In an old trunk in the school room along with some of her personal effects. The room has been used for storage for so long that I decided it was time to start going through it in preparation for Angus. There are masses of school books. I thought as they are so old and with Angus requiring new readers I would tidy things a little.'

Hamish drew his eyes away from the bangle. 'A good idea and I'm sorry. I had no idea there were any of Rose's personal effects left in the house. I did ask Mrs Cudlow to dispose of them after her death.'

'Well, if you wish to be rid of them I will ask one of the maids to tidy things up.'

'Yes, good.' The near forty years since Rose's passing disintegrated and her face came to him as clear as if she stood before him.

'Hamish, my dear, are you feeling unwell?'

'Not at all, merely . . . remembering.' For years after Rose's death he had suffered the most appalling dreams. It was as if she visited him nightly, for often the dreams were accompanied by footsteps outside his room and he would jump from his bed, lamp in hand only to find the hallway empty. It still staggered him that a woman, his own wife, could actually will herself to die. He had heard of such occurrences, of widowed women pining away, however his own wife, and all for the love of an Afghan? He looked again at the bracelet. 'Do you like it?'

Claire studied the bracelet. It was very pretty and a quick polish had revealed a wonderful golden gold, but did she like it? Just then she experienced the strangest of sensations.

'Not really.' She slid the bangle from her wrist and handed it to Hamish. He took it wordlessly. He would place it in his study for safekeeping, next to Abdullah Abishari's fob watch and chain. Perhaps, he mused, that would make Rose happy.

'Lee has taken control of the kitchen. I'm sure Cook is not impressed.' Hamish sipped the refreshing liquid, patting his immaculate moustache dry with a fine embroidered handkerchief.

'Well, I told him, my dear, that Cook was to do the dessert, which seemed like a perfectly fine compromise, until Cook disappeared and Lee discovered that Luke's latest raid had not only included raisins, but the cocoa powder as well.'

'I like constancy in my life,' Hamish grimaced, his moustache turning downwards.

Luke appeared from around the corner of the house, a dirty screaming bundle of rags under his arm. 'Now come on, Auntie Claire, I accept some blame, but not all.'

Nearing forty-five, Luke prided himself on his six foot height and enjoyed the sniggers of those who whispered that he acted as if he owned the world. Frankly, he reckoned if they ever got a gander at how things worked at Wangallon they would have a mighty different opinion.

'Your youngest I believe, Father,' he announced, holding his five-year-old half-brother Angus upside down by the ankle. 'He makes a terrible noise.' Luke twisted the boy around until he was upright, then plonked him feet first onto the verandah. Quick as a flash he felt a small kick in his shin. Luke grabbed the boy by his already torn shirt-collar, holding him still for parental inspection.

'Good heavens, Angus,' Claire gasped. 'What have you done to your face?'

Smiling sweetly, Angus lifted a filthy finger, licked it generously and then wiped it across his cheek before licking it again as if it were a boiled sweet.

'Cocoa powder,' Luke revealed.

'And the scratches?' Hamish bellowed, swinging both legs over his hammock to stare at his youngest.

'Well . . .' Angus hesitated, his small voice quavering.

Filling his pipe, Hamish glanced up at his son. 'You are a boy, are you not?'

'Yes, yes, Father,' he stammered.

'Well, then, speak up,' Hamish demanded between puffs of his pipe.

Angus thought quickly, his young mind searching for the right reply. 'I took the cocoa, but only because Luke did.' He shot a glance at his brother, his confidence rising. Luke hunched his shoulders in response. 'Then Cook chased me and followed me up the tree, but I had her cat . . .'

'Tied up,' Luke added.

'. . . and Cook scrambled along the branch and it broke,' Angus stated flatly, his eyes wide with indignation at his special place being intruded upon.

Trying not to laugh, Hamish leaned closer to his young boy. 'And?'

'We both fell,' Angus finished proudly.

'Oh dear!' Claire exclaimed. 'What about Cook?'

'Young Angus here,' Luke said, displaying a full set of tea-brown teeth, 'landed on Cook who is, as we speak, packing her bags.'

'Oh, Hamish,' Claire cried out, 'you must do something. Please?'

'What of the cat?' Hamish asked.

Angus clapped his mouth tightly shut. The cat was his hostage.

'Well . . .' Hamish rubbed his chin. 'Luke, fetch Cook's cat, and tell her that if she leaves, we'll eat it for dinner.'

'Hamish!' Claire smiled at her husband in reproach.

'Just tell her that. On the other hand, Lee used to make a pretty good cat stew back in Ridge Gully days,' he joked.

'Hamish,' Claire chided again, lifting a fine lace and bone fan to waft a gentle breeze about her face.

'Now, Angus, how important is it to be friends with the people who work for you?'

Angus dropped his head to stare at his bare feet. A burr stuck out from the side of his big toe, but it didn't hurt. He was used to running round and getting burrs. However, now that he knew it was there . . .

'Angus?'

His father's voice jolted him back to reality. 'Yes,' he answered in a quiet voice. It wasn't very good to be in trouble with his father. The last time his father had questioned him, he had received a sound whipping with an old riding crop. All he had done was smear honey on Lee's toes when the Chinese was asleep. The ants had come all by themselves.

'Lee, Lee, come out here, will you?' Hamish yelled impatiently.

'Yes, you want me?' Immediately Lee appeared from behind the house, shuffling down the verandah towards his boss.

'That was fast,' Hamish commented with a soft chuckle. His old friend was as wiry as ever, bow-legged and still voracious in his consumption of tobacco.

Lee bowed quickly. 'Cook going?' He rubbed his hands together in anticipation.

Hamish rolled his eyes.

'Come on, Lee.' Luke patted the Chinaman on the shoulder. 'Let's take Angus and see if we can find Cook's cat.'

'Cat very tasty,' Lee grinned, his near toothless smile widening as he followed Luke and Angus inside the house.

Hamish lay back in the hammock, his spine nestling comfortably in the soft canvas. With one foot on the floor he pushed gently so that a soft rocking motion lulled him into drowsiness. Feet away Claire wafted her fan, her eyes sleepy in the mid-afternoon heat. Wavy tendrils of her black hair moved slowly, twisting becomingly in the manufactured wind.

When Wilkinson & Cross first advised Hamish of Claire's determination to meet with her benefactor he had refused. It was true that in the aftermath of Rose's death he had thought of the young woman in his care, however he was used to controlling his own affairs and was somewhat put out by Claire Whittaker's resolve. However, the girl did not lack fortitude and he found himself amused by her insistence to travel north. It seemed she refused to be left at the whim of her benefactor and the possibility of being married off to a man not of her choosing.

After years of daydreaming and the gradual realisation that he wanted more of Claire than to purely care for her from a distance, her imminent arrival caused him some consternation; a rather unknown emotional state to him. What to expect was his main query. He certainly did not want to meet her and discover her to be like Mary, his first love. Nor find another replica of Rose. It was possible, Hamish knew, that he was simply not suited to women. And assisting and following Claire Whittaker's progress offered him contentment without angst. What he had not counted on was Claire.

Within a day of arriving at Wangallon for what was stipulated as a short visit, Claire, showing much tenacity, managed to tune the piano. Within two days she was out riding side saddle with him on one of his morning inspections and by month's end even Mrs Cudlow was grinning like a Cheshire cat. Hamish ordered her Sydney tutor to make the long journey north and at the end of three months, Claire and young Luke were comparing lessons and arguing over geography. Hamish could not have been more pleased. When they eventually kissed six months later Hamish felt as if he were finally home.

Claire still managed to delight him with her soft authority and great love for both him and the land that was theirs. Only last year, on a visit to Government House, his beloved wife had outshone them all in an off-the-shoulder gown of palest blue satin, complemented by long white court gloves giving only the most tantalising glimpse of flesh between glove and gown. She had carried an ostrich feather fan with an exquisitely carved ivory handle and worn an osprey feather entwined with fine seed pearls in her hair.

'Imperative, my darling, for these court presentations. You know that, my dear,' Claire whispered in reply to his compliments.

Then later, when many of the guests were long gone, they retired to the drawing room and, amidst champagne and the company of the titled, Claire played a little Chopin for the entertainment of the assembled guests.

'Just a trifle,' Claire announced to the admiring applause.

'Just a trifle,' Hamish repeated out loud, a contented smile curving his lips. Some assets, he had discovered, did not have to produce an income. Although they could ensure continuity, for Claire produced young Angus. Here was a boy made to inherit, to learn from both him and the still reckless Luke. Luke would not marry, he was not the kind. Hamish understood that. Wild and a loner, he spent his days as a boundary rider on Wangallon or droving their stock out on the great inland routes when the seasons turned against them. He had not been the same since the death of his brothers and mother some thirty years ago and, in truth, Hamish couldn't blame the lad for not fulfilling on the promise of ability so evident from an early age. Hamish scratched his chest. A lifetime ago that time seemed to him now.

The hurdles in his way had been numerous. Ridge Gully, the epic wool clip lost en route to England. That was a major loss. Hamish had banked everything on that clip and he nearly lost the property the following year when he found it difficult to repay the huge advance he had obtained. Yet he had managed it. There were yellowing pages in an old station ledger reflecting a large number of sheep being sold and then the miraculous return to normal stock numbers barely twelve months later. Old habits were hard to break, particularly when he and his men were so adept at moonlighting.

Then there was the tragic deaths of his boys, the contempt Abdullah Abishari showed towards Hamish's hospitality and Rose's tragic yet unstoppable demise. Yet it all slid into obscurity when compared with the death of his brother on the goldfields.

Still it had been worth it. Angus represented Wangallon's future and although Hamish's patience was strained after two stillbirths and a number of miscarriages, eventually young Angus presented himself. He firmly believed that a boy would come eventually to inherit and one did. As for daughters, there was only Elizabeth Sutton Russell. Matthew Reynolds' old house in Ridge Gully was hers, as was The General Store managed by her grandmother, Lorna. Town property was his daughter's gift, not the land, not the black soil encasing the Gordon lineage now and into the future. He had assured himself of a strong succession plan, and the girl had carried the surname of Sutton since Rose's death.

Sometimes if Hamish closed his eyes tightly, his imagination whisked him back in time to a life before the arrival of his beloved Claire. Dave and Jasperson crunching the dry dirt as they came to speak with him after dinner, his dead sons playing, Mrs Cudlow running breathlessly after Luke, the musty scent of Milly, the broken piano and the wallpaper of yellow roses. Most of all he remembered Charlie. He hoped his dead brother would be proud.

≪ *Spring, 1987* ≫

Wangallon Station

*A*ngus watched the figures assembled at the back gate to Wangallon homestead through the small square of the ambulance window, the faces of his family blurred by a light rain. He knew his return home was not expected, in fact at one stage even he doubted his mental ability to pull himself free of the abyss into which his injuries had flung him. Accepting the arm of an ambulance officer, Angus waited for the wheelchair to be unfolded, his eyes skimming his surroundings as he sucked in the fresh clean air of his land. The chair travelled roughly over uneven ground thick with shooting grasses. He raised a hand to halt their progression, noting the herbage coming through the grass, the small shoots of clover beginning to form indicative, finally, of the chance of a decent season coming their way. If only they could be fortunate enough to get another couple of inches of rain.

'All surprised I can see,' he challenged as he rose, cursing silently at his less than steady stance. 'I had a spritely nurse

468

attending to my rehabilitation so, as you can bloody well see, I'm not defunct yet.'

'Good to have you back, Dad.'

'Good to see you, Angus.'

'Hi, Grandfather.'

'That's better.' Accepting the handshakes and kisses with grudging reluctance – demonstrative examples of affection were never his style – he quickly gauged his family's wellbeing. Ronald looked tanned and fit and his broad smile that oozed relief proved that the rumours were indeed true: finally Sue was in a hospice. As for the flushed, soft look on his willowy granddaughter, well, Angus decided, he was starting to feel a whole lot better. 'Now I promised these two fine paramedics hot coffee and cake. Can we oblige them?'

'Absolutely,' Sarah beamed. 'I'll lead the way.'

Resuming his seat in the wheelchair, Angus meandered slowly up the back path behind his family. Two long months were behind him since the accident; weeks of pain and frustration. Weeks of forcing himself to eat when his body near damn well decided to pack it in, but he wasn't having any of that. The bastards could put their binoculars down if they expected a dismal curtain call behind a hospital screen. Nope, he would die when he was damn well good and ready, his way, at Wangallon.

'Well,' Angus nodded approvingly to where Anthony and Sarah waited at the back door. He noted Anthony's hand resting on his granddaughter's shoulder, 'I see you two have got your act together at last and you've even managed to make it rain.'

In response heavy droplets splashed on the corrugated iron roof. A contemplative haze of heat and moisture rose up from the cement path, signalling the beginnings of a heavy shower.

'There'll be a bloody flood next,' Angus stated.

Anthony thought of the open plains of Wangallon, of the fresh new herbage of the season and of the creeks and rivers still dust dry with thirst. 'I hope so. Just a small run-through will do.' Outside the homestead young joeys munched by their mothers' sides, ducklings called for food and a couple of young cattle pups growled with delight as they chased each other's tails in ever-decreasing circles up the back path. 'And here it comes.' Out to the west the welcome sight of darkening thunder clouds bursting with more rain, answered.

'Those pups belong to anyone?'

'They are Shrapnel's, Angus,' Anthony told him. 'Out of Pete's bitch, Molly. They should be good.' Scooping up the plump young animals, Anthony plonked both of them in Angus' lap. 'Pick one.'

'Old Shrapnel, eh. Well, Bullet,' Angus named the fattest of the two pups mauling his shirt, 'you have got a fair bit to live up to. Where is my old mate anyway?'

'He's buried in the cemetery, Grandfather,' Sarah answered.

'Good. Put me next to him when the time comes.' Picking the young pups up by the scruff of their necks, Angus dropped them both on the ground. 'They tell me, Sarah, that your work's been chosen for a photographic exhibition in Sydney.'

Sarah beamed. 'I know, it's just so exciting. It's a photo of the Wangallon Creek and it will be hanging in the Art Gallery. Can you believe it?'

'Yes, actually I can. Now about that coffee?'

Then he was being lifted up and into Wangallon homestead, to be wheeled to his place at the kitchen table. Finally, he was home.

Seated at the dining table under the piercing gaze of Hamish Gordon and the more reflective portrait of his wife Claire, Sarah, Anthony and Ronald waited as Angus sorted through the bundle of papers before him. Angus had wasted little time in re-establishing himself as boss of Wangallon although in the last couple of weeks since his return from hospital he'd graciously deferred to both Anthony and Ronald on two separate occasions, an occurrence not unnoticed by Sarah, who sensed a general winding down in her grandfather, both physically and mentally. He was tuning out, she realised with dismay, or perhaps at long last he was acknowledging the need to defer to others. All the more reason for Jim's presence to be made known immediately, she decided. Sarah looked directly at Anthony. They had spent last evening discussing when Jim's existence should be revealed. It wasn't exactly something that could be manoeuvred around lightly. Her father didn't know that Sarah knew about Jim, while her grandfather didn't know anything at all. With a deep breath and a nod of support from Anthony, Sarah opened her mouth to speak. She figured the only way to get Jim out in the open was to simply blurt it out.

'The last will and testament of Angus Gordon,' Angus read precisely, pausing to peer above his tortoiseshell reading glasses.

'Hey, Dad,' Ronald interrupted. 'This is a bit unusual, isn't it?'

'Well, why should I leave this to the bloody solicitor? He'll get his cut when the time comes and you'll all have to sit through this again anyway. But this is my will, nobody else's, and it's mine to damn well read out when I choose. Besides, I don't believe in surprises, not where Wangallon's involved. I'd rather everyone knew where they stood.'

'But, Grandfather,' Sarah interrupted, 'there's something you should know. Something Dad needs to know too. Something really important,' she emphasised, looking at Anthony for support.

'Yes, you should hear her out, sir, it may make a difference to all this.'

'I doubt it. You see, when I was in hospital I had a very enlightening conversation with a certain Scottish resident by the name of Mrs Catherine Jamieson.'

'What?' Sarah and her father asked in unison.

'Oh, this is interesting,' Angus chuckled, removing his reading glasses to twirl one arm of them between thumb and forefinger. 'I reckoned on you confronting your father about this, Sarah, but I see you've kept quiet about it.'

'Well I . . .'

'You know about Catherine Jamieson?' Ronald asked quietly.

'And Maggie Macken and your time in Tongue.' Angus cocked an eyebrow. 'Been busy in the past, haven't we?'

Sarah reached across the table to clasp her father's hand. 'I know about my half-brother, Jim.'

Ronald turned from puce to grey.

'Dad, it's okay, really.'

'Yes, well we've more half-brothers in this family than most,' Angus stated with a trademark scowl. He didn't need the proceedings to get all teary.

'You've met him?' Ronald looked ill.

'Of course.' Sarah squeezed her father's hand.

Angus cleared his throat. 'Back to business. I've a substantial parcel of shares and an amount of cash, this will be left jointly to you, Sarah and your father. Now for the best bit,' he said with a lightness belying the seriousness of the letter he was about to read aloud. 'Obviously I've had to add one of those codicil things but it's all legal. Not a loophole anywhere.'

'Don't think you'll be sitting, waiting with a smile on your faces. If you're hearing this, then I'm gone, which means I finally get the rest I deserve and you finally have to start working.'

'Nice tone to the beginning, don't you think?'

'Sarah, I leave you a thirty per cent share in Wangallon, contingent on you remaining and working on the property.

*If you leave, you're not entitled to a brass razoo. To Anthony, I
also leave a thirty per cent share, same conditions. He's family
enough to me and if you two swallow your pride and ignore
everyone else, the partnership will be sealed by marriage.'*

'I'm pleased to see that you two have finally come to your
senses in this regard. I would have haunted you for the rest of
your life, Sarah, if you had fucked up your inheritance.'

*'Ronald, it's time you returned to what you were born and bred
to. I appoint you as adviser to the partners of Wangallon and
leave you a ten per cent share in the property. Make sure you
work hard, I'll be watching. By the way, I've stipulated the
place can't be sold for fifty years. By that time, there should be
another generation to keep you people under control.'*

'So,' Angus looked up from the document at the expressionless faces at the table, 'no quibbles there I would imagine. Well,
I bet you're all asking who gets the other thirty per cent? Blood's
thicker than water. Grievances and country gossip aside, there are
some things that have to be done. I can only say I was saddened,
Ronald, that you chose not to tell me about my grandson in
Scotland. On the other hand, ever since Sue appeared on the
scene, followed quickly by her affair, I placed the blame squarely
on your shoulders for messing with Wangallon's future. So, in
fairness to you, I suppose you reckoned I'd just see Jim as another
problem caused by you. Well, you are wrong. I couldn't be prouder.
It is to him I leave the other thirty per cent if he wants it.'

'What?' Sarah and Anthony said in unison.

'He's a Gordon by birthright and more Scottish than us. So, if
you lot can't convince him to stay, well, you'll be working pretty
damn hard to buy him out. He's the only one who has that option,
mind. That's it.'

Ronald looked tentatively across at his daughter, then at his father. Jim was released from where he'd kept him in his heart. The rush of gratitude and relief caused his eyes to moisten.

'I'll leave you three to discuss things then.' Angus rose from the table, his knuckles whitening with the strain of heaving himself up and out of his chair.

'Thank you.' Anthony shook hands with Angus, conscious of the weight of responsibility passing to him as Angus placed a strong grip on his shoulder. 'I won't let you down.'

'I know that, lad, I know. Look after them for me,' he nodded towards Ronald and Sarah. 'And most of all . . .'

'I'll protect her, Angus.'

'She's a hard mistress. She'll test you until your back is broken and the banks are breathing down your neck. But if you tend her cautiously, conservatively, she'll reward you in the end. Now I'll see you two,' he smiled softly, 'later.'

'Thanks, Grandfather,' Sarah called out as he left the room.

Anthony laid a hand on Sarah's shoulder. 'I'll leave you two alone.'

'Good idea,' Ronald agreed.

'Bad idea,' Sarah disagreed. 'Sit down, Anthony. If we're all going to be running this place together,' she smiled at both Anthony and her father, 'then it's about time we were all honest with each other,' Sarah said, her eyes softening as Anthony sat beside her, taking her hand in his. 'I've met Jim. He is a fine man.'

'Does he know who you are?'

'Not yet, Dad, but he will. When the timing's right.'

Anthony interrupted them. 'Would he be interested in Wangallon?'

'Maybe. He does like the land,' Sarah offered. 'He's from the North Country and it's pretty ordinary up there, what with their small holdings.'

Ronald scratched his thinning head. 'One day Jim will have to be told of his share in Wangallon.'

Sarah opened her eyes wide. 'Firstly, Dad, don't you think he should meet his real father?'

'For this Jim bloke to become a part of Wangallon, we have to lose Angus,' Anthony interrupted. 'I'd only say, let's not have too much change too quickly.' He felt a little uncomfortable being present at such an emotional father–daughter discussion.

'Agreed,' Ronald replied quickly. Besides, no-one knew what Jim wanted, least of all if he wanted a new family. But he figured he would probably want his share, in one form or another.

'Dad, it's time for you to let go of Mum and come home. Help us, Dad. Help us run Wangallon like Grandfather wants you to.'

Ronald stared at the flat of his palms on the surface of the old table. The deep grain felt cool, welcoming to his skin. His grandparents had eaten here, raised their children. He himself, under the watchful tutelage of his mother, learned to read and write here. There was a patch of ink unable to be removed to prove it, as well as a deep scratch from his pocket knife when boredom and rebellion had set in. He ran his fingers across the wood.

'After Cameron died, Wangallon ceased to be home. It was a place that had taken my family's life. Maybe the knowledge of leaving another boy in Scotland added to my misery. My son, my mother Angie, even Sue, Wangallon took them all in some shape or form. I couldn't bring myself to stay and the flood provided the excuse I needed to escape.' Ronald met his daughter's eyes. 'I wanted to protect you as well, because for me the dream of continuing at Wangallon died with your brother.'

Sarah touched her father's hand. 'Dad, no-one is to blame for those deaths. Come home, Dad. We need you. Come home.'

'I don't think your mother will be coming back. She's too ill now. It would be too difficult.'

'I know it's hard, Dad, but it is best this way. The hospice she's in is very good.'

'Maybe we could find something a little closer to the water though. She loves the water, Sarah.'

Sarah took her father's hand, clasping it firmly in hers. Reaching out she felt the encompassing warmth of Anthony's strong grip. Sarah thought of the land about her, of those who had gone before and the length of time it had taken for her to finally realise her place in the world.

Angus held back a chuckle. Tiptoeing from behind the hall doorway until he was out of earshot, he poured himself a good shot of whiskey. At Sarah's bedroom he opened the drawer on his father's old chest and dropped a silk bag into it. Inside was a gold fob watch and chain he'd taken from his father's things upon his death. It was a beautiful piece with the surname Abishari engraved on it. Angus figured the Afghan merchant must have lost it to his father in a card game of some sort. Anyway, he knew Sarah would look after it.

Through the gauze of the verandah he watched willy-wagtails and topknot pigeons darting through the soft rain. The lawn, for months brittle dry, was now green and lush. It was done, he thought with satisfaction, as he positioned himself in one of the old squatter's chairs. Sarah and Anthony would marry and Wangallon would have an heir. He missed the boy, of course. Cameron was a fine lad, but he figured some things worked out the way they did for a reason.

Taking a good mouthful of whiskey, he swirled the contents

appreciatively around the inside of his mouth. The next sip didn't sit so well on his empty stomach and he tossed the contents through the gauze, the liquid forming glittering squares in the weak sunlight. If he had one regret it was the murder of Tom Conroy, Cameron's real father. Tom had been a mate. Yes, he had thought him a bit too smooth for the bush, but he had been a damn good wool buyer and honest as the day was long. That was the problem. Once Tom discovered he sired a son, he would have done the right thing and Angus could not bear the thought of his son's cuckolding being known. Then there were his succession plans, as well as the risk of Tom meddling with Wangallon's management. No, the public knowledge of a bastard heir would have destroyed their reputation. So he had organised his death: a simple stabbing, motive theft. Easy, the problem had gone. Sue, however, never seemed to get over it.

With the coming of the late afternoon, the rain was increasing in intensity. Across the miles of flat country, through the waving grasses, Angus could smell the tang of leaves fragrantly weeping the scent of eucalyptus. At the end of the garden, through the fence, wallabies were chewing tender stems, their small tongues seeking sweet juices. A fruit bat sailed through the air, landing suddenly as a fox crossed the wet lawn, its cloying pungence wafting to where Angus rested. Out in the garden he watched two female figures strolling amongst the trees and flowers. *Rose*, he called, *Angie, come in, you'll get wet*.

Finally as heavy rain began to fall, Angus felt himself drift away. It was a strange detached feeling, as if he were hovering above himself in the gathering twilight. The body below him took a long drawn-out breath and with that final exhalation he was sure he heard the heart of Wangallon sigh.

❧ Epilogue ❧

The wind lifted the day's dust from the old wilga and belah trees as a flock of white cockatoos screeched overhead. They stacked the campfire high. One of the men had trapped some rabbits for dinner and he whistled to himself as he skinned them deftly, the shiny blade splitting the carcasses with ease. As darkness descended, Hamish ate his rabbit hungrily, chewing the marrow from the bones with expert efficiency. Beside him his brother Charlie, unmarked by his mining accident, hummed contentedly, mesmerised by his nephew Luke, whose nimble fingers plaited a rawhide whip from kangaroo pelts, his old one nearly worn out from his numerous droving jobs.

Cameron called out into the rim of darkness surrounding the group, smiling delightedly as a deep voice answered. They had been waiting a long time for Angus. Accepting a chunk of rabbit meat, Angus sucked at the sweet flesh, after a time whistling into the darkness. The animal lumbered through the ring of men, snuffling at the rabbit bones as he went. In the glare from the campfire, a large jagged scar, a war wound from some ancient battle, was visible in the thinning hair. Finally Shrapnel sat down beside his master.

❧ Acknowledgements ❧

Thanks to my agent Tara Wynne and Vicki Guteirrez, my publisher Larissa Edwards, editor Chris Kunz and the welcoming team at Random House. It is a wonderful thing to be believed in. There have been many drafts of *The Bark Cutters*. Along the way I have received invaluable support from my family and friends, in particular my sister, Brooke, and my parents, Marita and Ian. A special mention to Catherine Hammond for her early advice and Professor Wally Woods at Central Queensland University (MLitt programme) for his encouragement in my writing endeavours. Thank you also to Bev Cranny at The Nook & Cranny Bookshop (Goondiwindi, QLD) for her enthusiasm and love of books, Margaret Adams for advice on the Kamilaroy tribe and David for understanding a writer's life.

∝ About the Author ∝

In the course of her career Nicole Alexander has worked both
in Australia and Singapore in financial services, fashion,
corporate publishing and agriculture. A fourth generation grazier
Nicole returned to her family's property in the late 1990s. She
is currently the business manager there and has a hands-on-role
in the running of the property. Nicole has a Master of Letters in
creative writing and her poetry, travel and genealogy articles have
been published in Australia, America and Singapore.

Visit www.nicolealexander.com.au

THE SAGA CONTINUES ...

A
CHANGING
LAND

Sequel to
The Bark Cutters out now,
keep reading for a sneak peek!

≪ Spring, 1987 ≫

Wangallon Station

Sarah stared at the headstones, at the ageing monuments silhouetted by the rising moon. The clearing was strangely quiet and she wondered whether the spirits of Wangallon were welcoming her grandfather, Angus, at some other sacred place on the property. Lifting the latch on the peeling wooden gate, she stepped through grass grown long by recent spring rains. Twigs and leaves crackled beneath her, the soft soil creating an imprint of her passing. The familiar pounding of a kangaroo echoed across the narrow stretch of water that formed the twisting Wangallon Creek, and with their movement a flock of lorikeets squawked in a tall gum tree before resettling for the night.

Sarah stopped first by her brother Cameron's grave, and then at the freshly turned mound that covered her beloved grandfather. For the first time the enormity of his passing settled on her slight shoulders. To have lost him, of all people, was incomprehensible, yet curled about her grief like a shroud was a sense of responsibility almost too great to imagine. She was now the beneficiary of a thirty per cent share in their family property, Wangallon. She was, as her father pointed out, the only legitimate Gordon left, apart from himself; nearly everyone else was buried here within the arms of the property that her great-grandfather, Hamish Gordon, founded in 1858. Sarah looked at the ancient head-stones: grandmother, brother, great uncle, wives, young children and Hamish Gordon. He that had amassed what was now one of the largest privately held properties left in north-western New South Wales.

Years ago Sarah had wished for such an opportunity, dreamt of it and could admit to resentment at having been passed over because of a chance of birth. Then Cameron died and Anthony– the hired help as her mother called him – eventually became manager. Now everything was different. As a direct descendent, Sarah knew the fates had anointed her as custodian of Wangallon and she felt ill-prepared for the future. She shook her head, hoping to clear a little of the fatigue and grief that had seeped into her veins over the last week. Soon they would be booking the contractors up for lamb marking, soon they would . . . but she couldn't recall what was scheduled next, she was too tired. Leaning against the trunk of a gum tree, Sarah rested her palms on the bark beneath her. Through the canopy of leaves above her, the sky was gun-metal blue. There were few stars, for what elements could compete with the moon that now blanketed her in a mantle of silver.

'Sarah?'

Anthony's voice startled her. She'd not heard the Landcruiser approach and was unsure how long she had been weeping beneath the moon's glow. Anthony took her hand and helped her to her feet, brushing the soil from her clothes.

'I didn't want to leave you out here any longer. I know you needed to say goodbye without the hordes that were here earlier but –'

Sarah kissed him on the cheek. 'It's okay. I'm okay.'

He looked at her tear-stained face and cocked an eyebrow.

'You've barely slept this last week.' He knew, for he had laid beside her and floated on the memory of sleep as she tossed and turned through each successive night. 'You should get some rest.'

Sarah allowed herself to be led from the graveyard, listened as the latch on the small gate clicked shut. Moon shadows followed their progress.

Anthony placed a supportive arm around her slight waist. His girl had lost weight in the week since old Angus's death. Anthony was worried about her. 'We need to sit down and work out the management plans for the next twelve to eighteen months. How does that sound?' Sarah looked at him blankly. 'We've the lambs to mark and . . .' He could tell she wasn't listening; her gaze was fixed somewhere out in the darkness of the countryside. 'Don't worry, I'll handle things until you feel more up to it.' Leading her around to the passenger-side door, Anthony helped her into her seat. 'Look, I brought a little friend for you.'

Sarah stroked the shiny fat pup Anthony placed in her lap. It was Bullet, one of the pups by Angus's dog Shrapnel. She hugged the little dog fiercely. 'Grandfather wanted this one.'

Reversing the Landcruiser away from the cemetery, Anthony headed in the direction of Wangallon Homestead. 'He's yours.'

Sarah rested her hand on Anthony's thigh.

'Everything will be fine, Sarah.' His grip tightened on her fingers.

The words were so familiar. Anthony uttered them after Cameron's death, after the flood of 1986, after her parents retired to the coast and once again when her mother went into respite care.

'Really, everything will be fine,' Anthony repeated.

Once is a comfort, Sarah thought, pressing the warm, wiggling pup against her cheek, twice is not.

As they drove away a lone fox moved stealthily through the ageing monuments. The animal padded carefully through tufts of grass, pausing to sniff the air. Finally he located the freshly turned soil of Angus Gordon's grave and curled up beside the mounded earth.

Tucked up in her bed, with Anthony's rhythmic breath marking out the long hours of the night, Sarah tried unsuccessfully to sleep. Her heart seemed to have taken on a life of its own and it fluttered erratically. At times during the night she found herself clutching at her chest, her breath catching in her throat, her eyes tearing in fright. She knew grief and uncertainty were causing the symptoms she experienced, yet common sense didn't ease her distress.

As the night dragged and the moon spread its glow through the open doors leading out onto the gauze verandah, Sarah watched dancing shapes flickering about her. Outlines of branches and leaves jostled for attention like paper puppets against the cream bedroom wall as she drifted through snippets of conversation shared with her grandfather. This moment was akin to the passing of her brother, for it heralded both unwanted change and an unknown future. Who would guide them now the wily Angus Gordon was no longer with them?

Near dawn Sarah felt a numbness begin to seep through her. With a sigh she rolled on her side, only just conscious of Anthony rising to meet the working day. As the morning sun penetrated the calming dark of the room, she pulled the bedclothes over her head and closed puffy eyes against all thoughts of her changed life. The house was quiet, too quiet. A scatter of leaves on the corrugated iron roof competed with morning birdsong. Sarah huddled further down beneath the covers, tears building. She sensed movement on the verandah and tried to calm herself with her grandfather's words: *It's only the old house stretching itself, girl*, he would say. Now more than ever, Sarah doubted his words. She was one of the custodians of Wangallon now and the spirits from the past were well aware of a newly delineated present.

≪ PART ONE ≫

❧ *Autumn, 1989* ❧

Wangallon Station

Forty emus raced across the road, their long legs stretching out from beneath thickly feathered bodies as their small erect heads fastened on the fence line some five hundred metres away. Sarah couldn't resist going up a gear on the quad bike. She pressed her right thumb down firmly on the accelerator lever and leant into the rushing wind. Bullet, her part-kelpie, part-blue cattle dog, pushed up tight against her back, squirrelling sideways until his head was tucked under her armpit. She swerved off the dirt road in pursuit of the emus, the bike tipping precariously to one side before righting itself. A jolt went through her spine as the quad tyres hit rough ground. Then the bike was airborne.

Bullet lost his balance on landing. He gave a warning yelp as Sarah grabbed at his thick leather collar, managing to drag him up onto her lap. Despite the urge to go faster, she slowed the bike down, the brown blur of feathers dodging trees and scrub to outrun her. Sarah loved emus, but not the damage they did to fences or the crops they trampled. Chasing them off Wangallon, albeit onto a neighbouring property, seemed a better alternative to breaking their eggs in the nest to cull numbers. She poked along slowly on the quad until she reached the fence. A number of emus had managed to push their prehistoric bodies through the wires, while the rest ran up and down the boundary trying to find a way out. Bullet whimpered. Sarah reached the fence as the last of the mob disappeared into the scrub, scattering merino sheep in their wake.

'Sorry.' Sarah apologised as the dog jumped from the bike, turning to stare at her. Bullet never had gone much on losing his footing and it was clear Sarah would not be forgiven quickly. He walked over to the nearest tree and lay down in protest.

Two bottom wires on the fence were broken and the telltale signs of snagged wool and emu feathers on the third wire suggested this wasn't a recent break. Sarah walked along the fence-side, stepping over fallen branches, clumps of galvanized burr and a massive ants' nest of mounded earth a good three feet in height. Eventually she located the two lengths of wire that had sprung back on breaking. Taking the bottom wire she tugged at it and threaded it through the holes on the iron fence posts until she was back near the original break. She did the same with the second wire and then walked back to the quad bike where an old plastic milk crate was secured with rope. Inside sat a pair of pliers and the fence strainers. Grabbing the tools, Sarah cut a couple of feet off the bottom wire, then interlaced it with the freshly cut piece until it looked like a rough figure eight. She pulled on it, feeling the strain in her back, until it tightened into a secure join, then she attached the strainers and pulled back and forwards on the lever. The action tightened the wire gradually. Once taut, Sarah used the pliers to join the ends. More wire was needed to repair the bottom run but at least it would baulk any more sheep from escaping.

Whistling to Bullet to rejoin her, Sarah followed the fence for some distance on the quad before cutting across the paddock. Little winter herbage could be seen between the tufts of grass. The rain long hoped for in March and April had not arrived and May was also proving to be a dry month. It was disappointing considering the rain which had fallen in early February. Within ten days of receiving nearly six inches, there was a great body of feed and then four weeks later, with a late heatwave of 42 degree days, the heavy grass cover sucked the land dry and the feed that would have easily carried their stock through a cold winter began to die off. The pattern of the next few months was trailing out before her like a dusty road. In one month they may have to begin supplementing the cattle with feed; in two they may have to be feeding the sheep corn. By mid-July they would begin the search for agistment or perhaps place a couple of mobs of cattle on the stock route.

Mice, lizards, bush quail and insects all disturbed into movement by her bike created a sporadic pattern of scampering life amid the tufts of grass. A flat expanse of open country lay ahead, punctuated occasionally by the encompassing arms of the wilga and box trees that dominated the landscape here. Ahead, the edge of a ridge was just visible; a hazy blur of distance and heat shimmering like an island. Soon the rich black soil began to be replaced by a sandier composition, the number of trees increasing, as did the birdsong.

The midmorning sunlight streamed into the woody stand of plants, highlighting saplings growing haphazardly along its edges. They were like wayward children, some scraggly and awkward in appearance, others plump and fresh with youth. Sarah drove the quad slowly, picking her way through the ridge, passing wildflowers and white flowering cacti. The trees thickening as she advanced deeper. The air grew cooler, birds fluttered and called out; the cloying scent of a fox wafted on the breeze. The path grew sandy and the quad's tyre tracks became indistinct as the edges collapsed in the dirt. Above, the dense canopy obliterated any speck of the blue sky.

Sarah halted in the small clearing. The tang of plant life untouched by the sun's rays filled the pine-tree-bordered enclosure. She breathed deeply, revelling in the musky solitude. Through the trees on her right were the remains of the old sawpit. The pale green paint of a steam engine from the 1920s could just be seen. It was here that her grandfather Angus had cut the long lengths of pine used to build the two station-hand cottages on Wangallon's western boundary. The sawpit, long since abandoned, also marked the original entrance to Wangallon Station. Long before gazetted roads and motor vehicles decided the paths that man could take, horses, drays and carriages bumped through this winding section of the property, straight through the ridge towards Wangallon Town.

Sarah continued onwards. Soon the tall pines began to thin out, the air lost its cool caress and within minutes a glimpse of sky gradually widened to a view of open country. She weaved away from the ridge through a tangle of closely growing black wattle trees and belahs, the thin branches whipping against her face.

She was in the start of the swamp country where a large paddock was cut by the twisting Wangallon River in one corner. The area was defined by scattered trees and bone-jarringly uneven ground. A ridge ran through the paddock and it was here that sandalwood stumps spiked upwards from the ground. Sarah stopped the bike and alighted.

Years had passed since she'd last been in this area alone. It was almost impossible to believe that her beloved brother had died here in her arms over seven years ago. Kneeling, Sarah touched the ground, her fingers kneading the soft soil.

In snatches the accident came back to her. His ankle trapped in the stirrup, his hands frantically clawing at the rushing ground, and then the sickening crunch as he struck the fallen log and the spear-like sandalwood stump pierced his stomach. Sarah swiped at the tears on her cheeks, her breathing laboured. Closing her eyes she heard the shallow rasp of his breath, like the rush of wind through wavering grasses.

Anthony caught up with her a kilometre from Wangallon Homestead. Sarah could tell by the lack of shadow on the ground that she was late. His welcome figure drew closer, just as it had when he had come searching for her and Cameron all those years ago. At the sight of him the tightness across her chest eased. As the white Landcruiser pulled up alongside her quad Sarah leant towards him for a kiss. Her forefinger traced the inverted crescent-shaped scar on his cheek, the end of which tapered into the tail of a question mark. Sometimes the eight years since his arrival at Wangallon only seemed a heartbeat ago.

'You're late,' Anthony admonished.

Sarah sat back squarely on the quad seat. *So much for the welcome*.

'I was worried. What's with all these long rides around the property?'

'It's his birthday.'

'Oh.' Each passing year Cameron faded a little more from Anthony's memory. He gave what he hoped was an understanding nod. 'Been fencing?' he nodded towards the milk crate. 'You don't have to do that stuff you know, Sarah.'

If she expected a few words of comfort, Anthony was not the person to rely on. He rarely delved past the necessary. She gave a weak smile. 'I am capable of fixing a few wires.'

'I don't want you to hurt yourself,' Anthony replied with a slight hint of annoyance. 'And what's with taking off and not letting me know where you're going or how long you'll be away?'

'Sorry.'

He scratched his forehead, the action tipping his akubra onto the back of his head. 'Well, no harm done. Let's go back to the house and have a coffee.'

'Would that be a flat white? Latte? Espresso?'

Anthony rolled his eyes. 'How about Nescafé?'

Bullet barked loudly. 'Sounds good.' Sarah pushed her hat down on her head and sped off down the dirt road with Bullet's back squarely against hers. She slowed when they passed some Hereford cows grazing close to the road. 'G'day girls,' she called above the bike's engine. Bullet whimpered over her shoulder and gave a single bark as they crossed one of the many bore drains feeding their land with water. These open channels provided a maze of life for Wangallon's stock and Sarah never failed to wonder at the effort gone into their construction nearly a century ago under the watchful command of her great-grandfather Hamish. Shifting up a gear, she raced through the homestead paddock gate to speed past the massive iron workshed and the machinery shed with its four quad-runners, three motorbikes, Landcruisers and mobile mechanic's truck. Weaving through the remaining trees of their ancient orchard, Sarah braked in a spurt of dirt outside Wangallon Homestead. She smiled, watching as Bullet walked through the open back gate, pausing to look over his shoulder at her.

'I'm coming.'

Bullet spiked his ears, lifted his tail and walked on ahead.